ISSUE ONE
"THE HYPNOCTOPUS"

DEDICATED TO MY LOVING PARENTS, FRIENDS,
AND THAT LITTLE GIRL WHO WAS OBSESSED
WITH CARTOONS AND DREAMED TO ONE DAY
WRITE STORIES OF HER OWN.

THERE WAS A GIRL NAMED MADISON
WHO LOVED TO PLAY IN SAND
ONE DAY SHE FOUND A MAGICAL WHALE
WASHED UP ON THE LAND

MADISON TICKLED THE WHALE
TILL IT ROLLED INTO THE SEA
THE WHALE WAS SO GRATEFUL
THAT IT FOUND SOMEONE TO BE

A FRIEND FOR MADISON

WRITTEN AND ILLUSTRATED BY
JEANINE-JONEE

CONTENT EDITED BY
EMILY BRIGOLIN

ADDITIONAL COLORING BY
KYLE P. HOLLAND

BRYAN SEATON: PUBLISHER/ CEO
SHAWN GABBORIN: EDITOR IN CHIEF
JASON MARTIN: PUBLISHER-DANGER ZONE
NICOLE D'ANDRIA: MARKETING DIRECTOR/EDITOR
DANIELLE DAVISON: EXECUTIVE ADMINISTRATOR
CHAD CICCONI: OFFICIAL NARWHAL WRANGLER
SHAWN PRYOR: PRESIDENT OF CREATOR RELATIONS

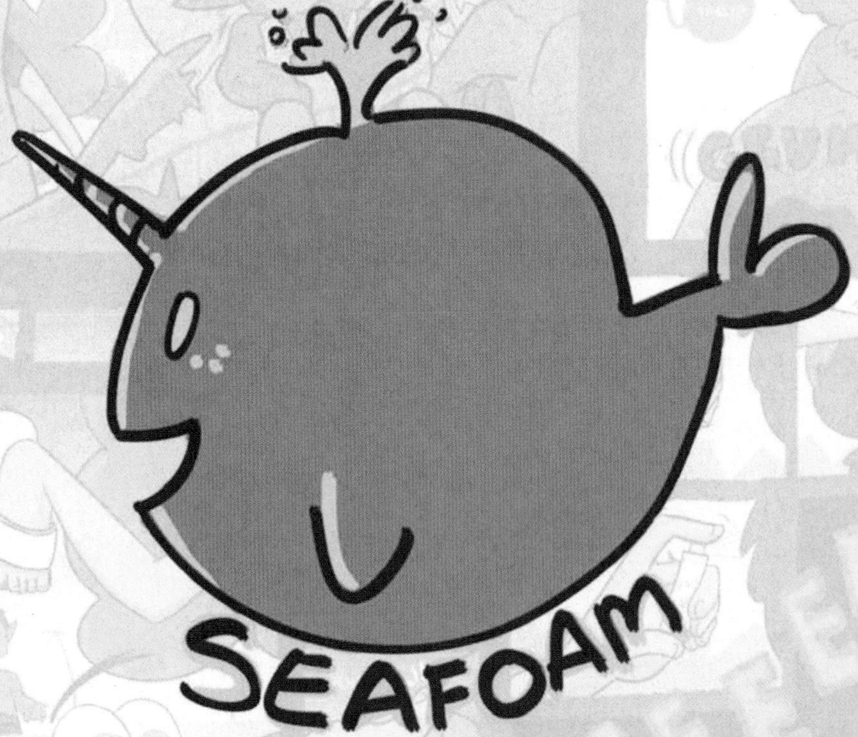
SEAFOAM

For information regarding the CPSIA on this printed material, call: (203) 595-3636 and provide reference #RICH - 844161.

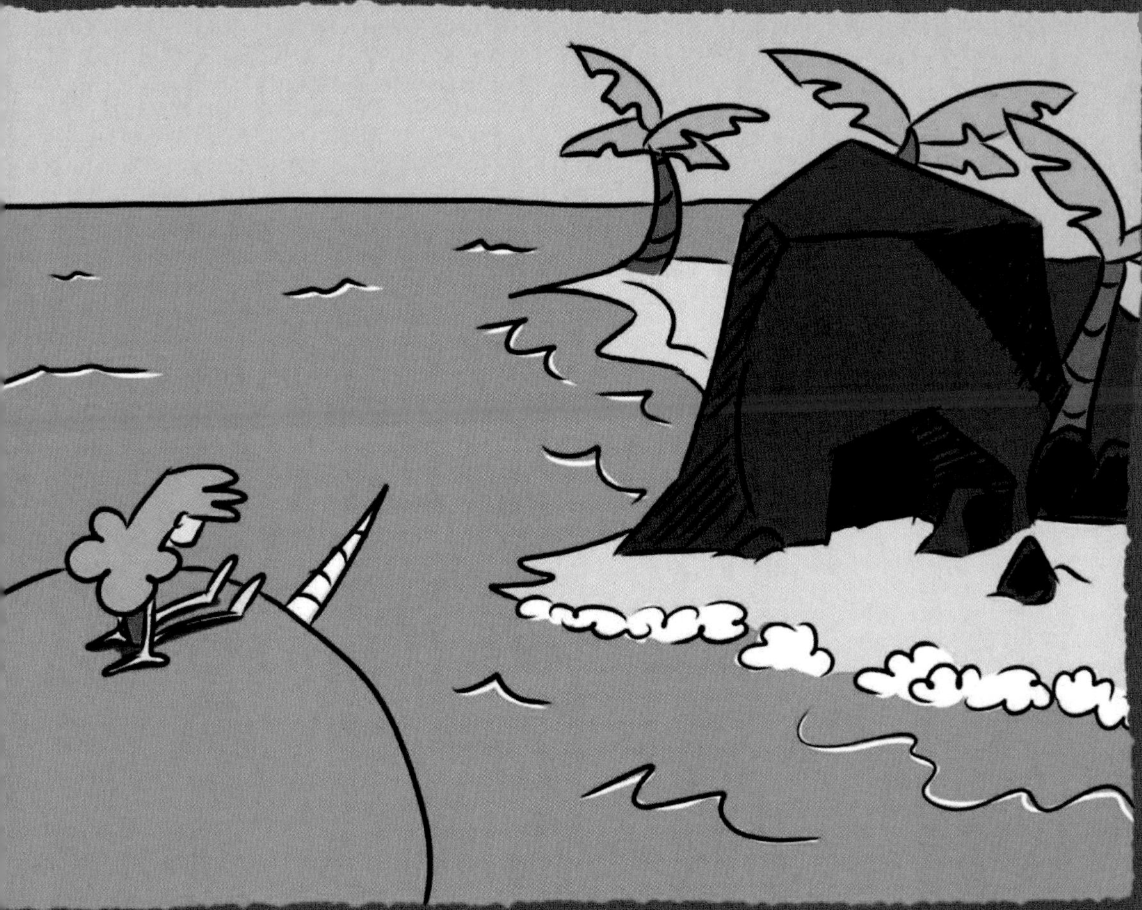

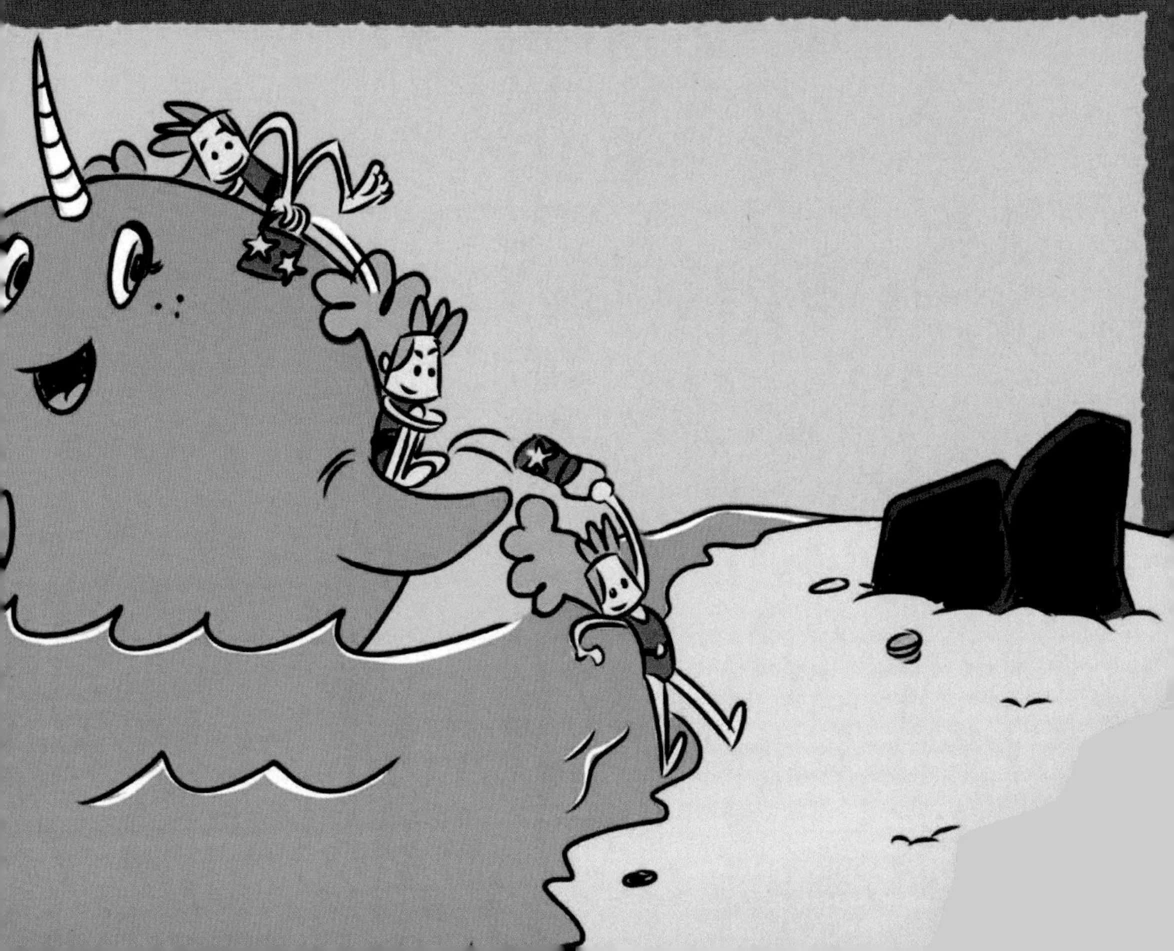

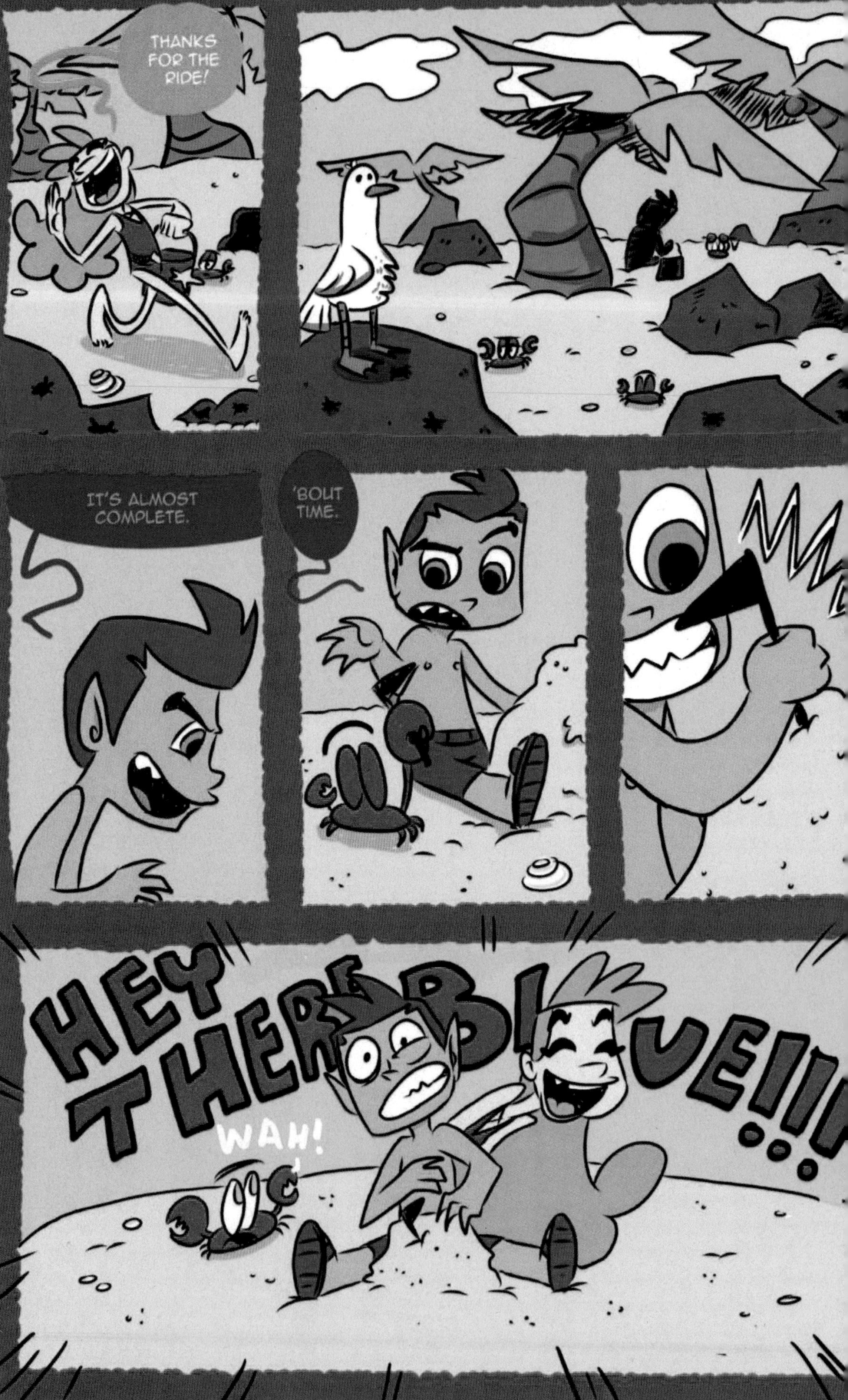

THANKS FOR THE RIDE!
IT'S ALMOST COMPLETE.
'BOUT TIME.
HEY THERE, BLUE!!!
WAH!

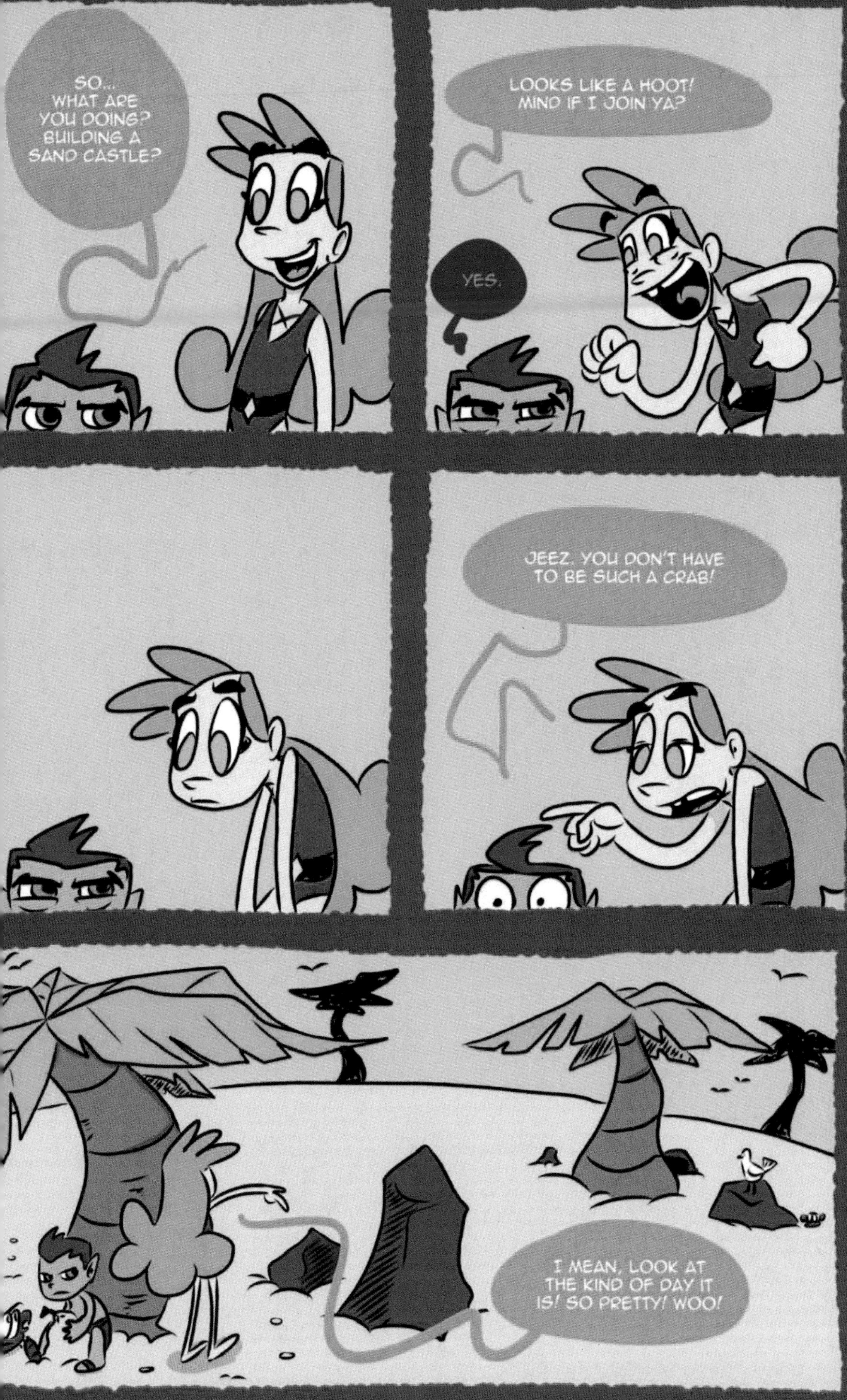
SO... WHAT ARE YOU DOING? BUILDING A SAND CASTLE?
LOOKS LIKE A HOOT! MIND IF I JOIN YA?
YES.
JEEZ. YOU DON'T HAVE TO BE SUCH A CRAB!
I MEAN, LOOK AT THE KIND OF DAY IT IS! SO PRETTY! WOO!

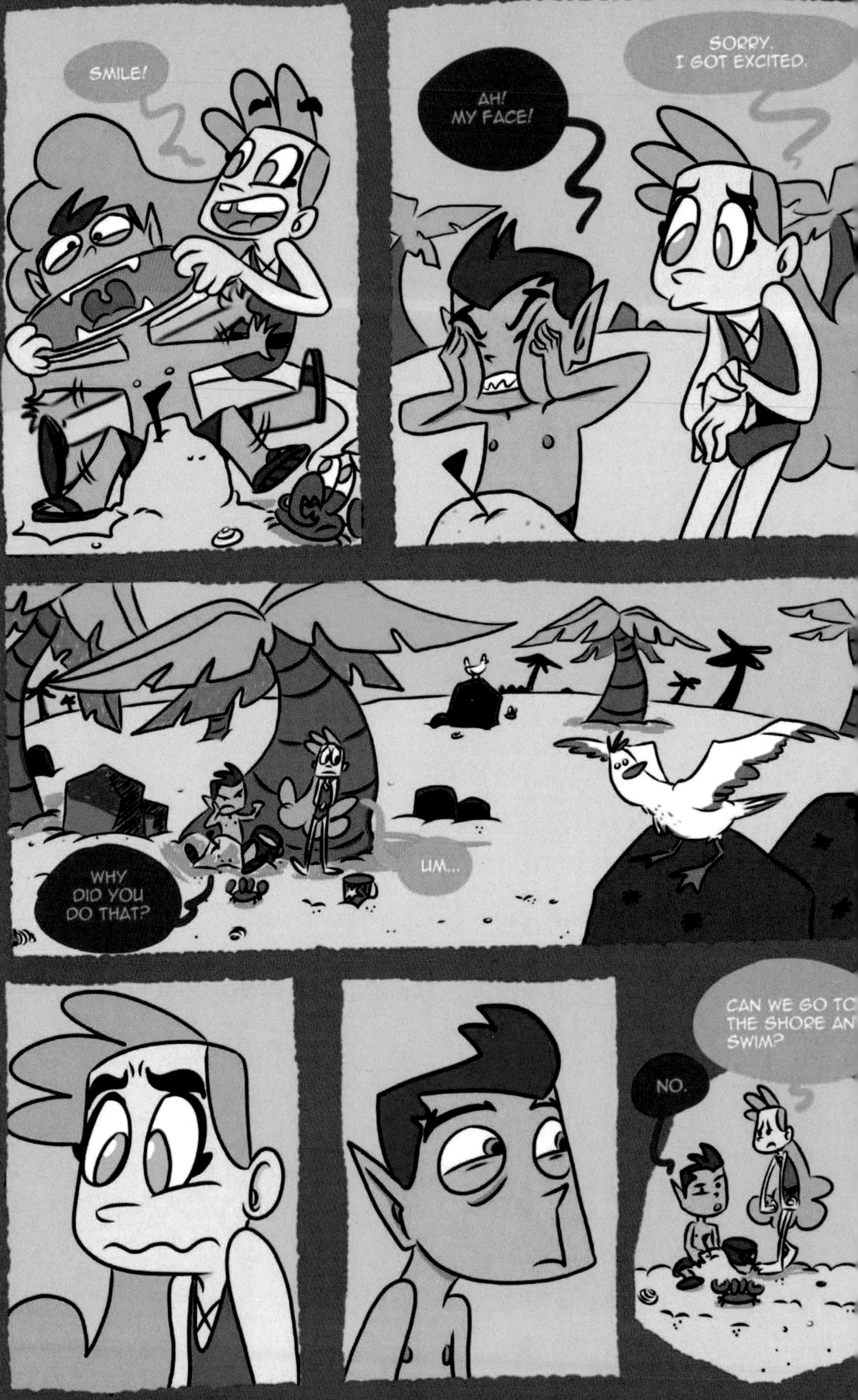
SMILE!
AH!
MY FACE!
SORRY.
I GOT EXCITED.
WHY
DID YOU
DO THAT?
UM...
CAN WE GO TO
THE SHORE AN
SWIM?
NO.

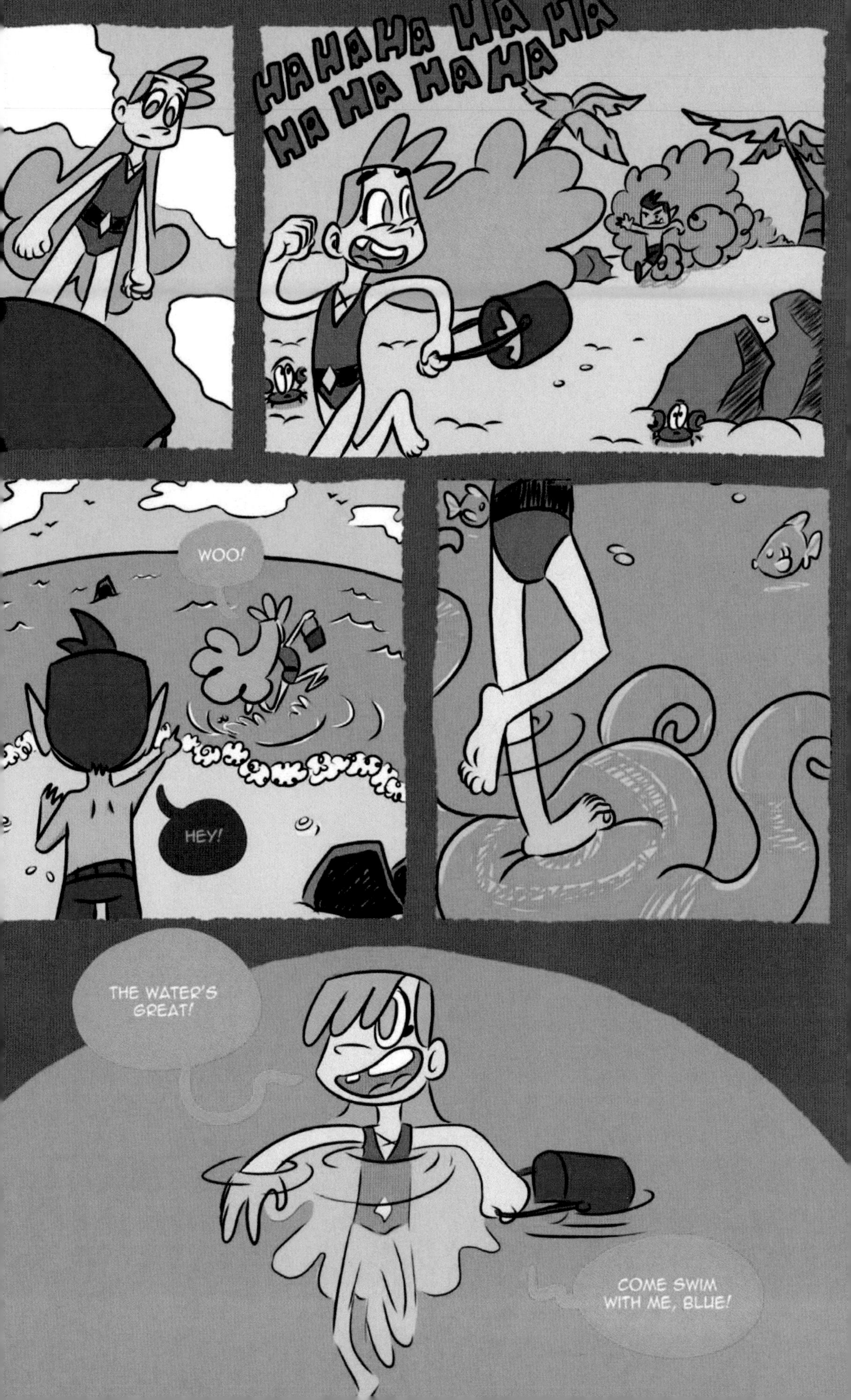
HAHAHA HA HA
HA HA HA HA HA
WOO!
HEY!
THE WATER'S GREAT!
COME SWIM WITH ME, BLUE!

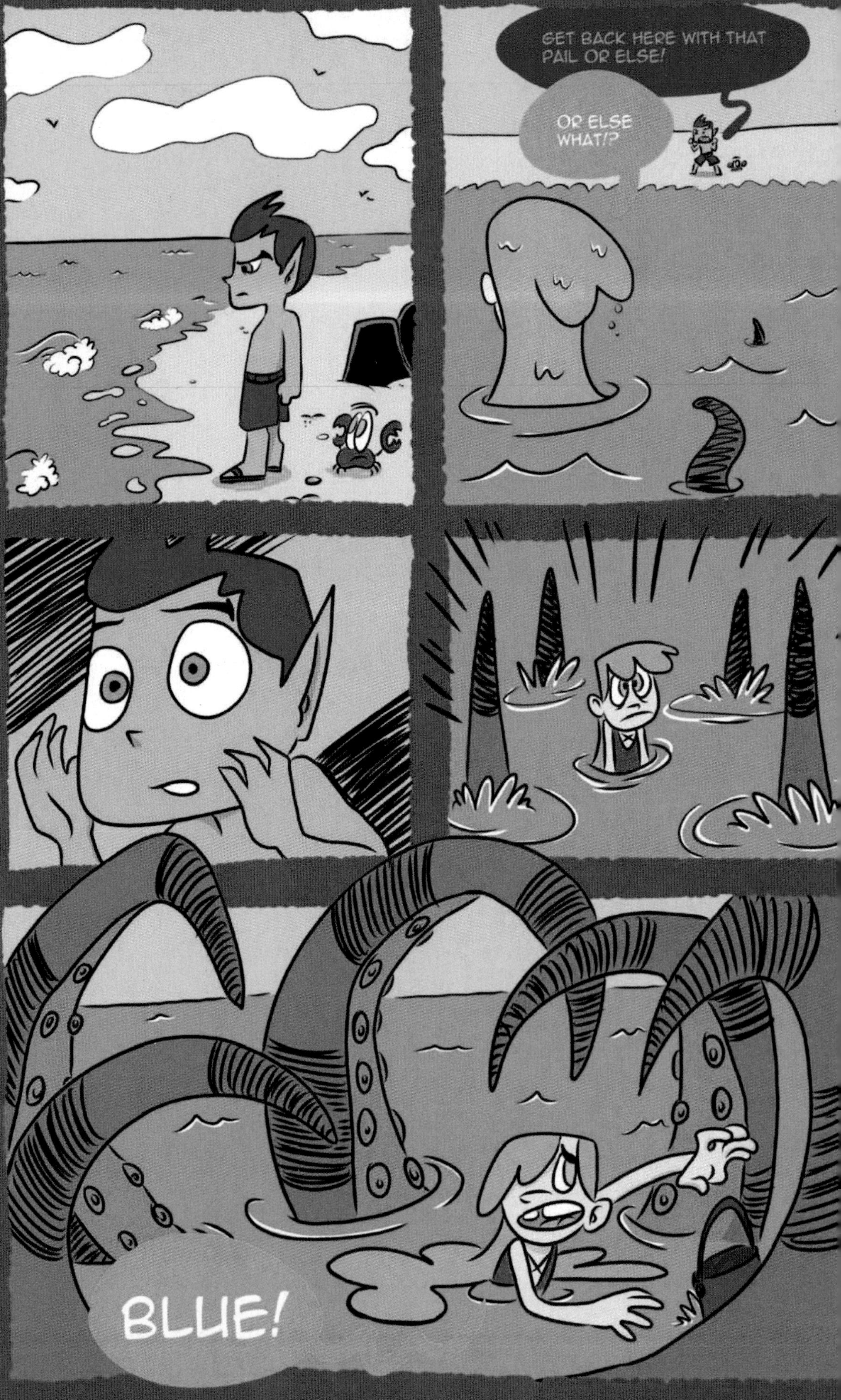
GET BACK HERE WITH THAT PAIL OR ELSE!
OR ELSE WHAT!?
BLUE!

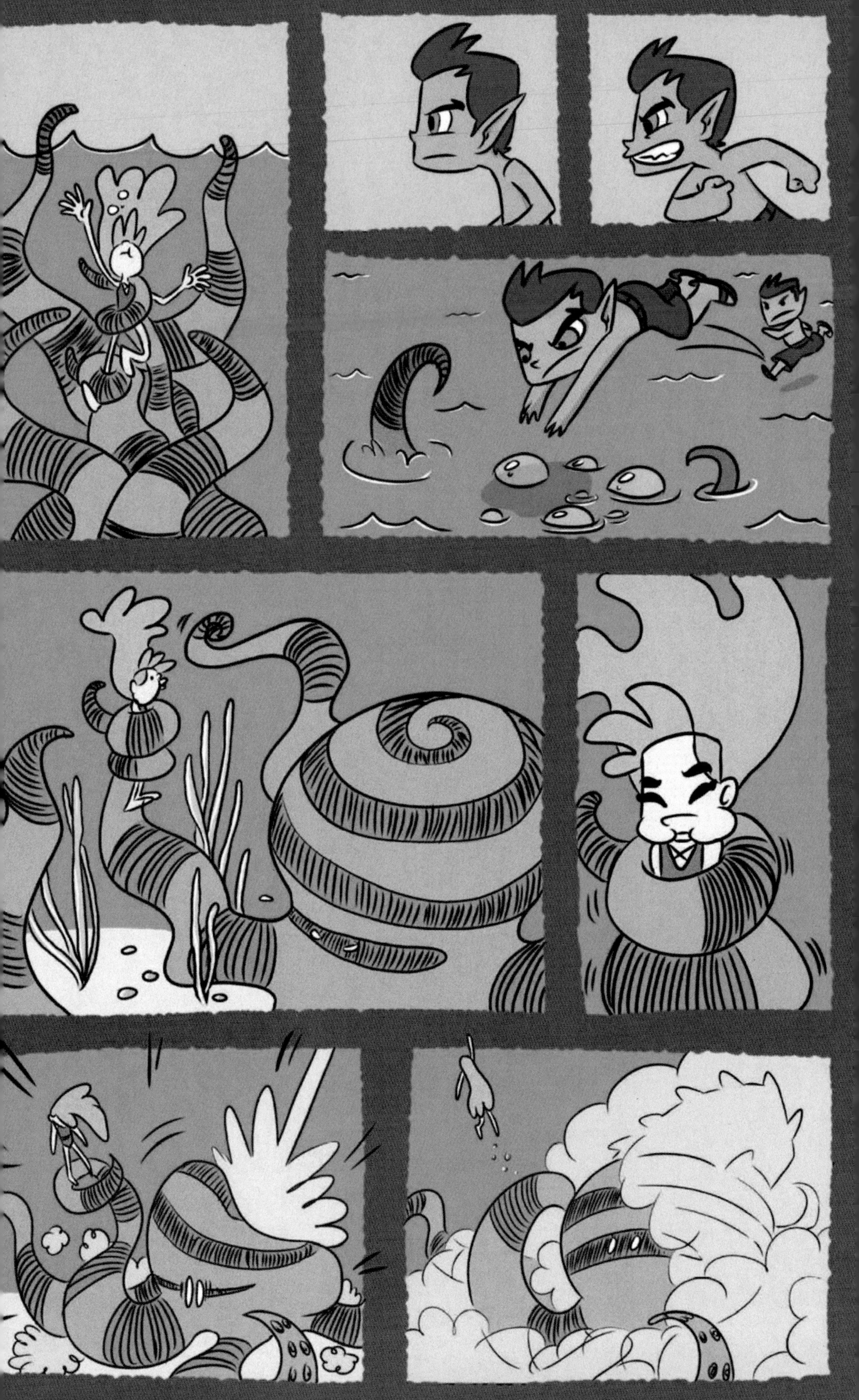

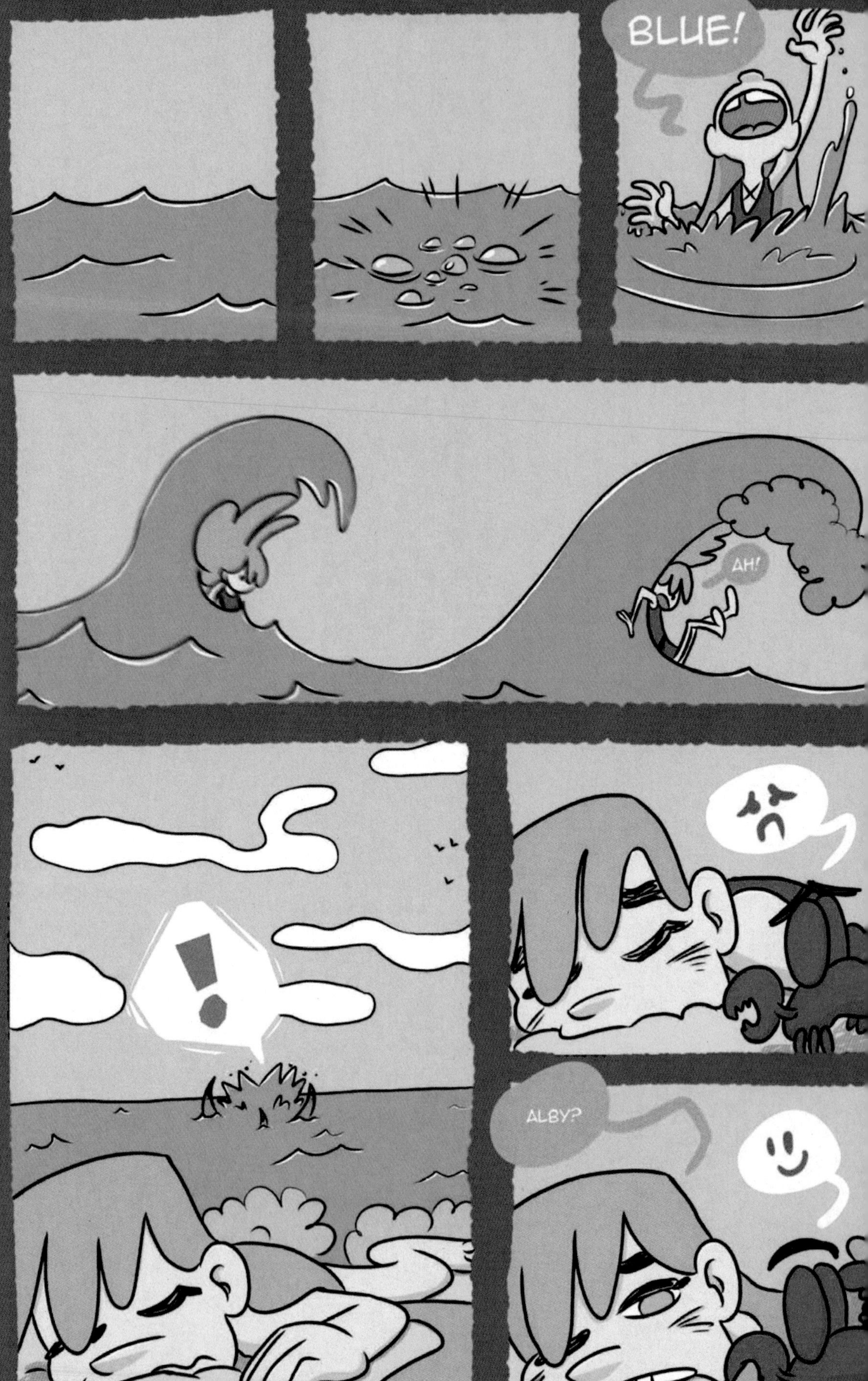
BLUE!
AH!
ALBY?

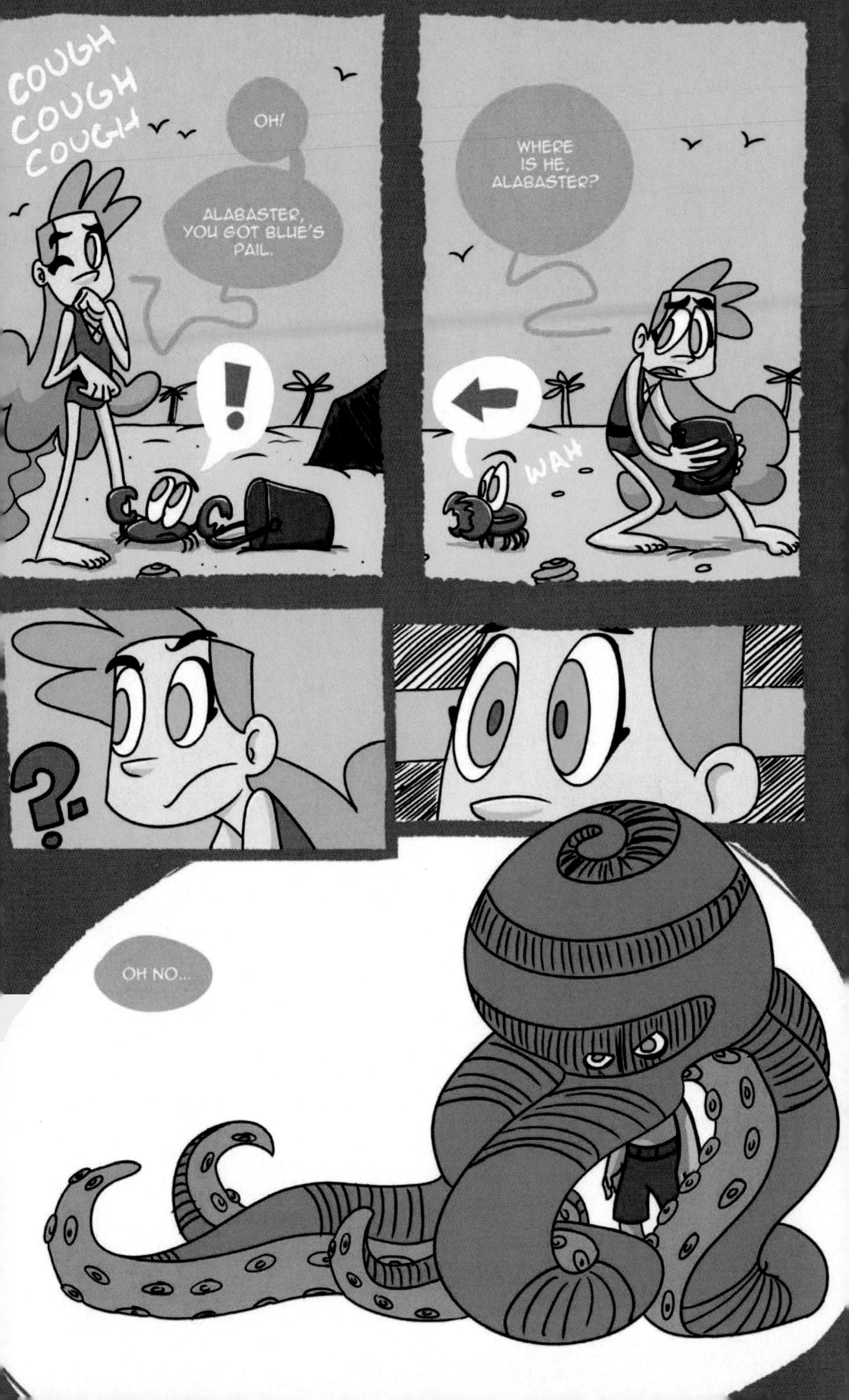
COUGH
COUGH
COUGH
OH!
ALABASTER, YOU GOT BLUE'S PAIL.
!
WHERE IS HE, ALABASTER?
WAH
?
OH NO...

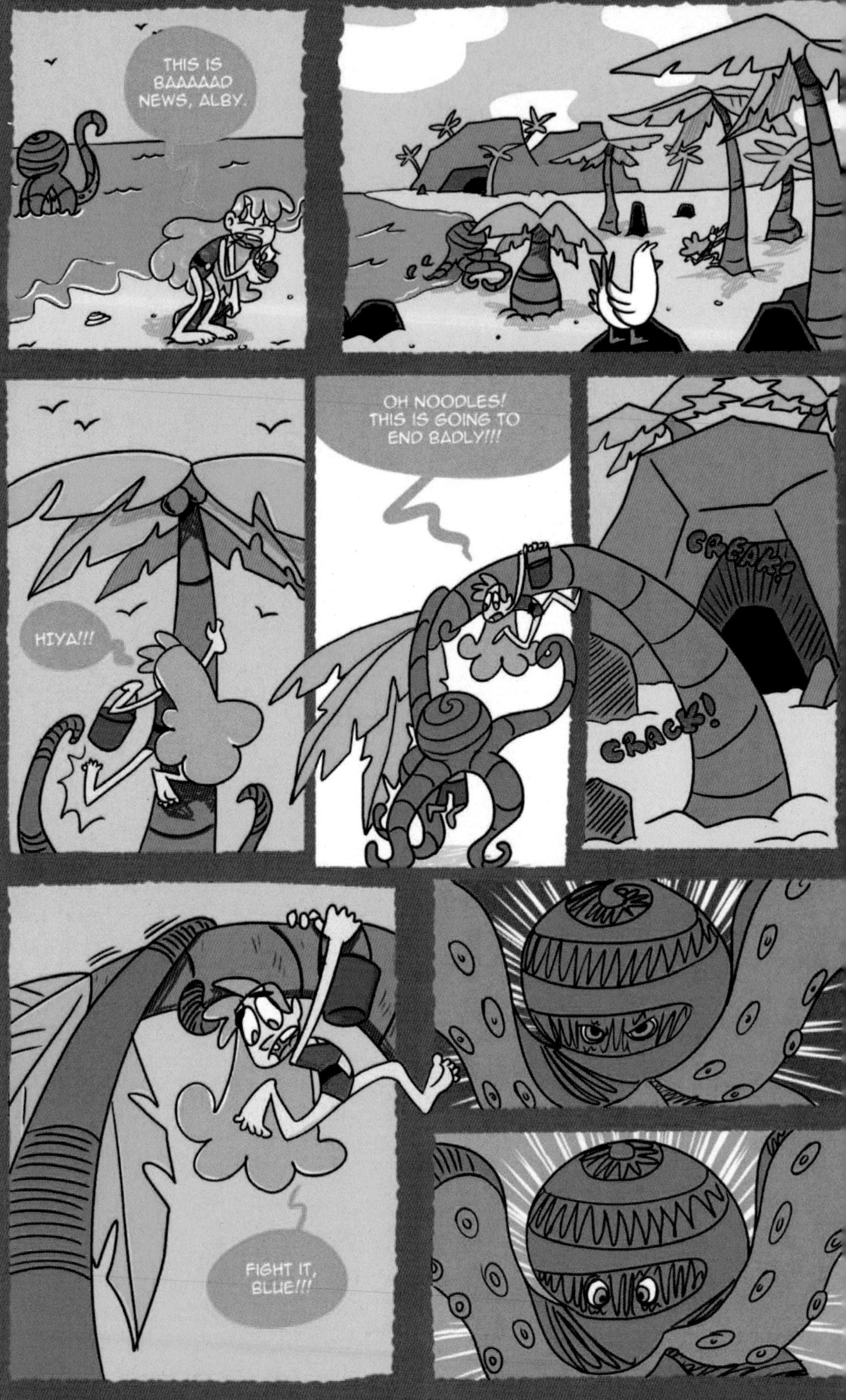
THIS IS BAAAAAD NEWS, ALBY.
HIYA!!!
OH NOODLES! THIS IS GOING TO END BADLY!!!
CREAK!
CRACK!
FIGHT IT, BLUE!!!

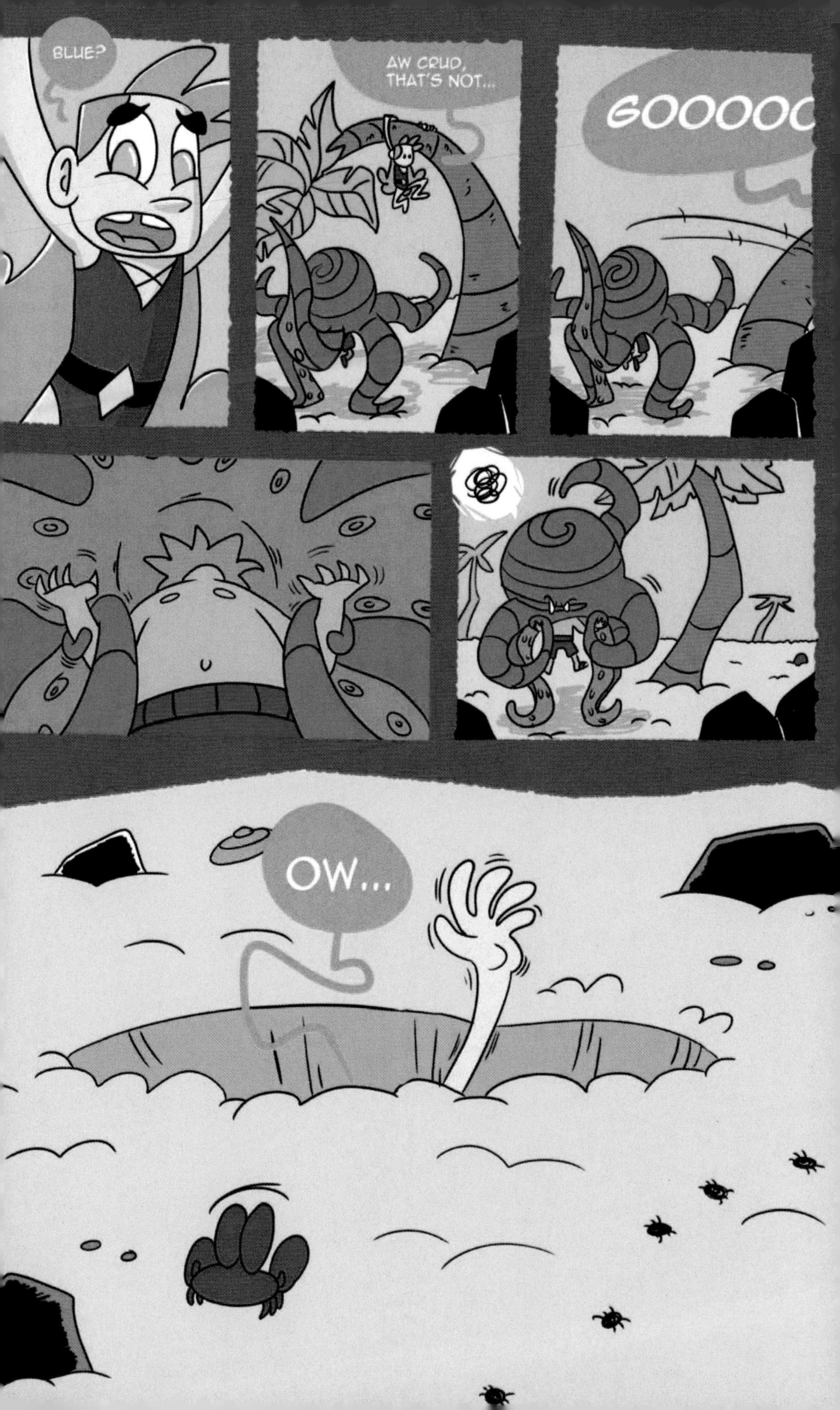

BLUE?
AW CRUD, THAT'S NOT...
GOOOOO
OW...

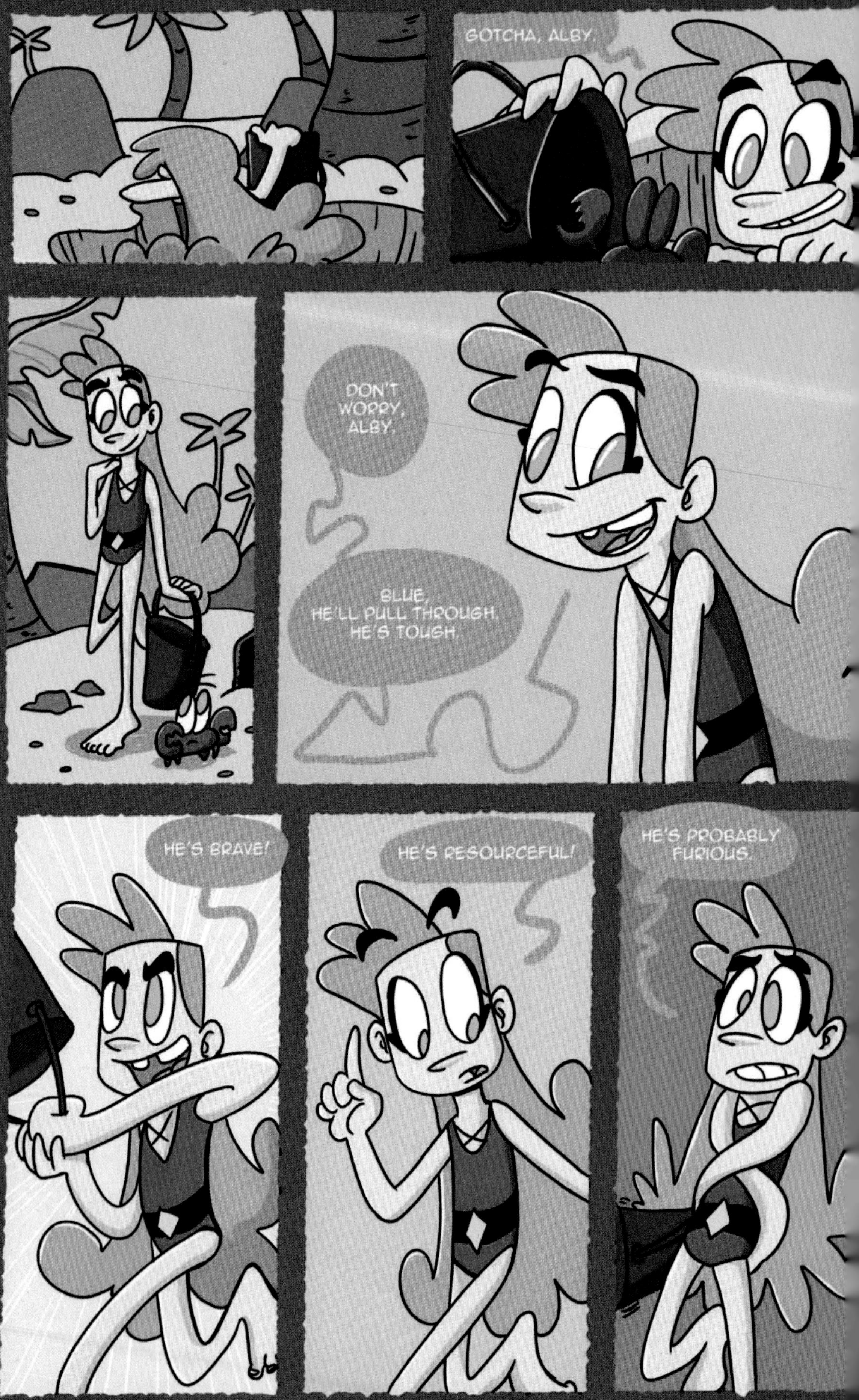
GOTCHA, ALBY.
DON'T WORRY, ALBY.
BLUE, HE'LL PULL THROUGH. HE'S TOUGH.
HE'S BRAVE!
HE'S RESOURCEFUL!
HE'S PROBABLY FURIOUS.

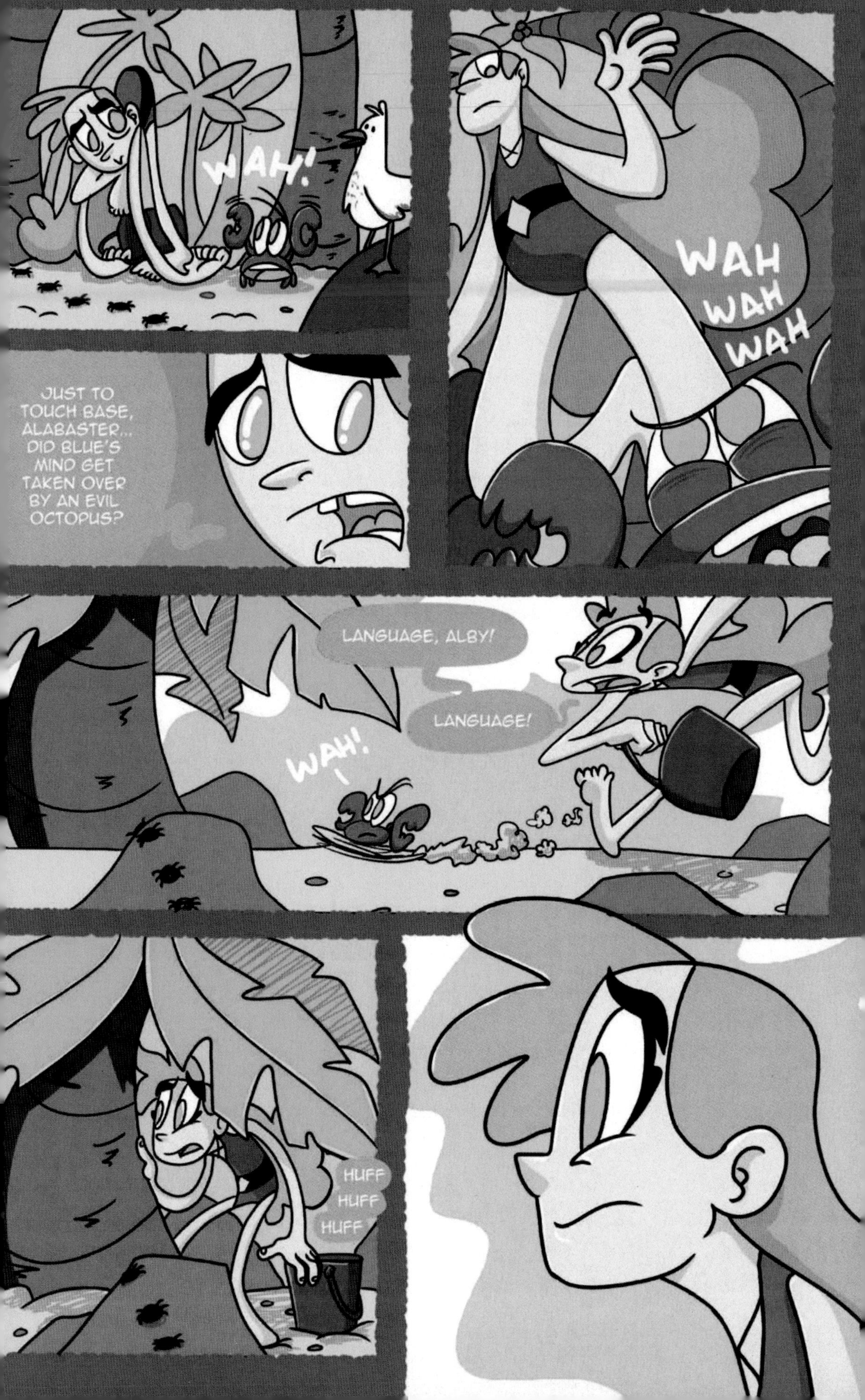
WAH!
WAH
WAH
WAH
JUST TO TOUCH BASE, ALABASTER... DID BLUE'S MIND GET TAKEN OVER BY AN EVIL OCTOPUS?
LANGUAGE, ALBY!
LANGUAGE!
WAH!
HUFF
HUFF
HUFF

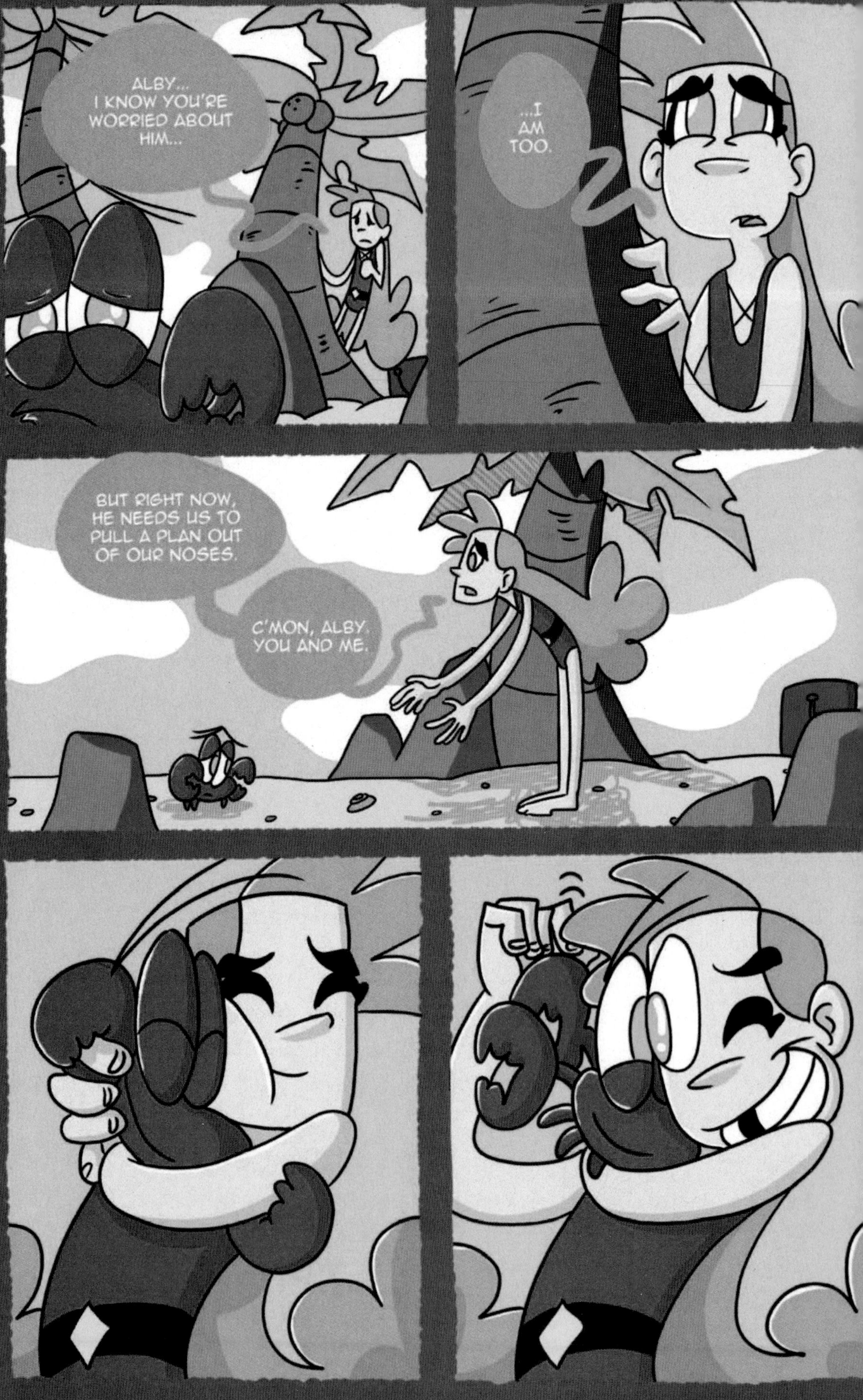
ALBY... I KNOW YOU'RE WORRIED ABOUT HIM...
...I AM TOO.
BUT RIGHT NOW, HE NEEDS US TO PULL A PLAN OUT OF OUR NOSES.
C'MON, ALBY. YOU AND ME.

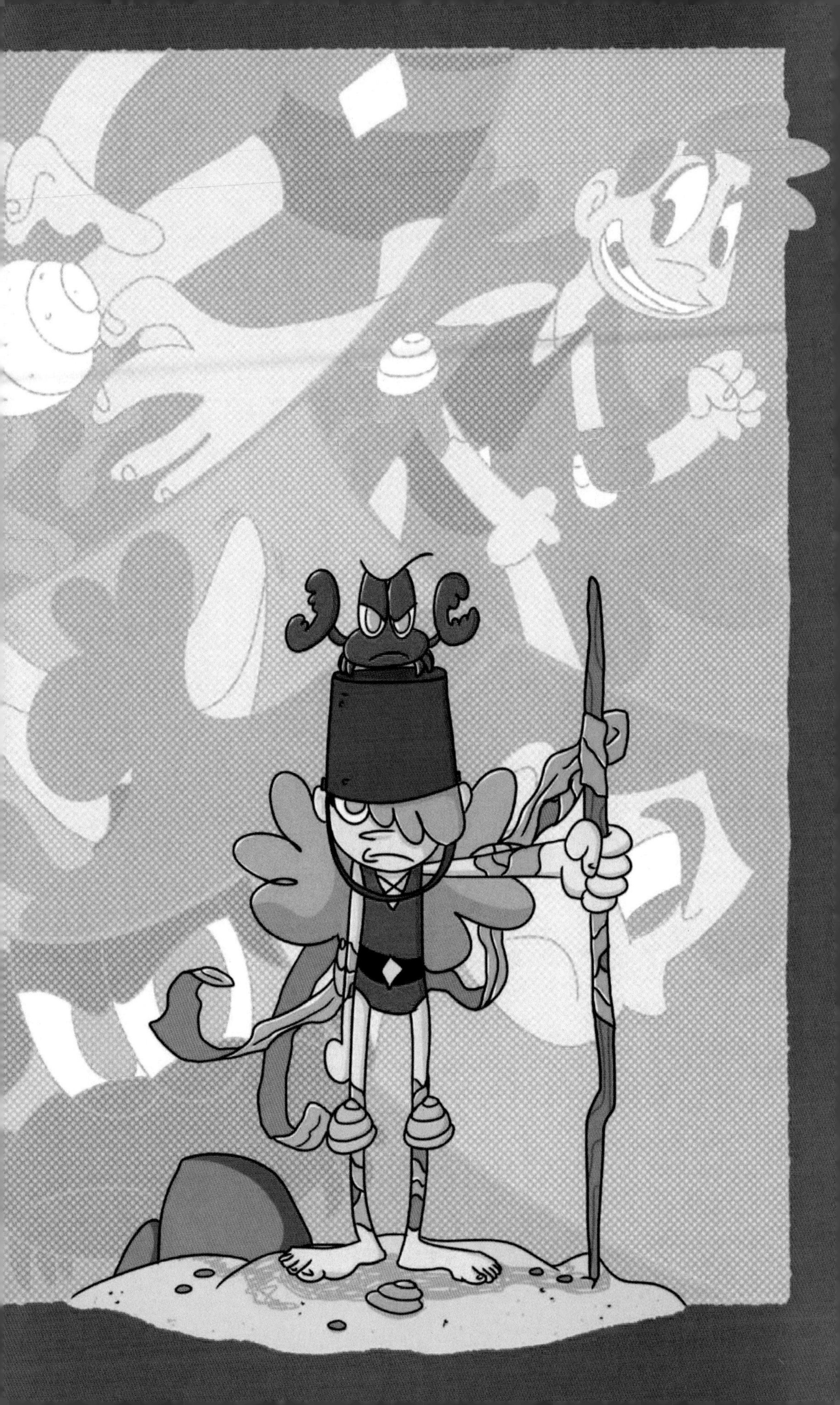

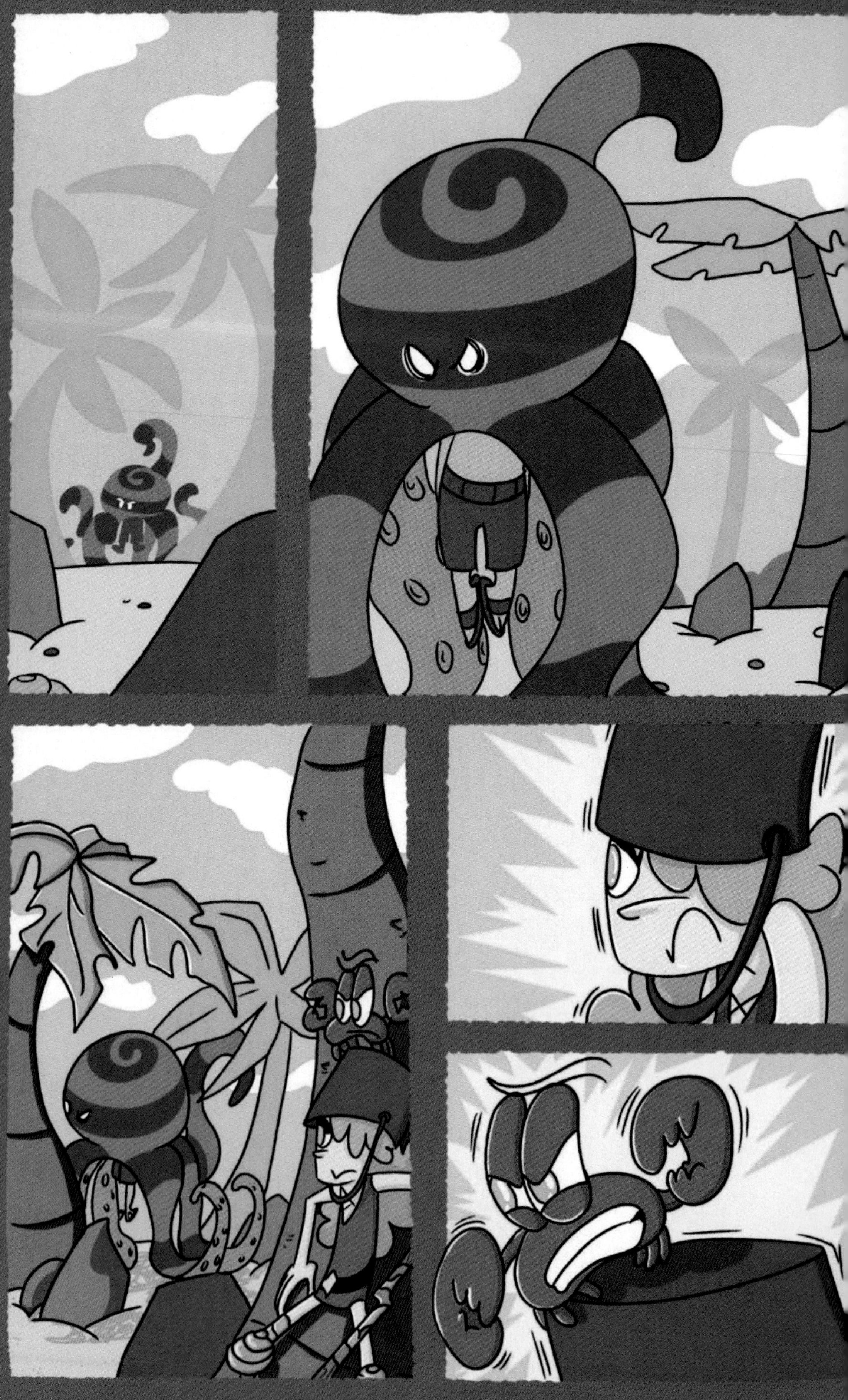

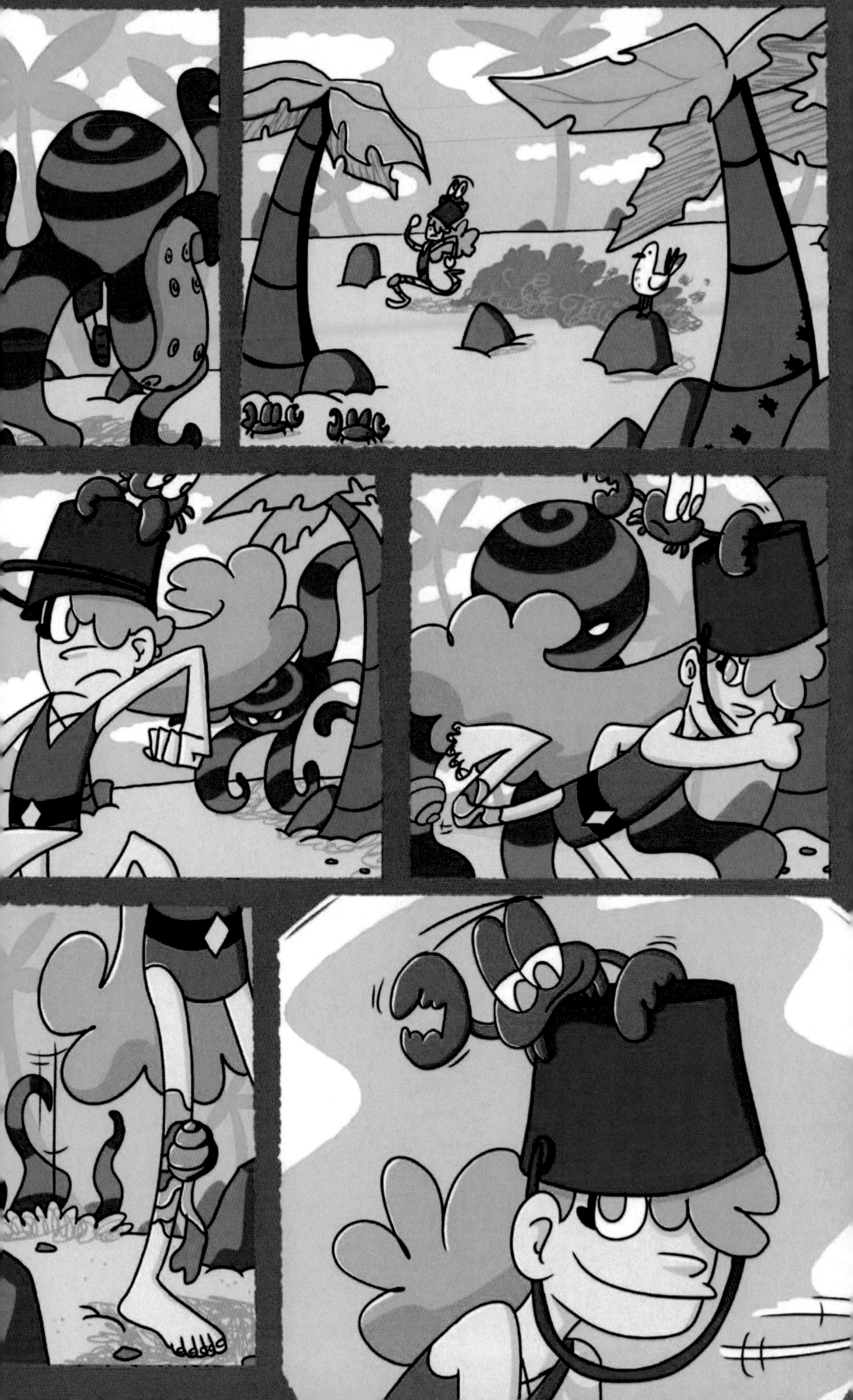

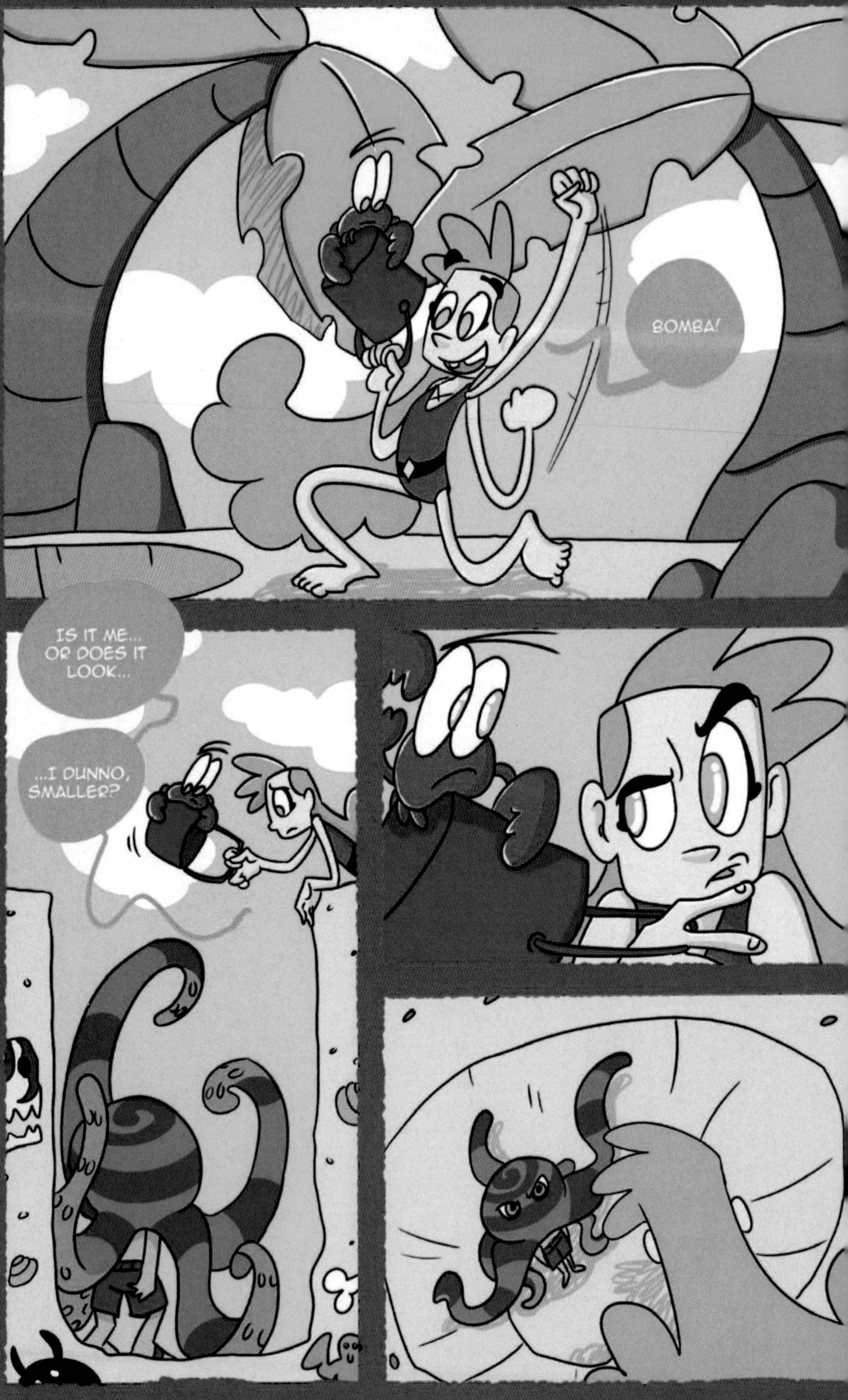
BOMBA!
IS IT ME... OR DOES IT LOOK...
...I DUNNO, SMALLER?

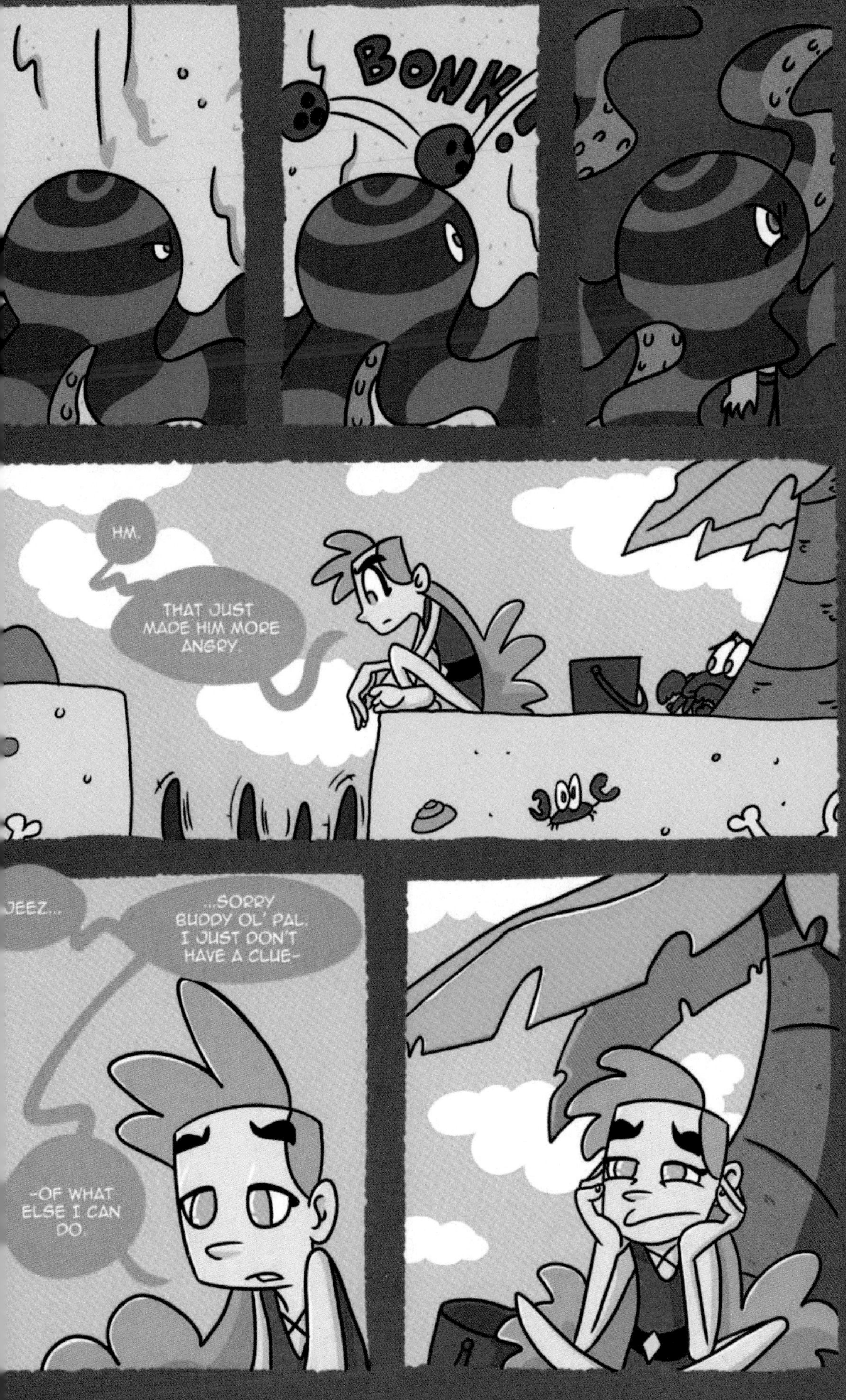

BONK
HM.
THAT JUST MADE HIM MORE ANGRY.
JEEZ...
...SORRY BUDDY OL' PAL. I JUST DON'T HAVE A CLUE-
-OF WHAT ELSE I CAN DO.

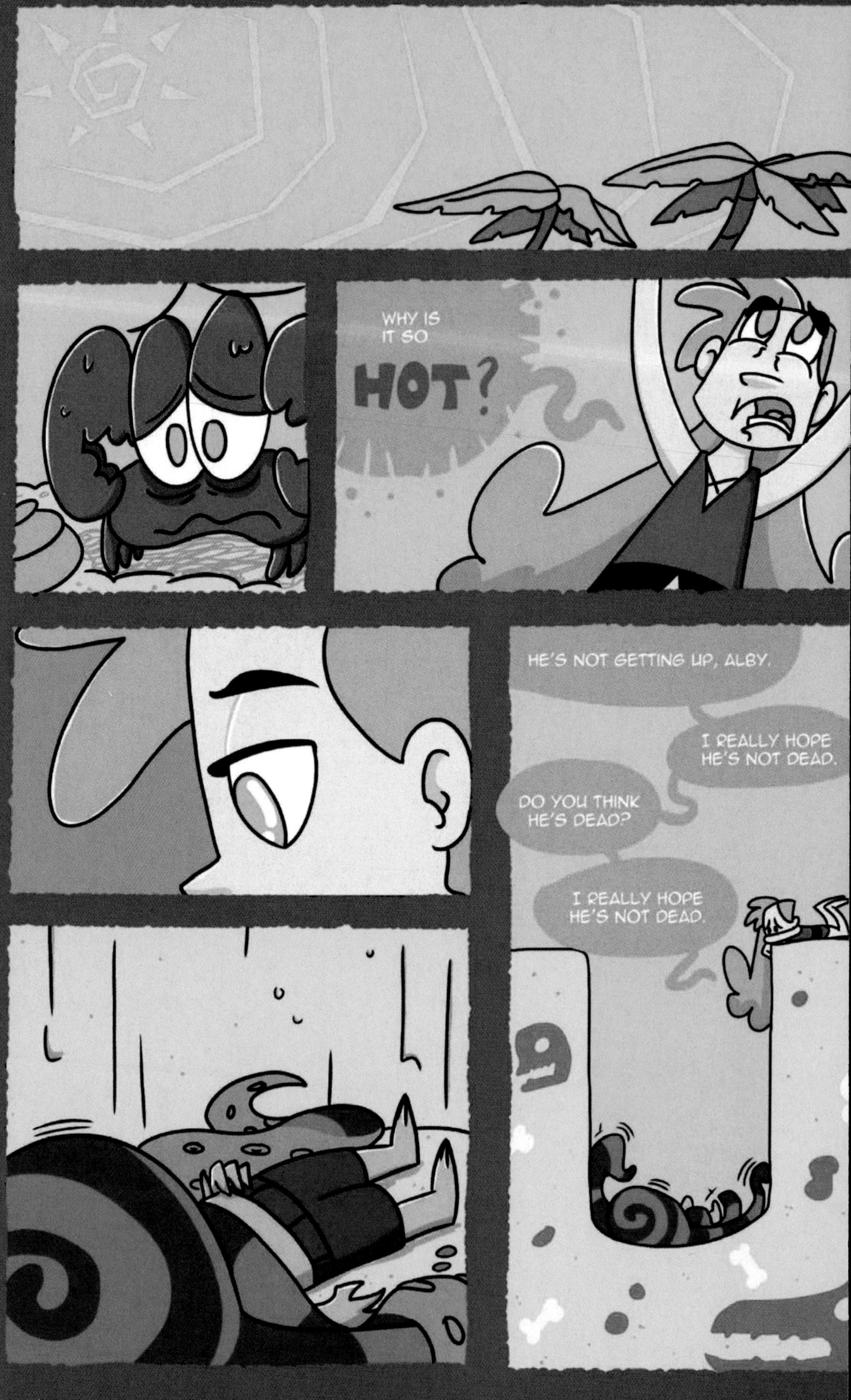

WHY IS IT SO HOT?
HE'S NOT GETTING UP, ALBY.
I REALLY HOPE HE'S NOT DEAD.
DO YOU THINK HE'S DEAD?
I REALLY HOPE HE'S NOT DEAD.

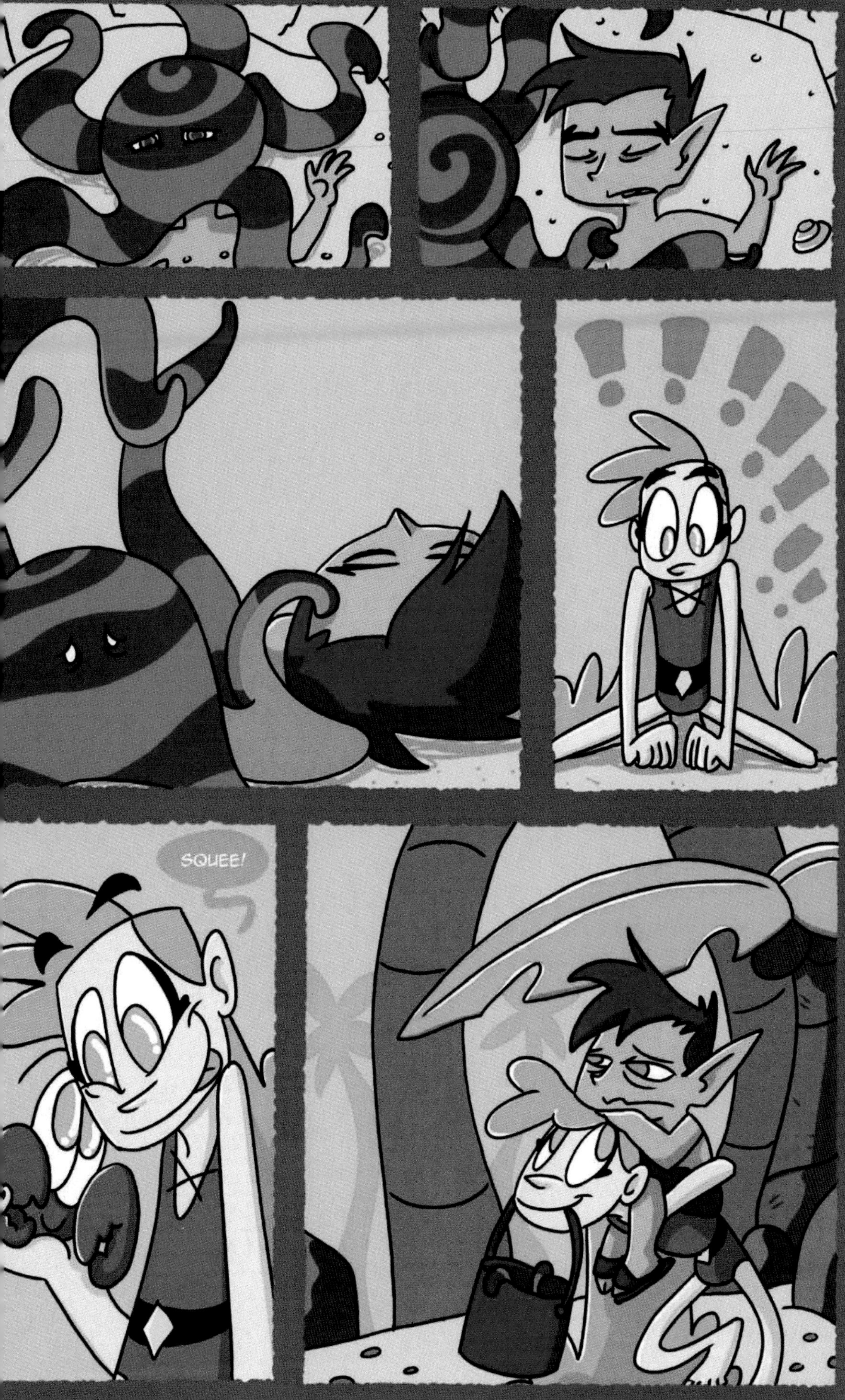
SQUEE!

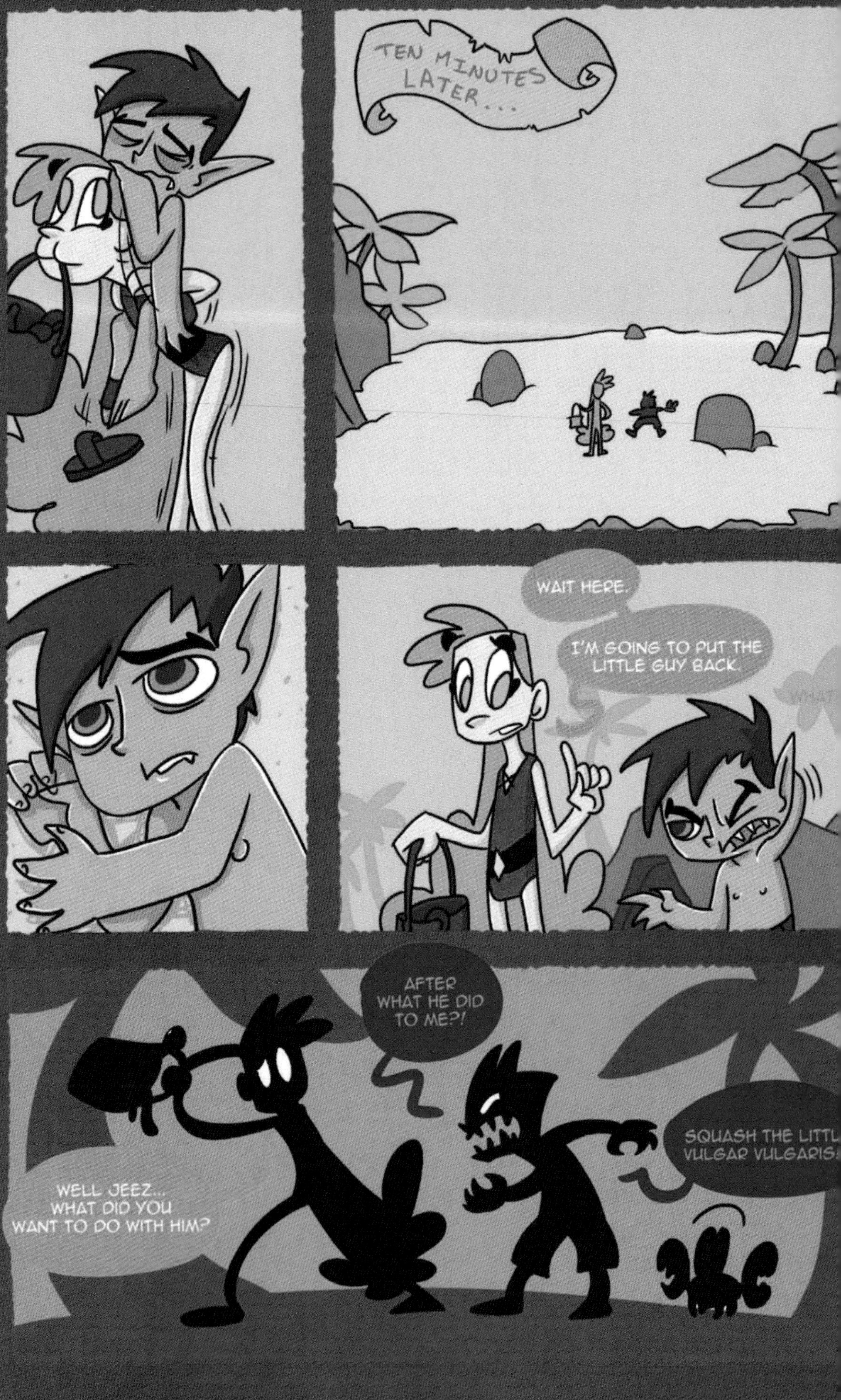

TEN MINUTES LATER...
WAIT HERE.
I'M GOING TO PUT THE LITTLE GUY BACK.
AFTER WHAT HE DID TO ME?!
WELL JEEZ... WHAT DID YOU WANT TO DO WITH HIM?
SQUASH THE LITTL
VULGAR VULGARIS

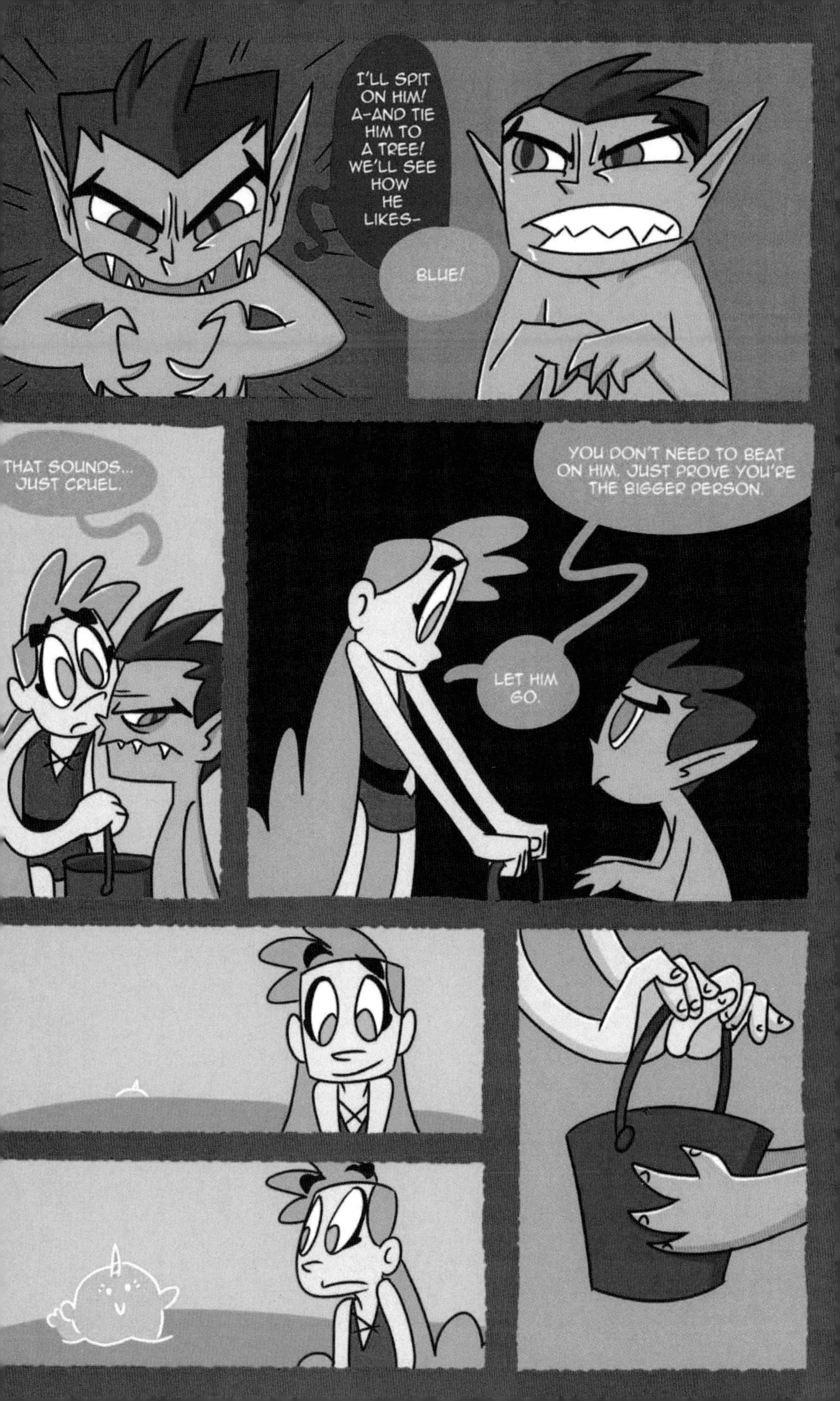
I'LL SPIT ON HIM! A-AND TIE HIM TO A TREE! WE'LL SEE HOW HE LIKES-
BLUE!
THAT SOUNDS... JUST CRUEL.
YOU DON'T NEED TO BEAT ON HIM. JUST PROVE YOU'RE THE BIGGER PERSON.
LET HIM GO.

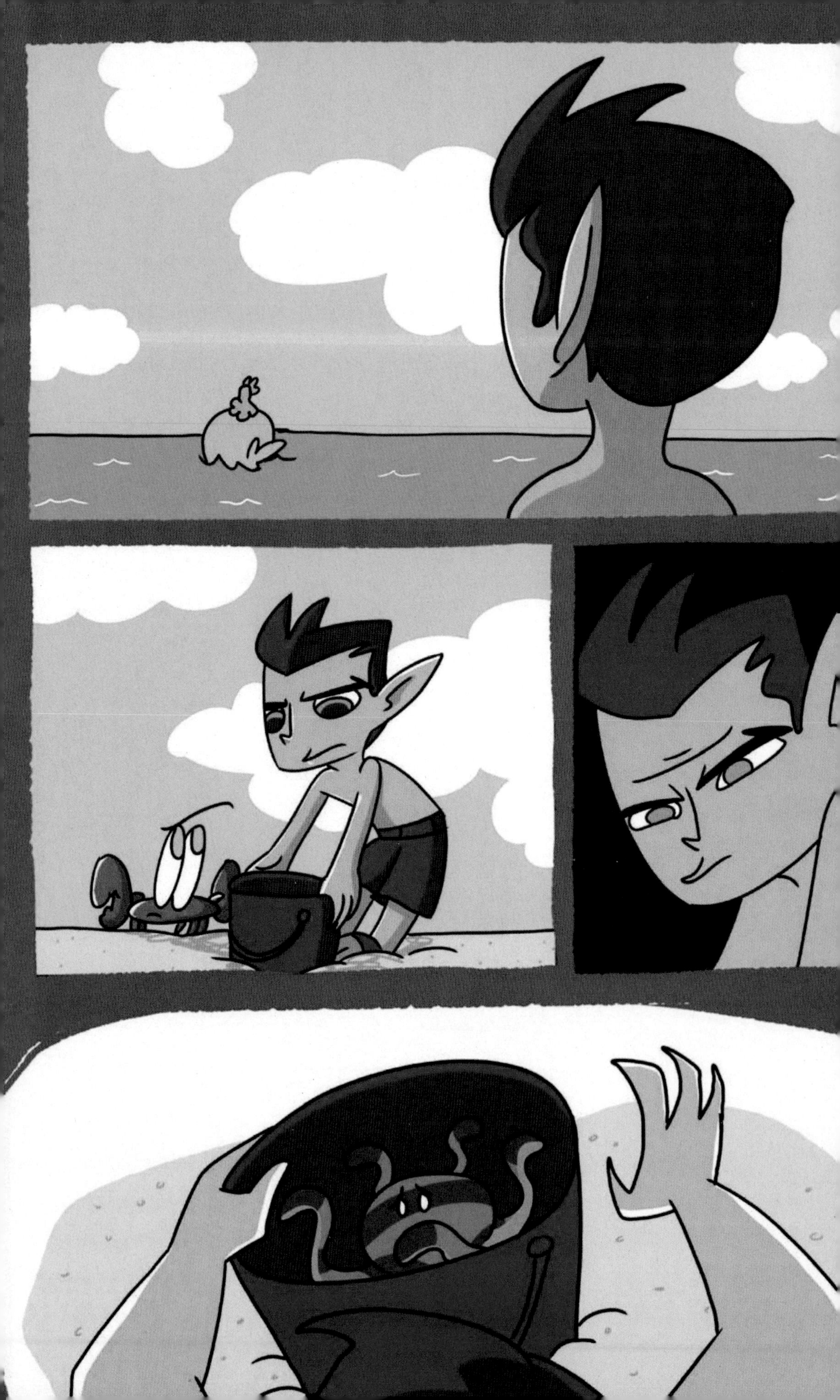

CONCEPT ART

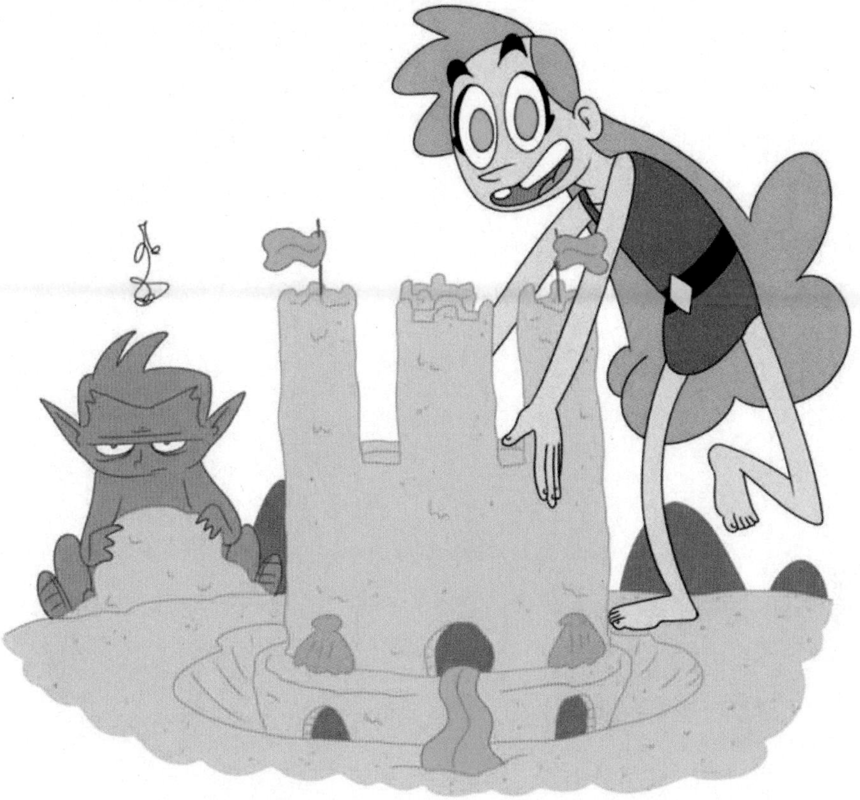

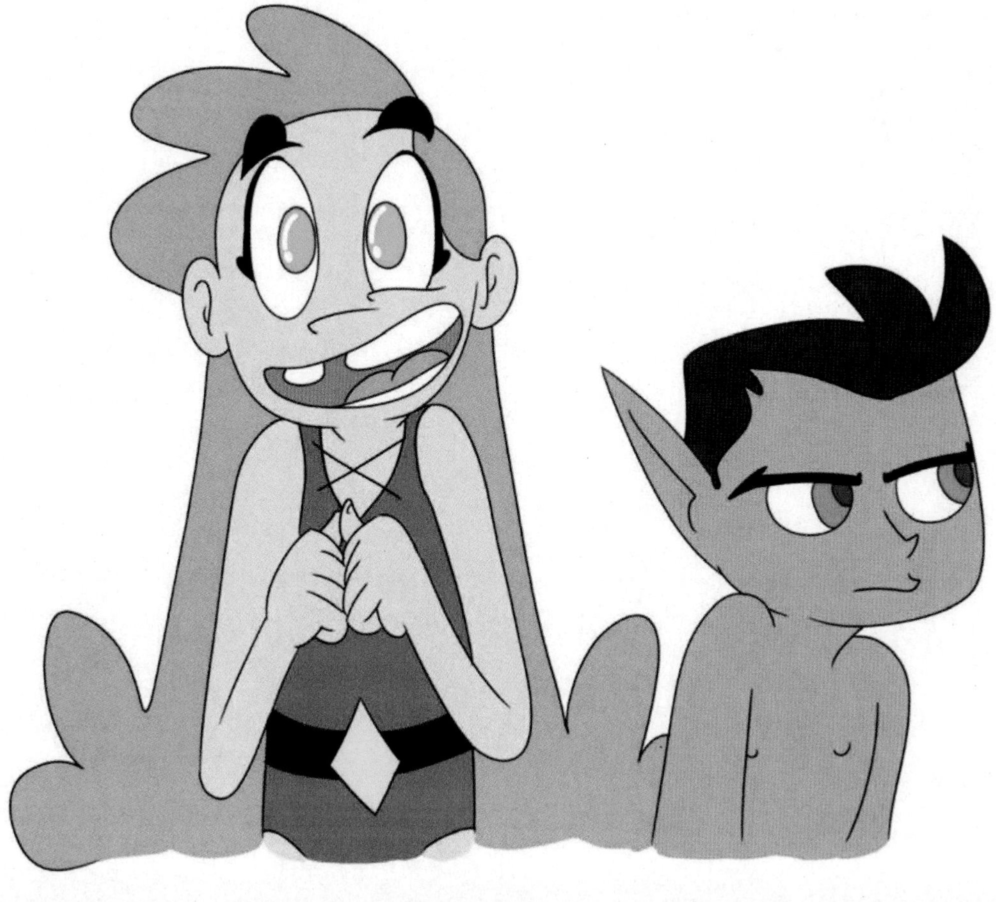

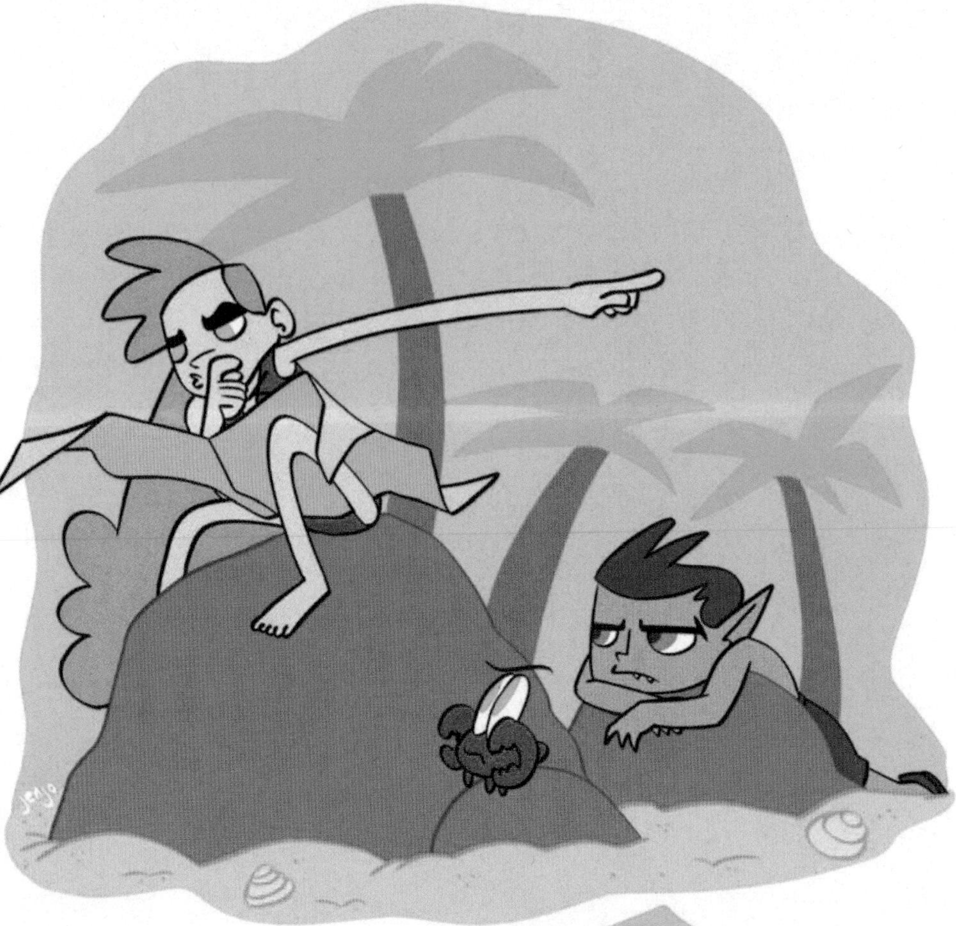

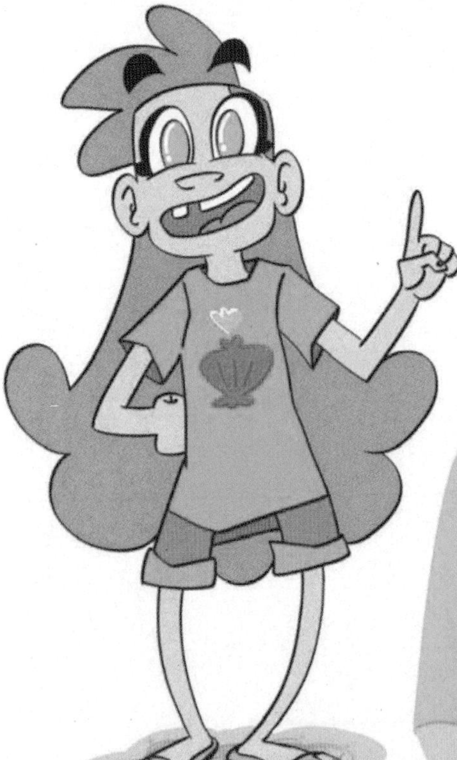

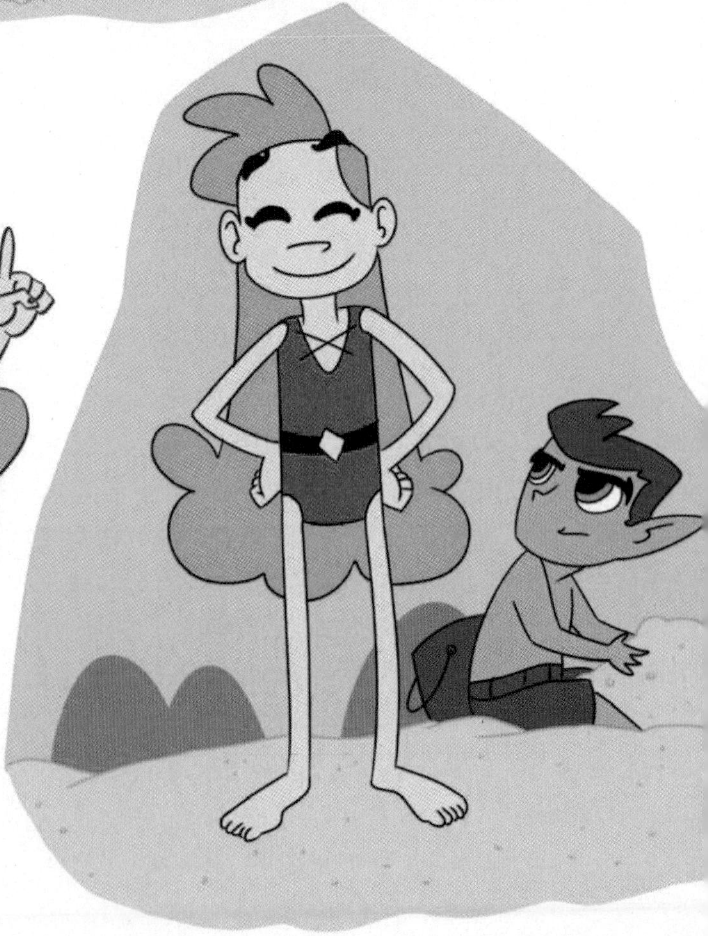

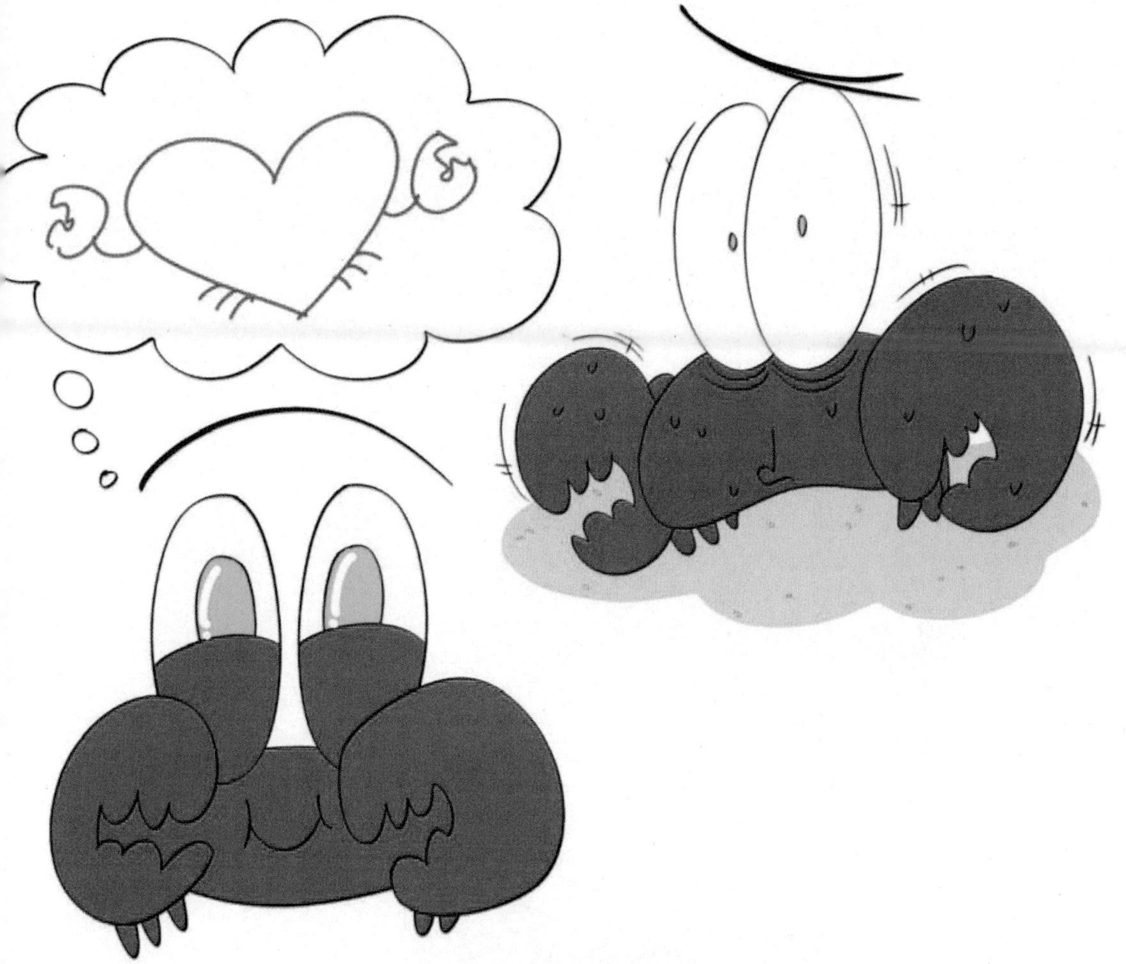

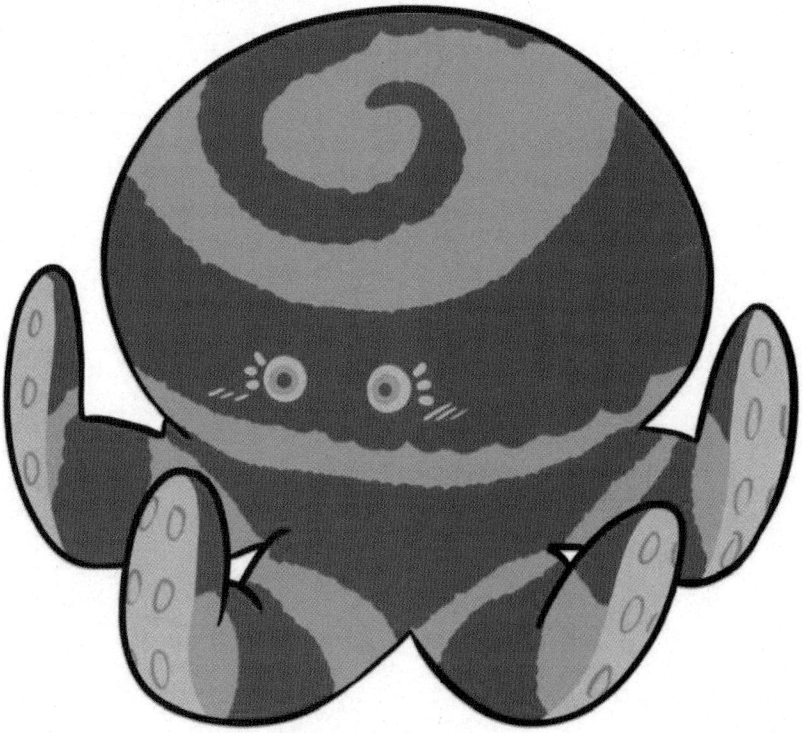

SEAFOAM

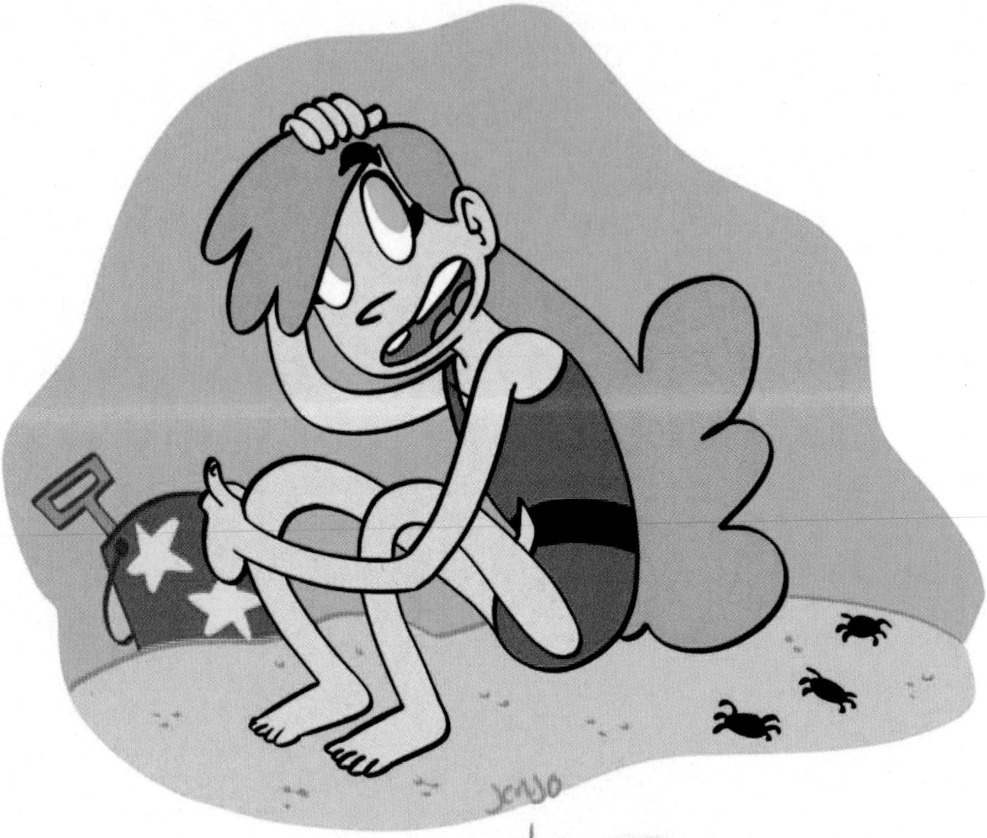

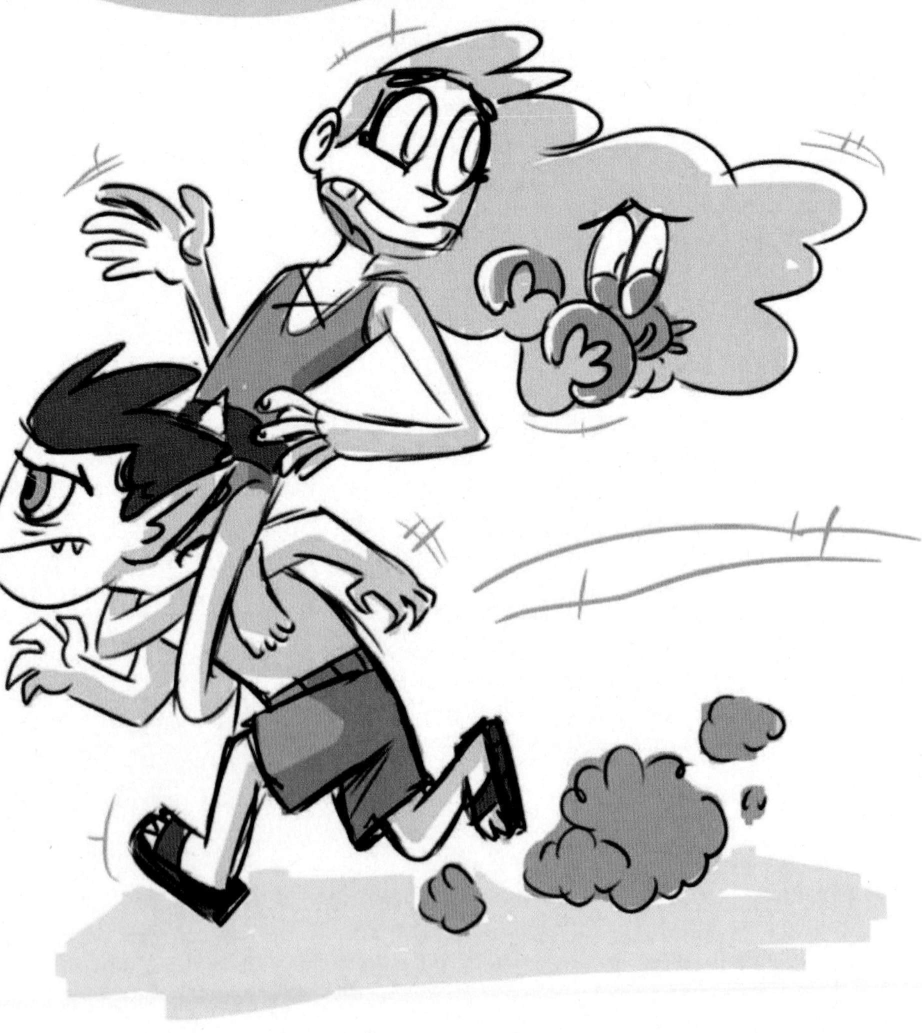

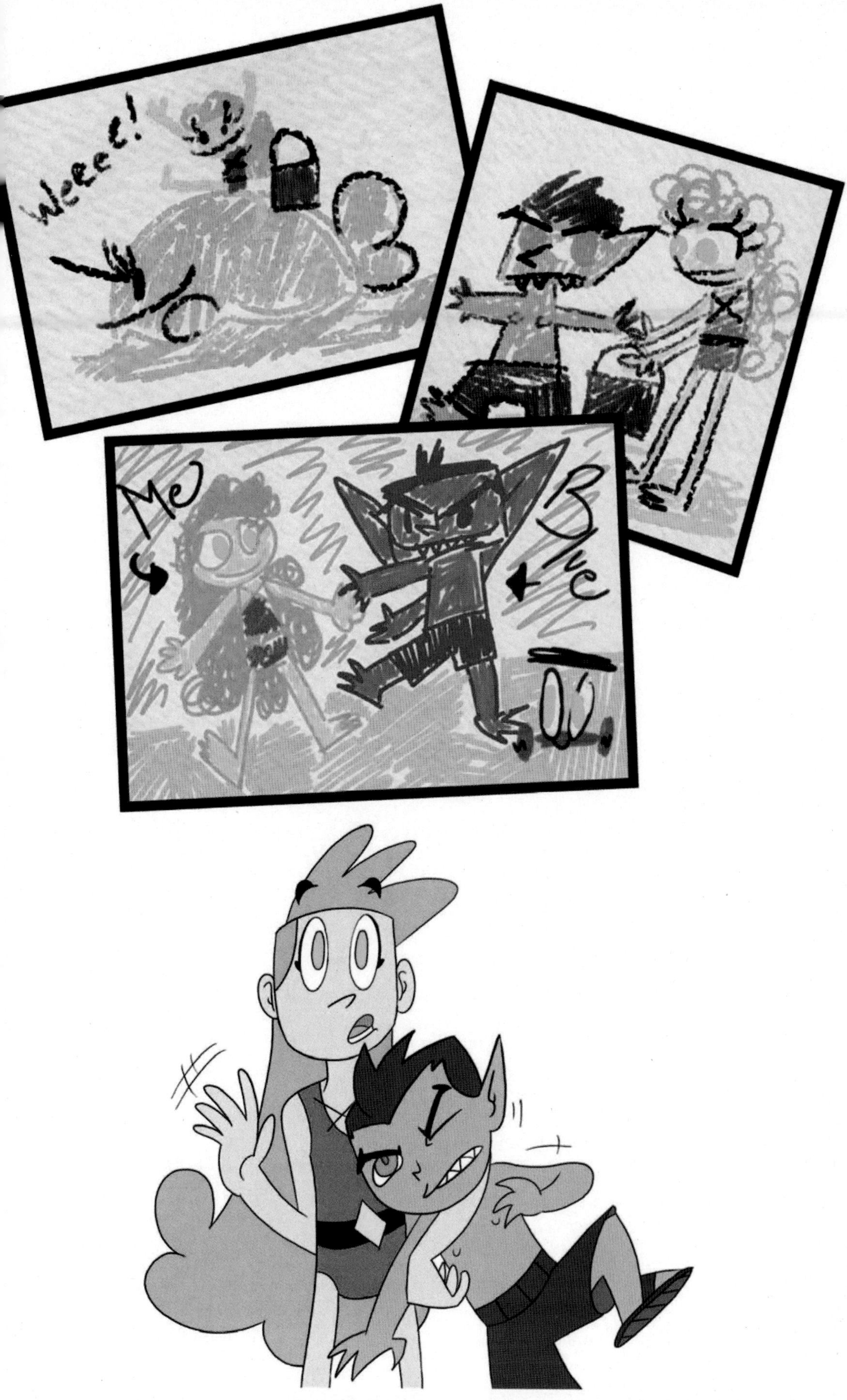
Weeee!
Me
Blue

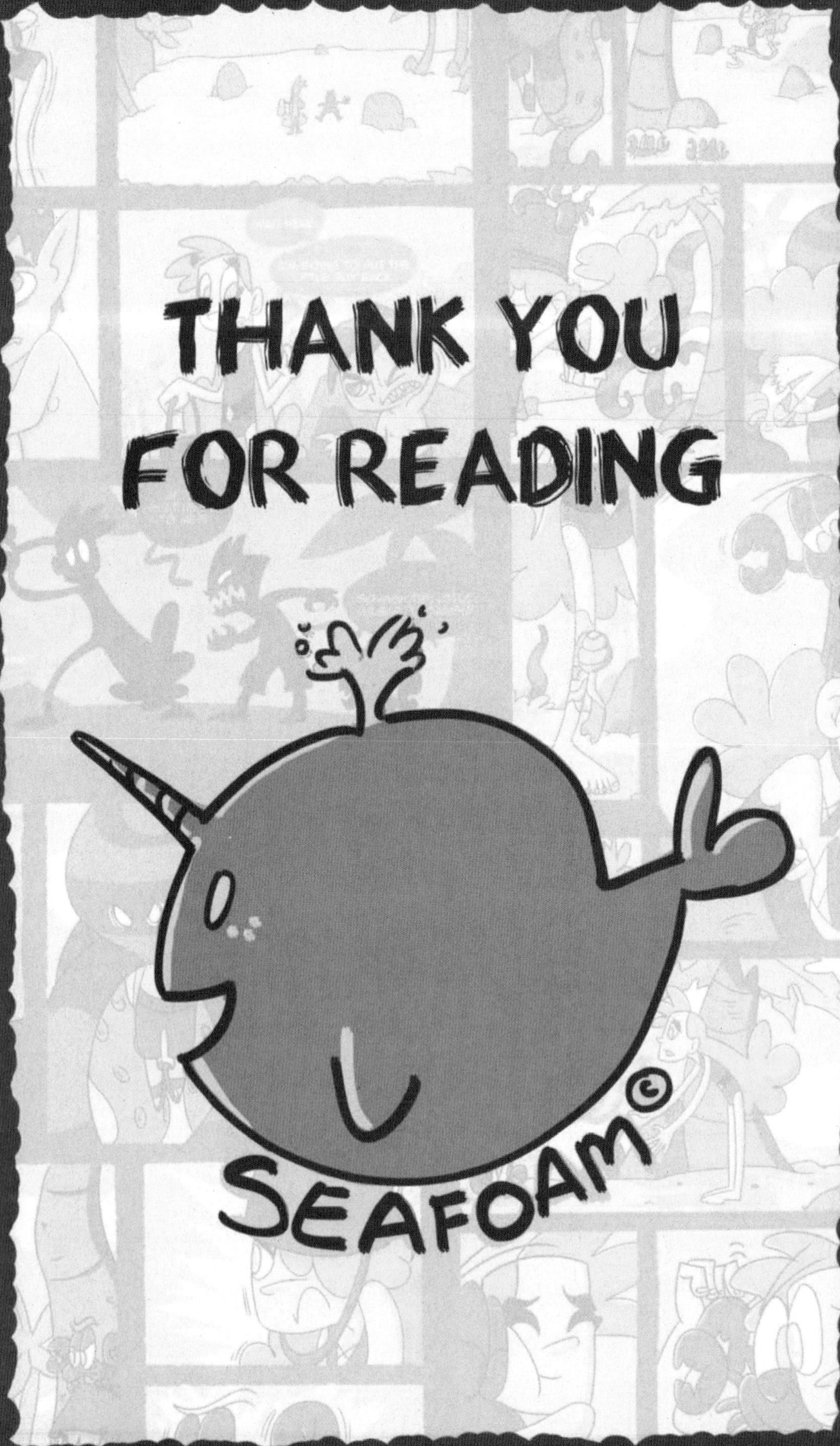
THANK YOU
FOR READING
SEAFOAM©

ISSUE TWO
"A DEVIOUS DJINN"

THERE WAS A GIRL NAMED MADISON
WHO LOVED TO PLAY IN SAND
ONE DAY SHE FOUND A MAGICAL WHALE
WASHED UP ON THE LAND

SO MADISON TICKLED THE WHALE
TILL IT ROLLED INTO THE SEA
THE WHALE WAS SO GRATEFUL
THAT IT FOUND SOMEONE TO BE
A FRIEND FOR MADISON

NOW EVERYDAY SHE JOURNEYS
TO A MAGICAL LAND

TODAY SHE FINDS HERSELF FACING
A DJINN WITH A DEVIOUS PLAN

WRITTEN AND ILLUSTRATED BY

JEANINE-JONEE

CONTENT EDITED BY

EMILY BRIGOLIN
NICOLE D'ANDRIA

ADDITIONAL COLORING BY

KYLE P. HOLLAND

BRYAN SEATON: PUBLISHER/ CEO
SHAWN GABBORIN: EDITOR IN CHIEF
JASON MARTIN: PUBLISHER-DANGER ZONE
NICOLE D'ANDRIA: MARKETING DIRECTOR/EDITOR
JESSICA LOWRIE: SOCIAL MEDIA CZAR
DANIELLE DAVISON: EXECUTIVE ADMINISTRATOR
CHAD CICCONI: OFFICIAL NARWHAL WRANGLER
SHAWN PRYOR: PRESIDENT OF CREATOR RELATIONS

SEAFOAM

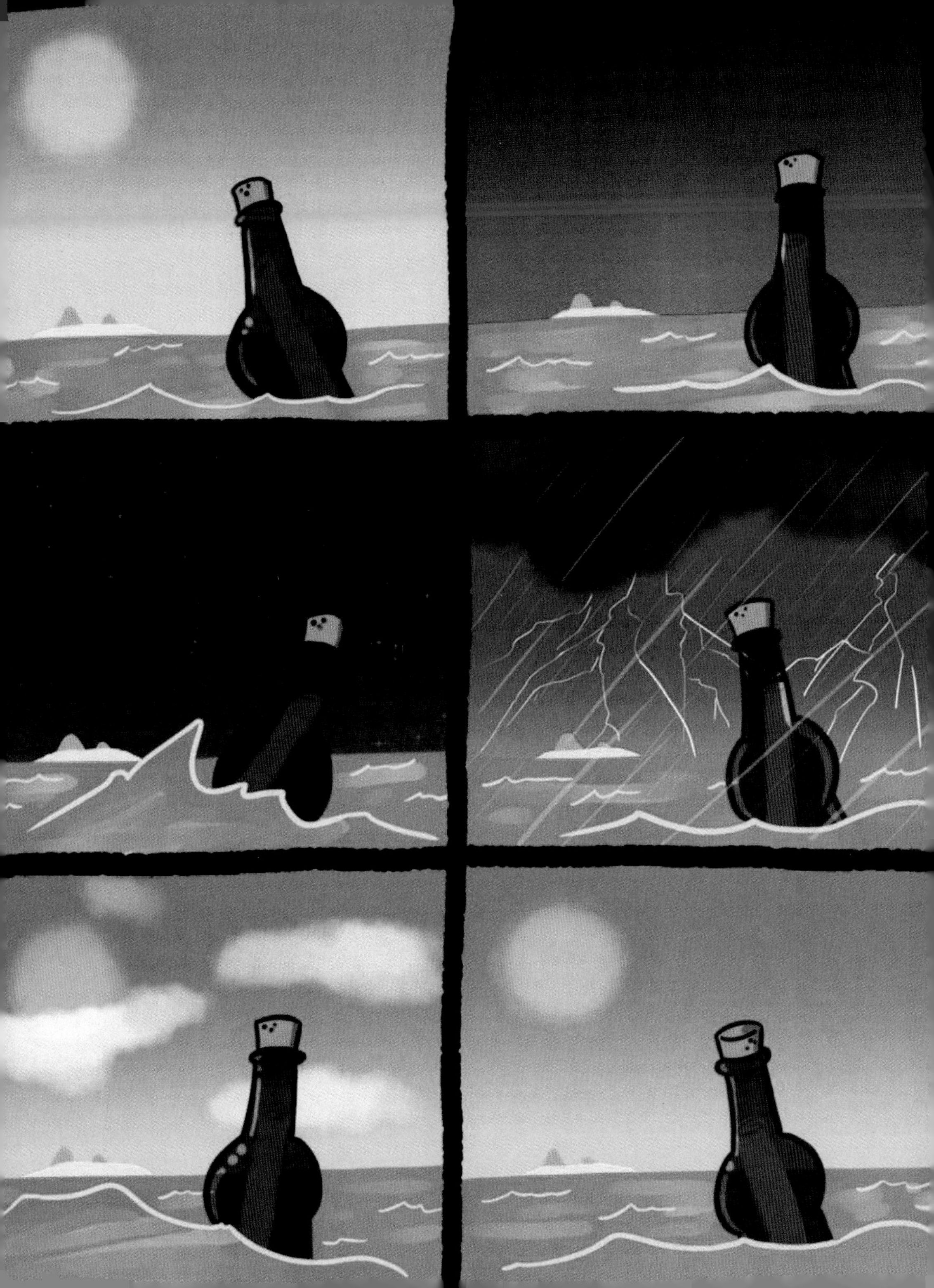

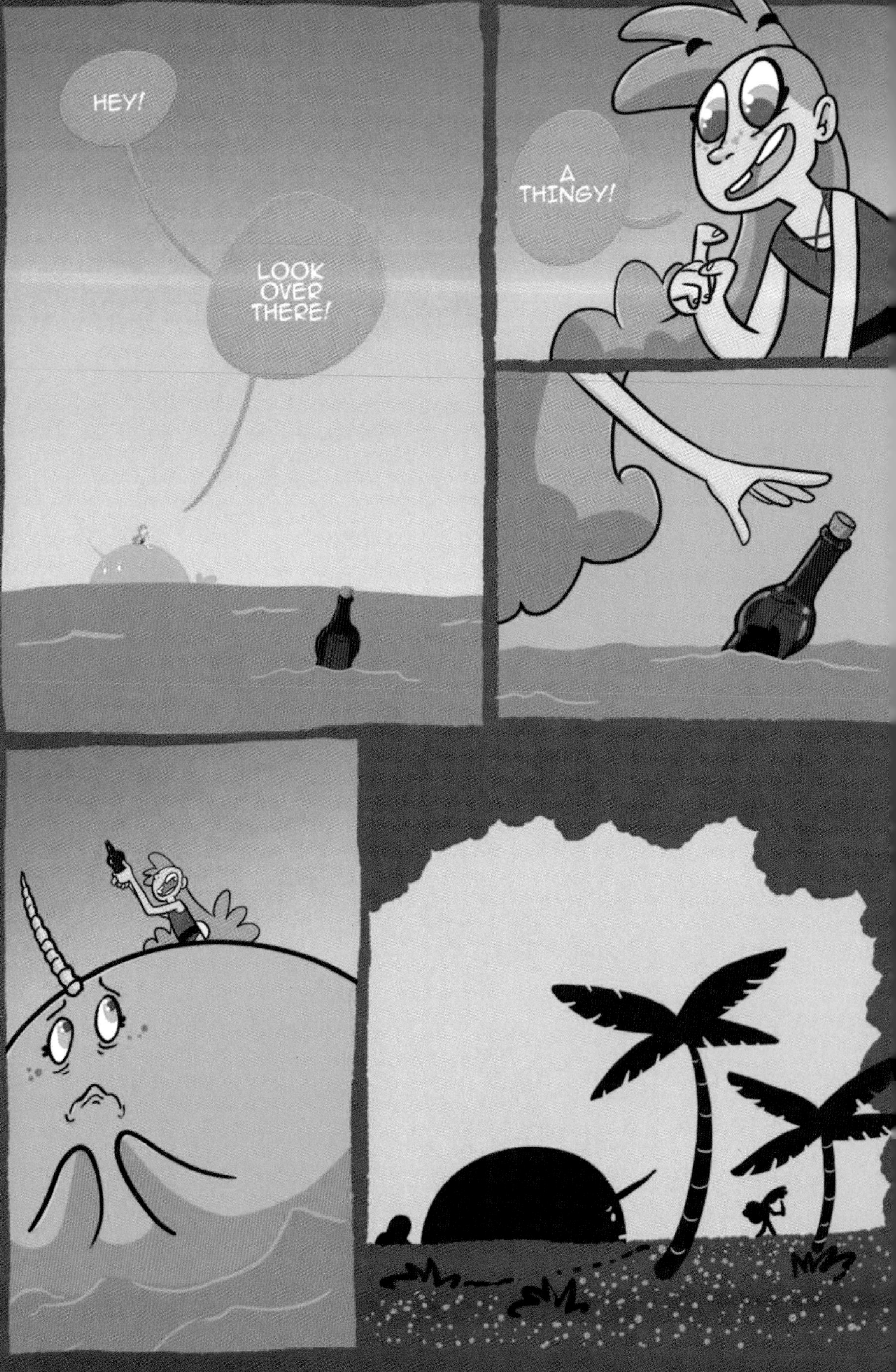
HEY!
LOOK OVER THERE!
A THINGY!

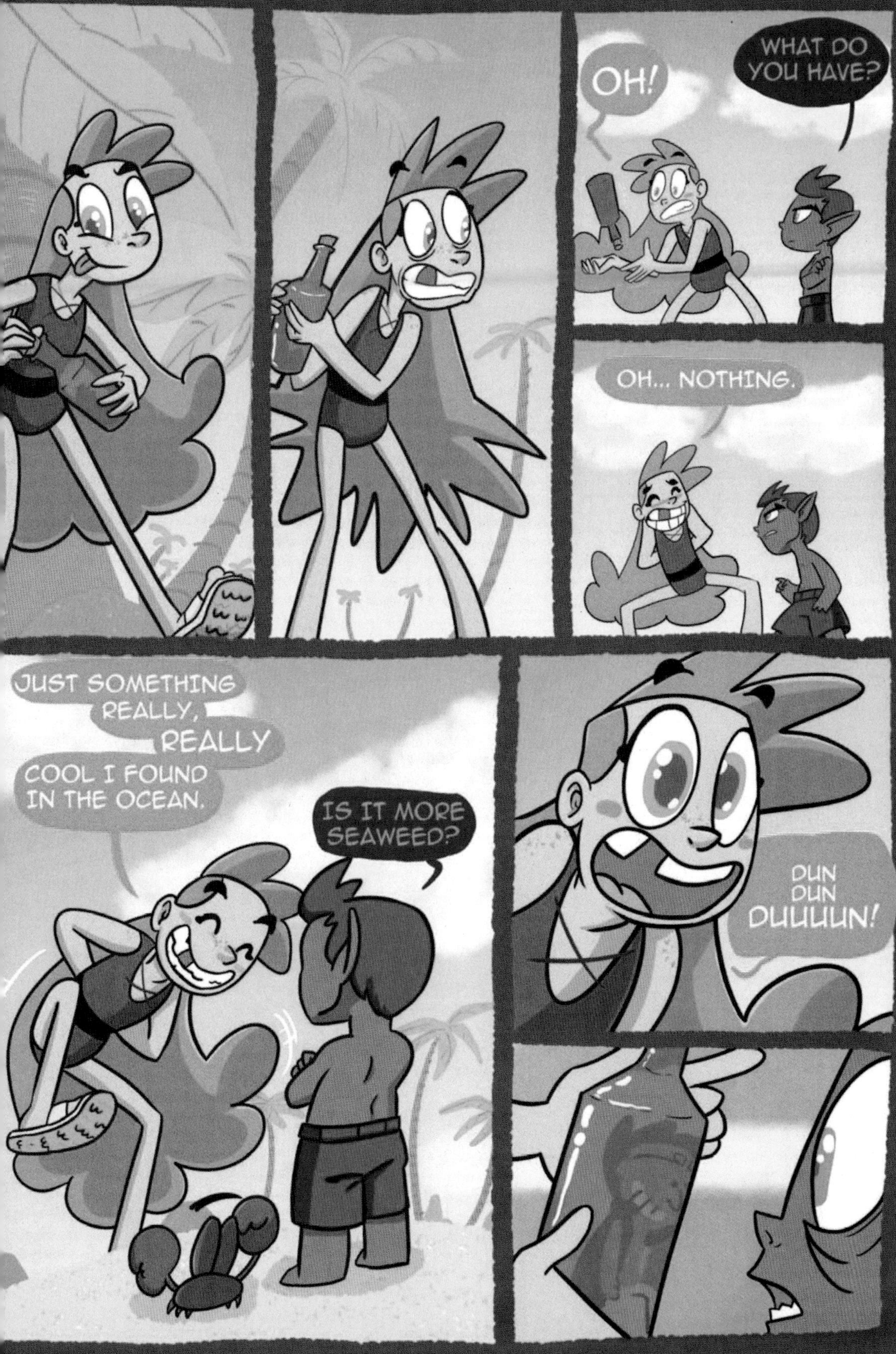
OH!
WHAT DO YOU HAVE?
OH... NOTHING.
JUST SOMETHING REALLY, REALLY COOL I FOUND IN THE OCEAN.
IS IT MORE SEAWEED?
DUN DUN DUUUUN!

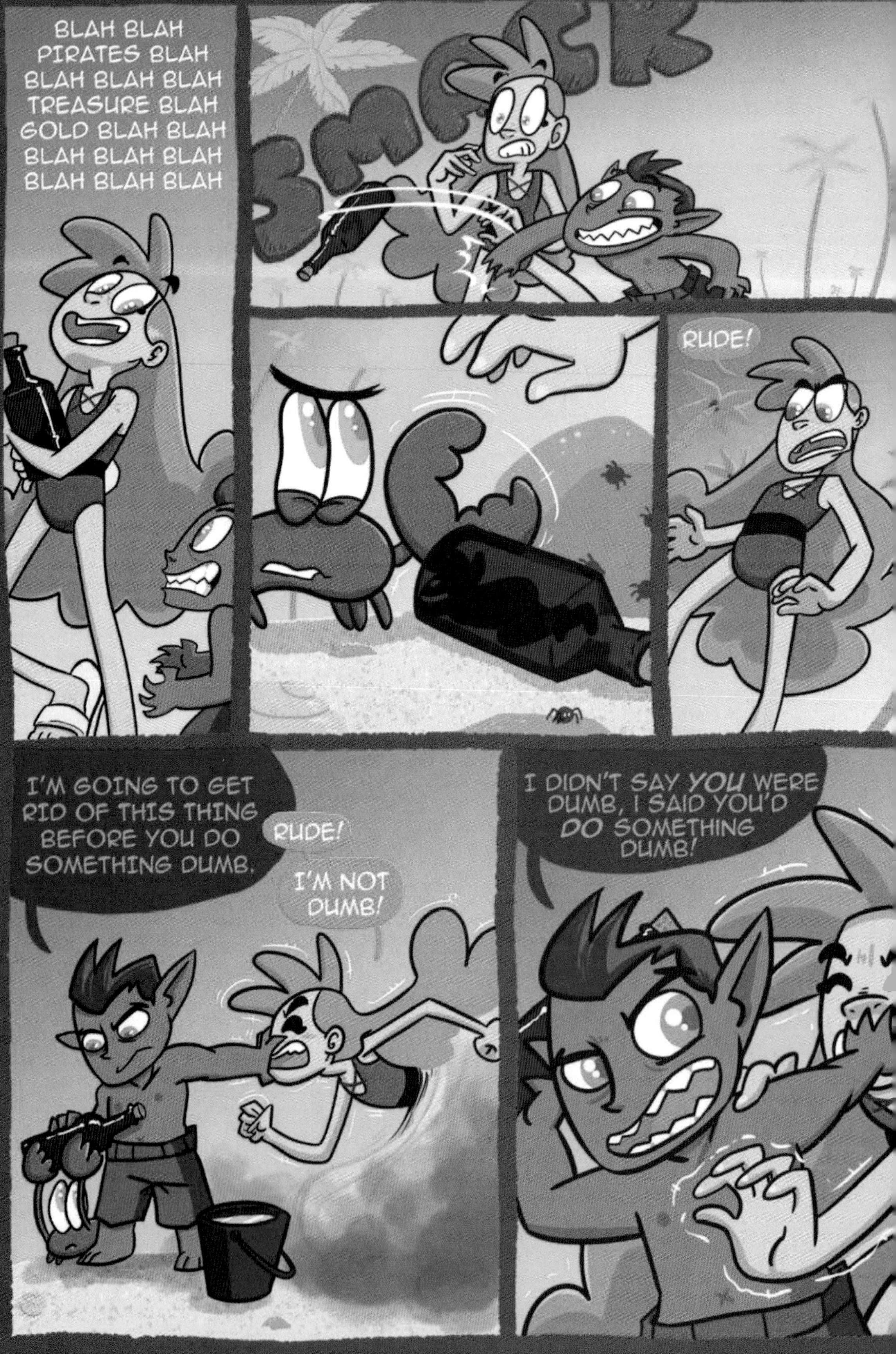
BLAH BLAH PIRATES BLAH BLAH BLAH BLAH TREASURE BLAH GOLD BLAH BLAH BLAH BLAH BLAH BLAH BLAH BLAH
SMACK
RUDE!
I'M GOING TO GET RID OF THIS THING BEFORE YOU DO SOMETHING DUMB.
RUDE!
I'M NOT DUMB!
I DIDN'T SAY *YOU* WERE DUMB, I SAID YOU'D *DO* SOMETHING DUMB!

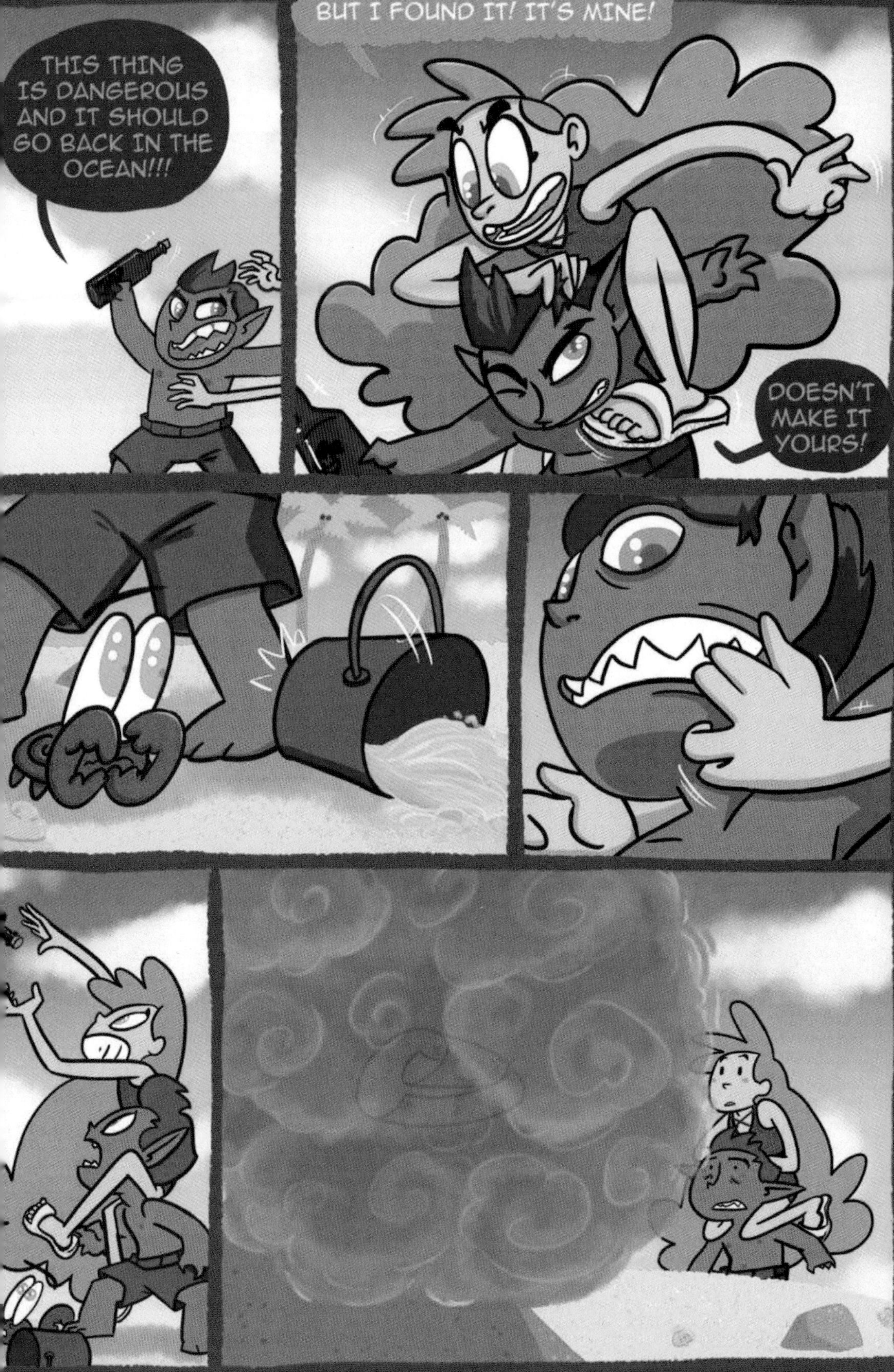
THIS THING IS DANGEROUS AND IT SHOULD GO BACK IN THE OCEAN!!!
BUT I FOUND IT! IT'S MINE!
DOESN'T MAKE IT YOURS!

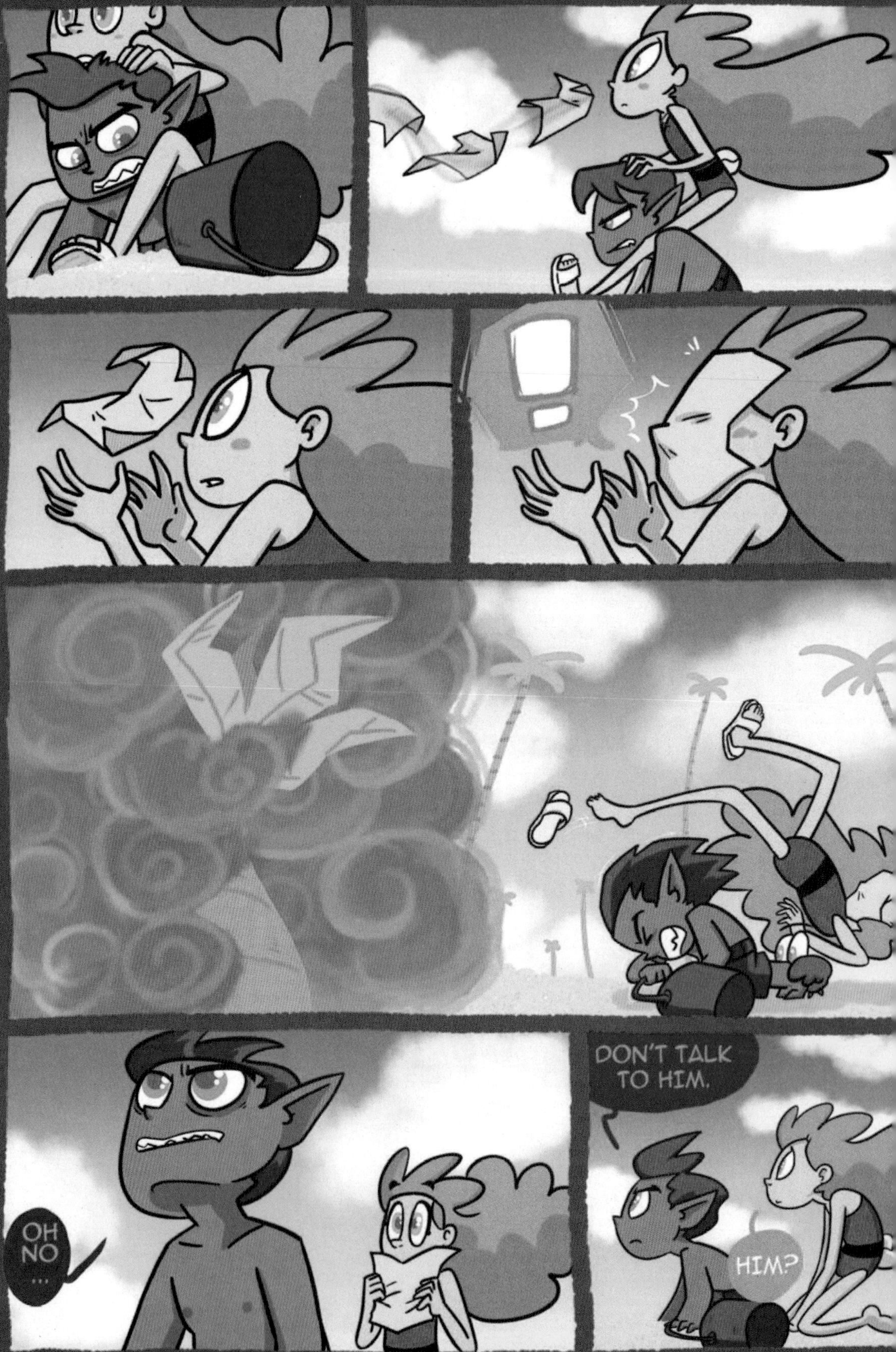
OH NO ...
DON'T TALK TO HIM.
HIM?

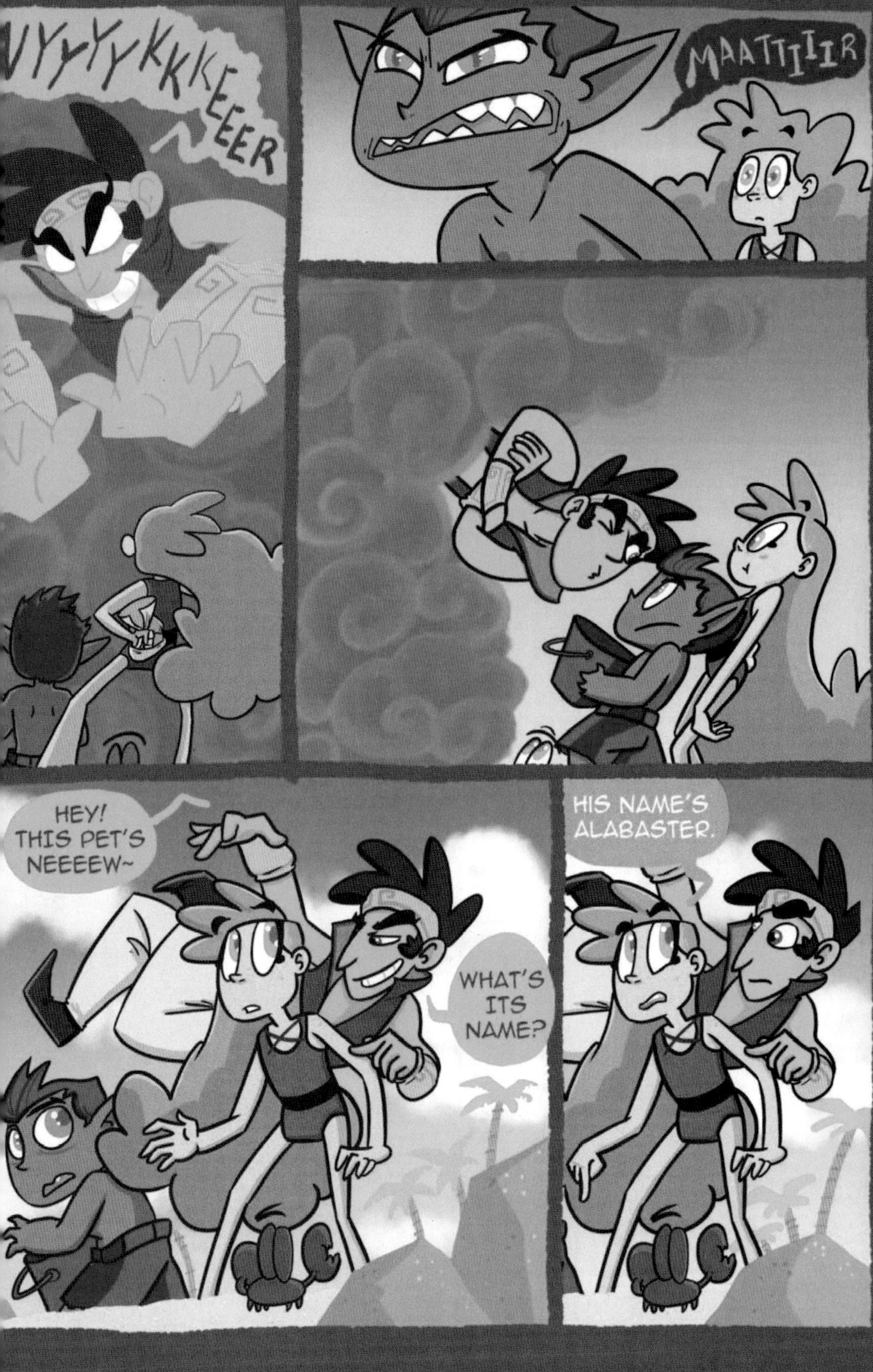

YYYYYKKKEEER
MAATTIIIR
HEY! THIS PET'S NEEEEW~
WHAT'S ITS NAME?
HIS NAME'S ALABASTER.

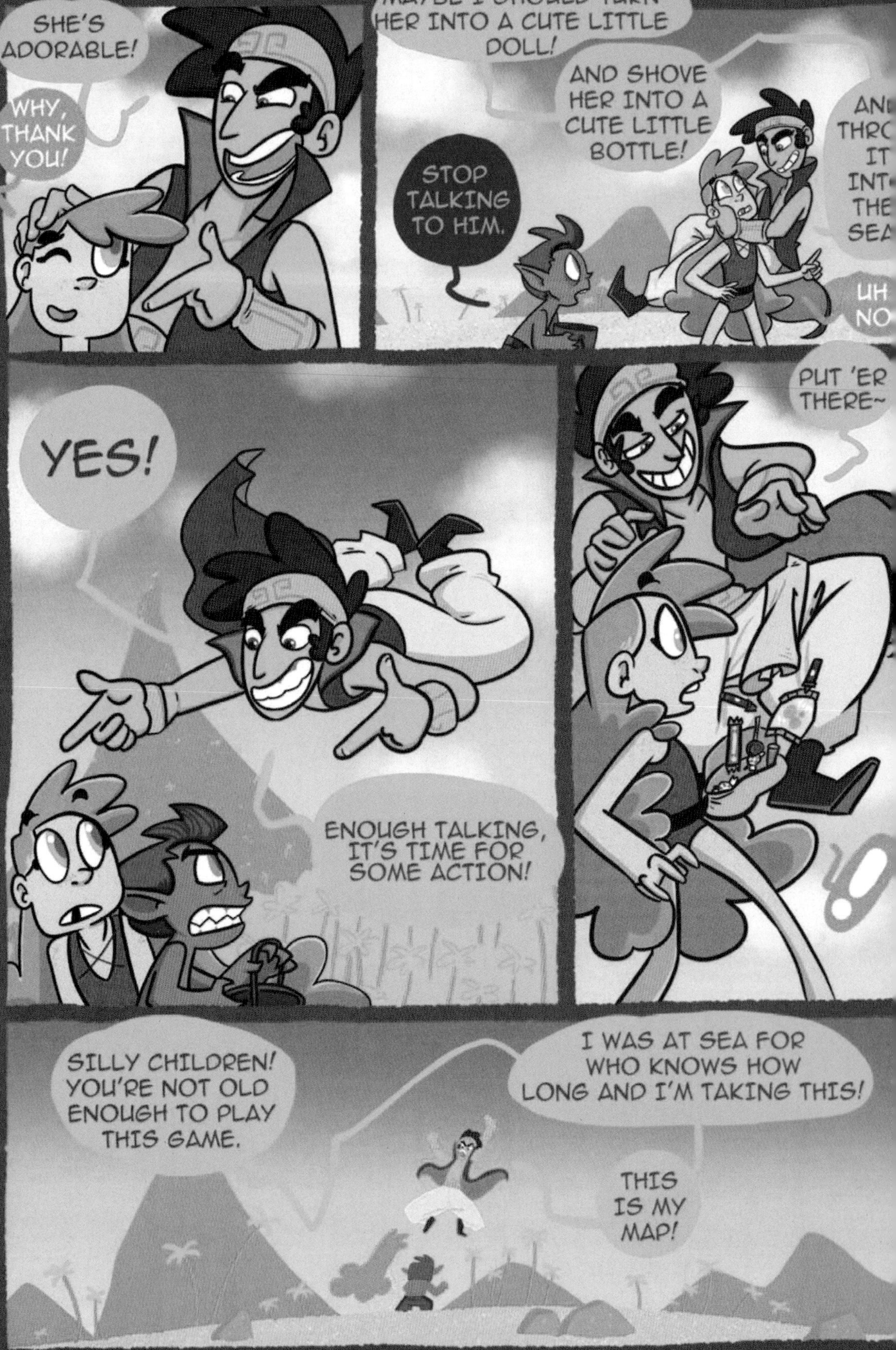

SHE'S ADORABLE!
WHY, THANK YOU!
MAYBE I SHOULD TURN HER INTO A CUTE LITTLE DOLL!
AND SHOVE HER INTO A CUTE LITTLE BOTTLE!
STOP TALKING TO HIM.
YES!
ENOUGH TALKING, IT'S TIME FOR SOME ACTION!
PUT 'ER THERE~
!
SILLY CHILDREN! YOU'RE NOT OLD ENOUGH TO PLAY THIS GAME.
I WAS AT SEA FOR WHO KNOWS HOW LONG AND I'M TAKING THIS!
THIS IS MY MAP!

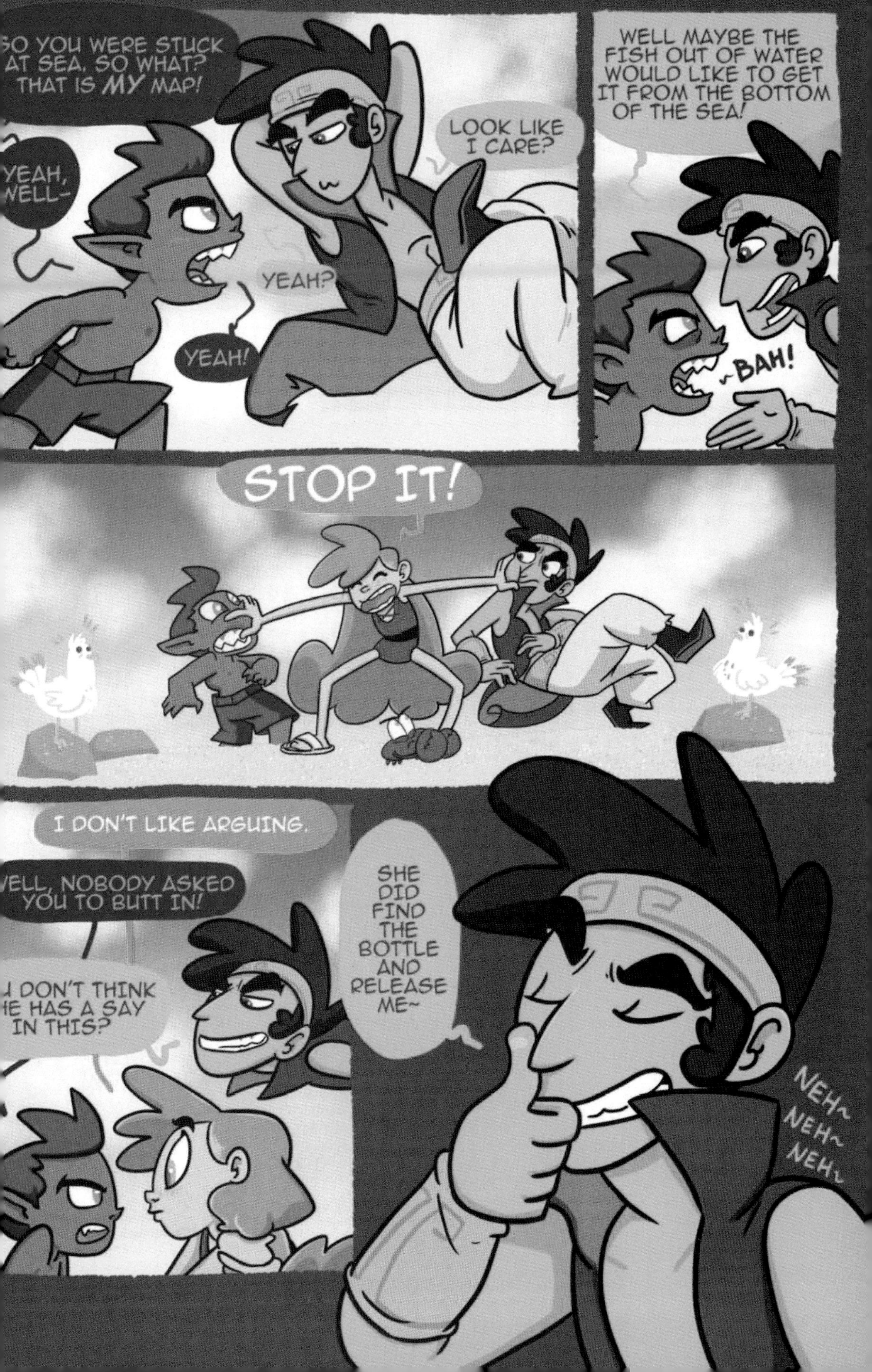

SO YOU WERE STUCK AT SEA, SO WHAT? THAT IS MY MAP!
YEAH, WELL-
LOOK LIKE I CARE?
YEAH?
YEAH!
WELL MAYBE THE FISH OUT OF WATER WOULD LIKE TO GET IT FROM THE BOTTOM OF THE SEA!
~BAH!
STOP IT!
I DON'T LIKE ARGUING.
WELL, NOBODY ASKED YOU TO BUTT IN!
I DON'T THINK HE HAS A SAY IN THIS?
SHE DID FIND THE BOTTLE AND RELEASE ME~
NEH~ NEH~ NEH~

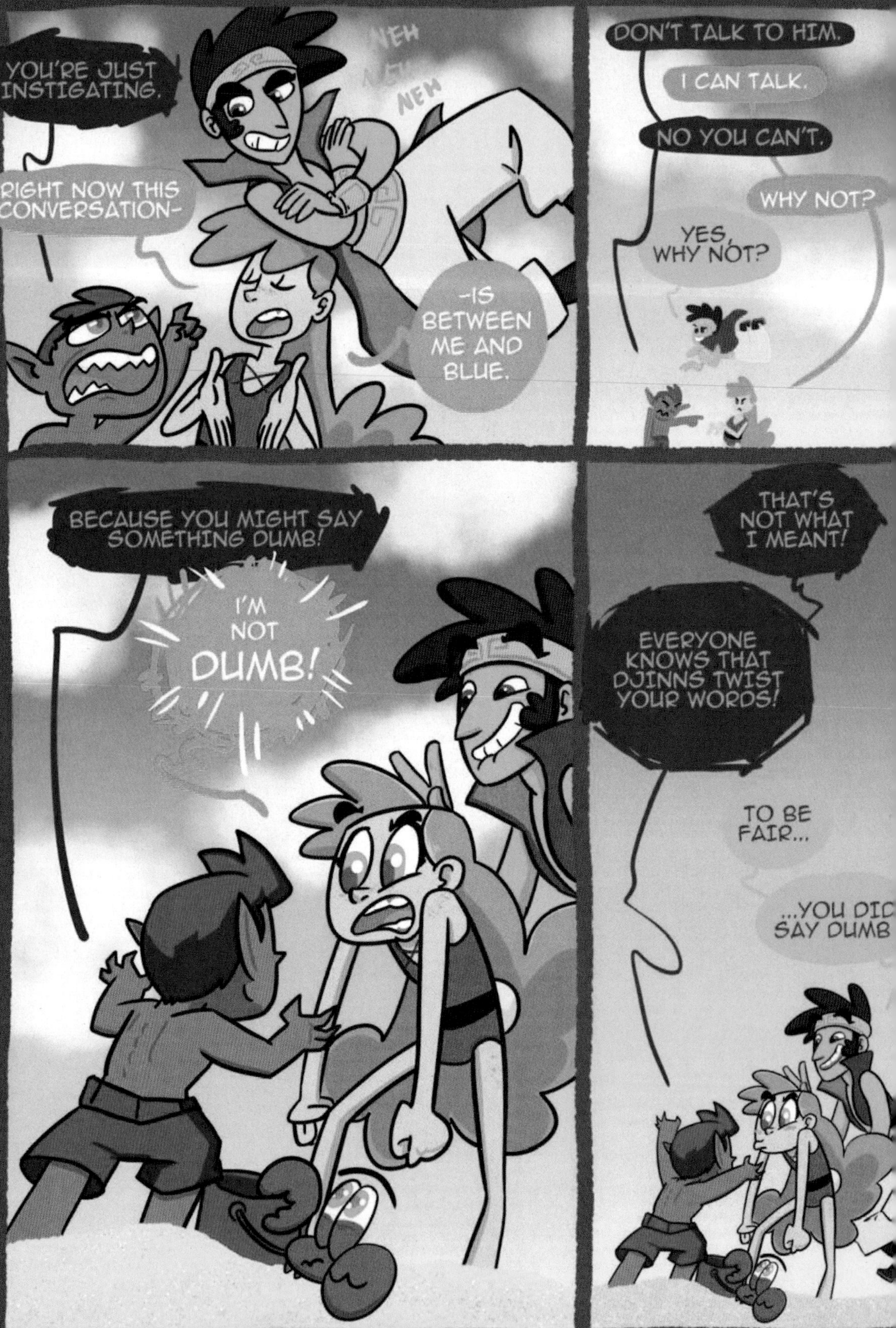
YOU'RE JUST INSTIGATING.
RIGHT NOW THIS CONVERSATION-
NEH NEH NEH
-IS BETWEEN ME AND BLUE.
DON'T TALK TO HIM.
I CAN TALK.
NO YOU CAN'T.
WHY NOT?
YES, WHY NOT?
BECAUSE YOU MIGHT SAY SOMETHING DUMB!
I'M NOT DUMB!
THAT'S NOT WHAT I MEANT!
EVERYONE KNOWS THAT DJINNS TWIST YOUR WORDS!
TO BE FAIR...
...YOU DID SAY DUMB

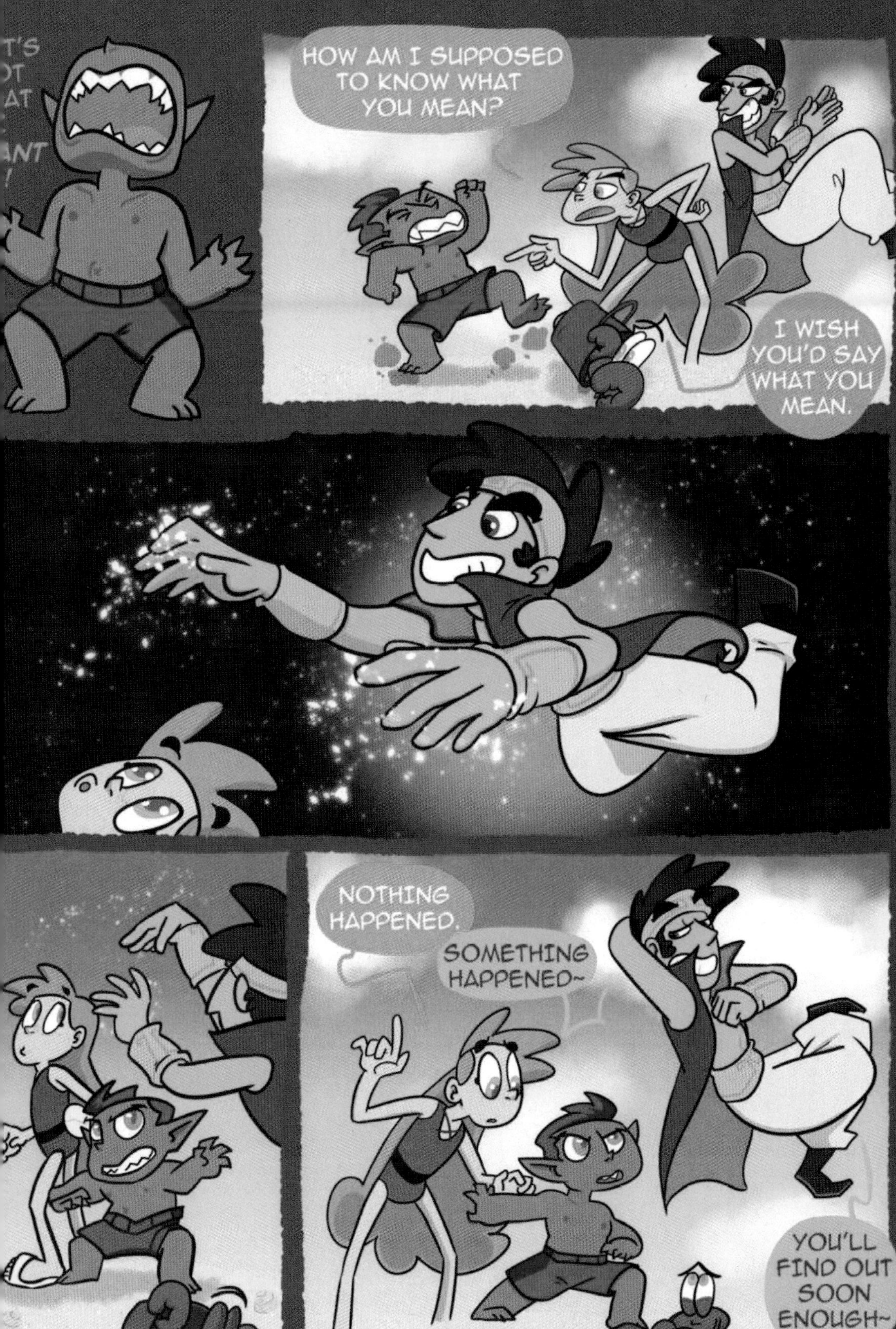
HOW AM I SUPPOSED TO KNOW WHAT YOU MEAN?
I WISH YOU'D SAY WHAT YOU MEAN.
NOTHING HAPPENED.
SOMETHING HAPPENED~
YOU'LL FIND OUT SOON ENOUGH~

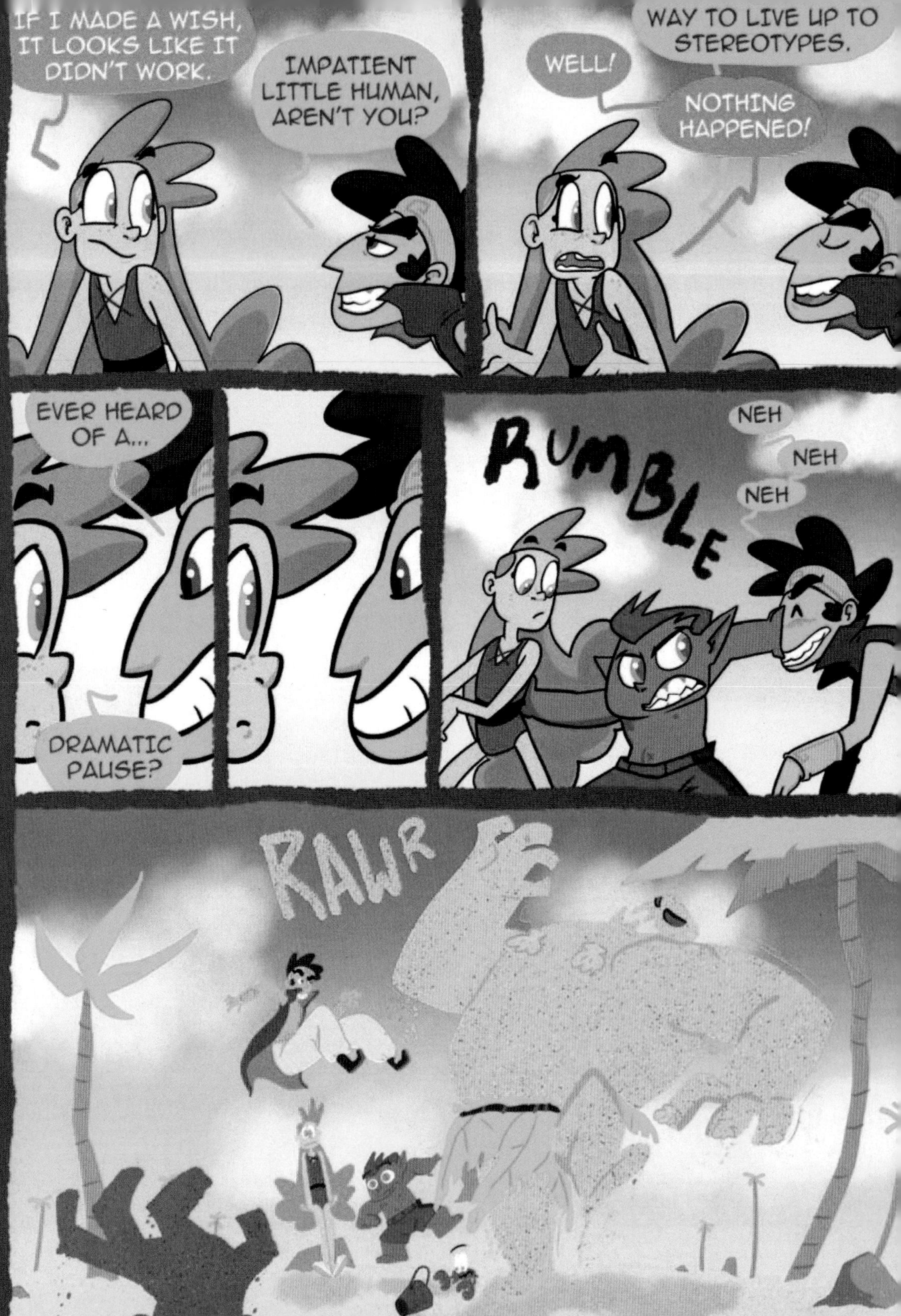
IF I MADE A WISH, IT LOOKS LIKE IT DIDN'T WORK.
IMPATIENT LITTLE HUMAN, AREN'T YOU?
WELL!
NOTHING HAPPENED!
WAY TO LIVE UP TO STEREOTYPES.
EVER HEARD OF A...
DRAMATIC PAUSE?
RUMBLE
NEH
NEH
NEH
RAWR

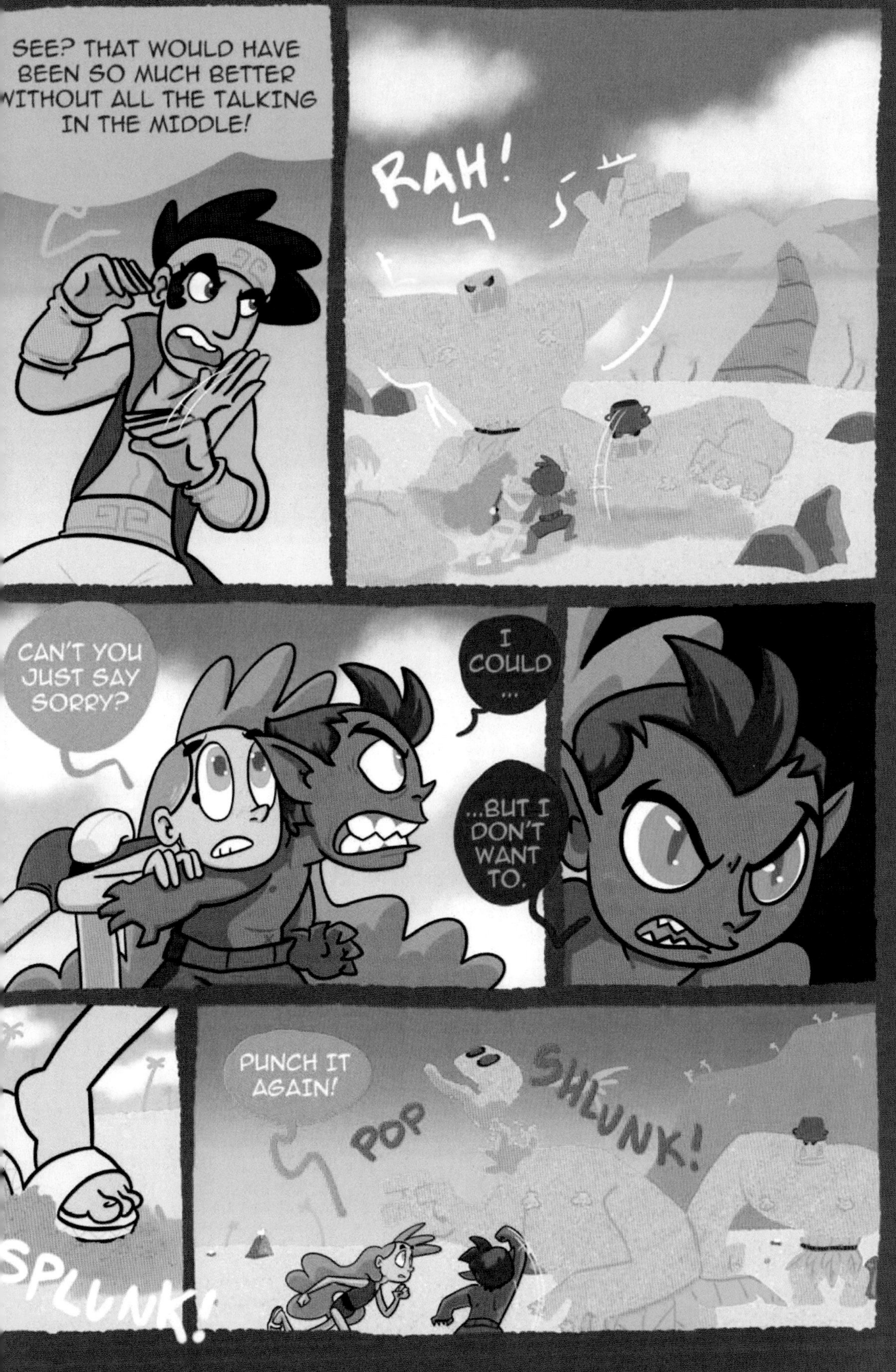

SEE? THAT WOULD HAVE BEEN SO MUCH BETTER WITHOUT ALL THE TALKING IN THE MIDDLE!
RAH!
CAN'T YOU JUST SAY SORRY?
I COULD ...
...BUT I DON'T WANT TO.
SPLUNK!
PUNCH IT AGAIN!
POP
SHLUNK!

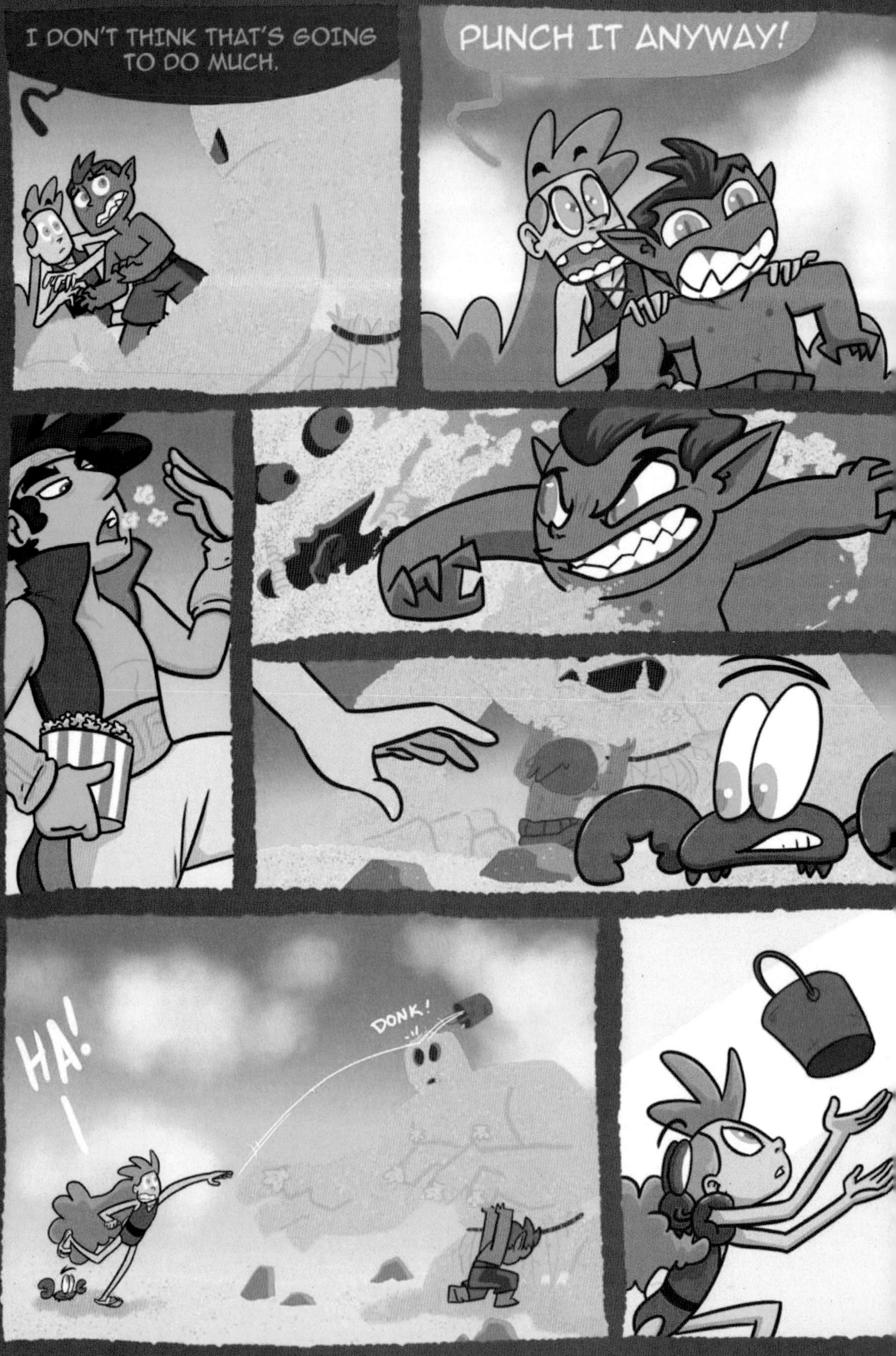
I DON'T THINK THAT'S GOING TO DO MUCH.
PUNCH IT ANYWAY!
HA!
DONK!

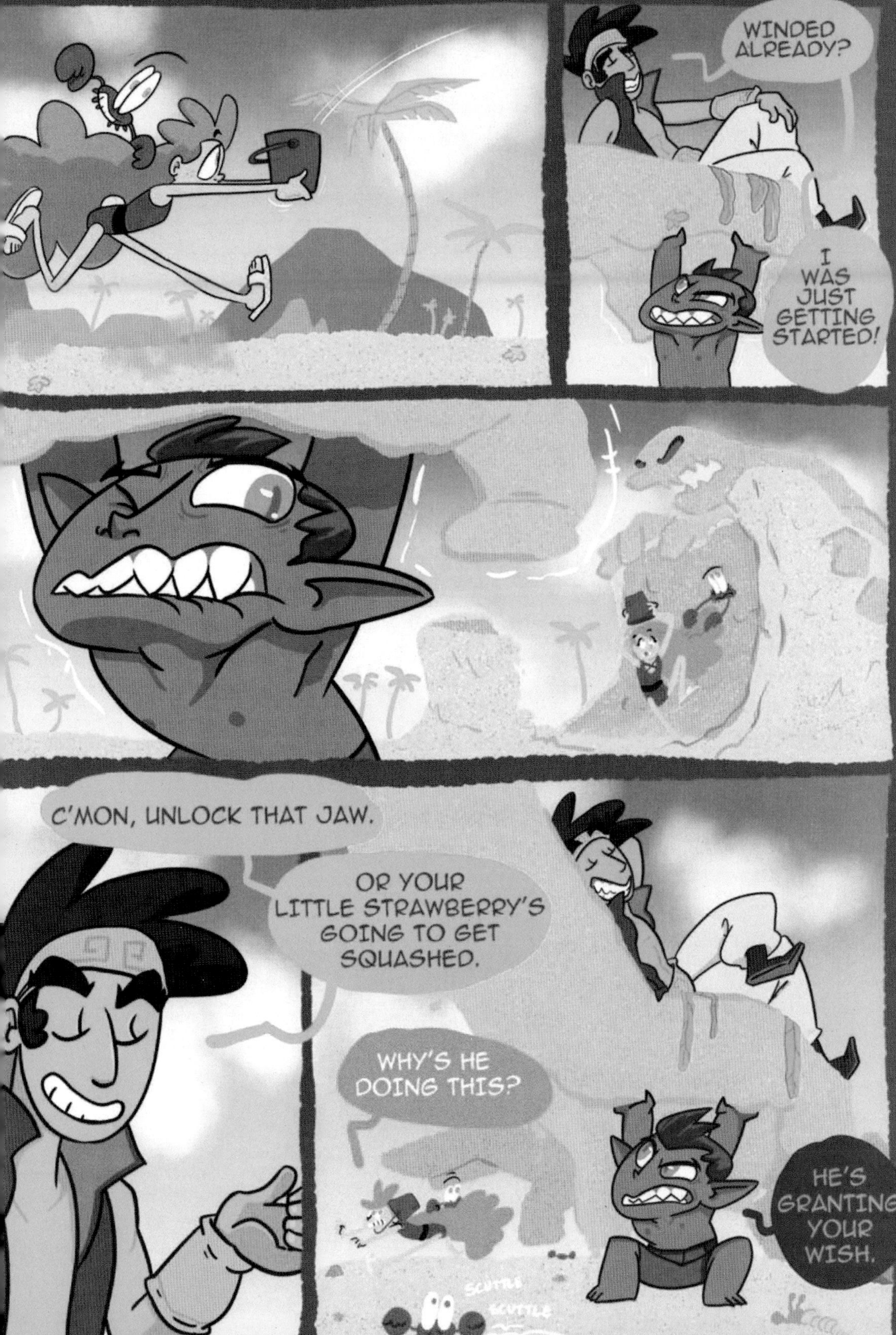
WINDED ALREADY?
I WAS JUST GETTING STARTED!
C'MON, UNLOCK THAT JAW.
OR YOUR LITTLE STRAWBERRY'S GOING TO GET SQUASHED.
WHY'S HE DOING THIS?
HE'S GRANTING YOUR WISH.
SCUTTLE
SCUTTLE

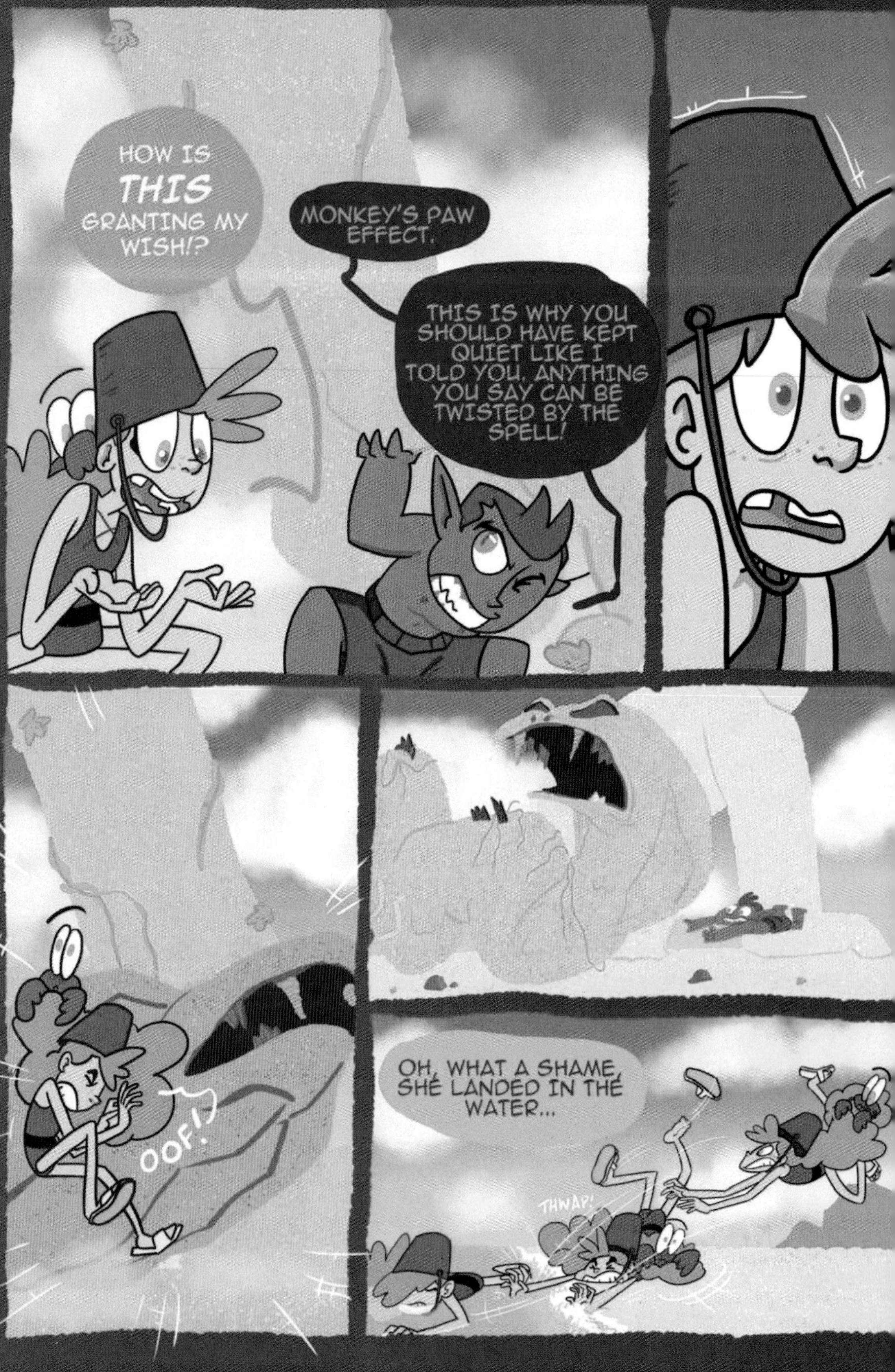
HOW IS THIS GRANTING MY WISH!?
MONKEY'S PAW EFFECT.
THIS IS WHY YOU SHOULD HAVE KEPT QUIET LIKE I TOLD YOU. ANYTHING YOU SAY CAN BE TWISTED BY THE SPELL!
OOF!
OH, WHAT A SHAME, SHE LANDED IN THE WATER...
THWAP!

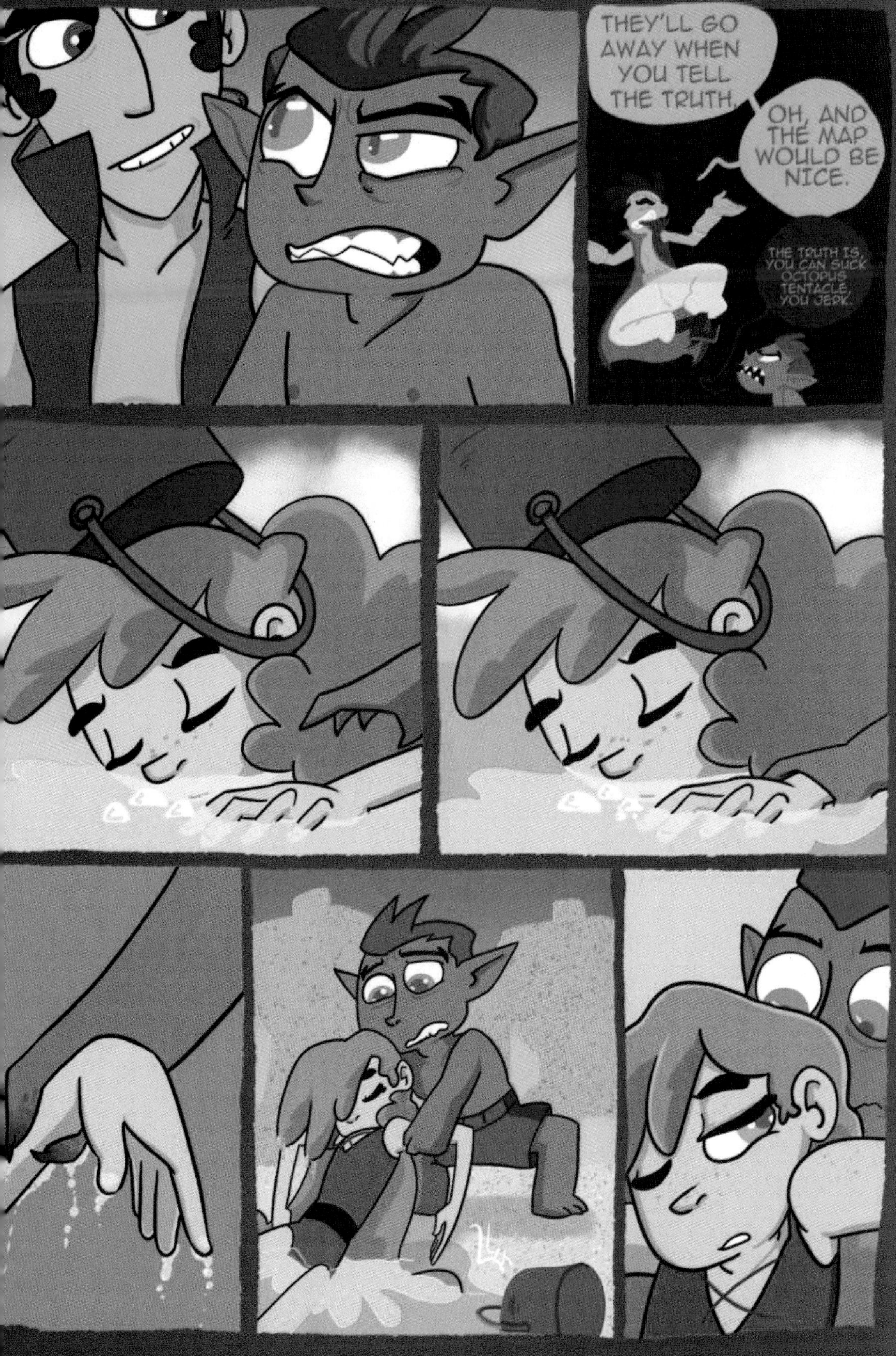
THEY'LL GO AWAY WHEN YOU TELL THE TRUTH.
OH, AND THE MAP WOULD BE NICE.
THE TRUTH IS, YOU CAN SUCK OCTOPUS TENTACLE, YOU JERK.

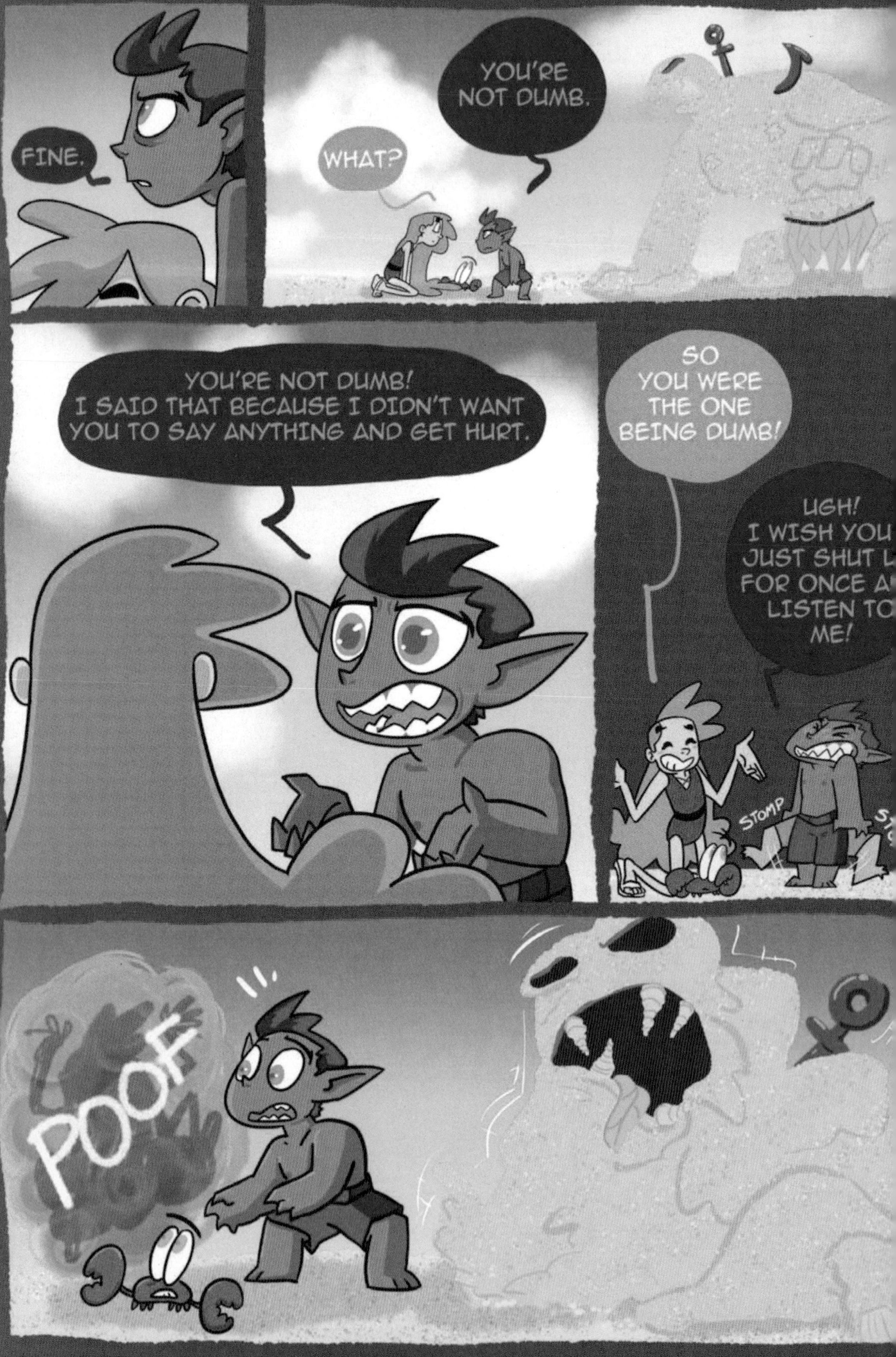
FINE.
WHAT?
YOU'RE NOT DUMB.
YOU'RE NOT DUMB! I SAID THAT BECAUSE I DIDN'T WANT YOU TO SAY ANYTHING AND GET HURT.
SO YOU WERE THE ONE BEING DUMB!
UGH! I WISH YOU JUST SHUT FOR ONCE LISTEN ME!
STOMP
POOF

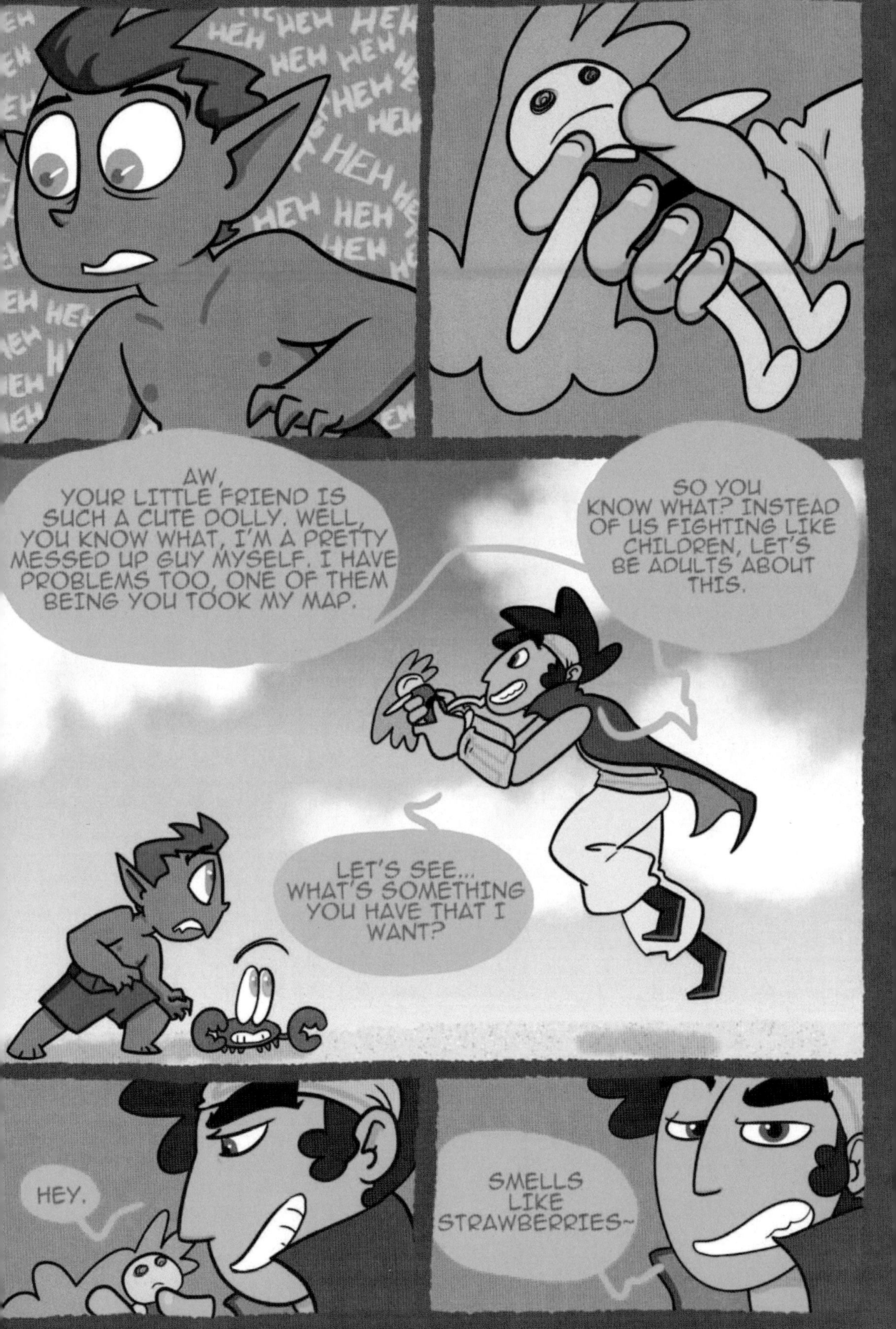
HEH HEH HEH HEH HEH HEH HEH HEH HEH HEH HEH
AW, YOUR LITTLE FRIEND IS SUCH A CUTE DOLLY. WELL, YOU KNOW WHAT, I'M A PRETTY MESSED UP GUY MYSELF. I HAVE PROBLEMS TOO, ONE OF THEM BEING YOU TOOK MY MAP.
SO YOU KNOW WHAT? INSTEAD OF US FIGHTING LIKE CHILDREN, LET'S BE ADULTS ABOUT THIS.
LET'S SEE... WHAT'S SOMETHING YOU HAVE THAT I WANT?
HEY.
SMELLS LIKE STRAWBERRIES~

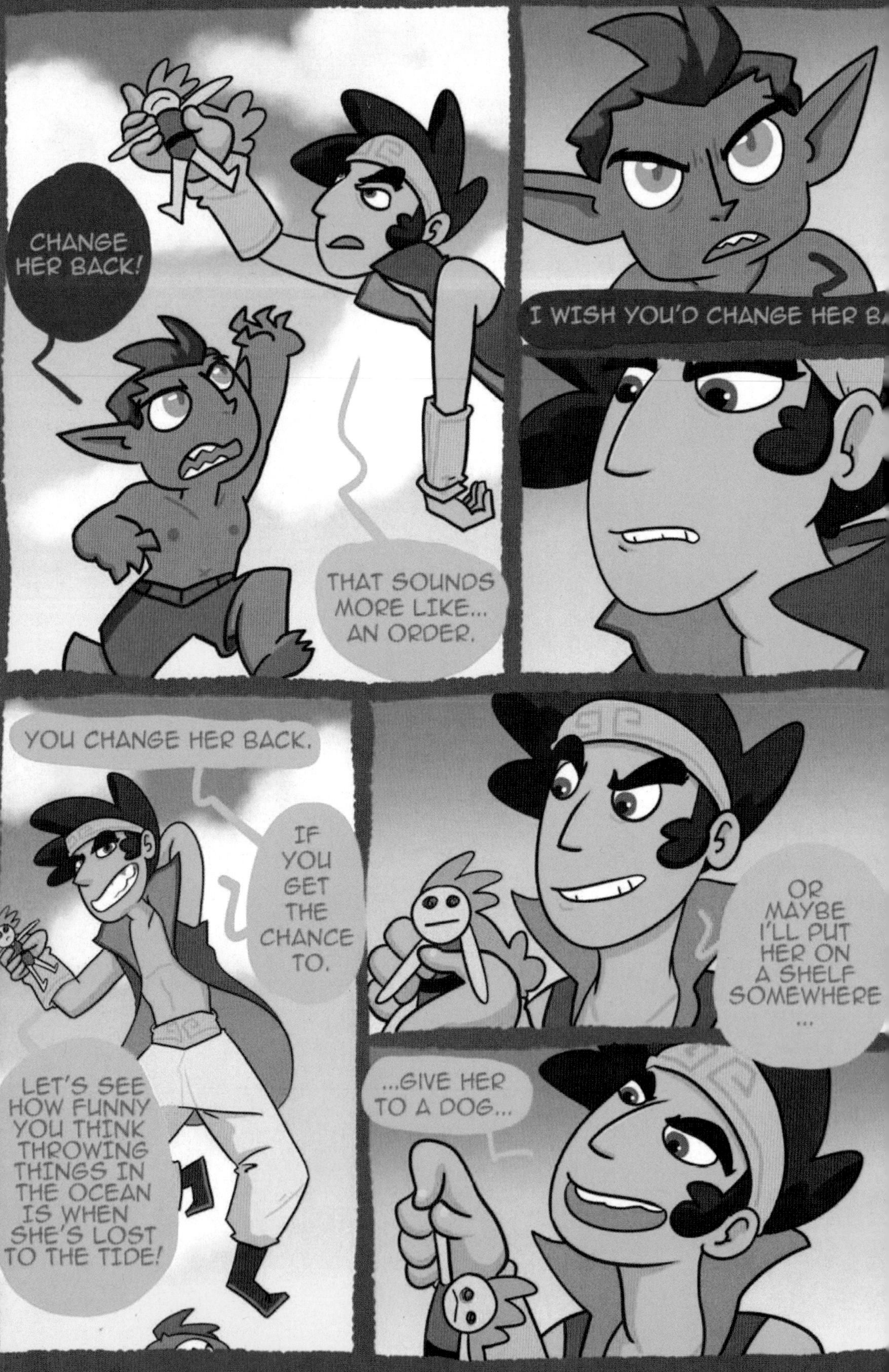

CHANGE HER BACK!
THAT SOUNDS MORE LIKE... AN ORDER.
I WISH YOU'D CHANGE HER BA
YOU CHANGE HER BACK.
IF YOU GET THE CHANCE TO.
LET'S SEE HOW FUNNY YOU THINK THROWING THINGS IN THE OCEAN IS WHEN SHE'S LOST TO THE TIDE!
OR MAYBE I'LL PUT HER ON A SHELF SOMEWHERE ...
...GIVE HER TO A DOG...

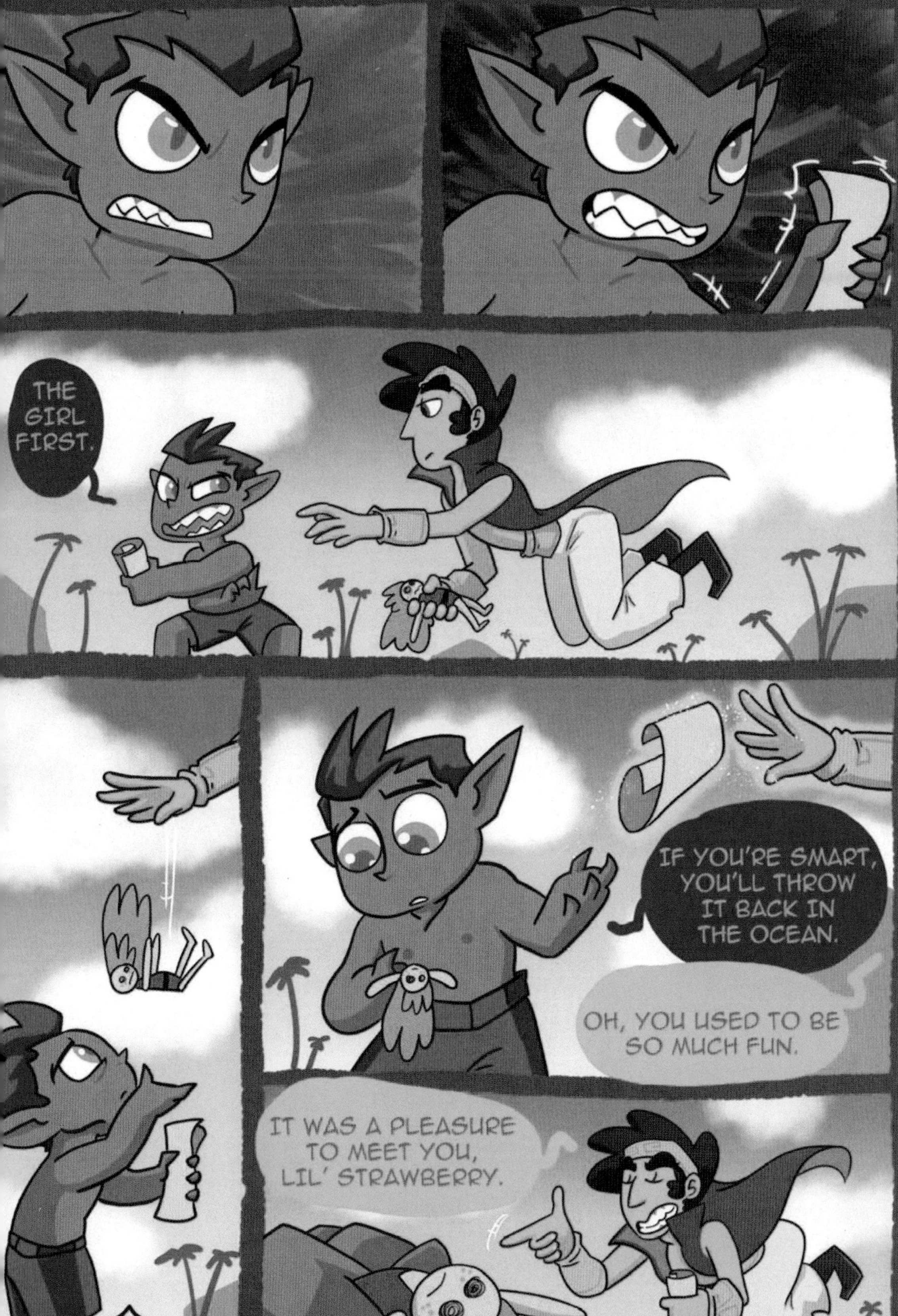
THE GIRL FIRST.
IF YOU'RE SMART, YOU'LL THROW IT BACK IN THE OCEAN.
OH, YOU USED TO BE SO MUCH FUN.
IT WAS A PLEASURE TO MEET YOU, LIL' STRAWBERRY.

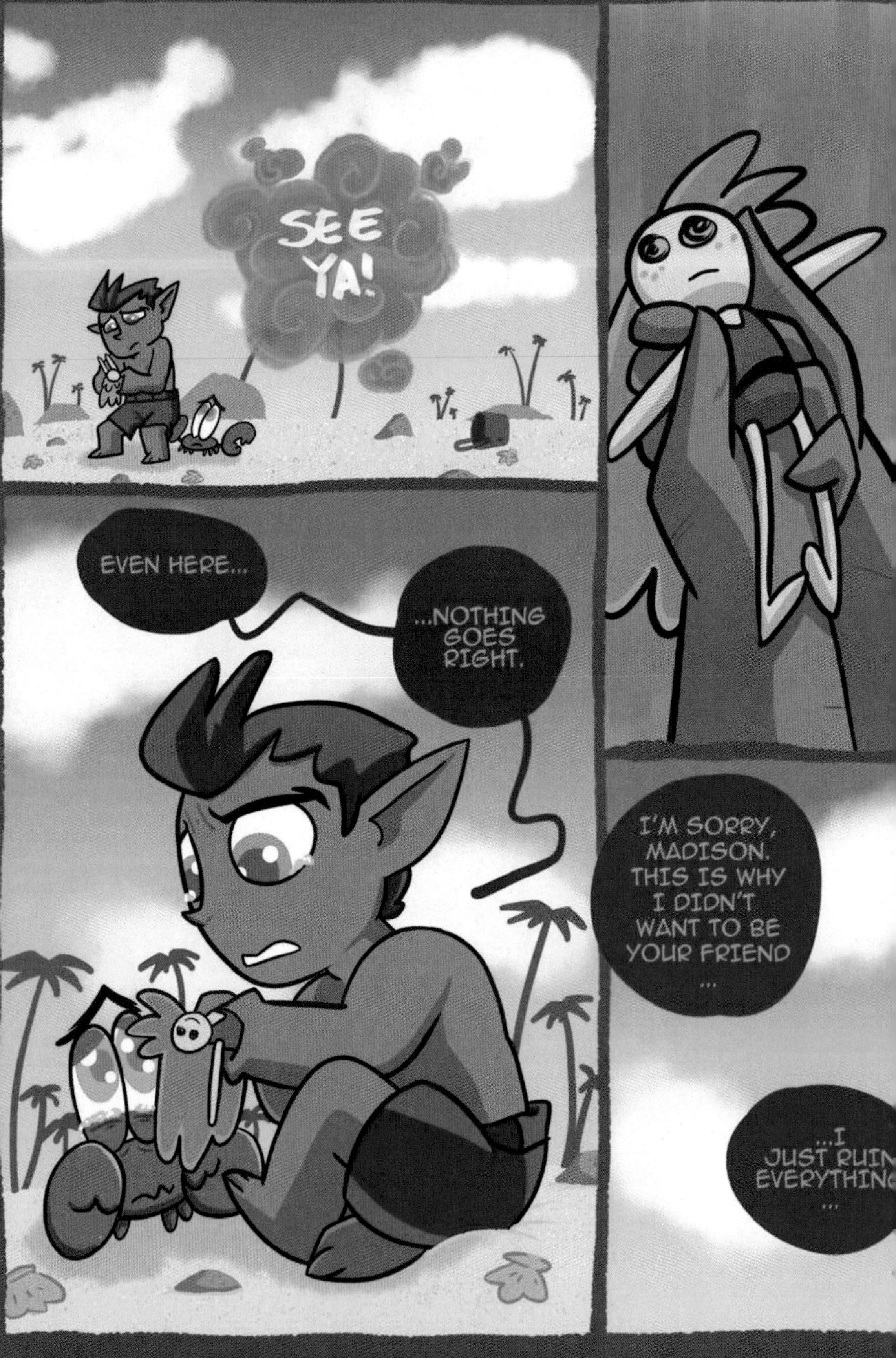
SEE YA!
EVEN HERE...
...NOTHING GOES RIGHT.
I'M SORRY, MADISON. THIS IS WHY I DIDN'T WANT TO BE YOUR FRIEND ...
...I JUST RUIN EVERYTHING ...

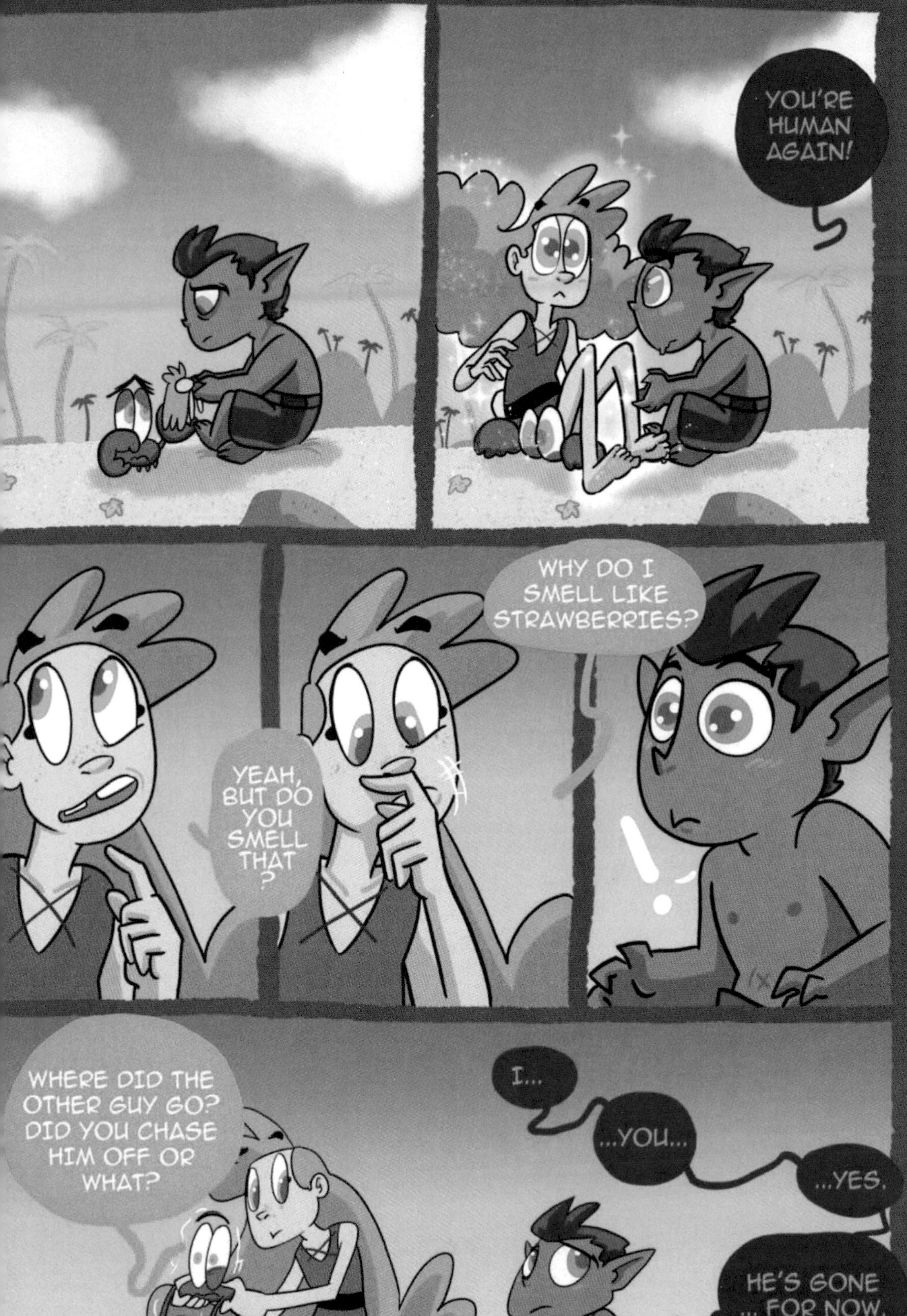

YOU'RE HUMAN AGAIN!
WHY DO I SMELL LIKE STRAWBERRIES?
YEAH, BUT DO YOU SMELL THAT?
WHERE DID THE OTHER GUY GO? DID YOU CHASE HIM OFF OR WHAT?
I...
...YOU...
...YES.
HE'S GONE ... FOR NOW.

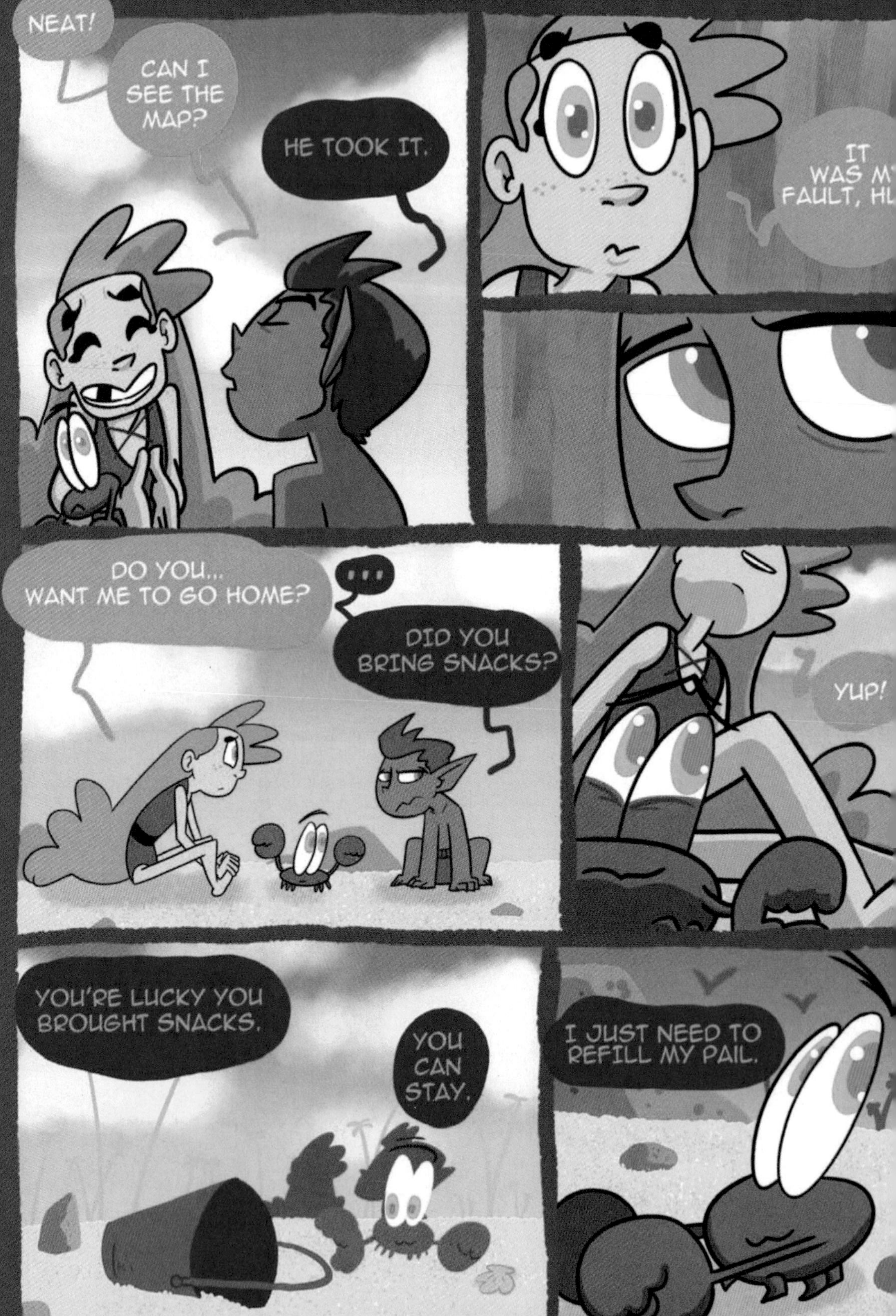

NEAT!
CAN I SEE THE MAP?
HE TOOK IT.
IT WAS M
FAULT, HU
DO YOU... WANT ME TO GO HOME?
...
DID YOU BRING SNACKS?
YUP!
YOU'RE LUCKY YOU BROUGHT SNACKS.
YOU CAN STAY.
I JUST NEED TO REFILL MY PAIL.

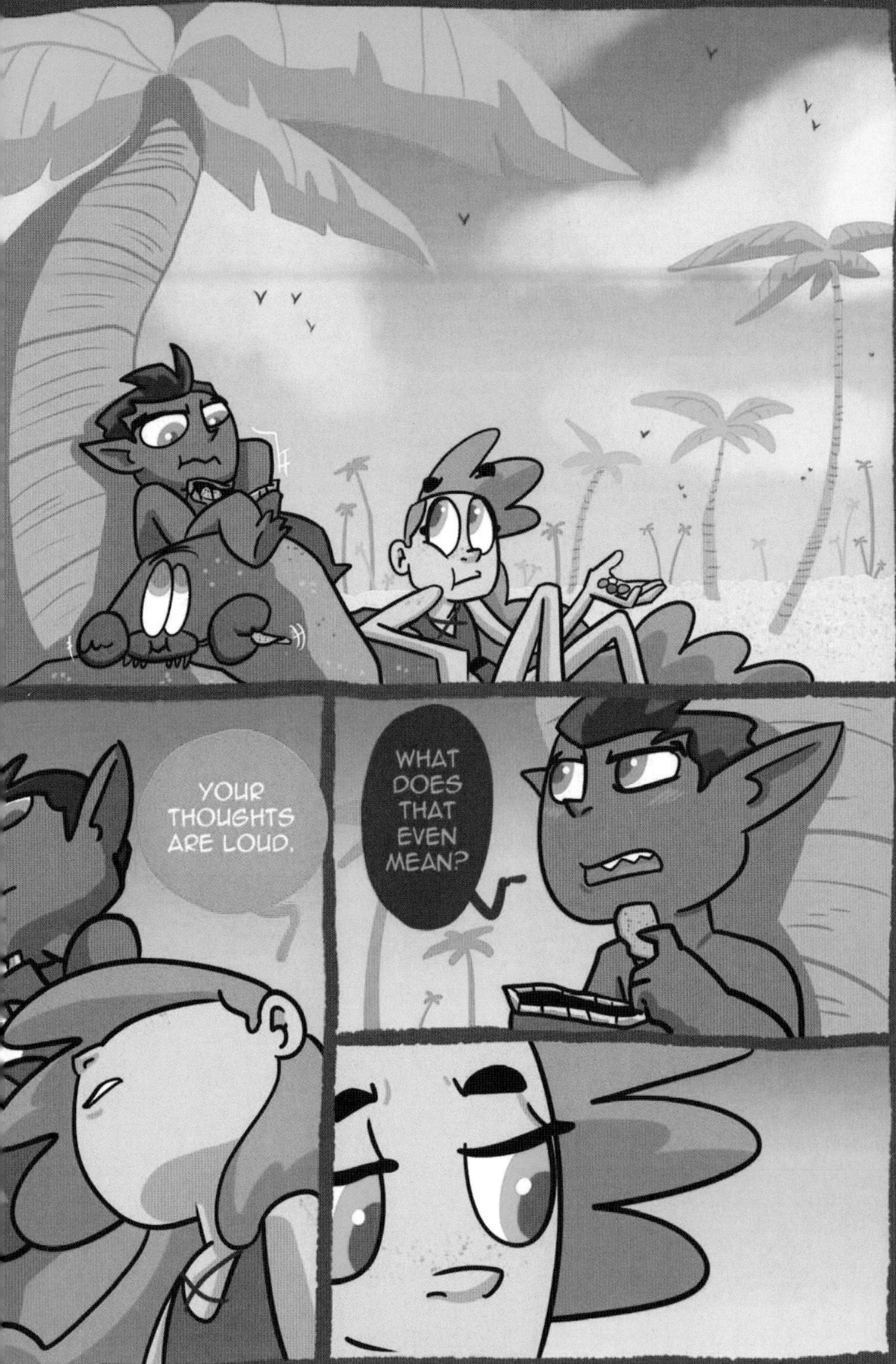
YOUR THOUGHTS ARE LOUD.
WHAT DOES THAT EVEN MEAN?

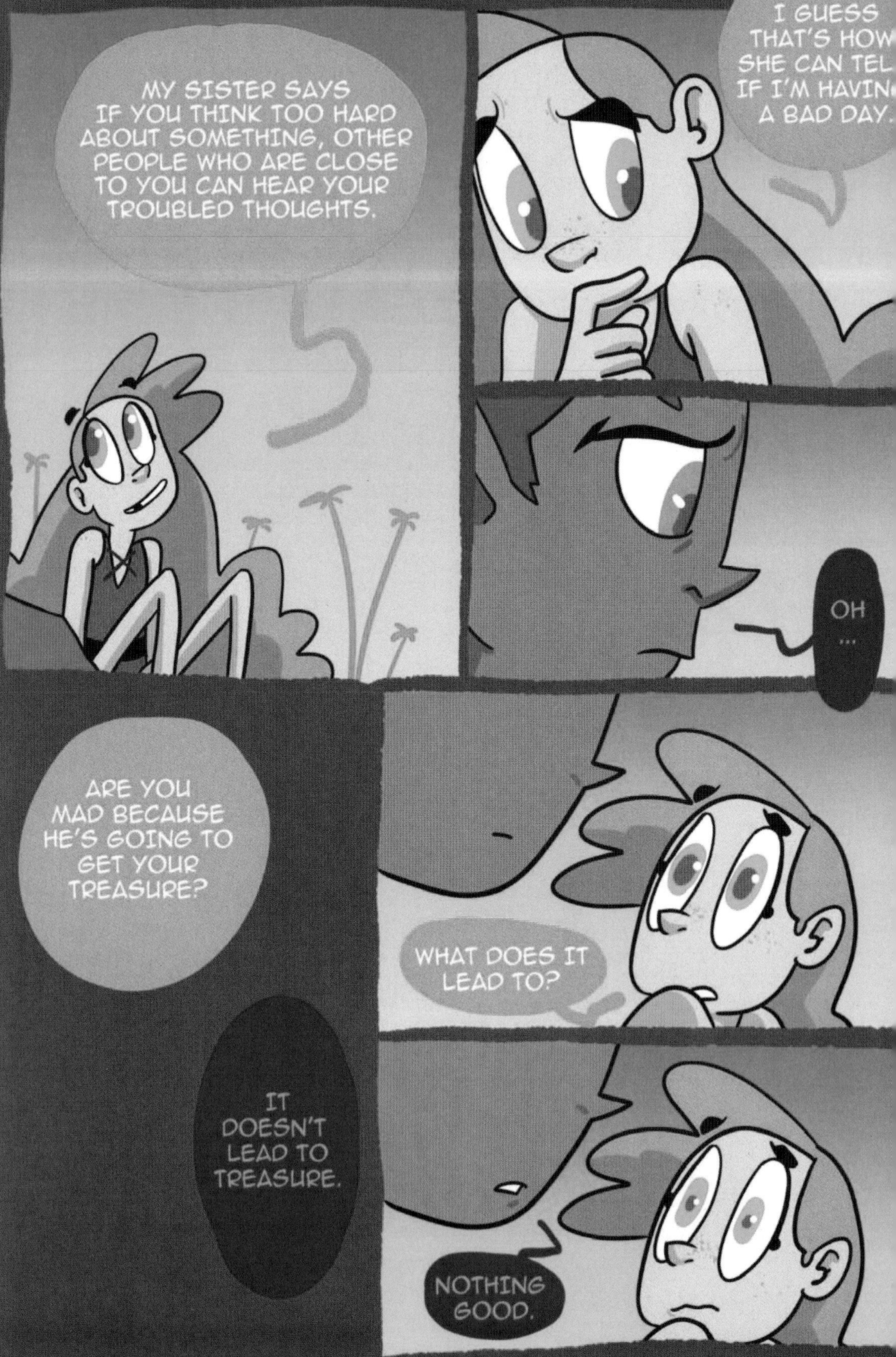
MY SISTER SAYS IF YOU THINK TOO HARD ABOUT SOMETHING, OTHER PEOPLE WHO ARE CLOSE TO YOU CAN HEAR YOUR TROUBLED THOUGHTS.
I GUESS THAT'S HOW SHE CAN TEL IF I'M HAVIN A BAD DAY.
OH ...
ARE YOU MAD BECAUSE HE'S GOING TO GET YOUR TREASURE?
WHAT DOES IT LEAD TO?
IT DOESN'T LEAD TO TREASURE.
NOTHING GOOD.

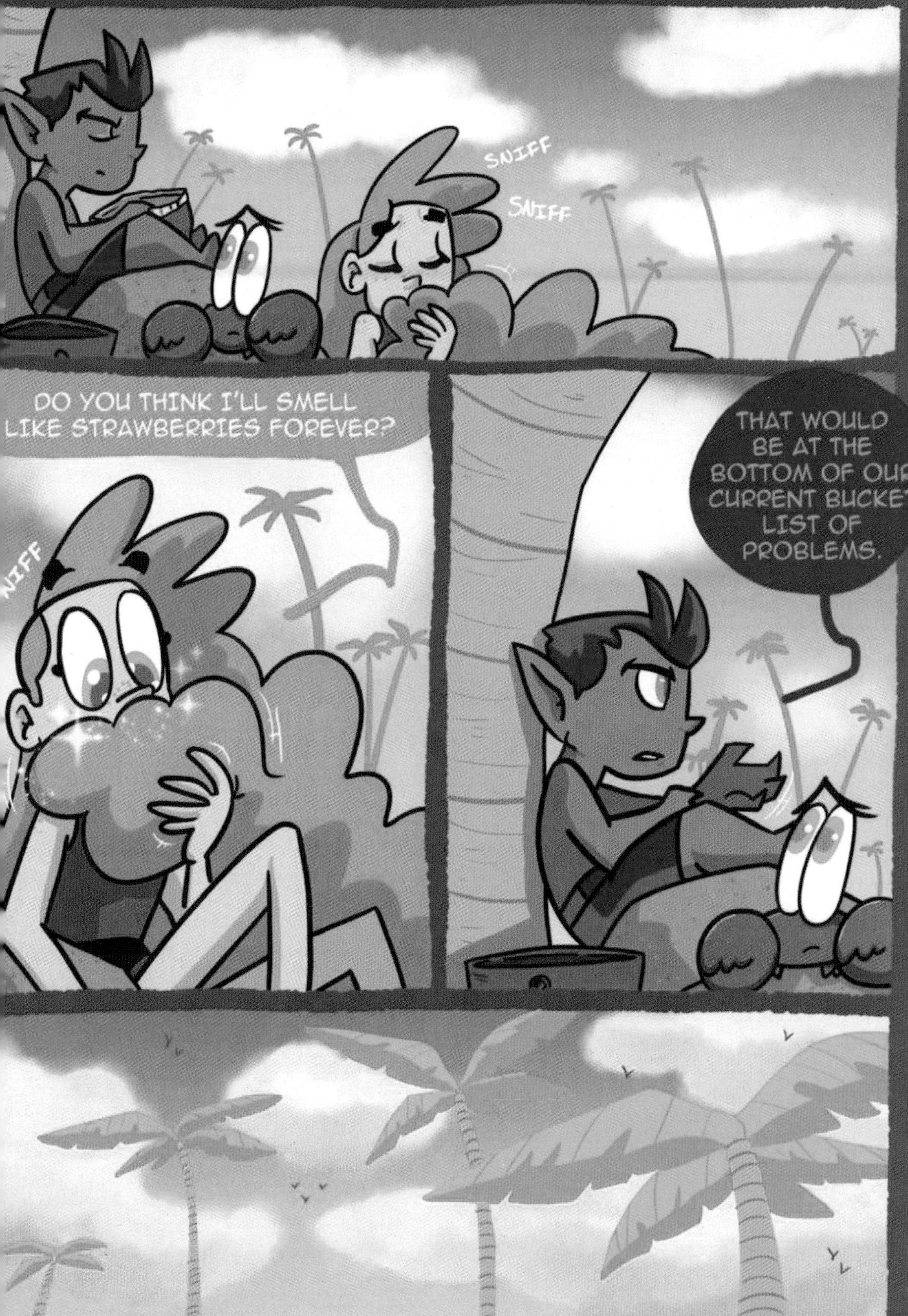
SNIFF
SNIFF
DO YOU THINK I'LL SMELL LIKE STRAWBERRIES FOREVER?
THAT WOULD BE AT THE BOTTOM OF OUR CURRENT BUCKET LIST OF PROBLEMS.

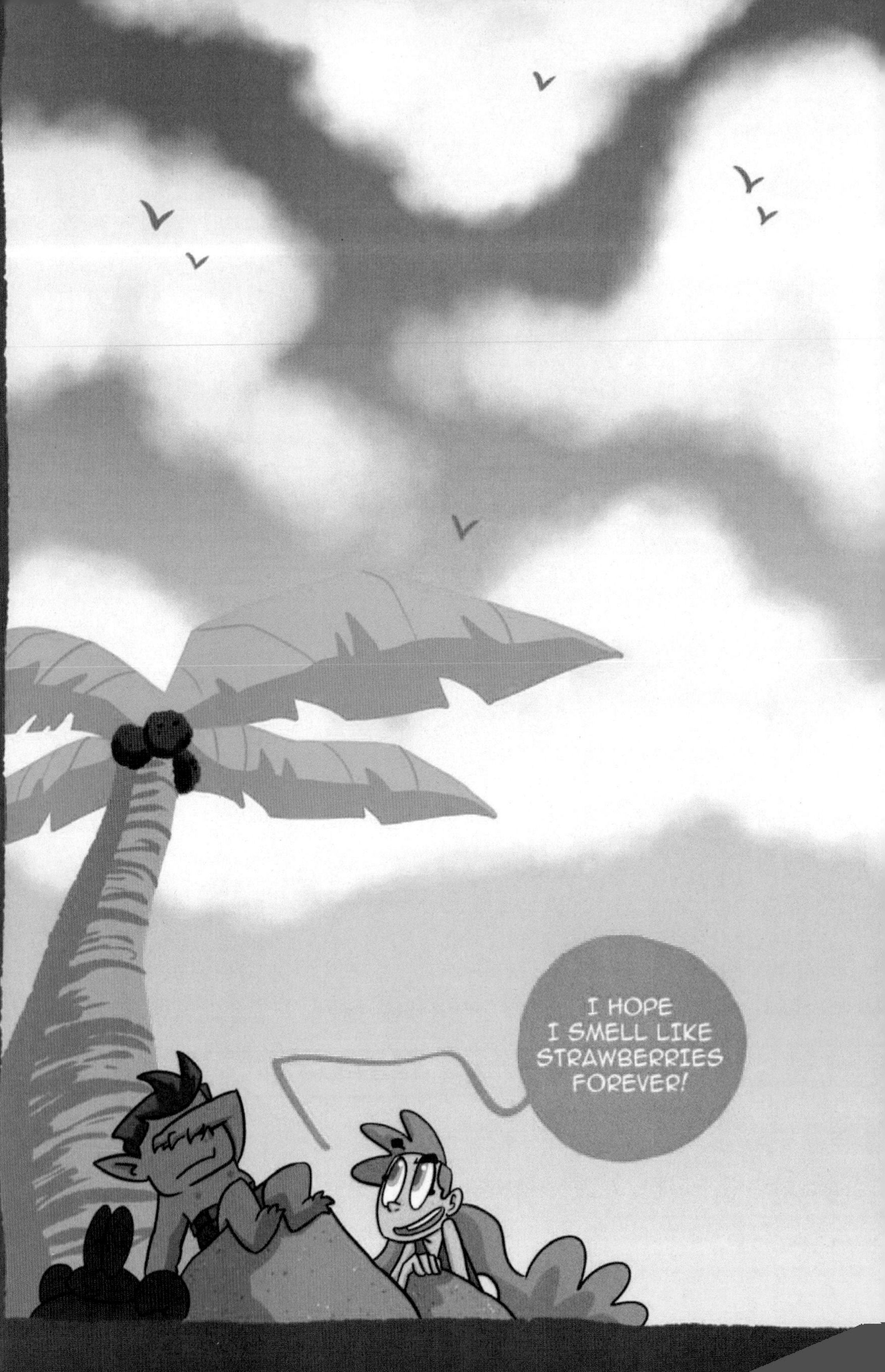
I HOPE I SMELL LIKE STRAWBERRIES FOREVER!

CONCEPT ART

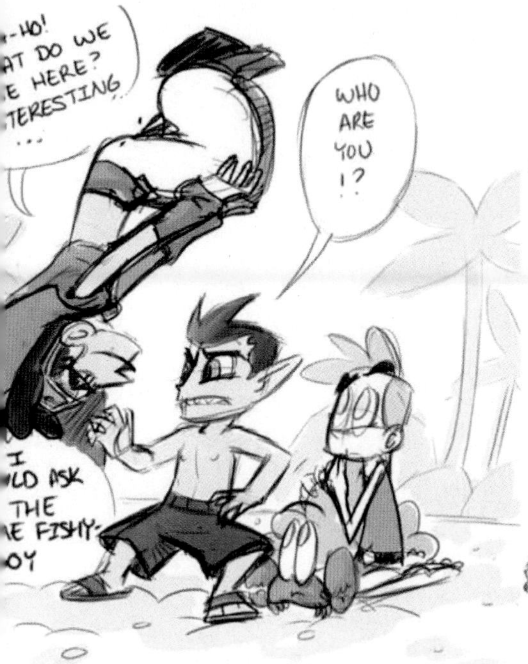
-HO!
AT DO WE
E HERE?
TERESTING
...
WHO ARE YOU !?
I
LD ASK
THE
E FISHY-
OY

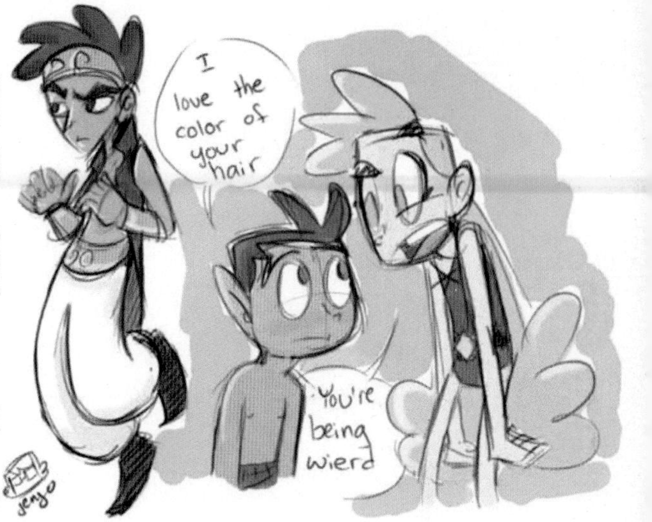
I love the color of your hair
You're being wierd

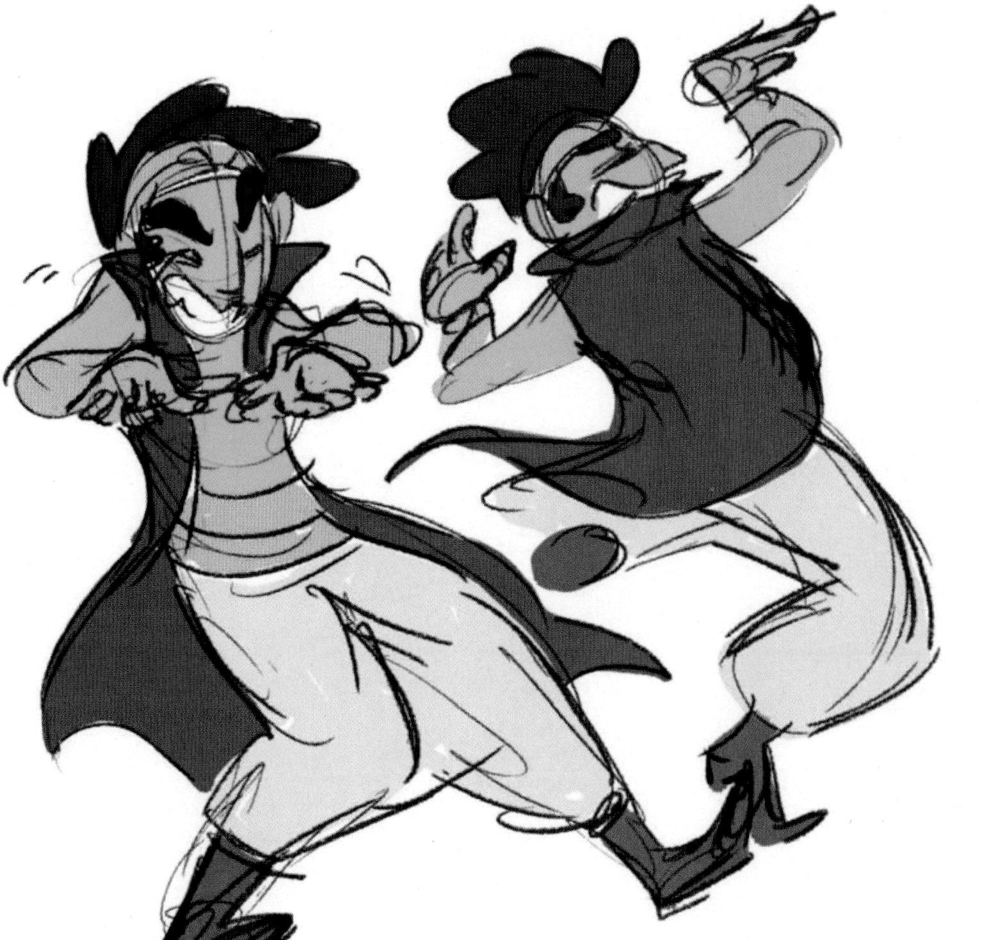

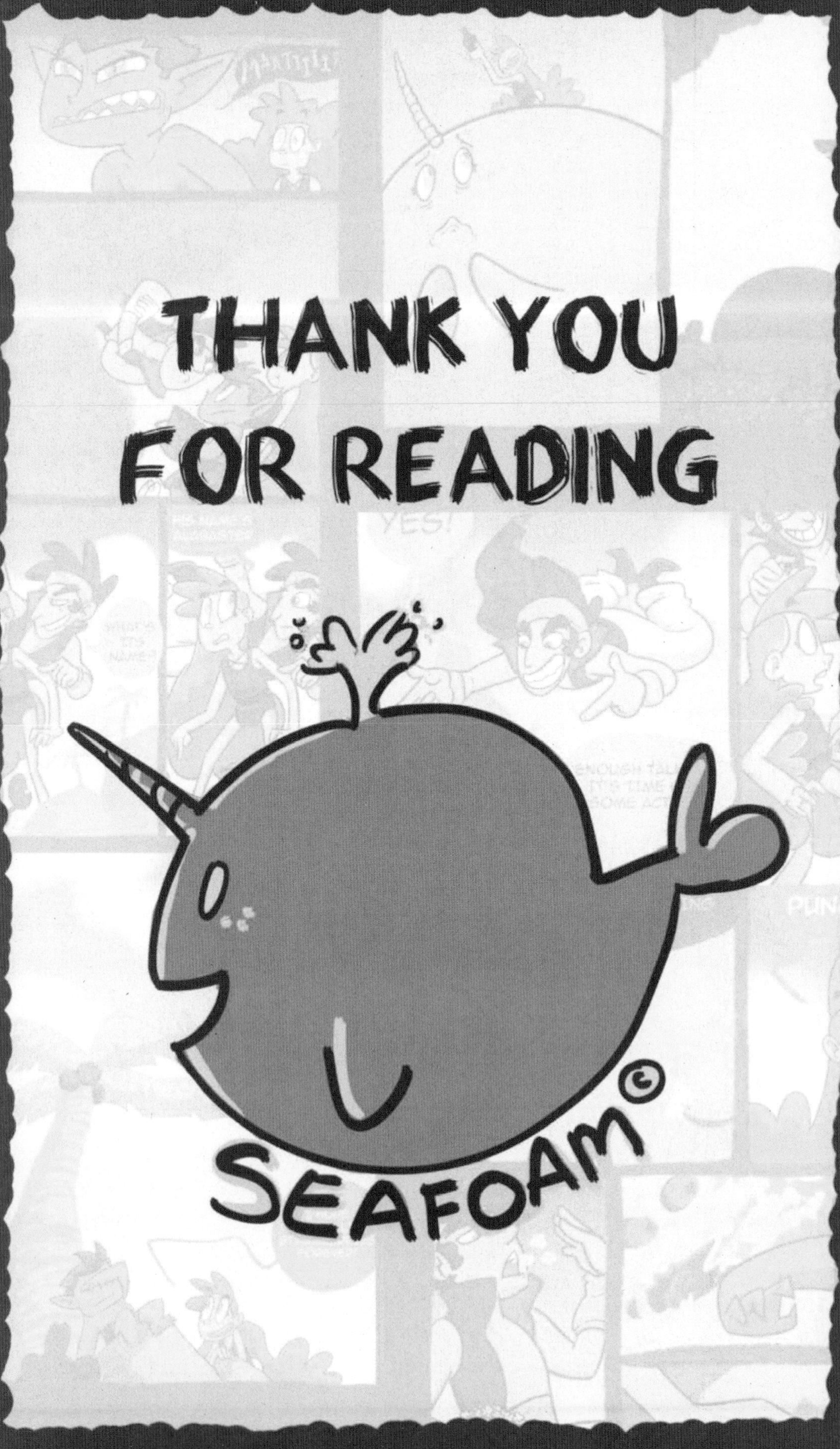
THANK YOU
FOR READING
SEAFOAM©

ISSUE THREE
"THE NATIVES AREN'T SO FRIENDLY"

THERE WAS A GIRL NAMED MADISON
WHO LOVED TO PLAY IN SAND

ONE DAY SHE FOUND A MAGICAL WHALE
WASHED UP ON THE LAND
SO MADISON TICKLED THE WHALE
TILL IT ROLLED INTO THE SEA

THE WHALE WAS SO GRATEFUL
THAT IT FOUND SOMEONE TO BE
A FRIEND FOR MADISON

SPEARS START FLYING FROM THE TREES
DISRUPTING THE COOL ISLAND BREEZE
BLUE KNOWS BETTER THAN TO TRUST
CREATURES FROM THE FOREST MUCH

NOT ALL ARE BAD IN THE END
SOME JUST NEED A HELPING HAND

WRITTEN AND ILLUSTRATED BY

JEANINE-JONEE

CONTENT EDITED BY

EMILY BRIGOLIN

NICOLE D'ANDRIA

ADDITIONAL COLORING BY

KYLE P. HOLLAND

BRYAN SEATON: PUBLISHER/ CEO
SHAWN GABBORIN: EDITOR IN CHIEF
JASON MARTIN: PUBLISHER-DANGER ZONE
NICOLE D'ANDRIA: MARKETING DIRECTOR/EDITOR
JESSICA LOWRIE: SOCIAL MEDIA CZAR
DANIELLE DAVISON: EXECUTIVE ADMINISTRATOR
CHAD CICCONI: OFFICIAL NARWHAL WRANGLER
SHAWN PRYOR: PRESIDENT OF CREATOR RELATIONS

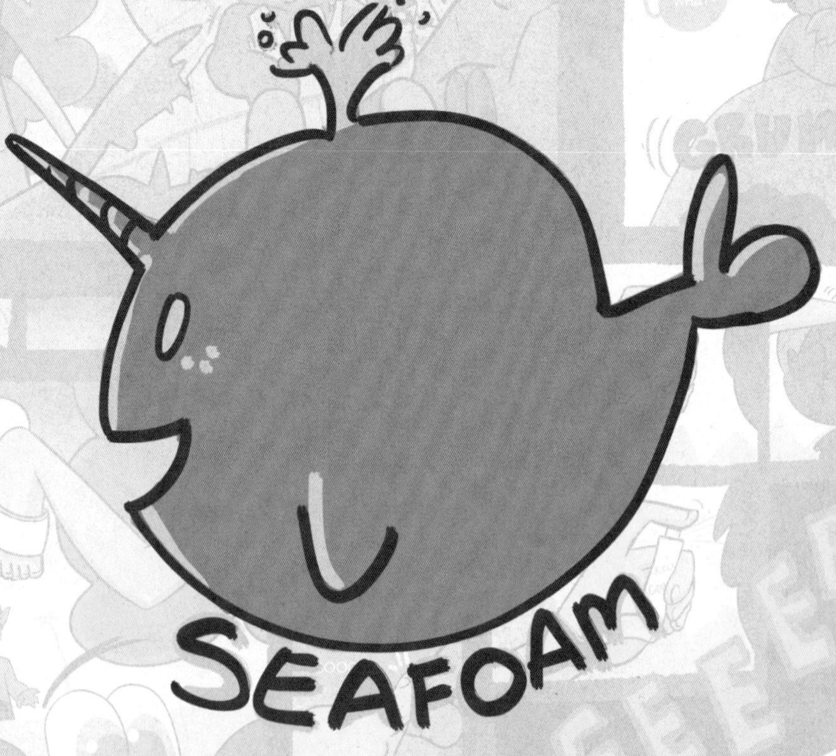
SEAFOAM

For information regarding the CPSIA on this printed material, call: (203) 595-3636 and provide reference #RICH - 852937.

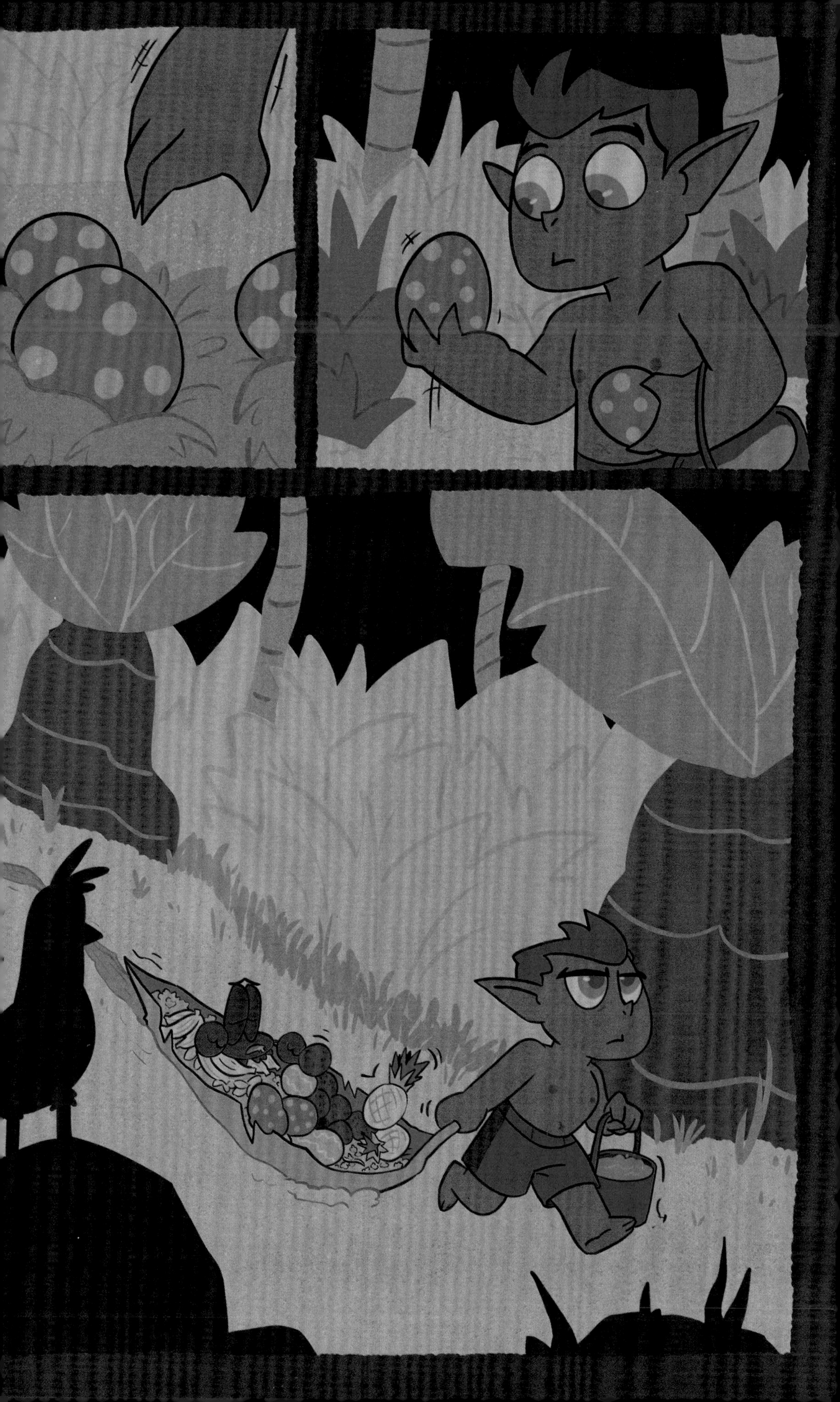

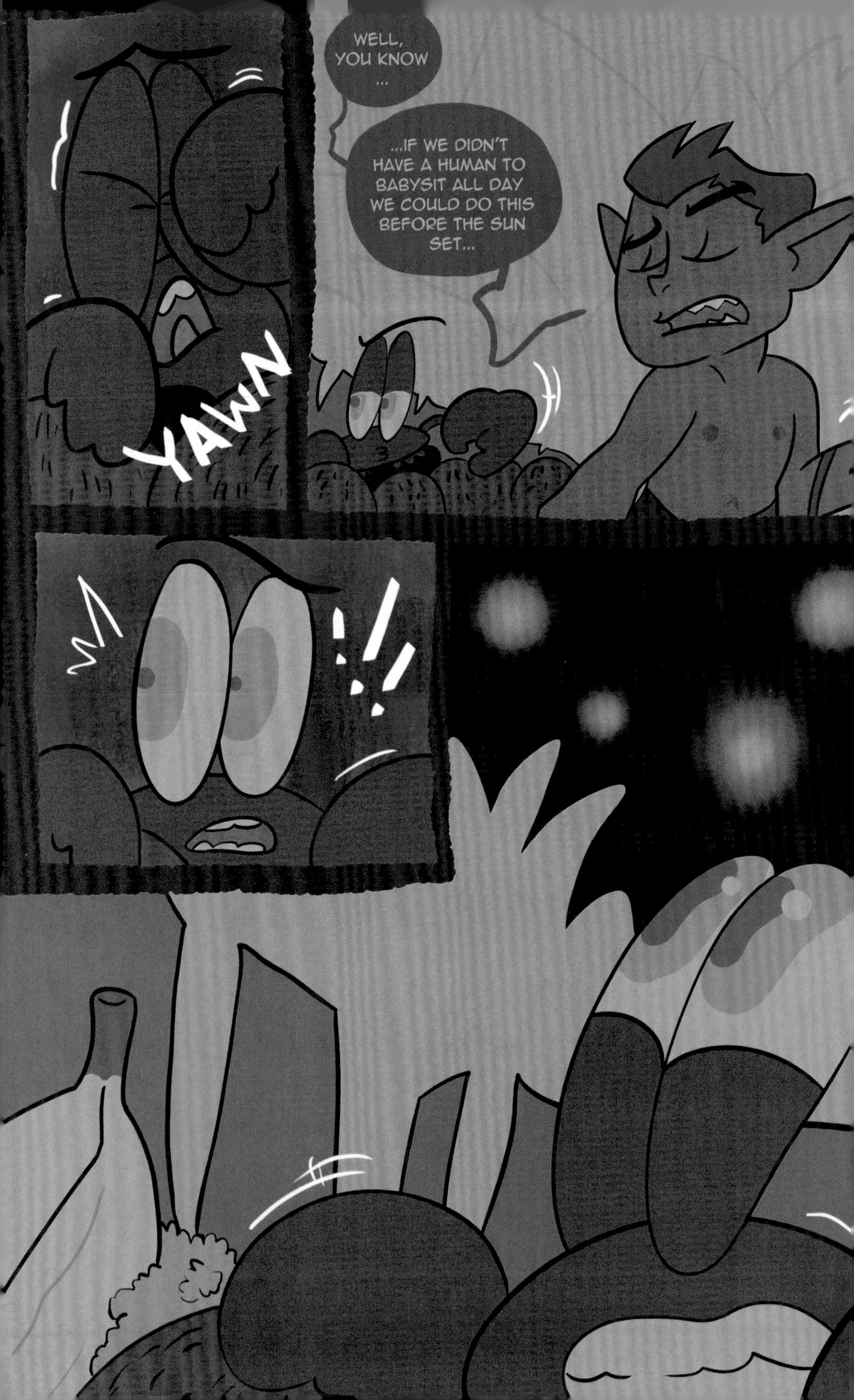
YAWN
WELL, YOU KNOW ...
...IF WE DIDN'T HAVE A HUMAN TO BABYSIT ALL DAY WE COULD DO THIS BEFORE THE SUN SET...

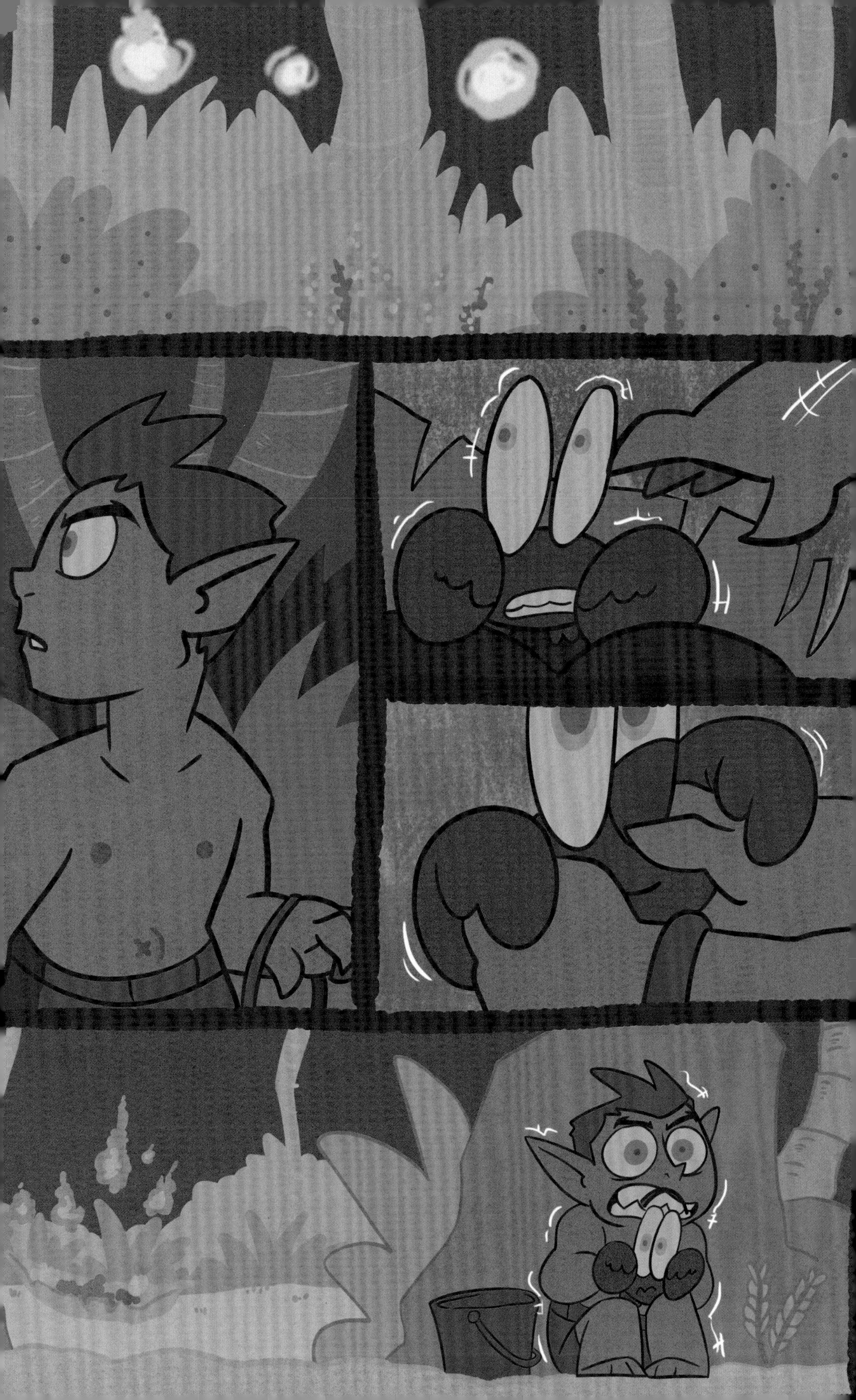

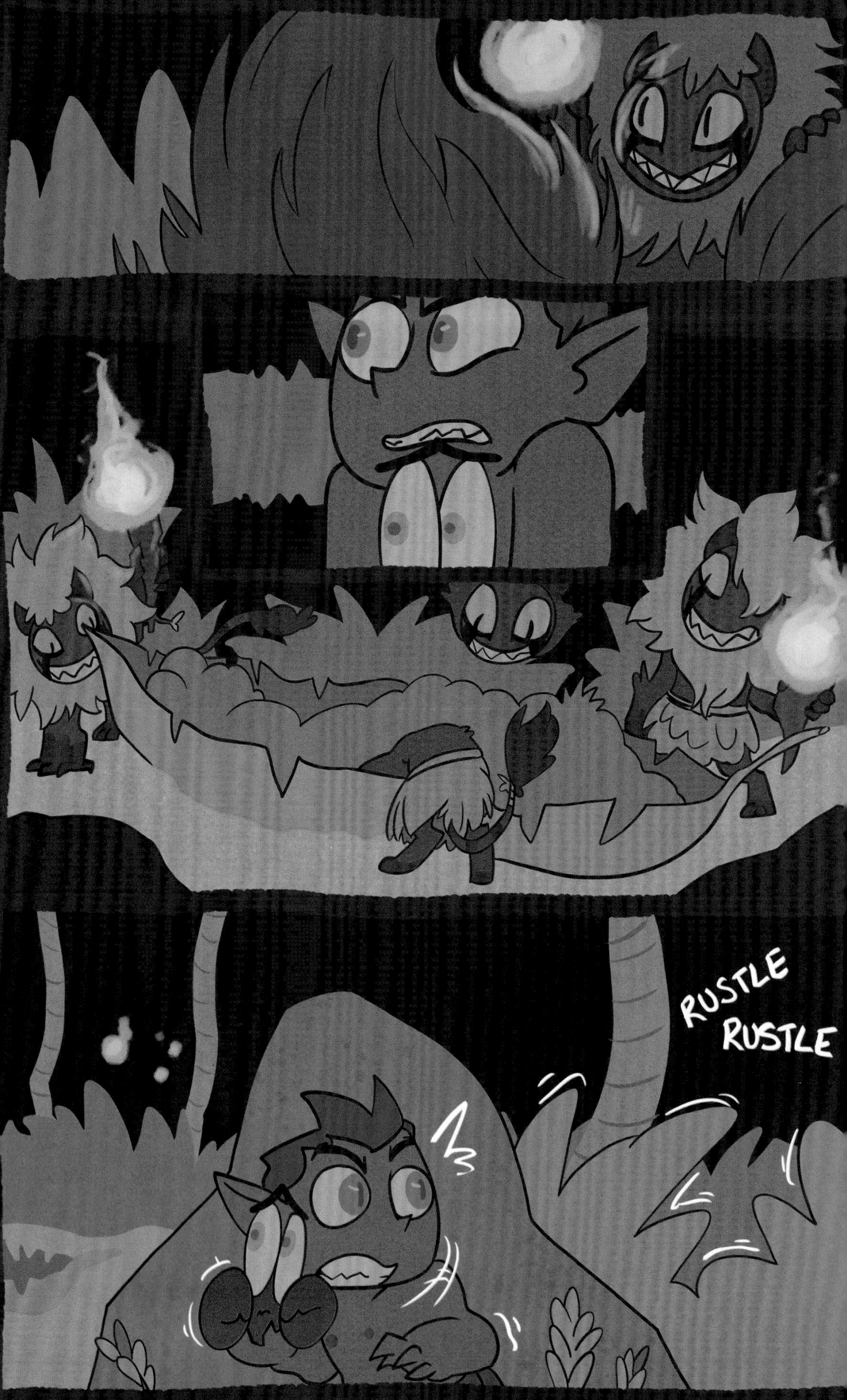
RUSTLE
RUSTLE

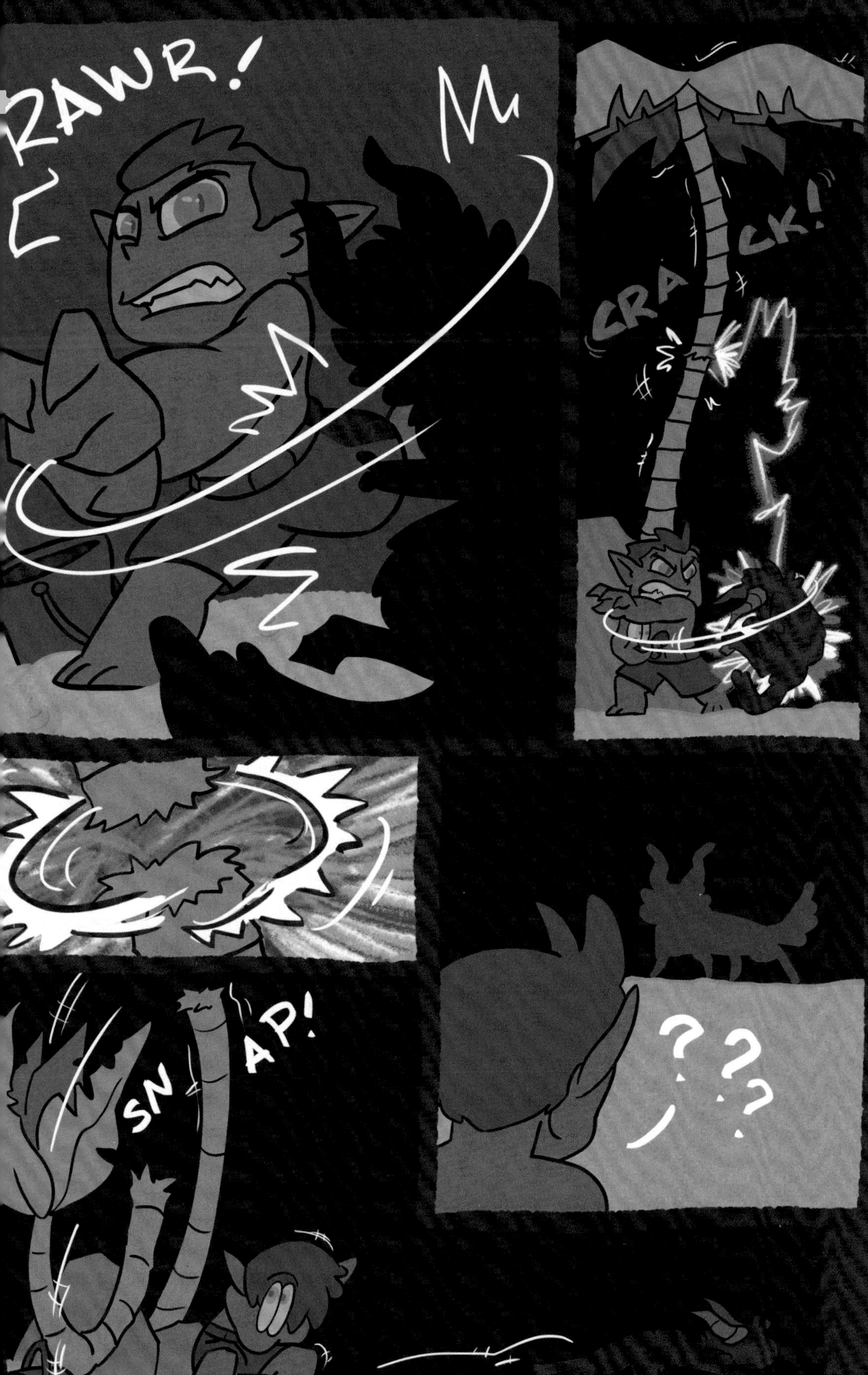
RAWR!
CRACK!
SNAP!
???

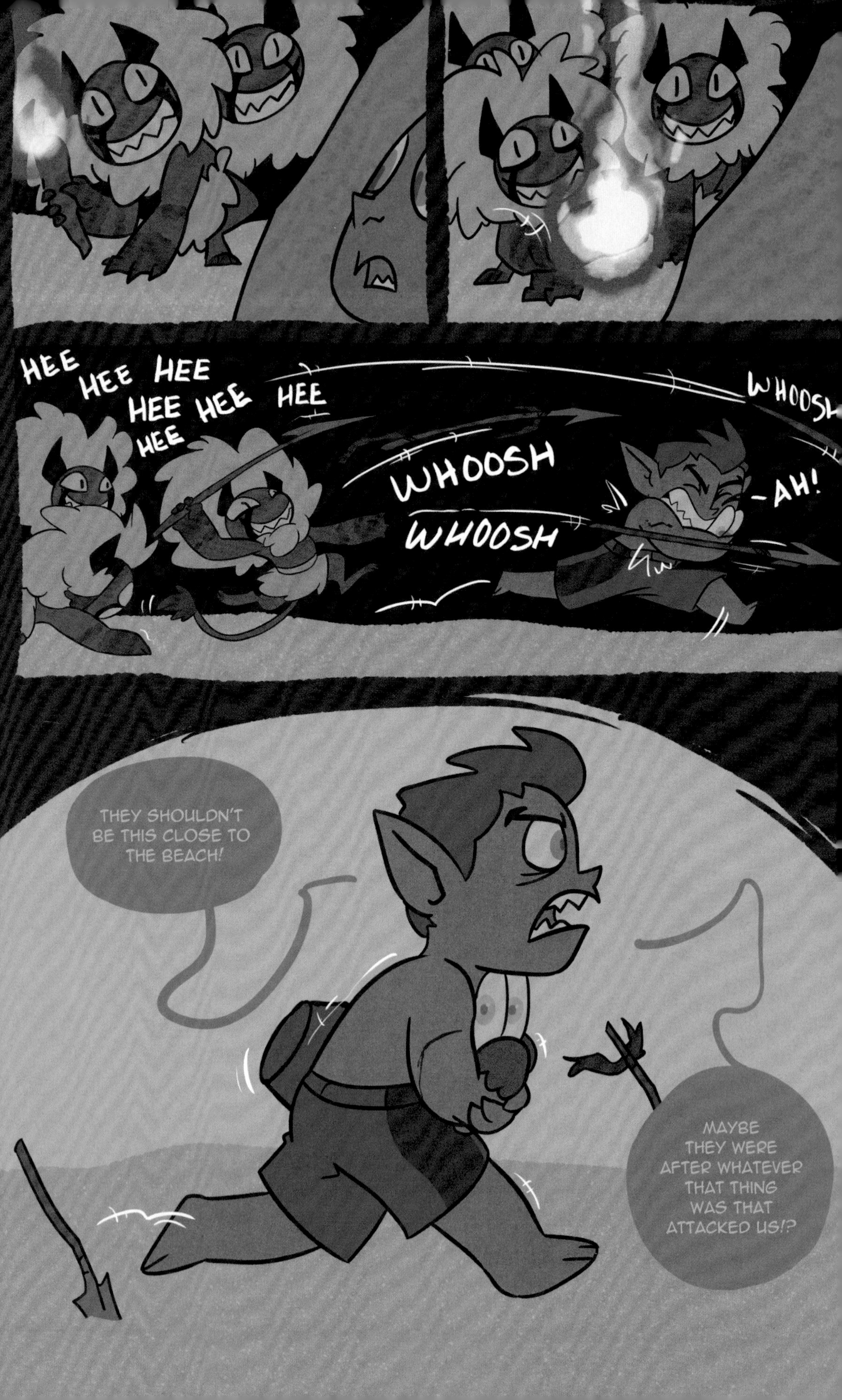
HEE
HEE HEE
HEE HEE HEE
HEE
WHOOSH
WHOOSH
WHOOSH
-AH!
THEY SHOULDN'T BE THIS CLOSE TO THE BEACH!
MAYBE THEY WERE AFTER WHATEVER THAT THING WAS THAT ATTACKED US!?

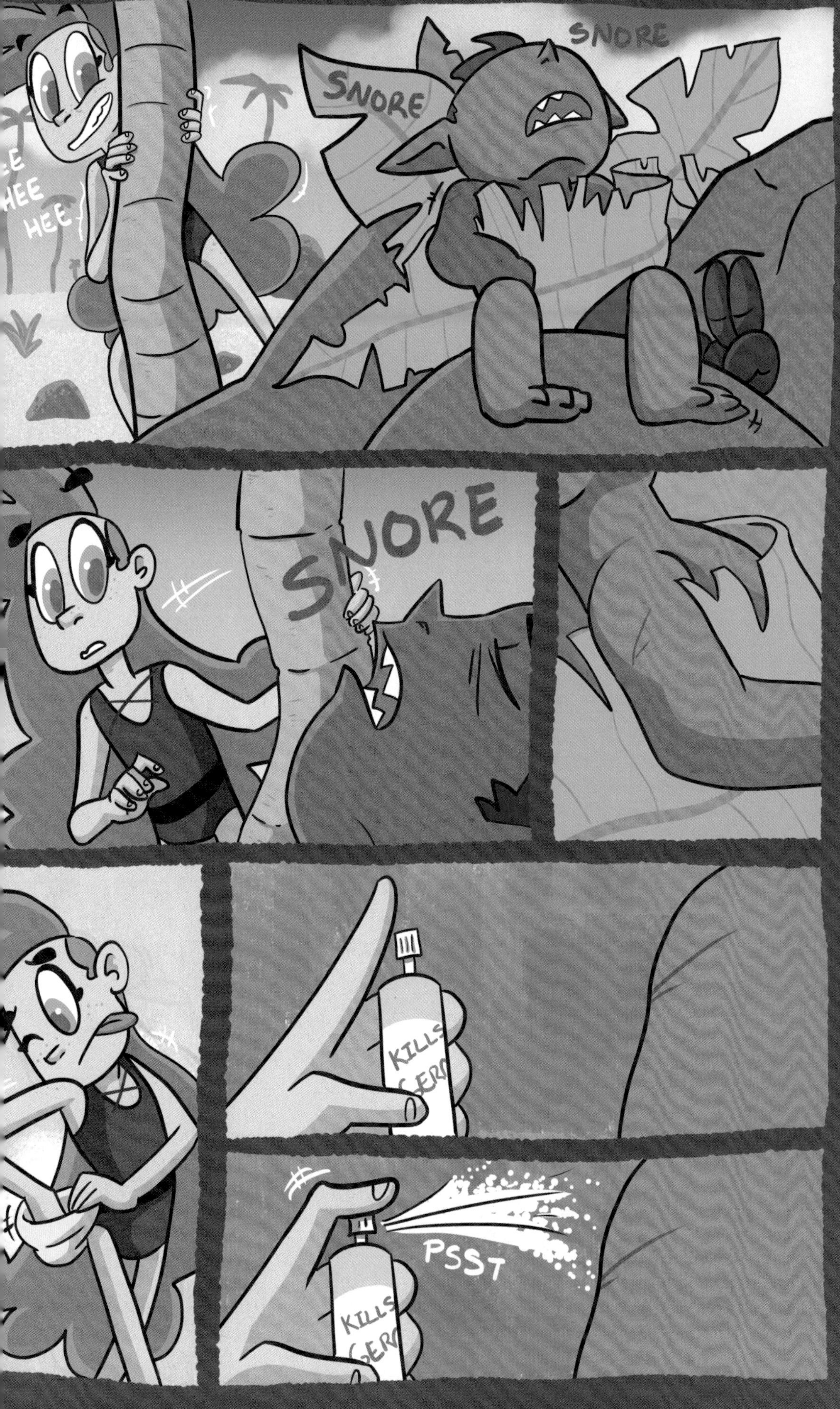
HEE HEE HEE
SNORE
SNORE
SNORE
KILLS GERM
PSST
KILLS GERM

WHAT DO YOU EXPECT WHEN YOU ATTACK ME *WHILE I'M SLEEPING!?*

YAWN

WOAH!

RELAX, IT'S JUST A LITTLE SPRAY. SO IT DOESN'T GET INFECTED.

YOU'RE SO RUDE!

SMACK

I WASN'T TRYING—

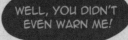

WELL, YOU DIDN'T EVEN WARN ME!

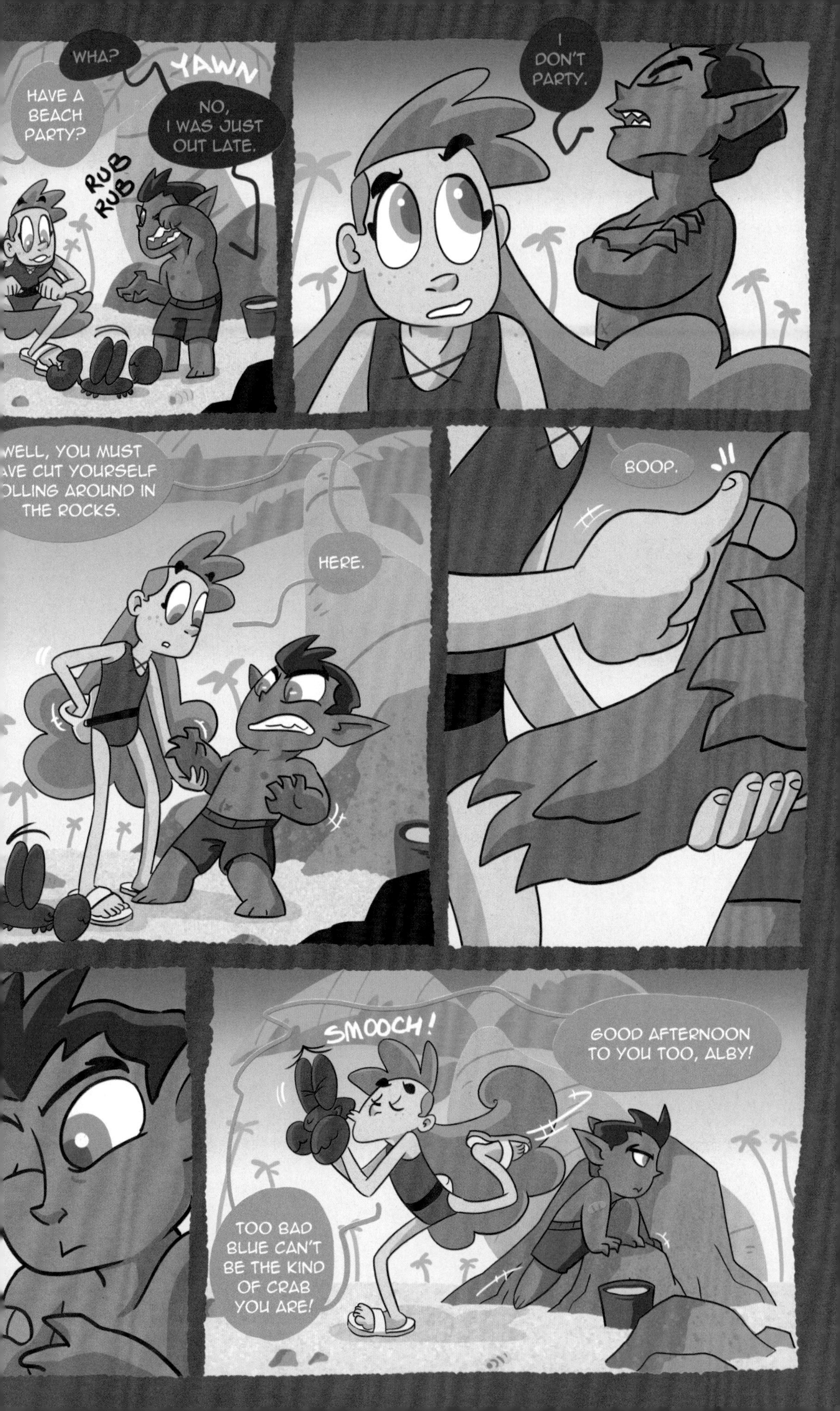
HAVE A BEACH PARTY?
WHA?
YAWN
NO, I WAS JUST OUT LATE.
RUB RUB
I DON'T PARTY.
WELL, YOU MUST AVE CUT YOURSELF OLLING AROUND IN THE ROCKS.
HERE.
BOOP.
SMOOCH!
GOOD AFTERNOON TO YOU TOO, ALBY!
TOO BAD BLUE CAN'T BE THE KIND OF CRAB YOU ARE!

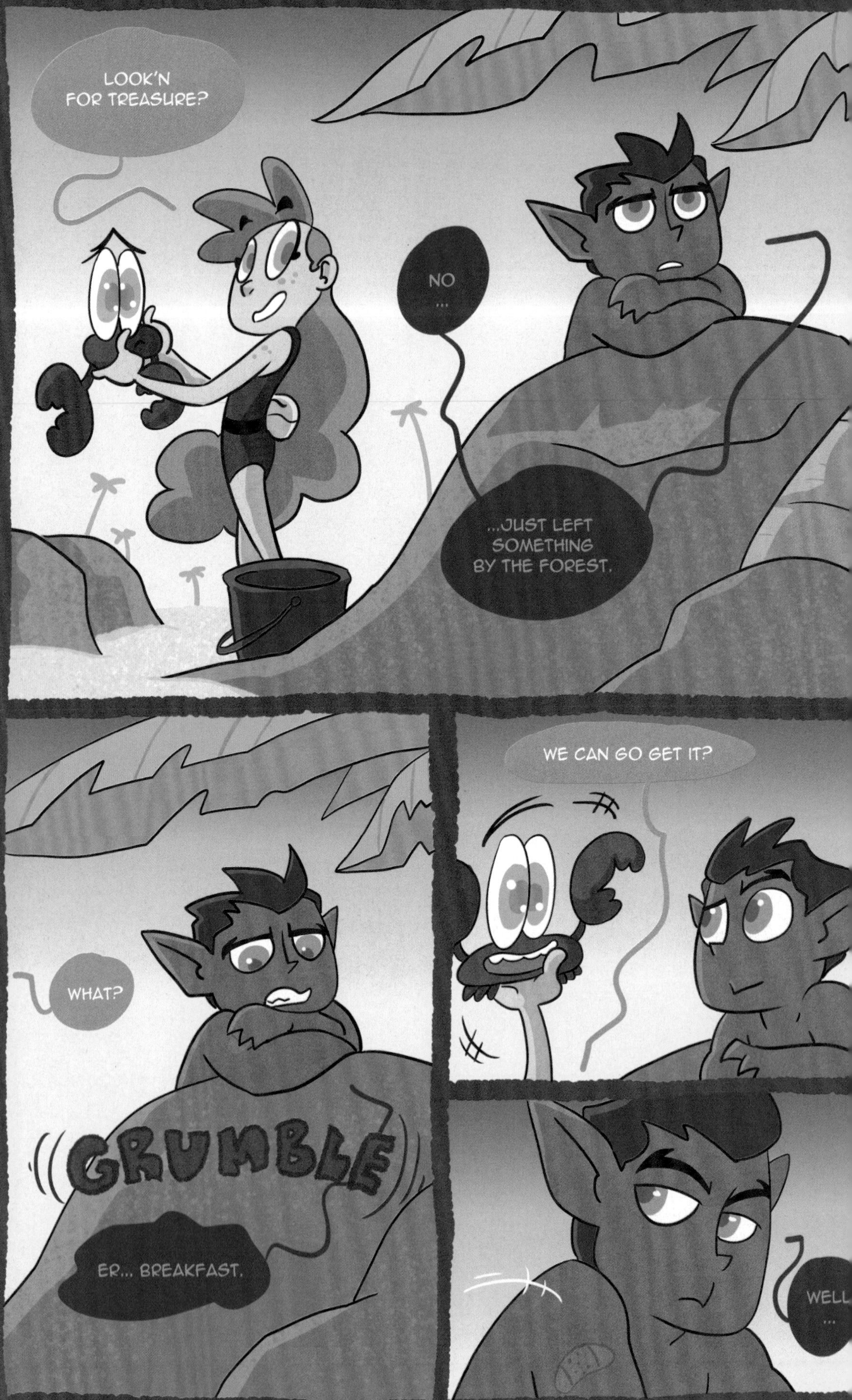
LOOK'N FOR TREASURE?
NO ...
...JUST LEFT SOMETHING BY THE FOREST.
WHAT?
GRUMBLE
ER... BREAKFAST.
WE CAN GO GET IT?
WELL ...

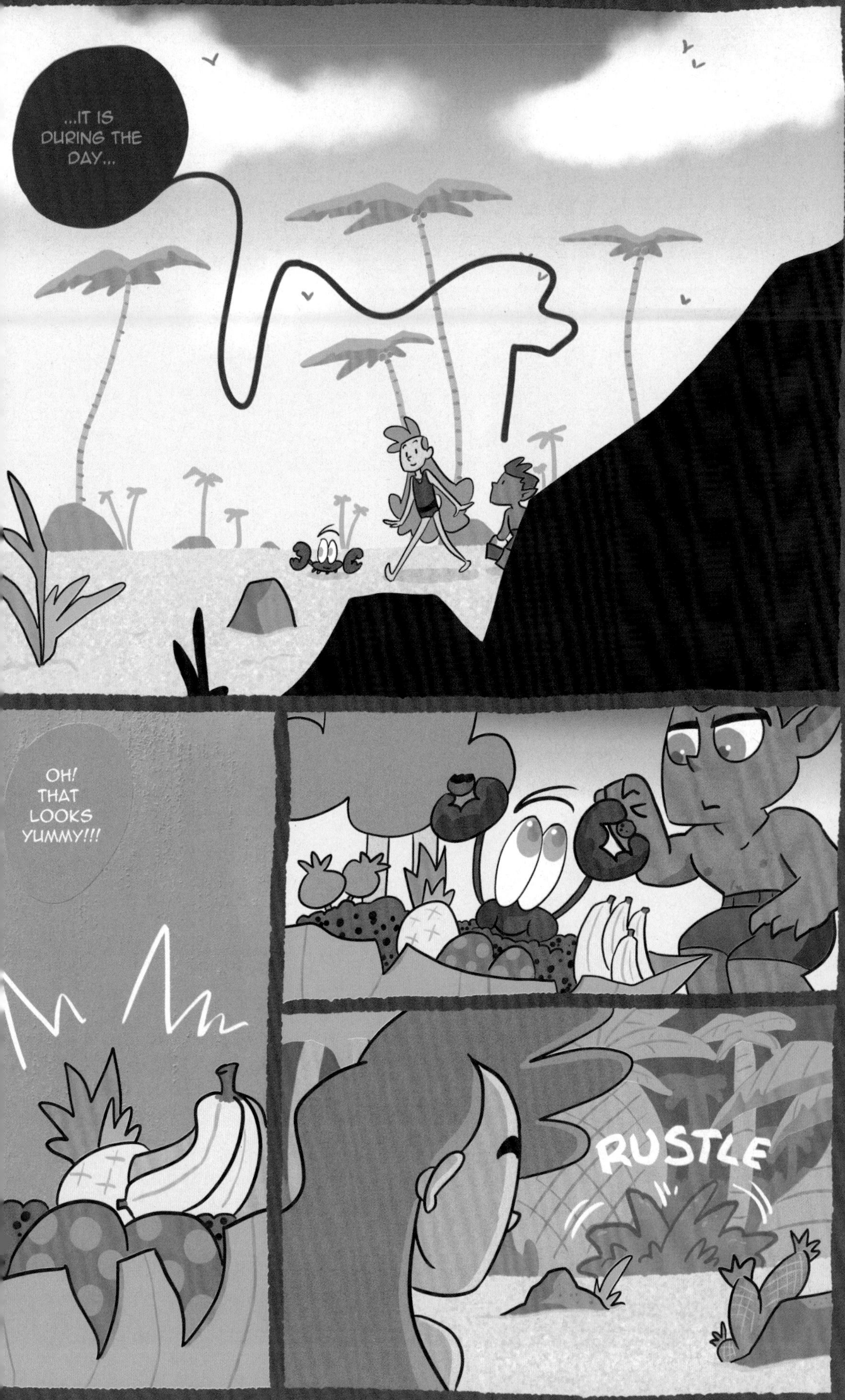
...IT IS DURING THE DAY...
OH! THAT LOOKS YUMMY!!!
RUSTLE

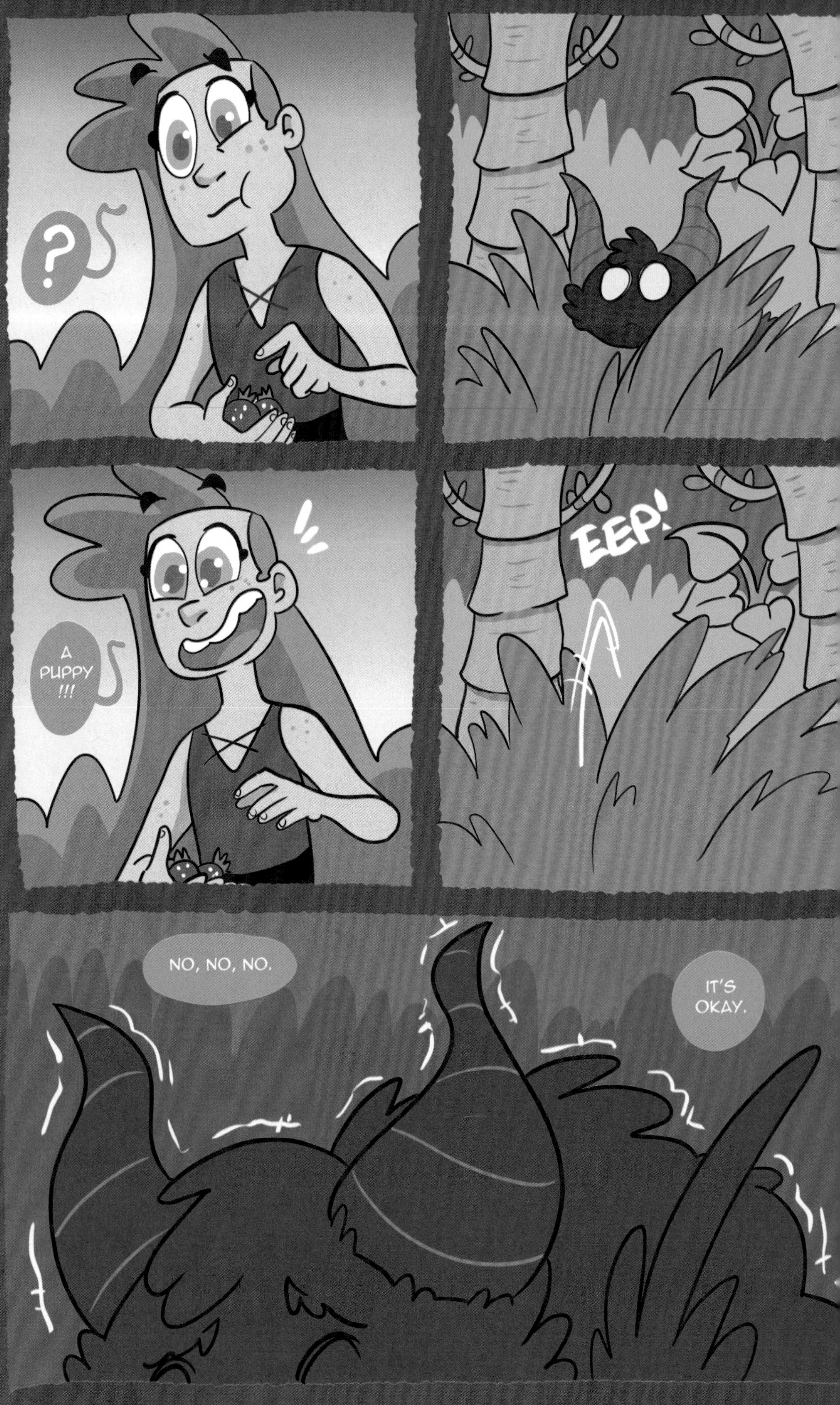
?
A PUPPY !!!
EEP!
NO, NO, NO.
IT'S OKAY.

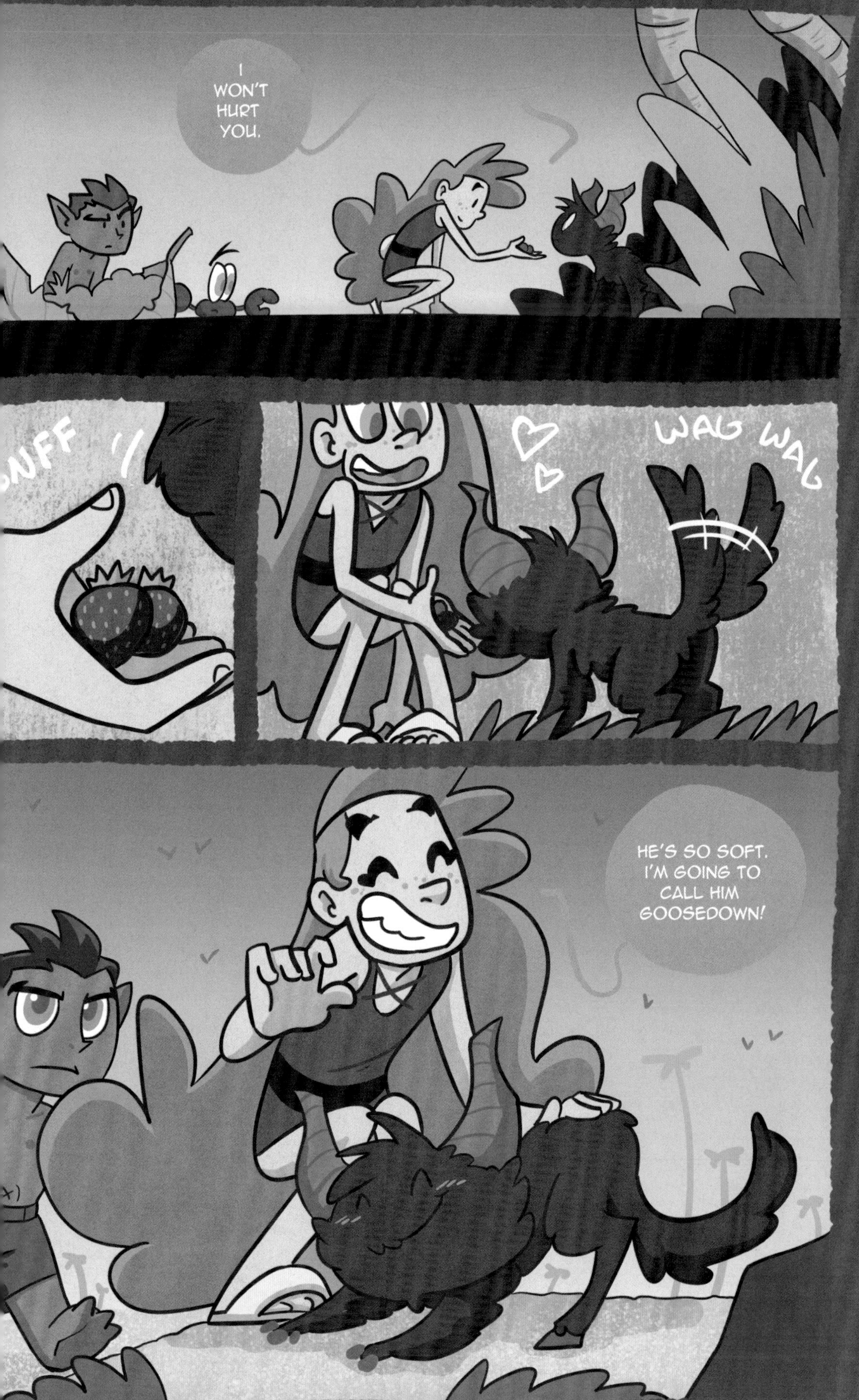
I WON'T HURT YOU.
SNFF
WAG WAG
HE'S SO SOFT. I'M GOING TO CALL HIM GOOSEDOWN!

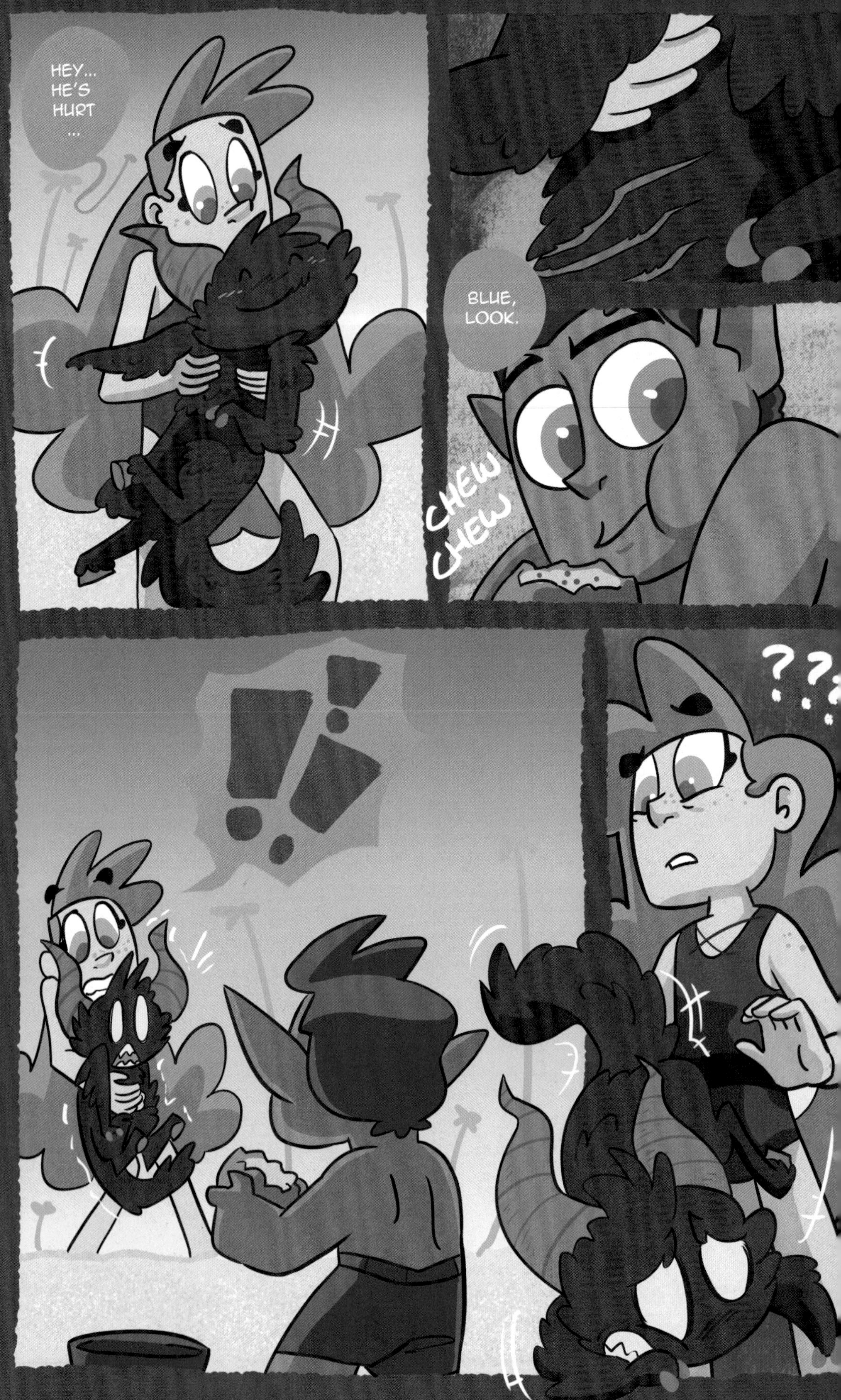
HEY... HE'S HURT ...
BLUE, LOOK.
CHEW CHEW
!!
???

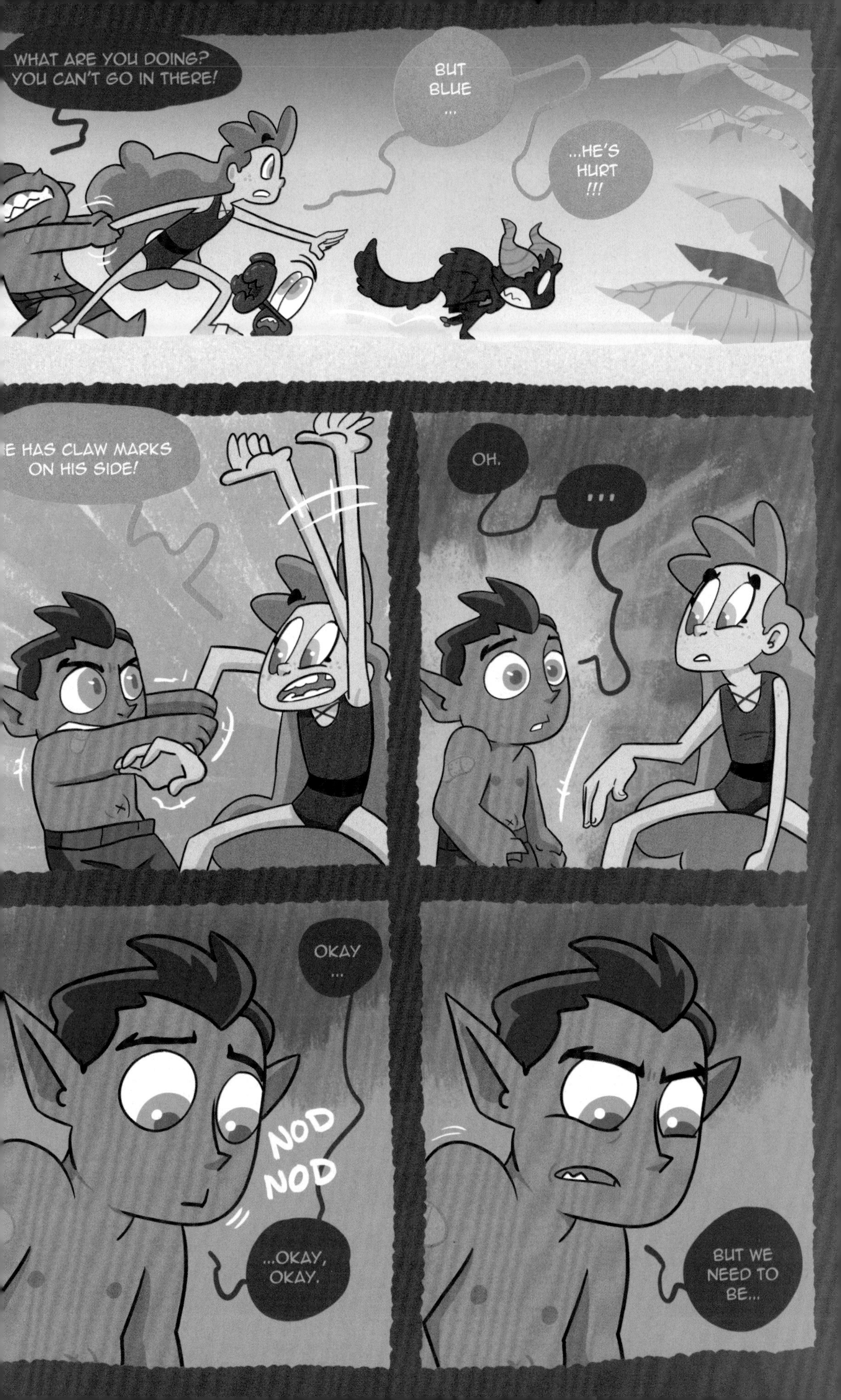
WHAT ARE YOU DOING?
YOU CAN'T GO IN THERE!
BUT BLUE ...
...HE'S HURT !!!
E HAS CLAW MARKS ON HIS SIDE!
OH.
...
OKAY ...
NOD NOD
...OKAY, OKAY.
BUT WE NEED TO BE...

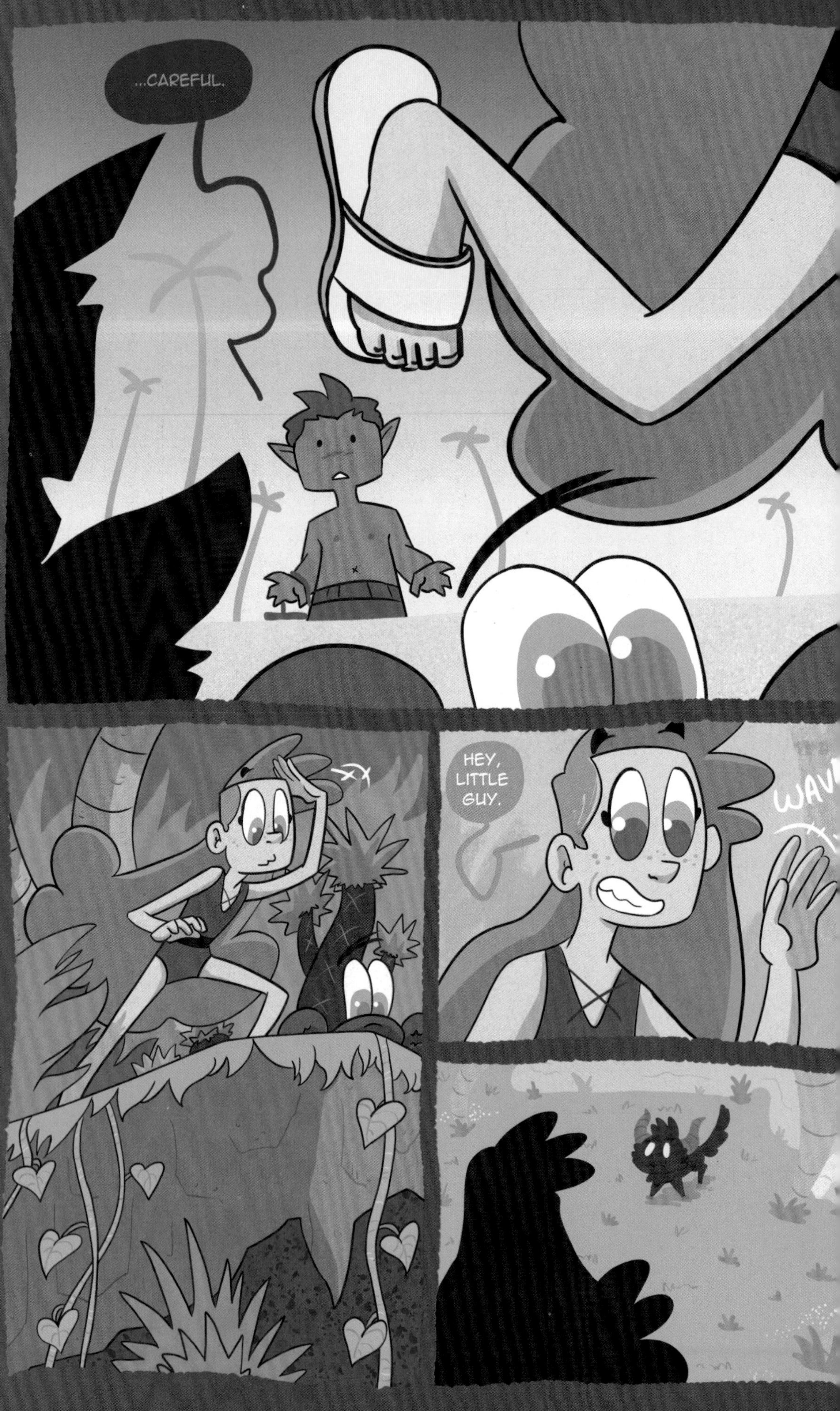
...CAREFUL.
HEY, LITTLE GUY.
WAV

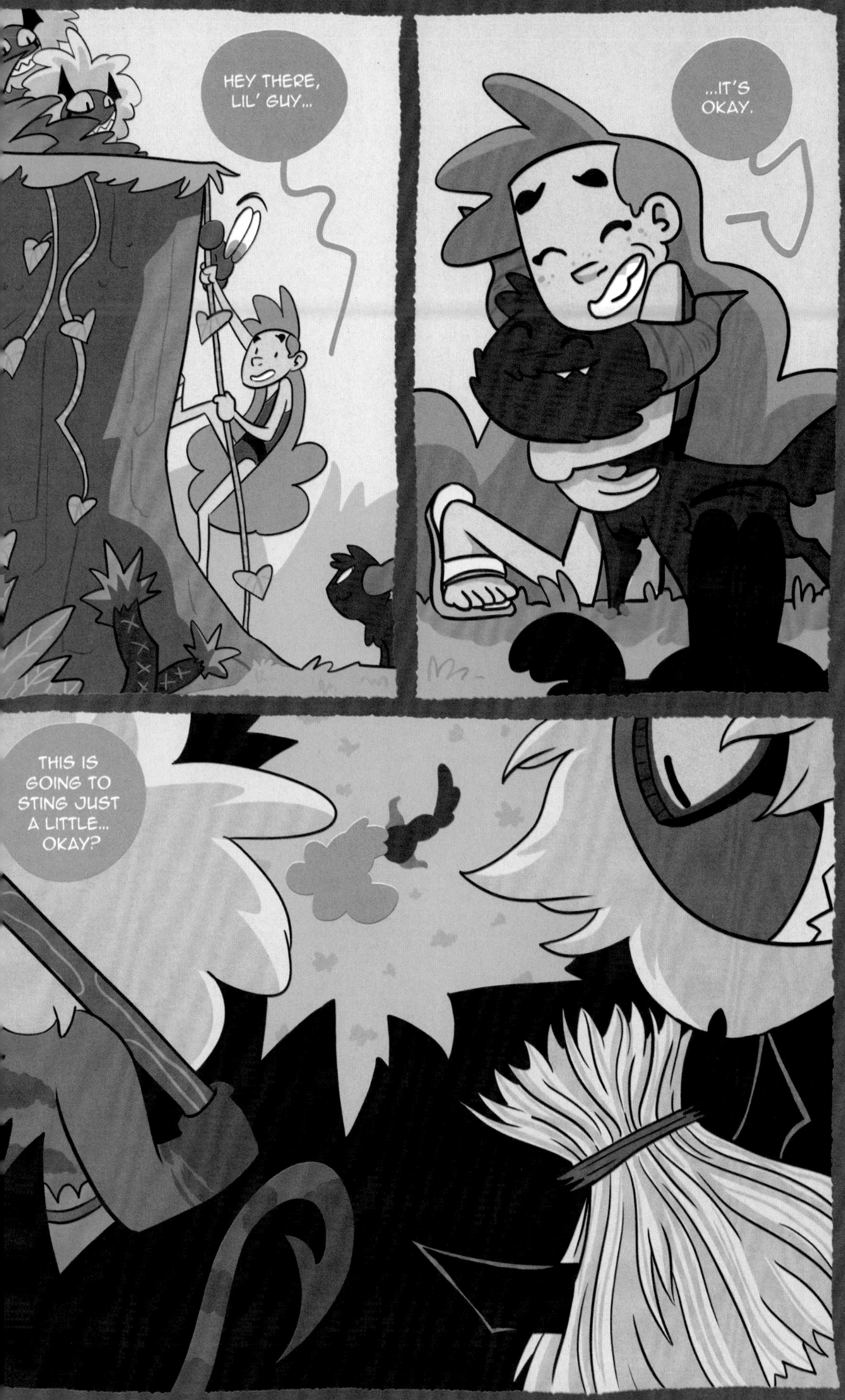
HEY THERE, LIL' GUY...
...IT'S OKAY.
THIS IS GOING TO STING JUST A LITTLE... OKAY?

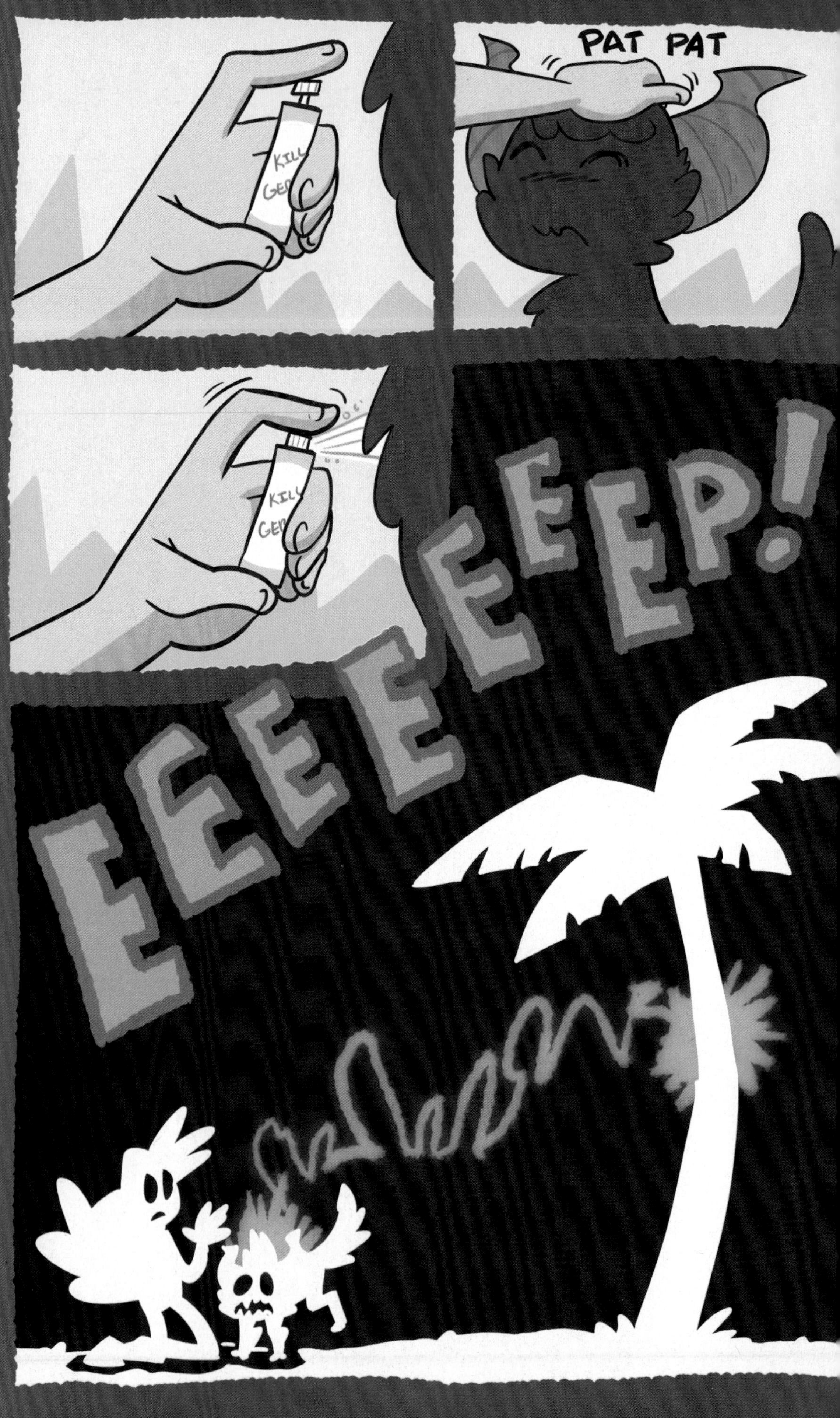

KILL
PAT PAT
KILL
EEEEEEEEP!

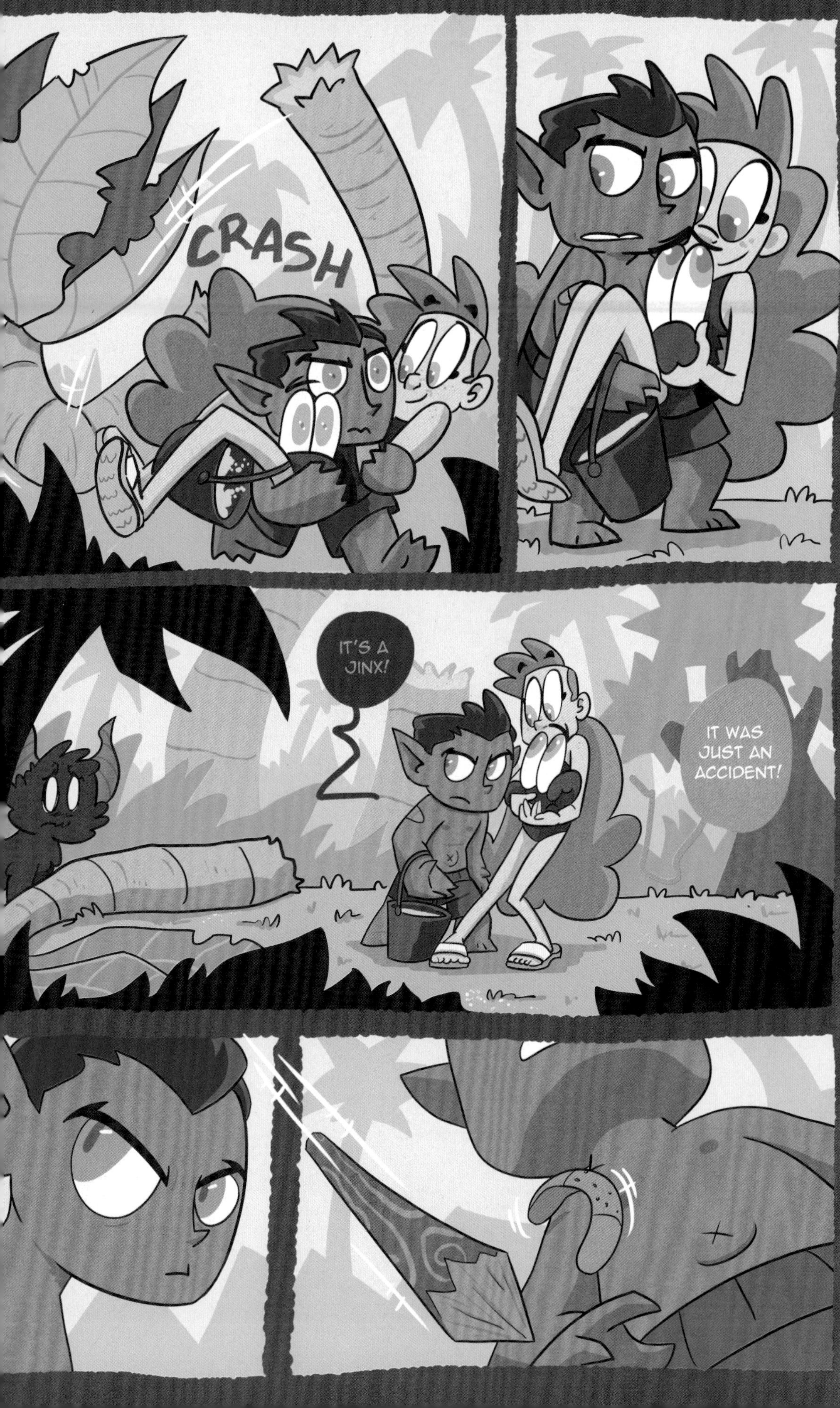
CRASH
IT'S A JINX!
IT WAS JUST AN ACCIDENT!

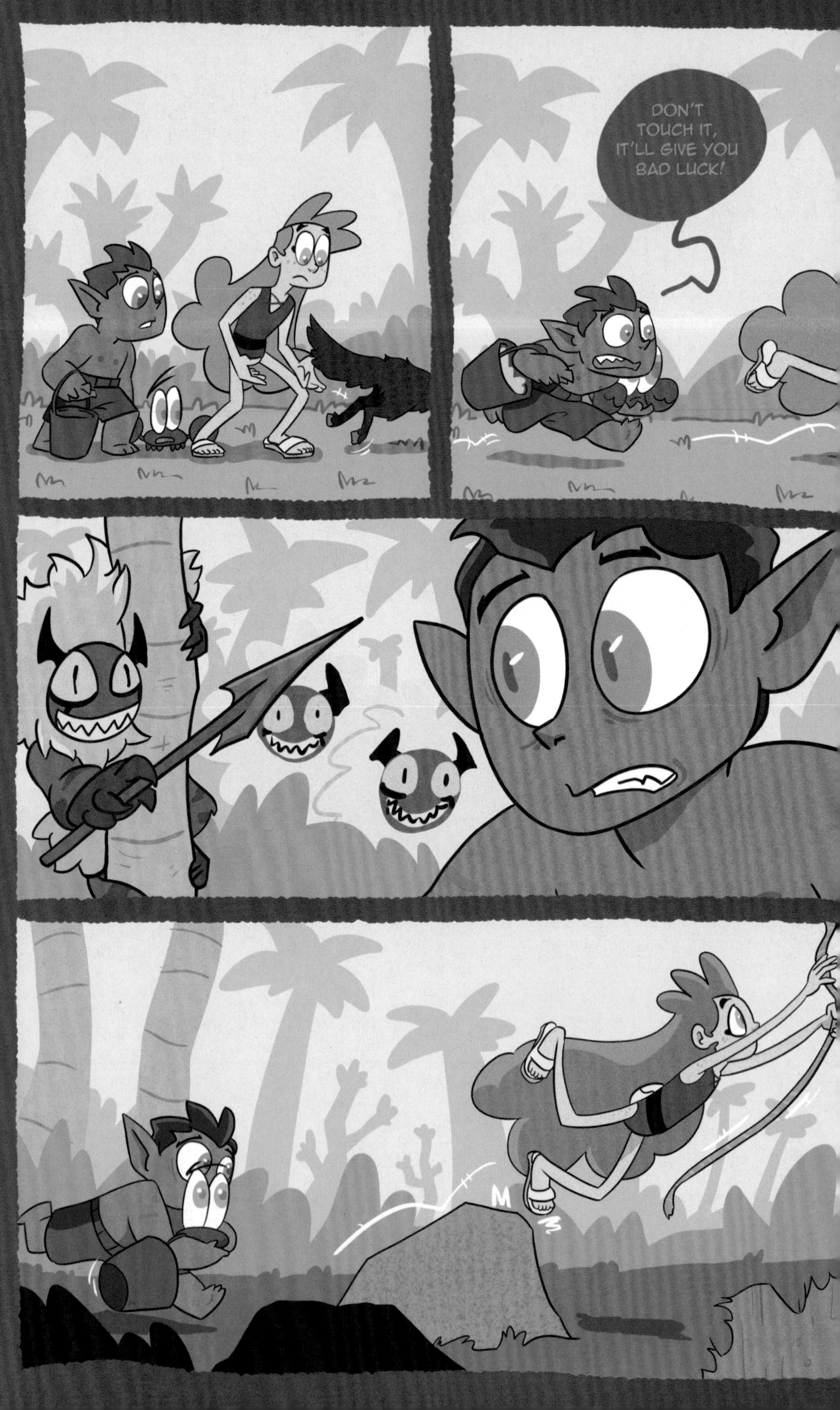
DON'T TOUCH IT, IT'LL GIVE YOU BAD LUCK!
M

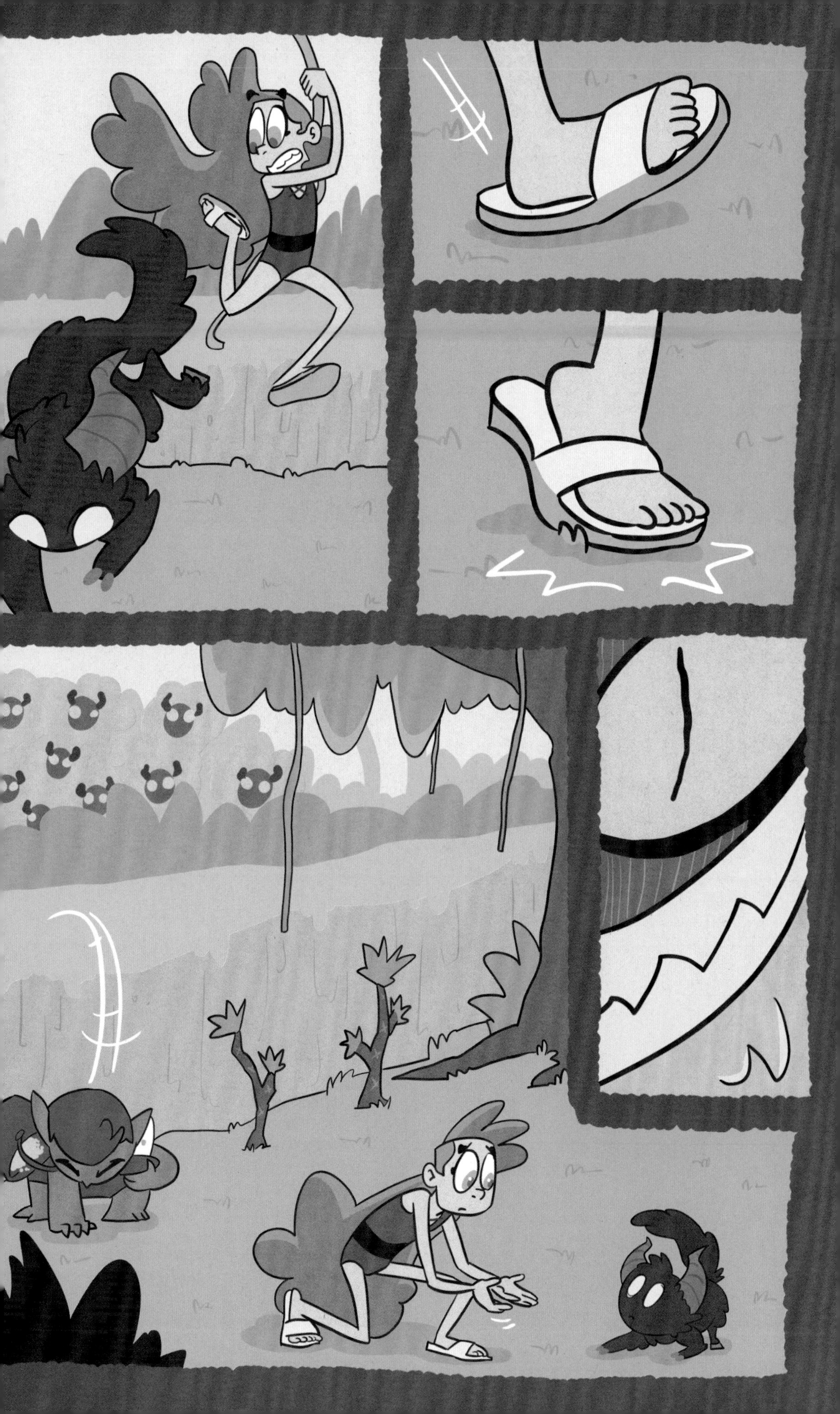

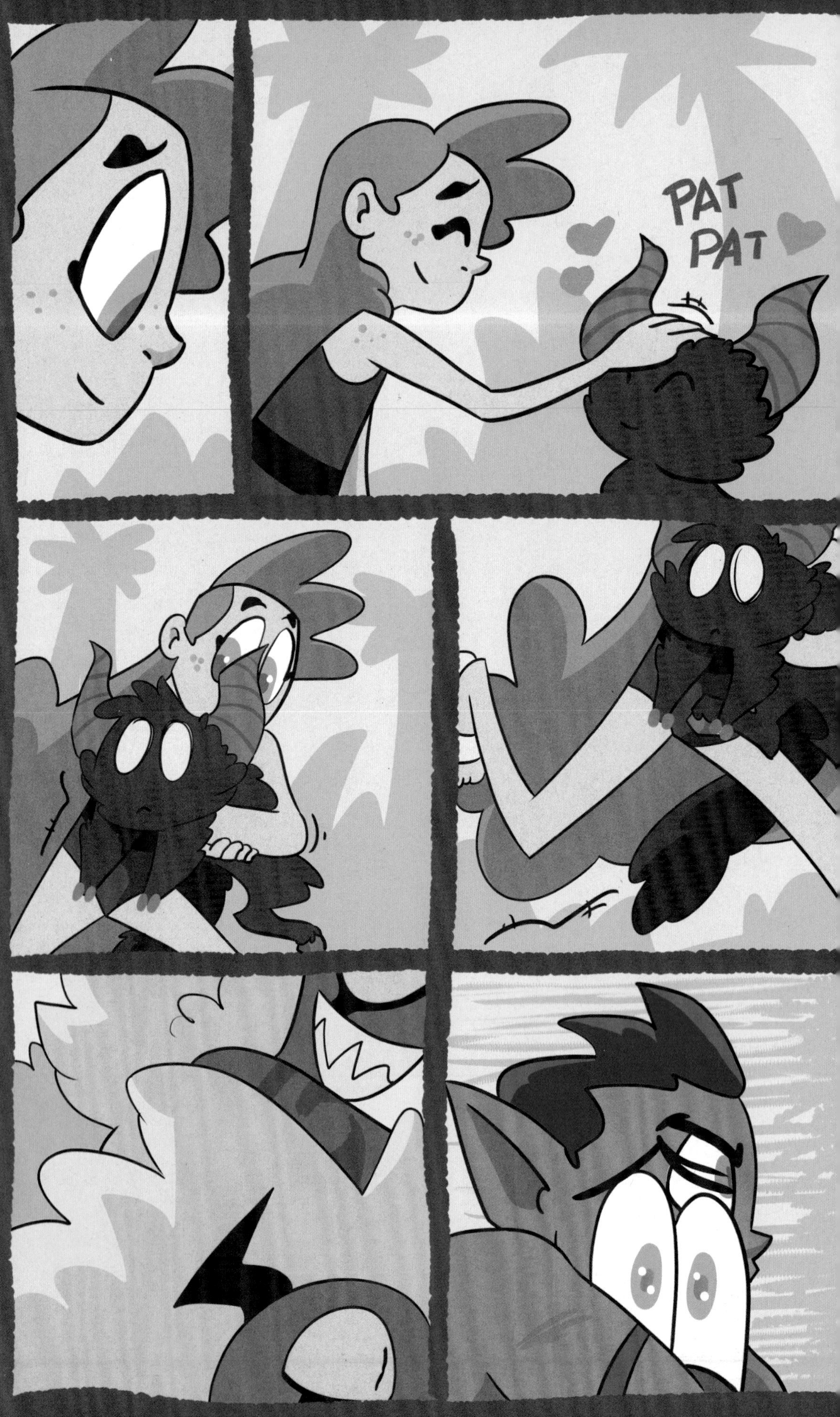
PAT
PAT

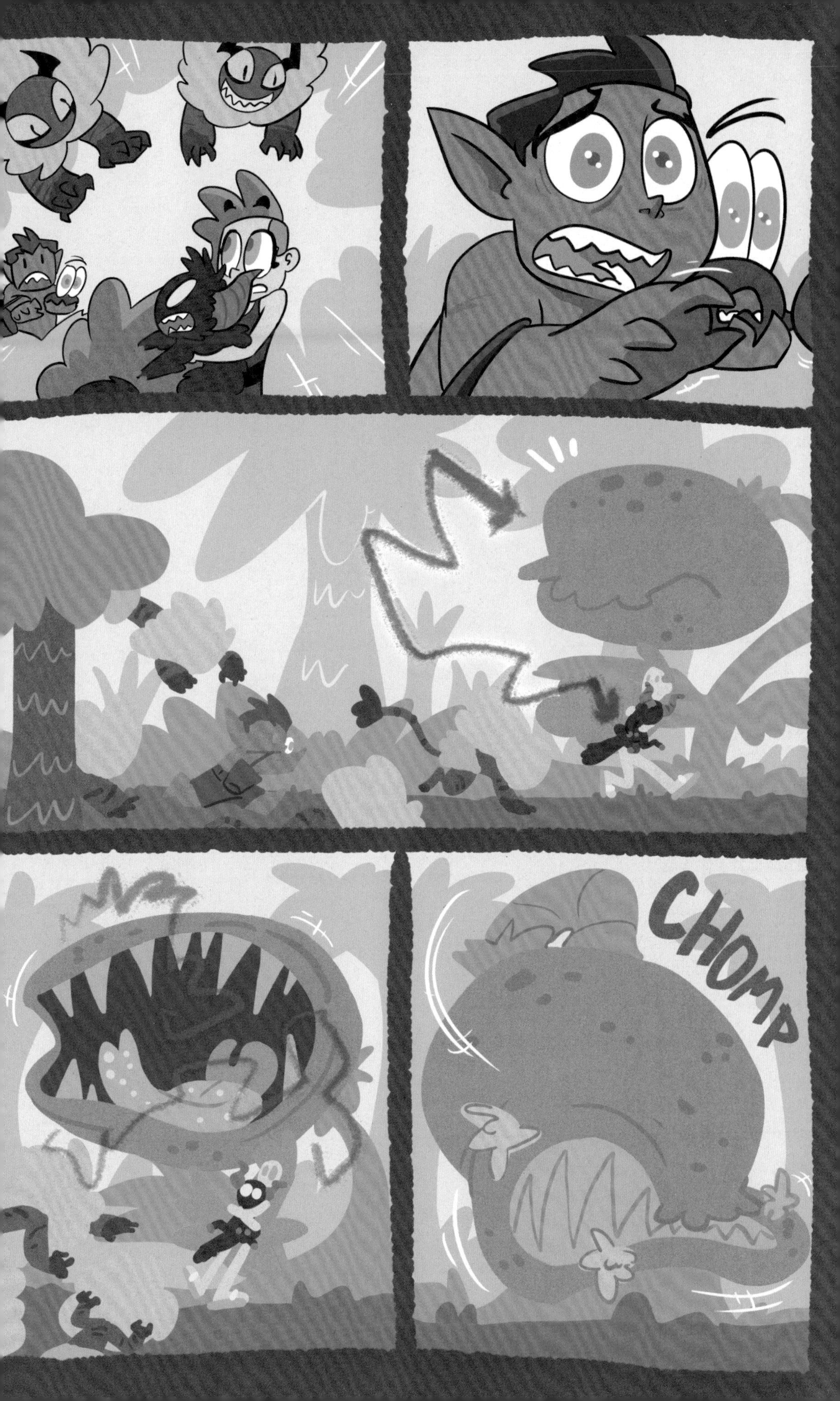
CHOMP

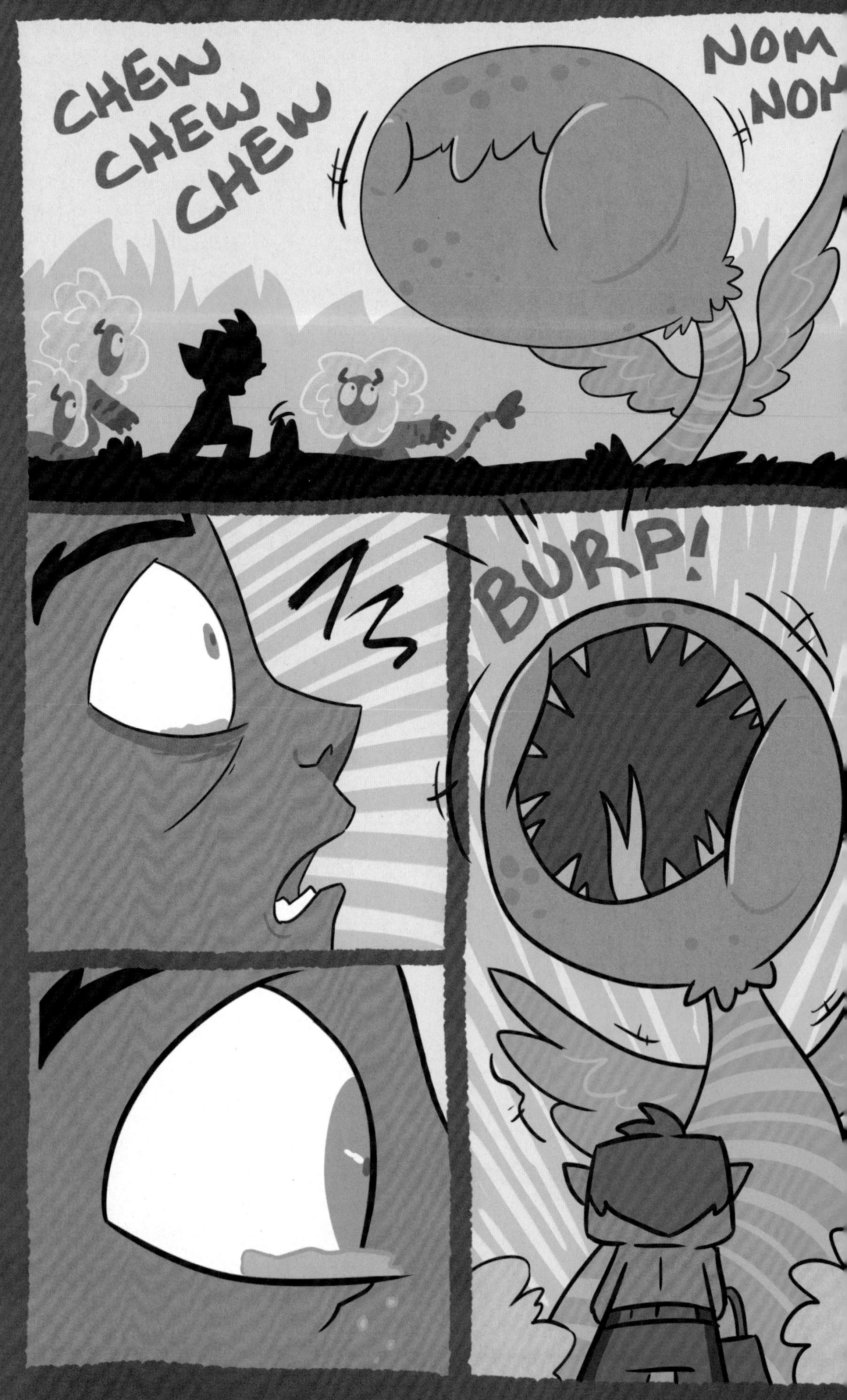
CHEW
CHEW
CHEW
NOM
NOM
BURP!

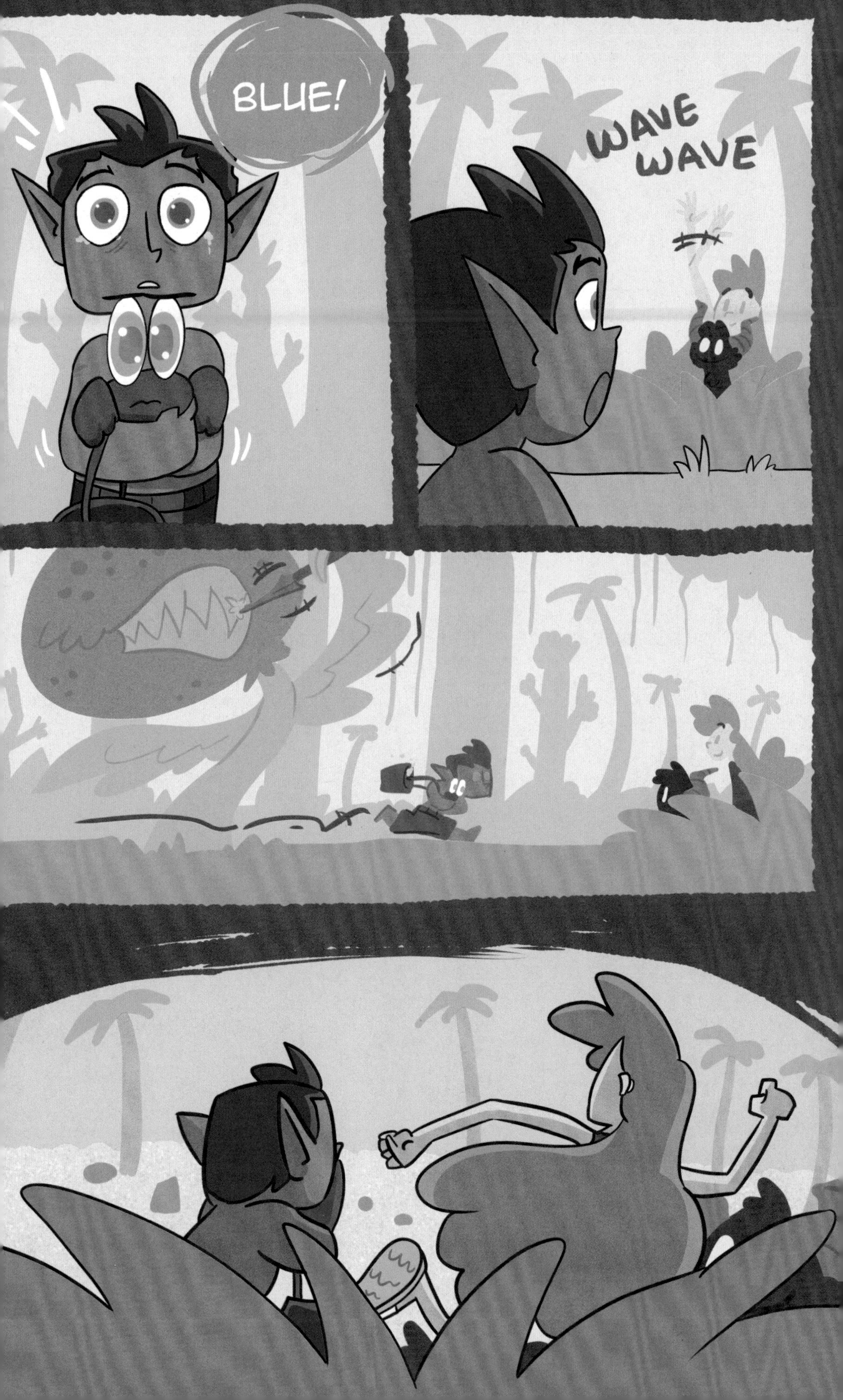
BLUE!
WAVE
WAVE

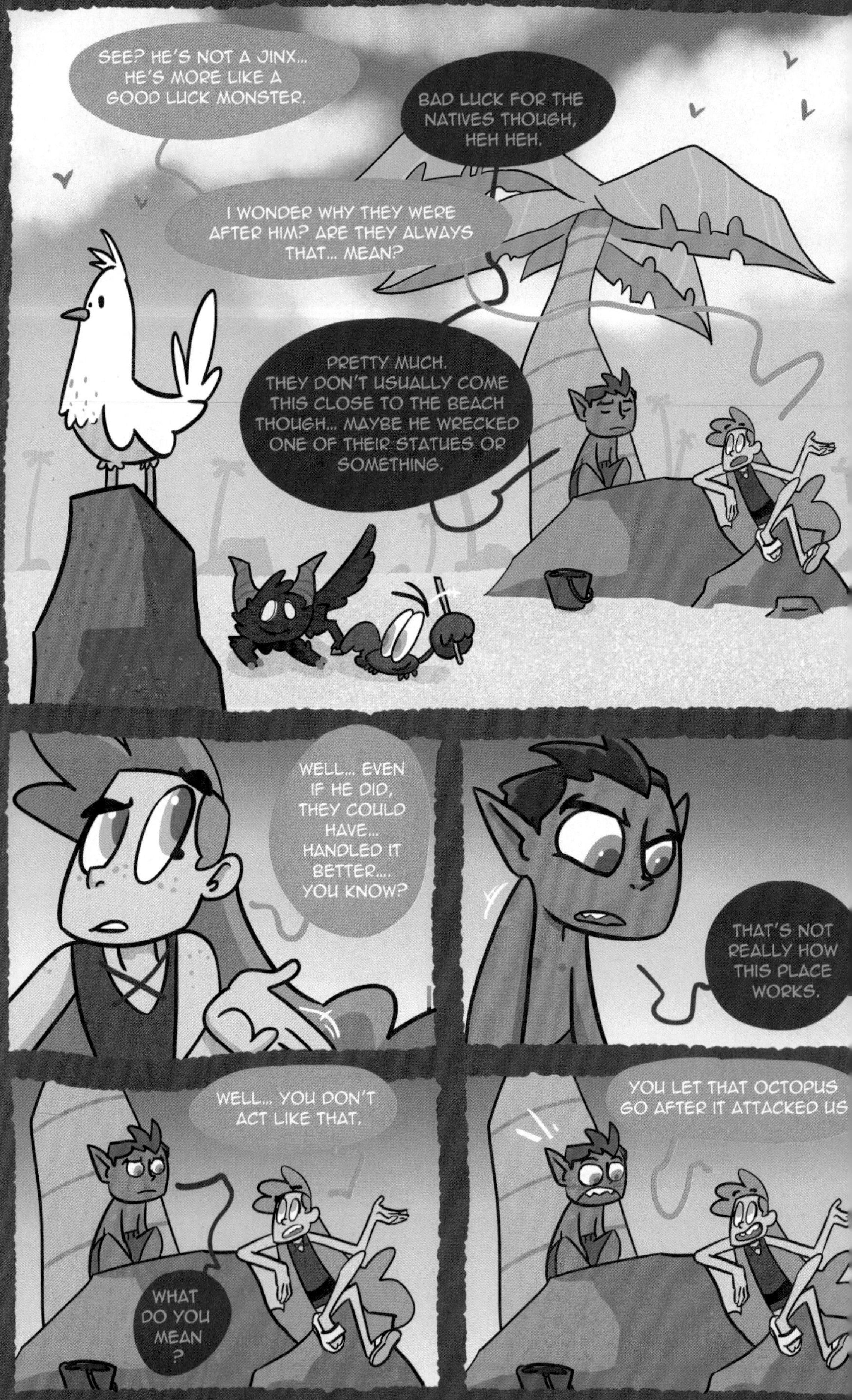
SEE? HE'S NOT A JINX... HE'S MORE LIKE A GOOD LUCK MONSTER.
BAD LUCK FOR THE NATIVES THOUGH, HEH HEH.
I WONDER WHY THEY WERE AFTER HIM? ARE THEY ALWAYS THAT... MEAN?
PRETTY MUCH. THEY DON'T USUALLY COME THIS CLOSE TO THE BEACH THOUGH... MAYBE HE WRECKED ONE OF THEIR STATUES OR SOMETHING.
WELL... EVEN IF HE DID, THEY COULD HAVE... HANDLED IT BETTER.... YOU KNOW?
THAT'S NOT REALLY HOW THIS PLACE WORKS.
WELL... YOU DON'T ACT LIKE THAT.
WHAT DO YOU MEAN ?
YOU LET THAT OCTOPUS GO AFTER IT ATTACKED US

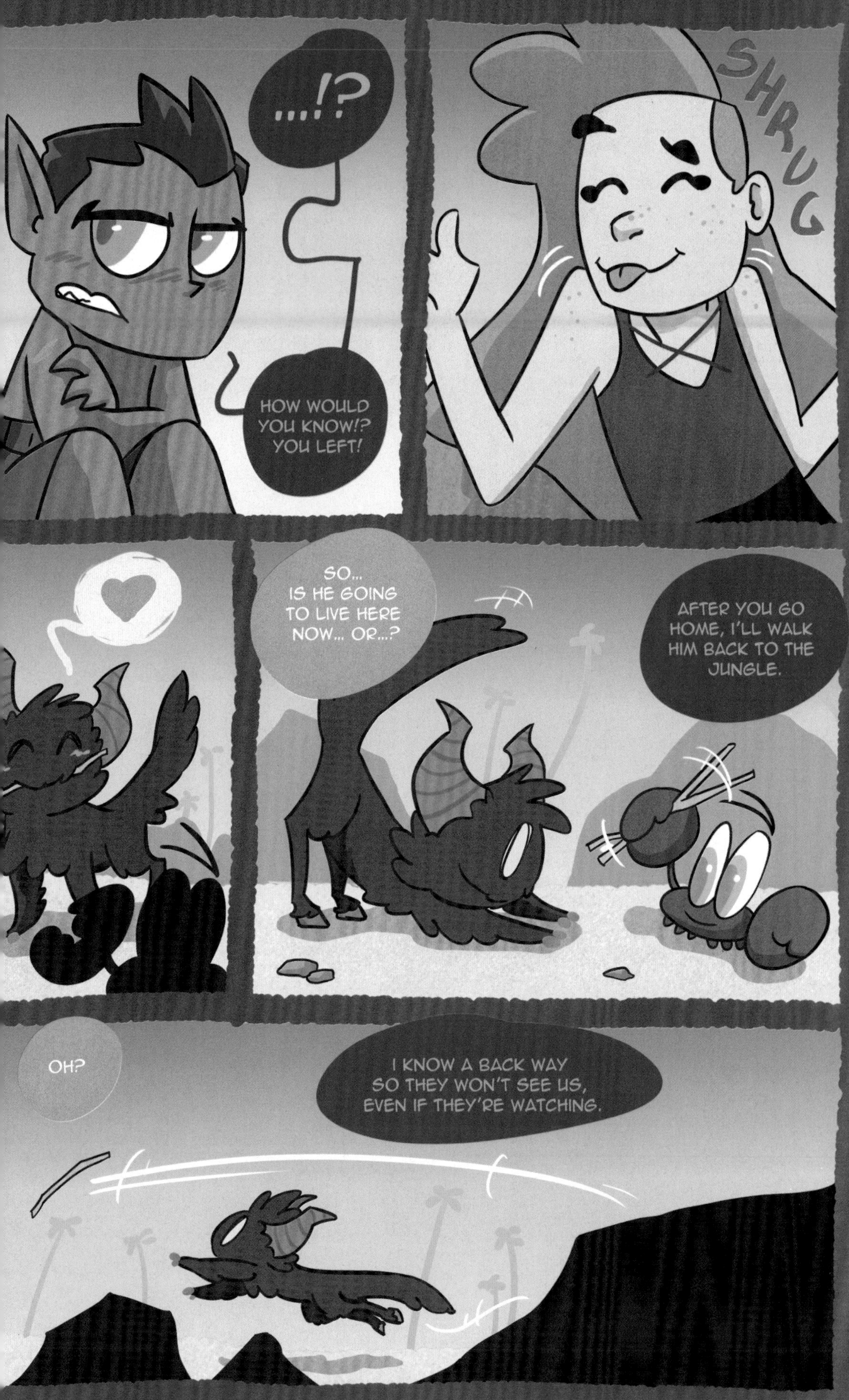
...!?
HOW WOULD YOU KNOW!? YOU LEFT!
SHRUG
SO... IS HE GOING TO LIVE HERE NOW... OR...?
AFTER YOU GO HOME, I'LL WALK HIM BACK TO THE JUNGLE.
OH?
I KNOW A BACK WAY SO THEY WON'T SEE US, EVEN IF THEY'RE WATCHING.

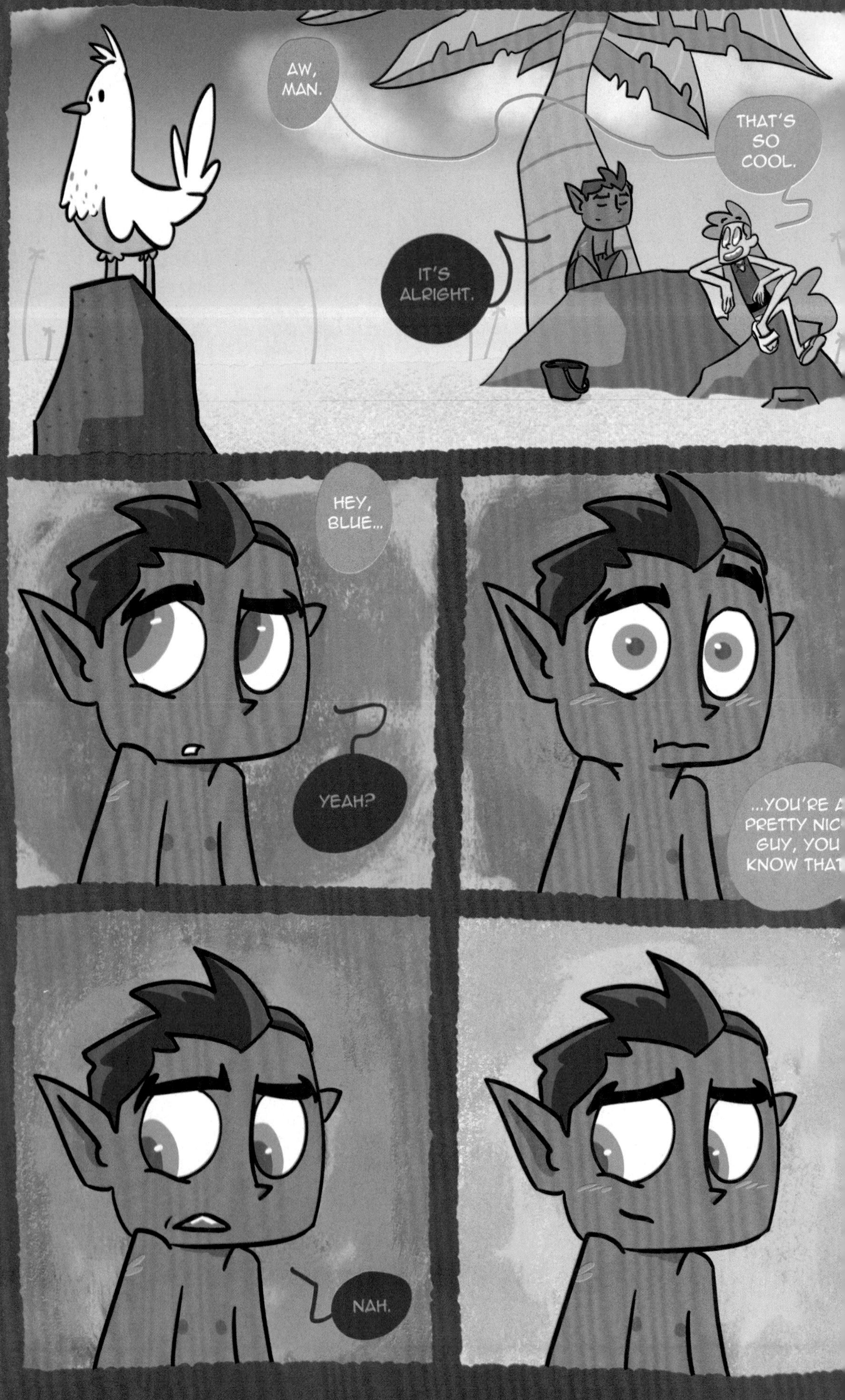
AW, MAN.
THAT'S SO COOL.
IT'S ALRIGHT.
HEY, BLUE...
YEAH?
...YOU'RE A PRETTY NIC GUY, YOU KNOW THAT
NAH.

CONCEPT ART

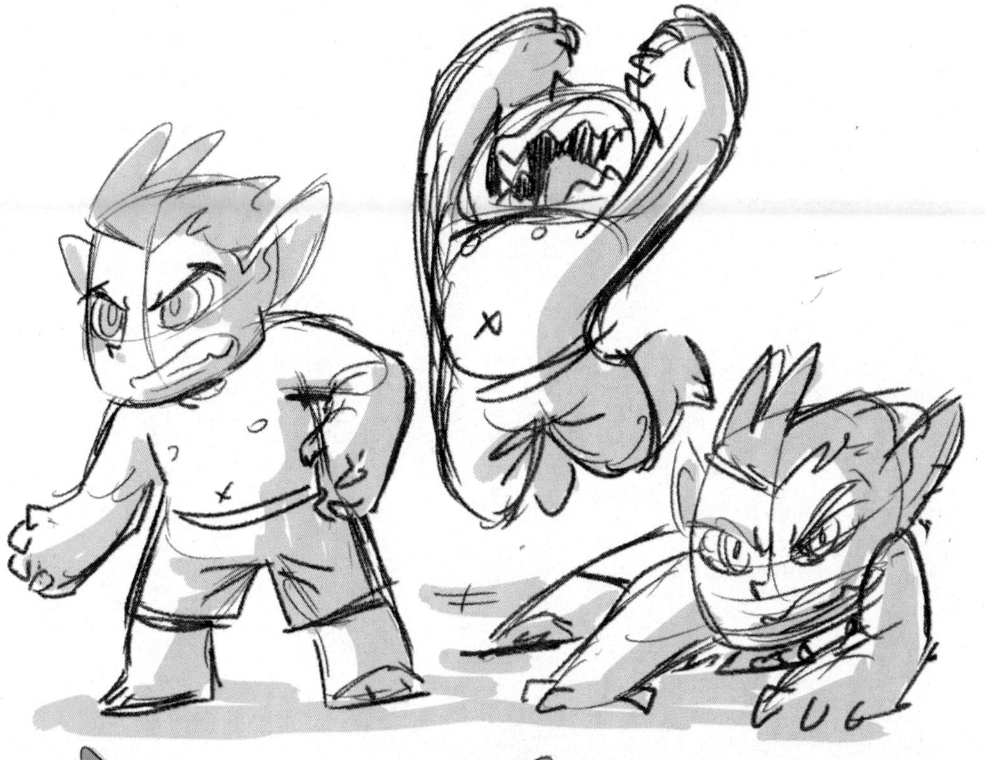

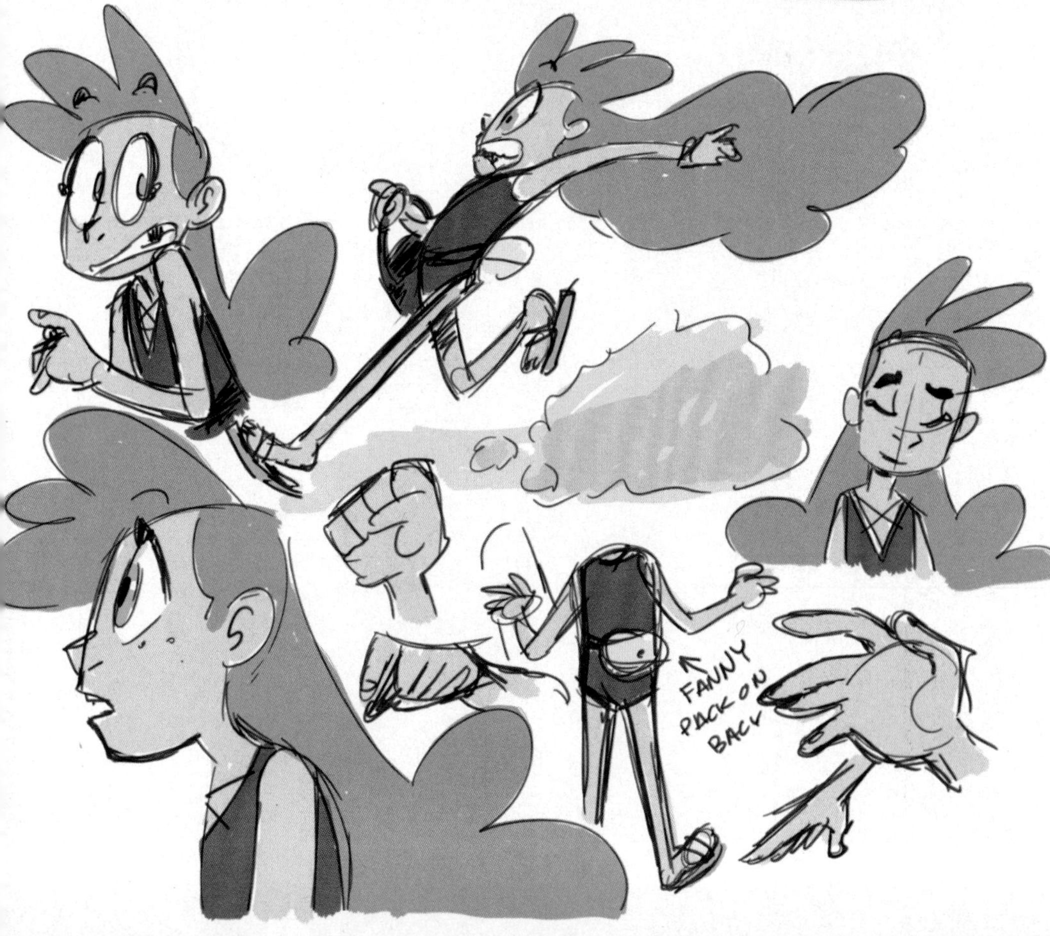
FANNY PACK ON BACK

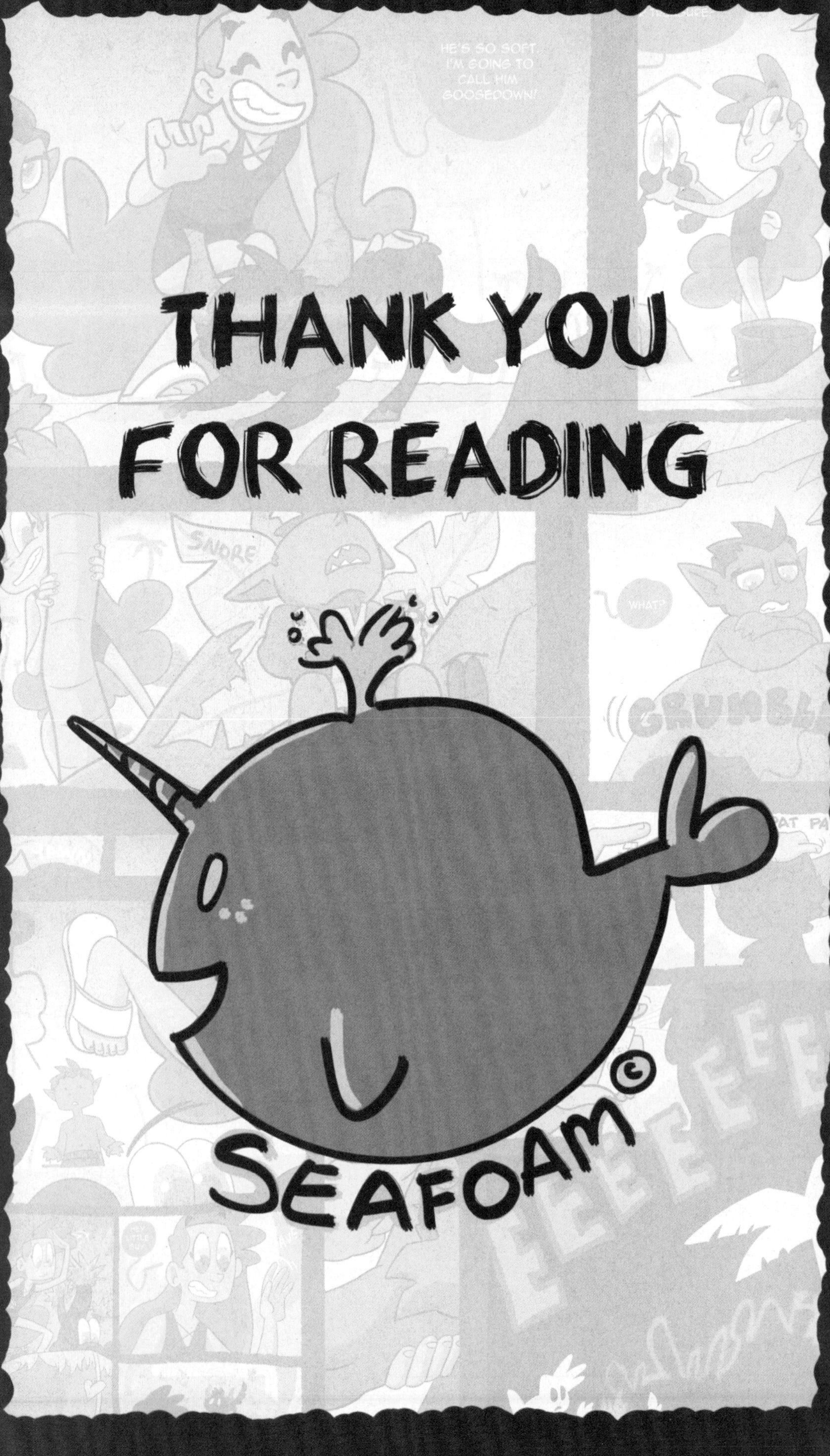
HE'S SO SOFT. I'M GOING TO CALL HIM GOOSEDOWN!
THANK YOU FOR READING
SNORE
WHAT?
SEAFOAM ©

ISSUE FOUR
"ISLAND SHADOWS"

THERE WAS A GIRL NAMED MADISON
WHO LOVED TO PLAY IN SAND

ONE DAY SHE FOUND A MAGICAL WHALE
WASHED UP ON THE LAND

SO MADISON TICKLED THE WHALE
TILL IT ROLLED INTO THE SEA

THE WHALE WAS SO GREATFUL
THAT IT FOUND SOMEONE TO BE

A FRIEND FOR MADISON

AND THAT FRIEND LIVES ALL ALONE
ON THE ISLAND HE CALLS HOME

IT'S DARK AND COLD AS SHE VISITS
BRINGING SMILES AND PRESENTS

WRITTEN AND ILLUSTRATED BY
JEANINE-JONEE

CONTENT EDITED BY
EMILY BRIGOLIN
NICOLE D'ANDRIA

ADDITIONAL COLORING BY
KYLE P. HOLLAND

BRYAN SEATON: PUBLISHER/ CEO
SHAWN GABBORIN: EDITOR IN CHIEF
JASON MARTIN: PUBLISHER-DANGER ZONE
NICOLE D'ANDRIA: MARKETING DIRECTOR/EDITOR
JESSICA LOWRIE: SOCIAL MEDIA CZAR
DANIELLE DAVISON: EXECUTIVE ADMINISTRATOR
CHAD CICCONI: OFFICIAL NARWHAL WRANGLER
SHAWN PRYOR: PRESIDENT OF CREATOR RELATIONS

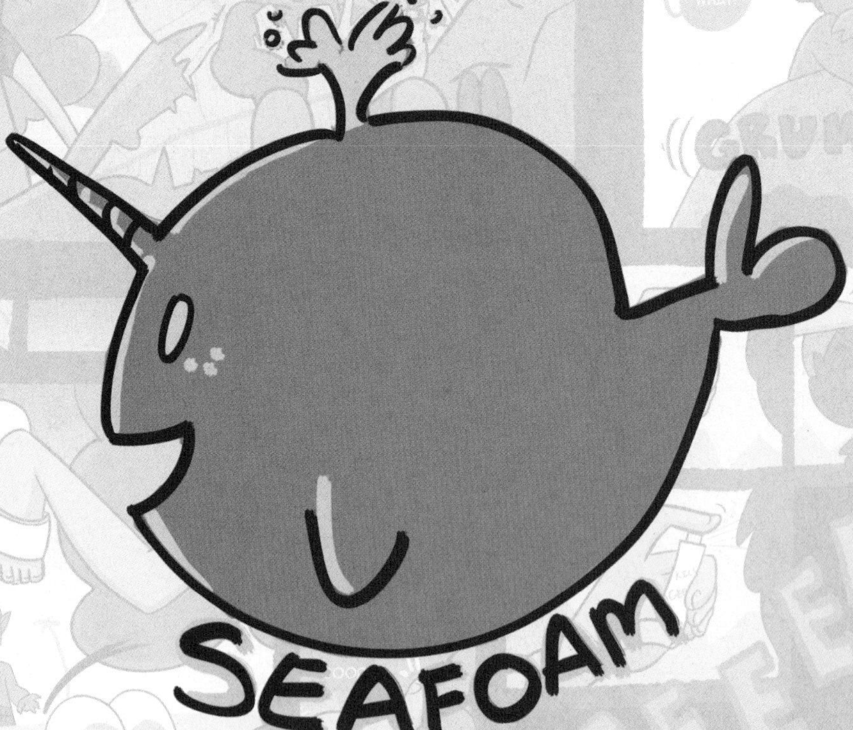
SEAFOAM

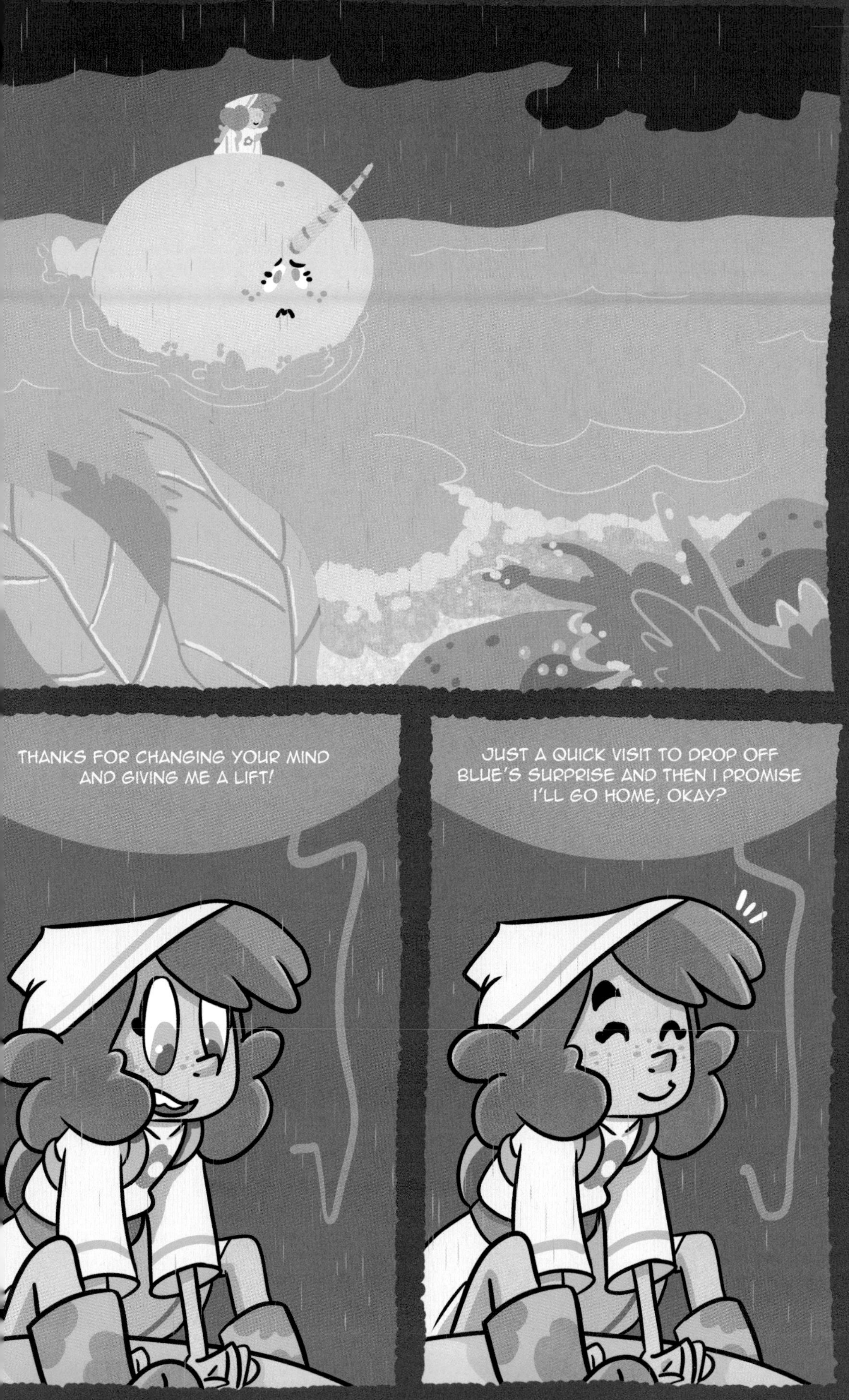
THANKS FOR CHANGING YOUR MIND AND GIVING ME A LIFT!
JUST A QUICK VISIT TO DROP OFF BLUE'S SURPRISE AND THEN I PROMISE I'LL GO HOME, OKAY?

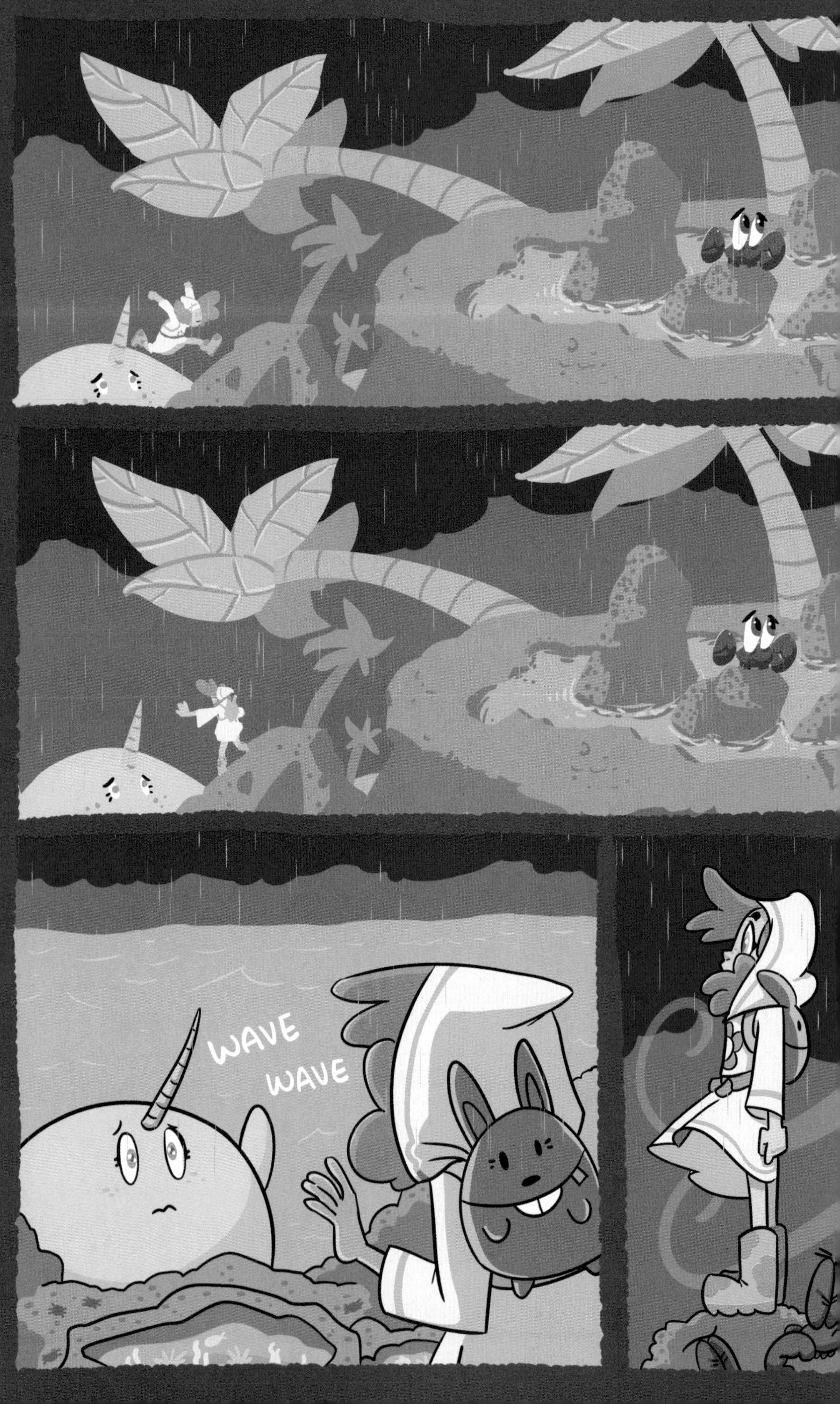
WAVE
WAVE

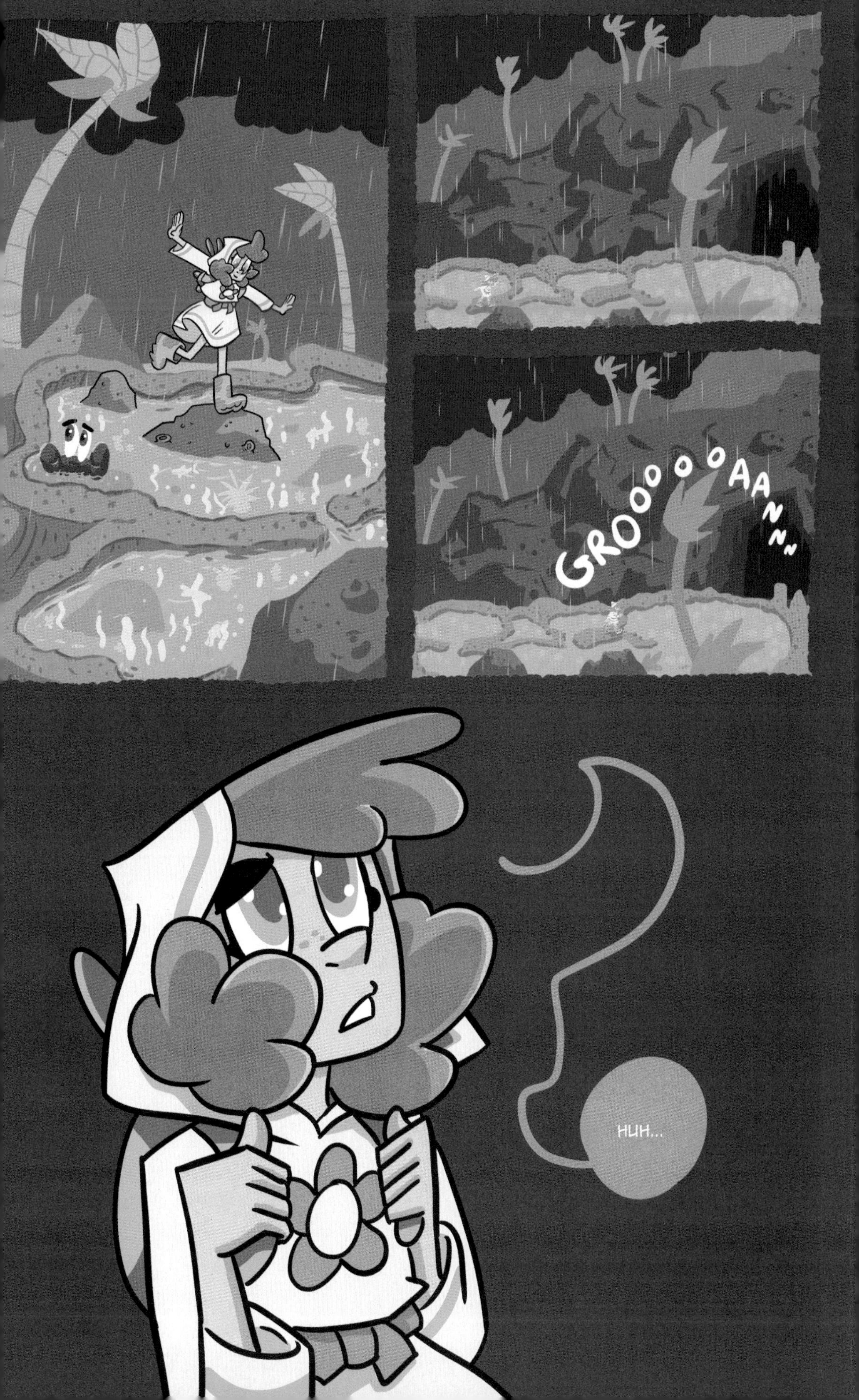
GROOOOOAANNN
HUH...

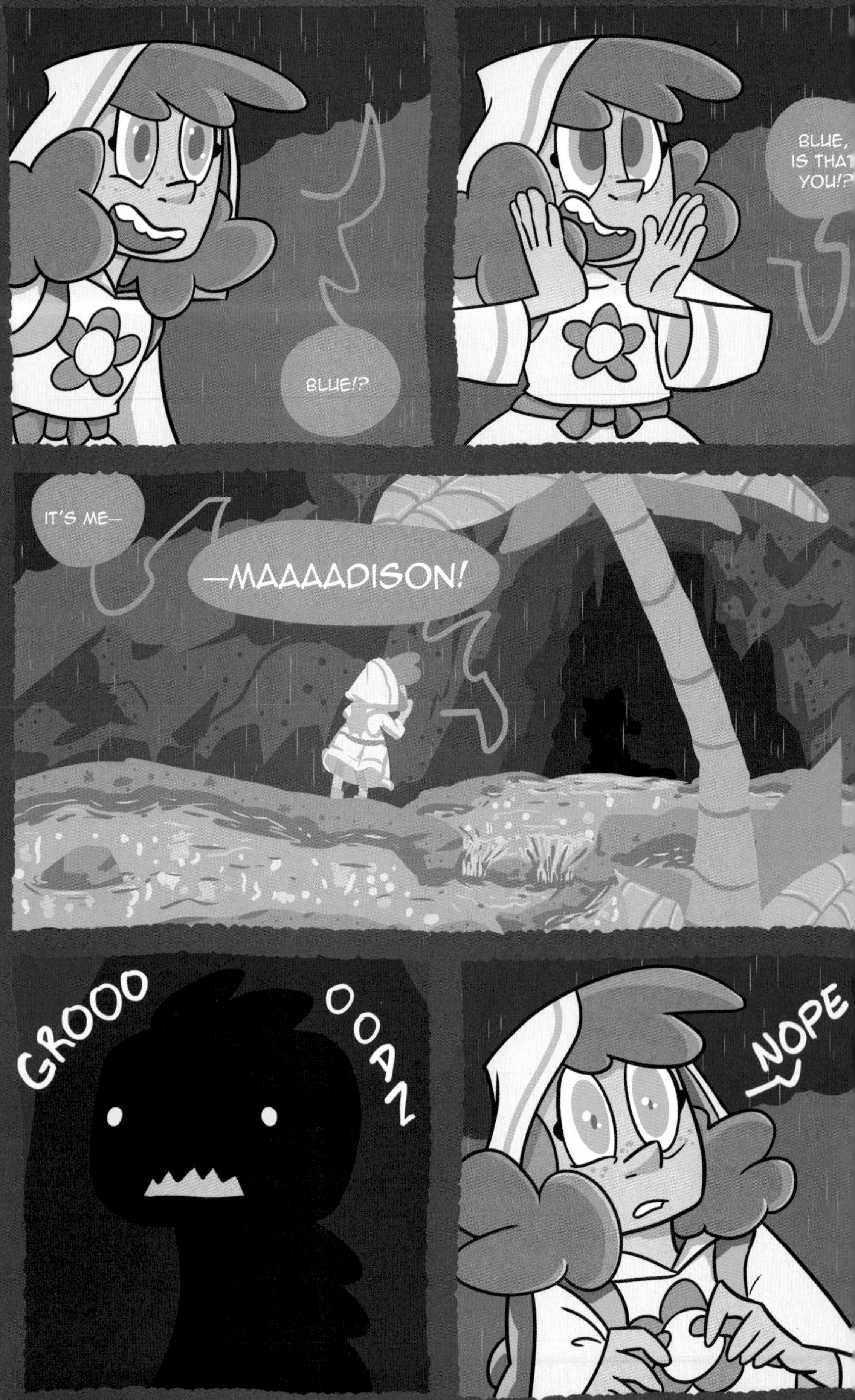
BLUE!?
BLUE, IS THAT YOU!?
IT'S ME—
—MAAAADISON!
GROOO OOAN
—NOPE

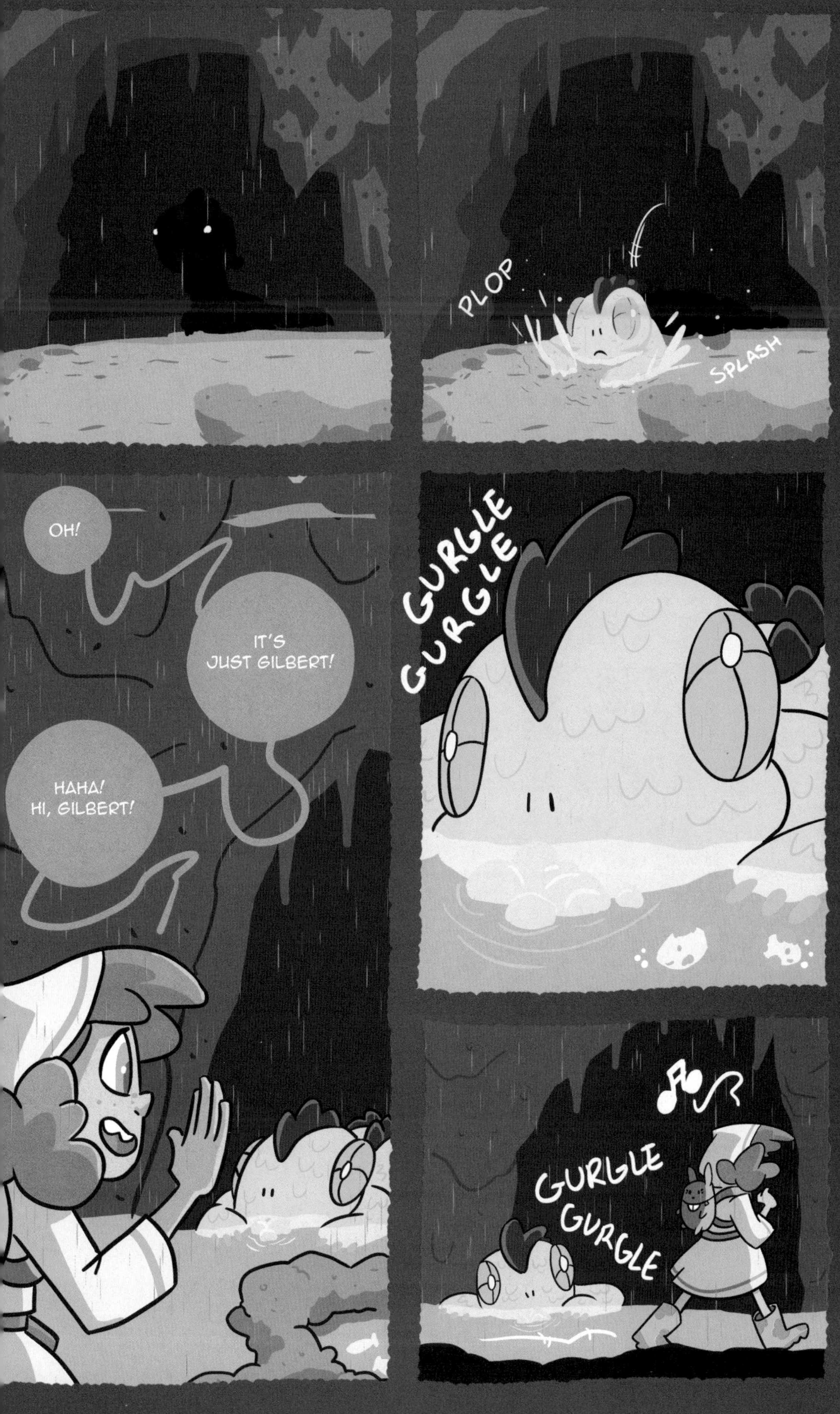
PLOP
SPLASH
OH!
IT'S JUST GILBERT!
HAHA! HI, GILBERT!
GURGLE GURGLE
GURGLE GURGLE

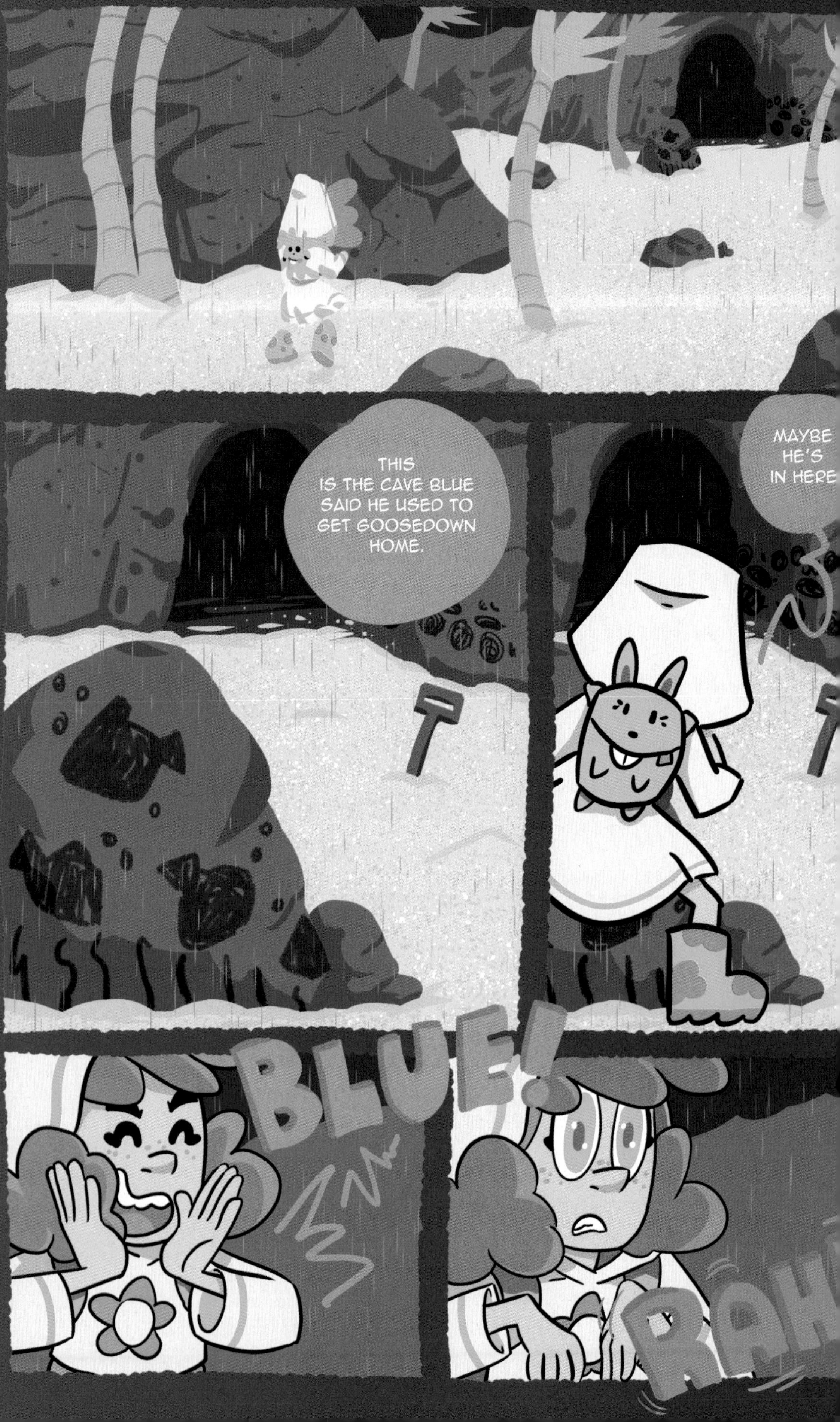
THIS IS THE CAVE BLUE SAID HE USED TO GET GOOSEDOWN HOME.
MAYBE HE'S IN HERE
BLUE!

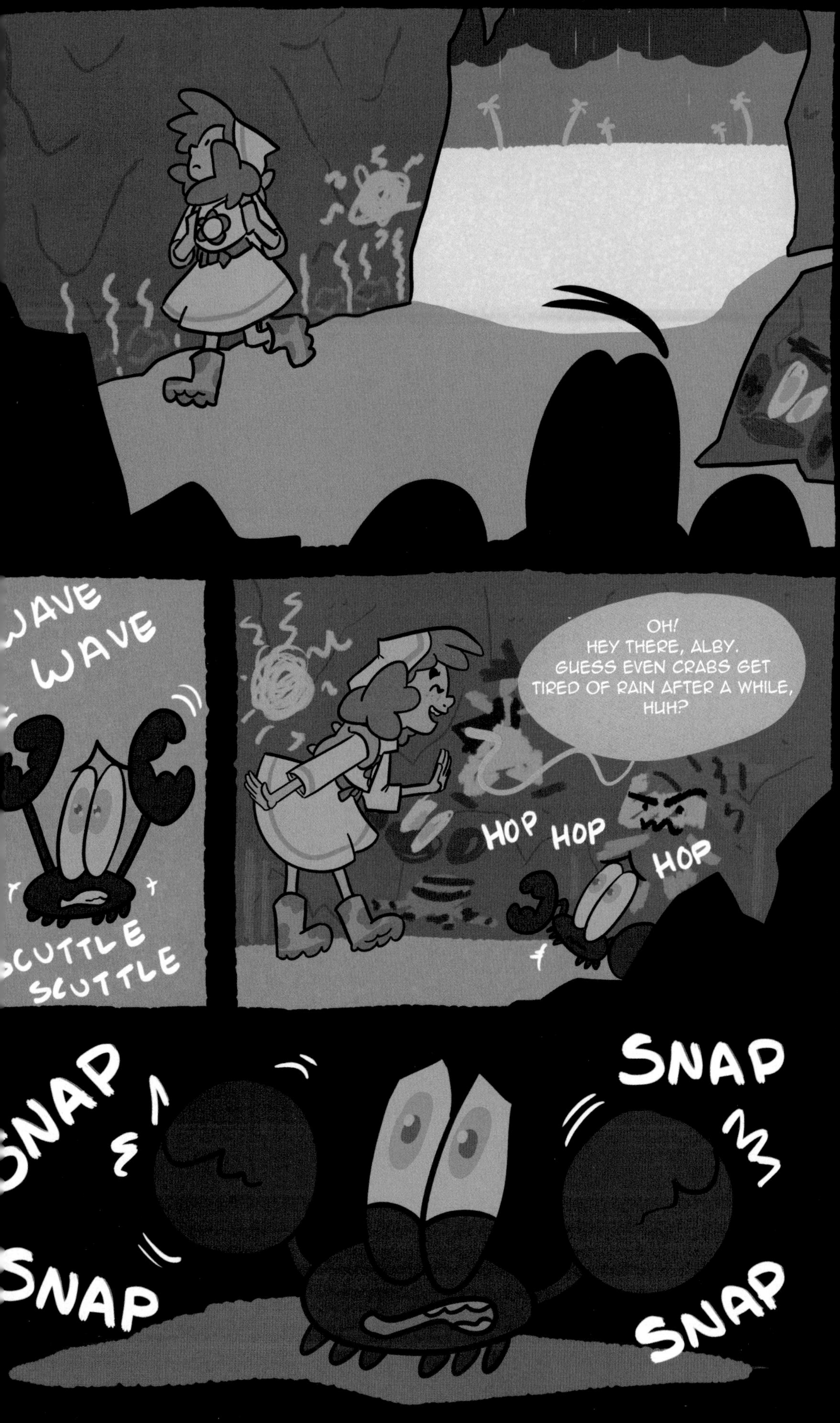
WAVE
WAVE
SCUTTLE
SCUTTLE
OH!
HEY THERE, ALBY.
GUESS EVEN CRABS GET
TIRED OF RAIN AFTER A WHILE,
HUH?
HOP
HOP
HOP
SNAP
SNAP
SNAP
SNAP

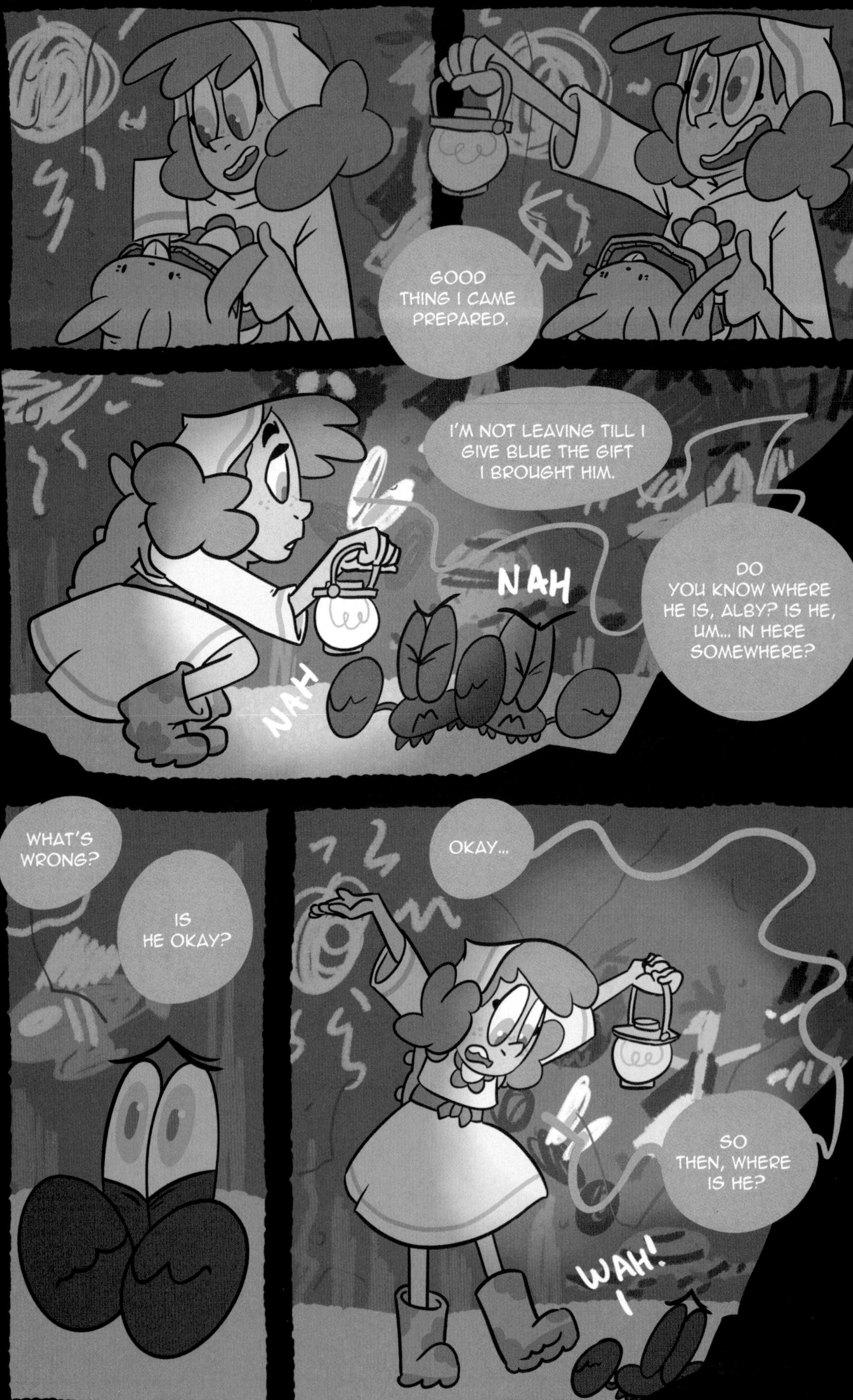
GOOD THING I CAME PREPARED.
I'M NOT LEAVING TILL I GIVE BLUE THE GIFT I BROUGHT HIM.
NAH
NAH
DO YOU KNOW WHERE HE IS, ALBY? IS HE, UM... IN HERE SOMEWHERE?
WHAT'S WRONG?
IS HE OKAY?
OKAY...
SO THEN, WHERE IS HE?
WAH! !

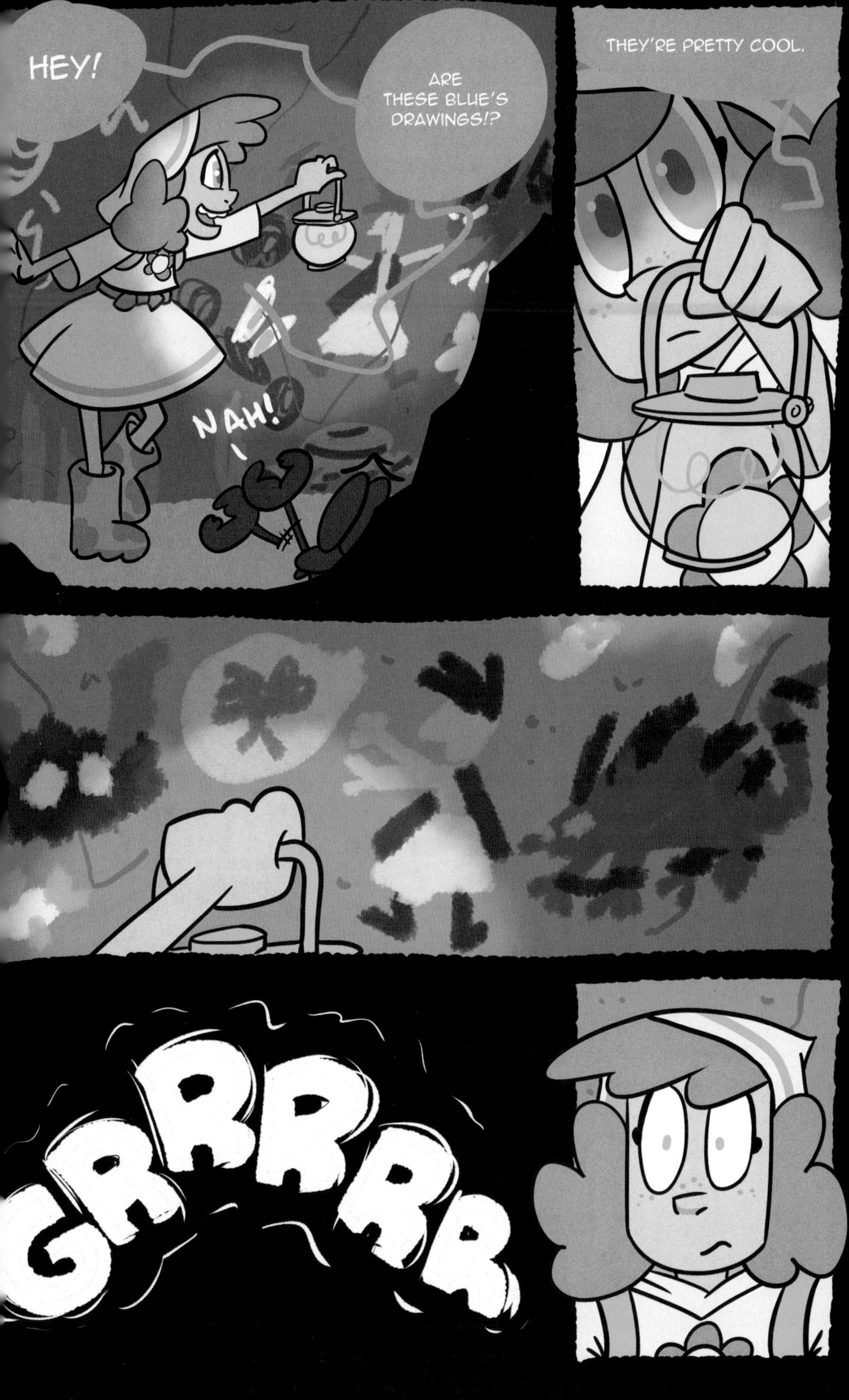
HEY!
ARE THESE BLUE'S DRAWINGS!?
NAH!
THEY'RE PRETTY COOL.
GRRRRR

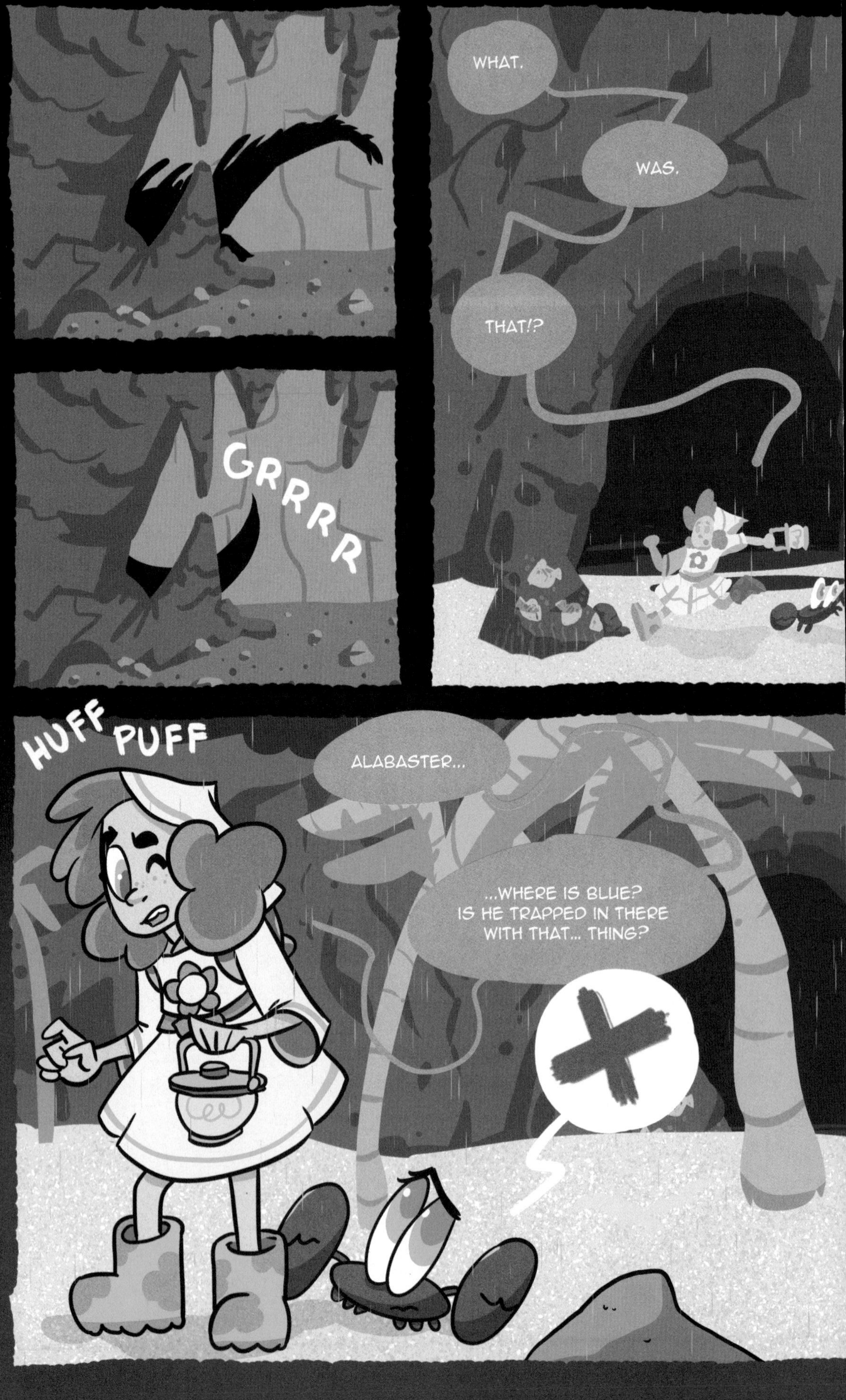
GRRRRR
WHAT.
WAS.
THAT!?
HUFF PUFF
ALABASTER...
...WHERE IS BLUE?
IS HE TRAPPED IN THERE
WITH THAT... THING?

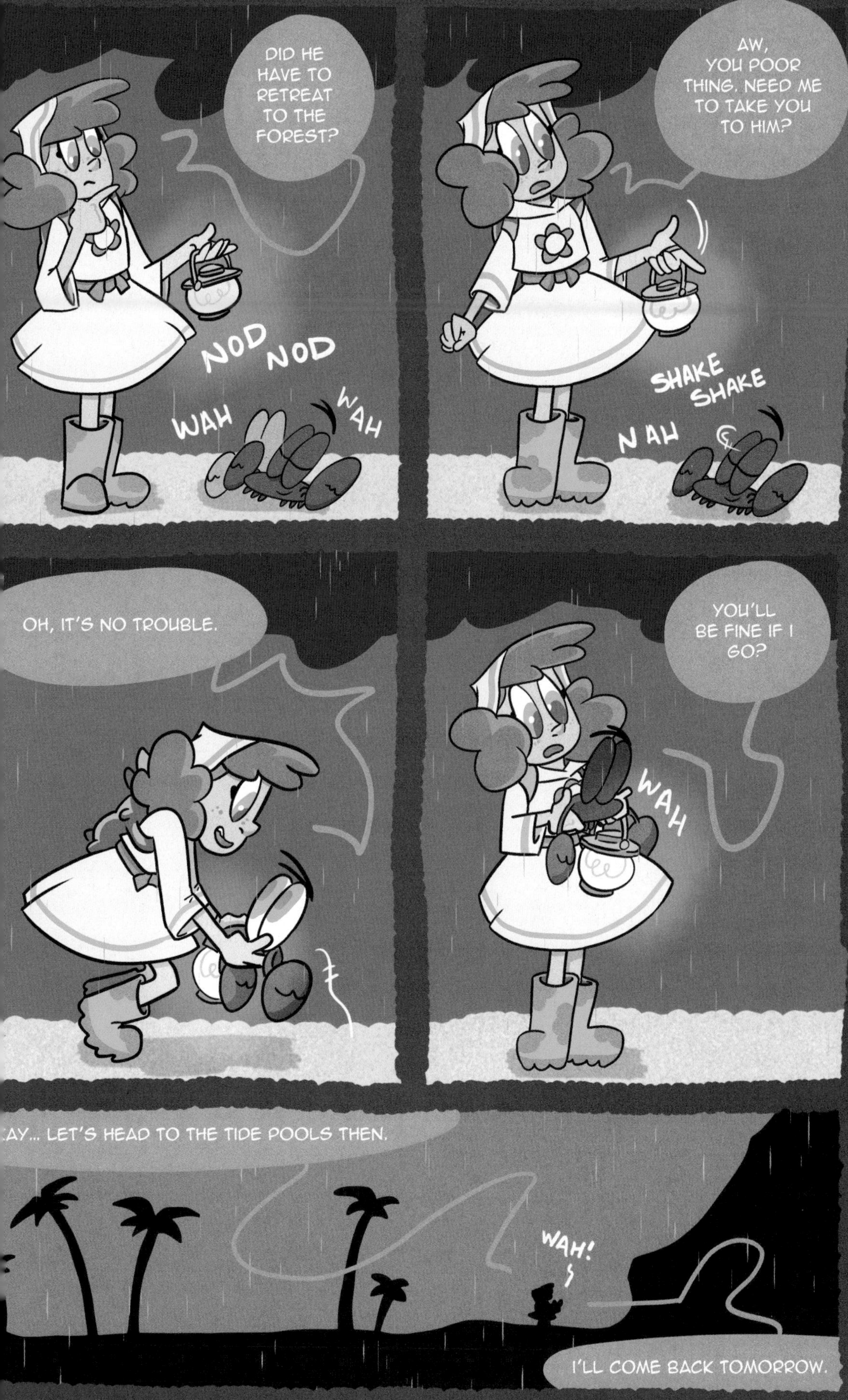
DID HE HAVE TO RETREAT TO THE FOREST?
NOD NOD
WAH WAH
AW, YOU POOR THING. NEED ME TO TAKE YOU TO HIM?
SHAKE SHAKE
NAH
OH, IT'S NO TROUBLE.
YOU'LL BE FINE IF I GO?
WAH
AY... LET'S HEAD TO THE TIDE POOLS THEN.
WAH!
I'LL COME BACK TOMORROW.

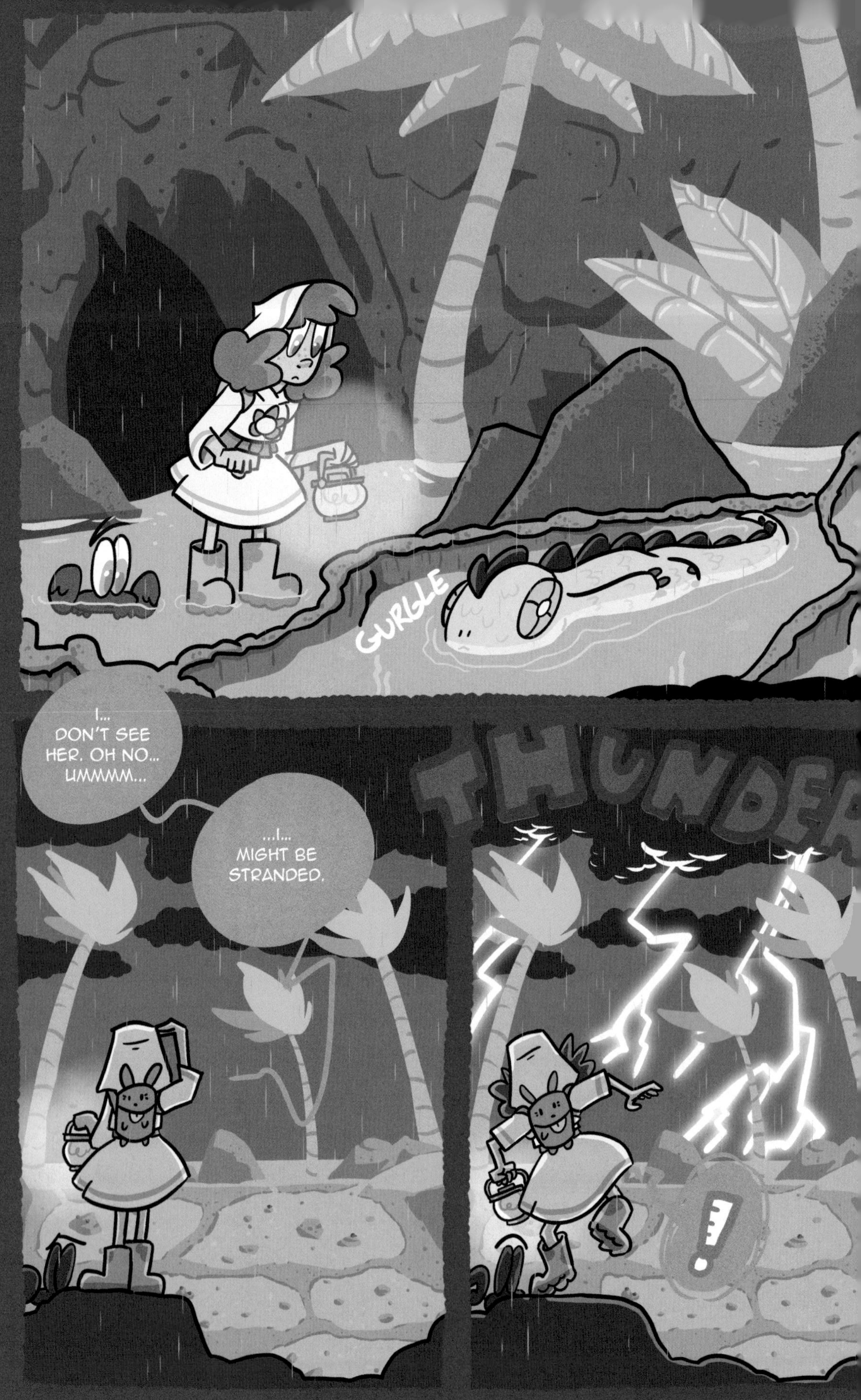
GURGLE
I... DON'T SEE HER. OH NO... UMMMM...
...I... MIGHT BE STRANDED.
THUNDER
!

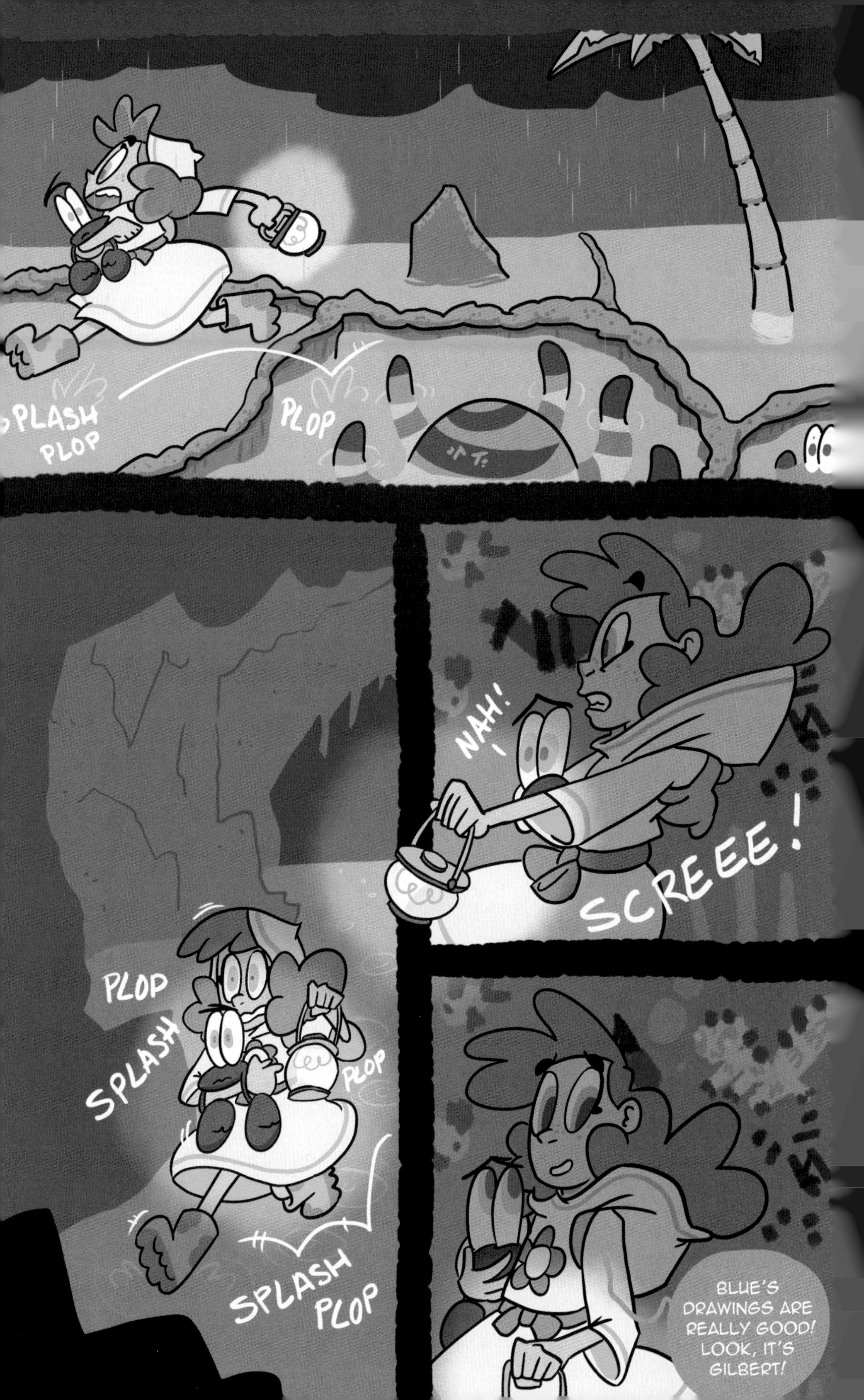
SPLASH
PLOP
PLOP
NAH!
SCREEE!
PLOP
SPLASH
PLOP
SPLASH
PLOP
BLUE'S DRAWINGS ARE REALLY GOOD! LOOK, IT'S GILBERT!

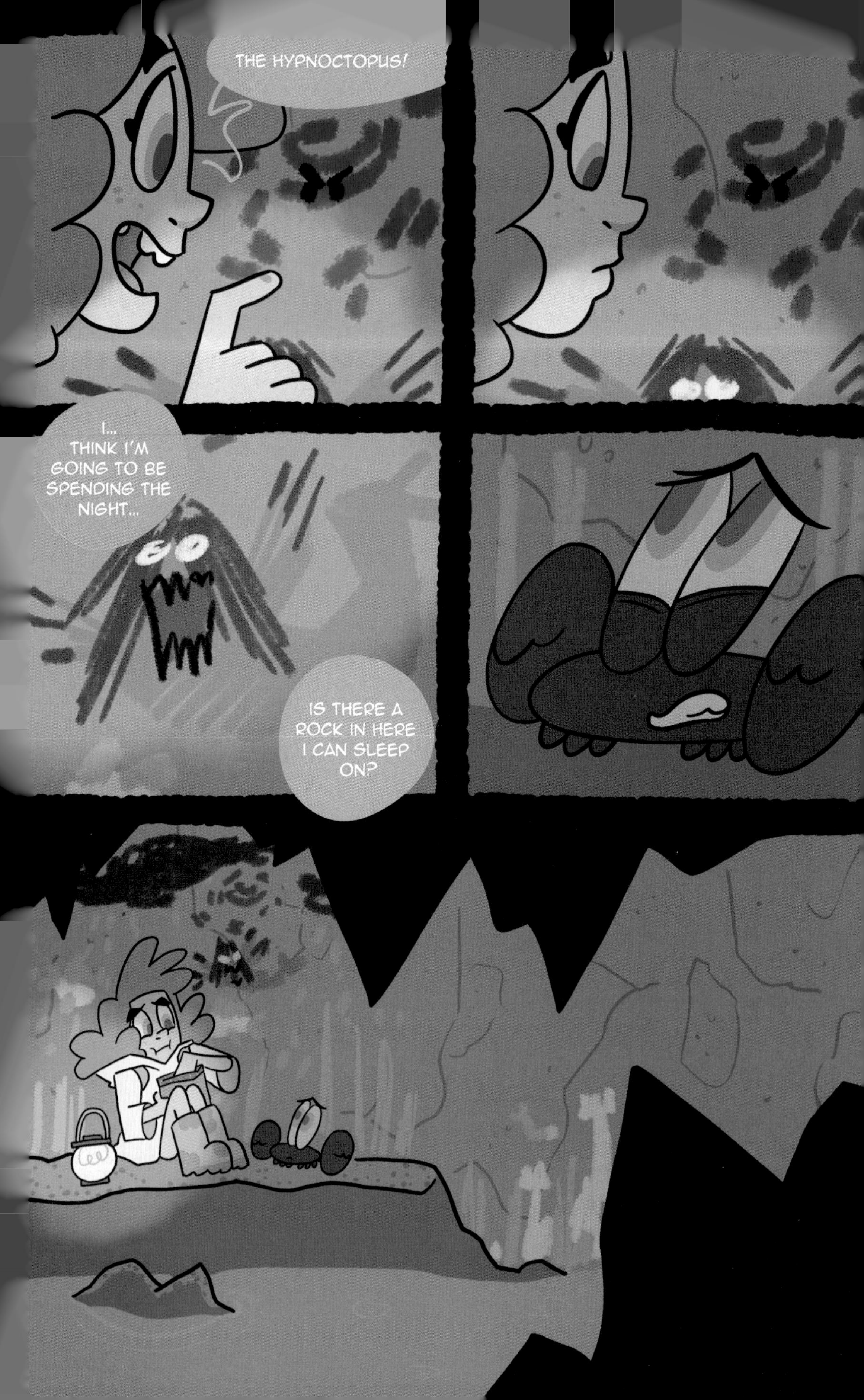
THE HYPNOCTOPUS!
I... THINK I'M GOING TO BE SPENDING THE NIGHT...
IS THERE A ROCK IN HERE I CAN SLEEP ON?

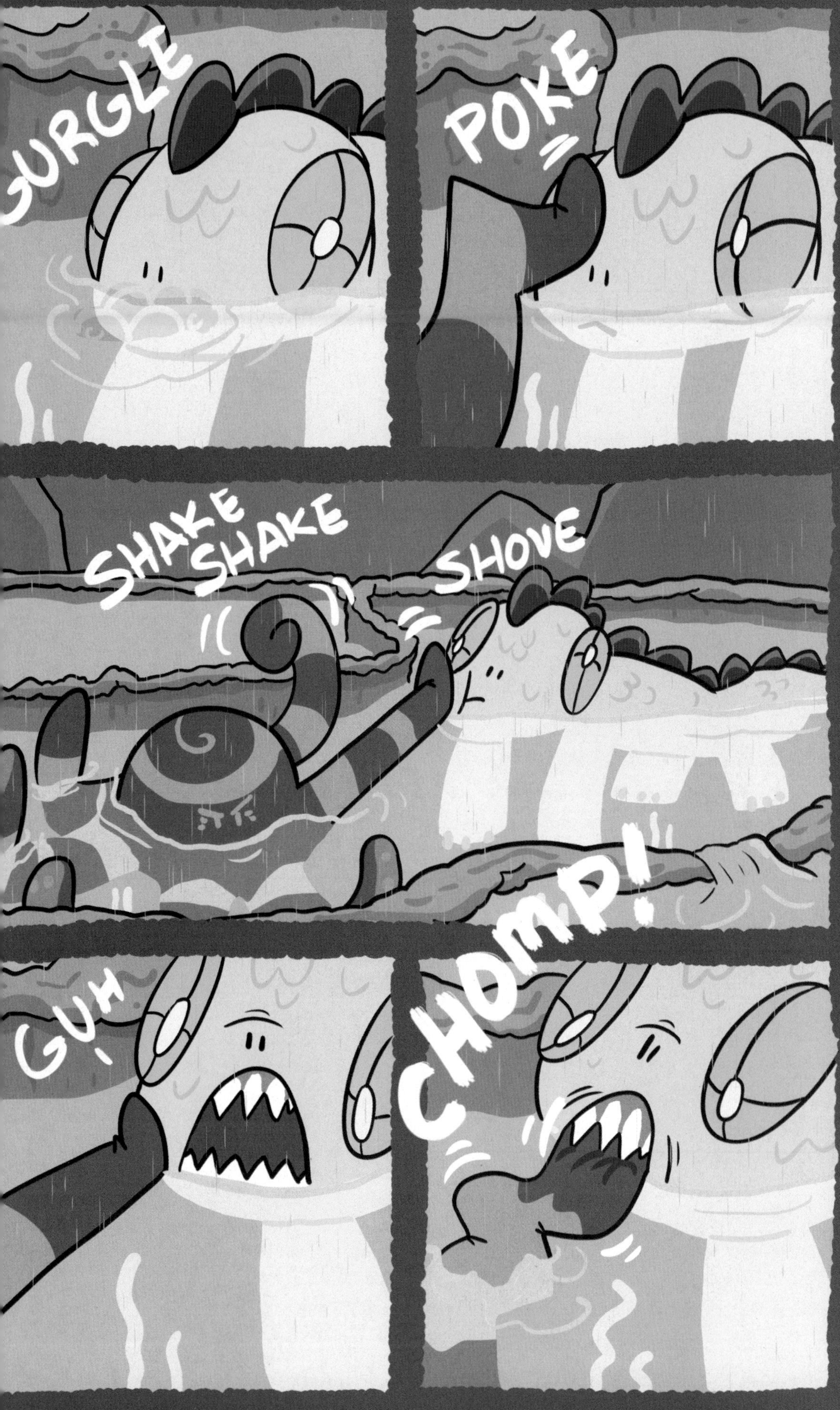
GURGLE
POKE
SHAKE SHAKE
SHOVE
GUH
CHOMP!

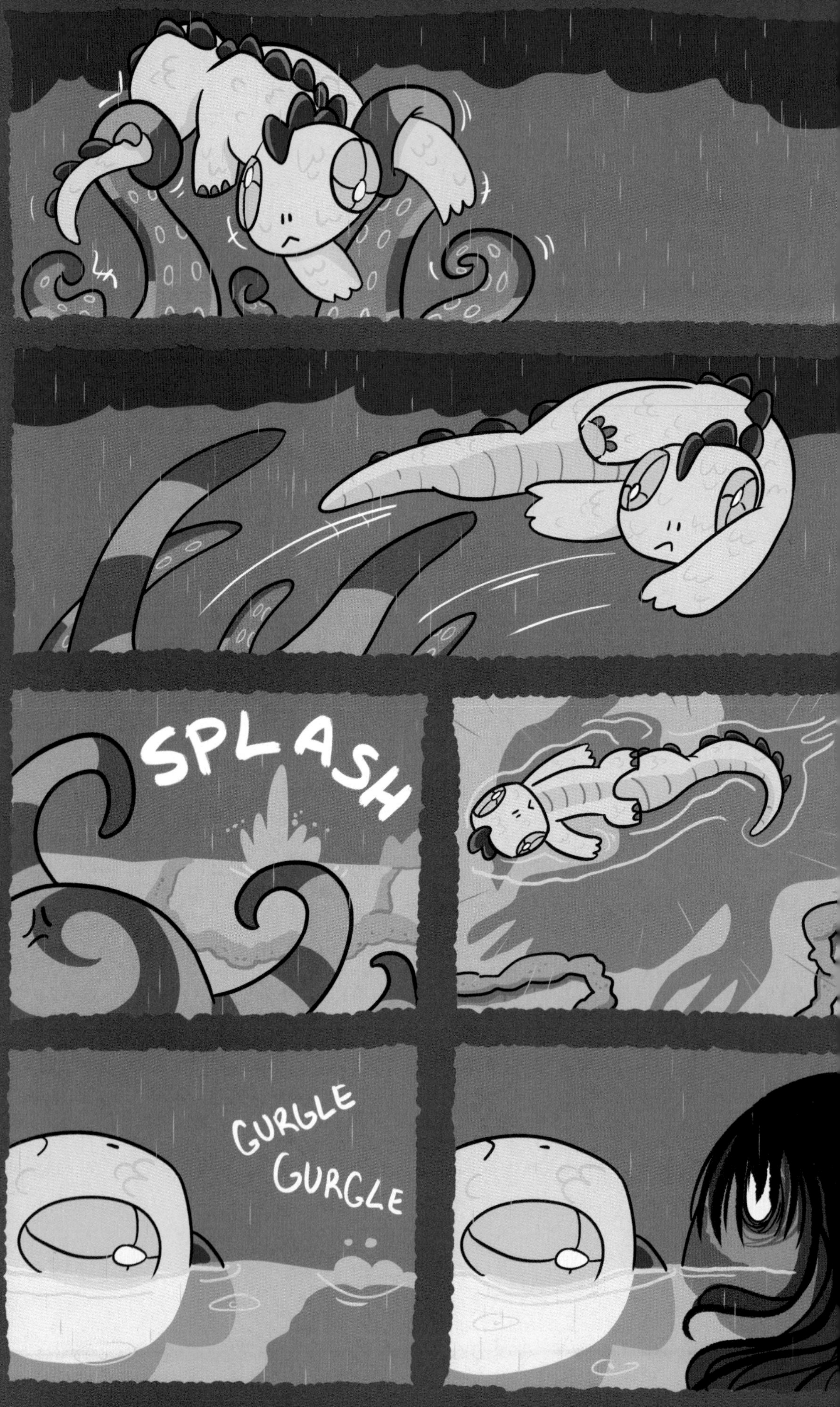
SPLASH
GURGLE
GURGLE

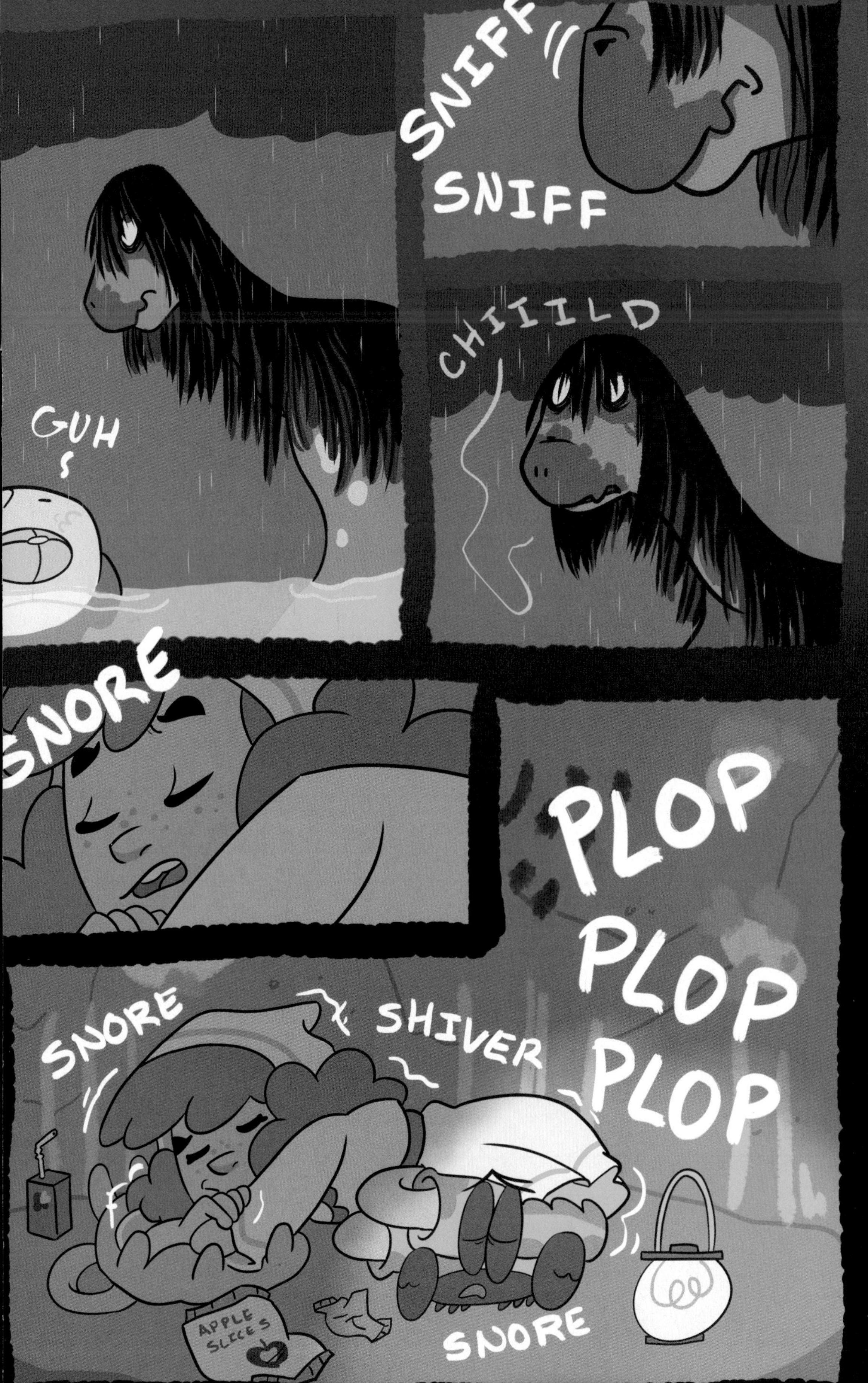
SNIFF
SNIFF
GUH
CHIIILD
SNORE
PLOP
PLOP
PLOP
PLOP
SNORE
SHIVER
APPLE SLICES
SNORE

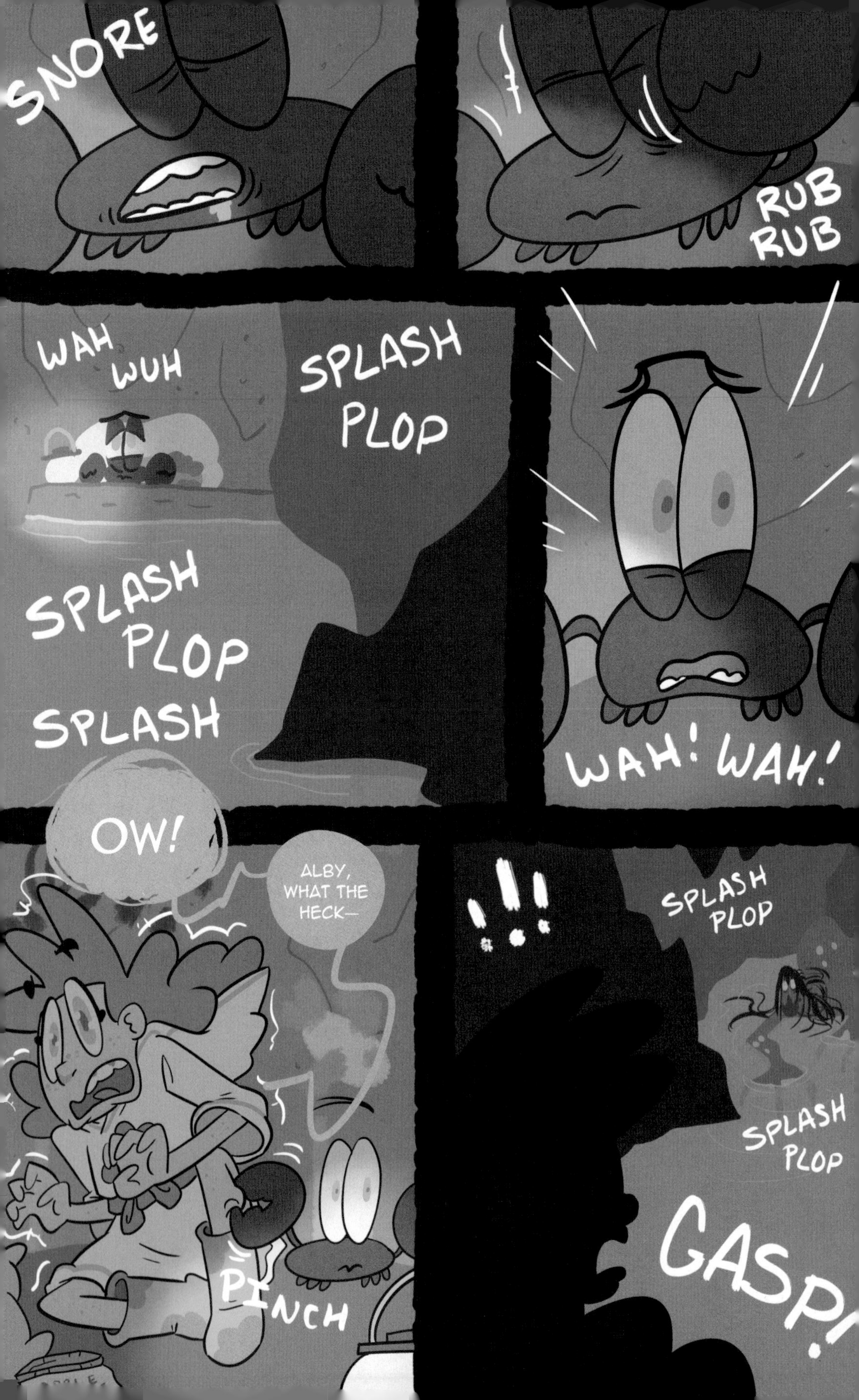
SNORE
RUB RUB
WAH WUH
SPLASH PLOP
SPLASH PLOP SPLASH
WAH! WAH!
OW!
ALBY, WHAT THE HECK—
PINCH
!!!
SPLASH PLOP
SPLASH PLOP
GASP!

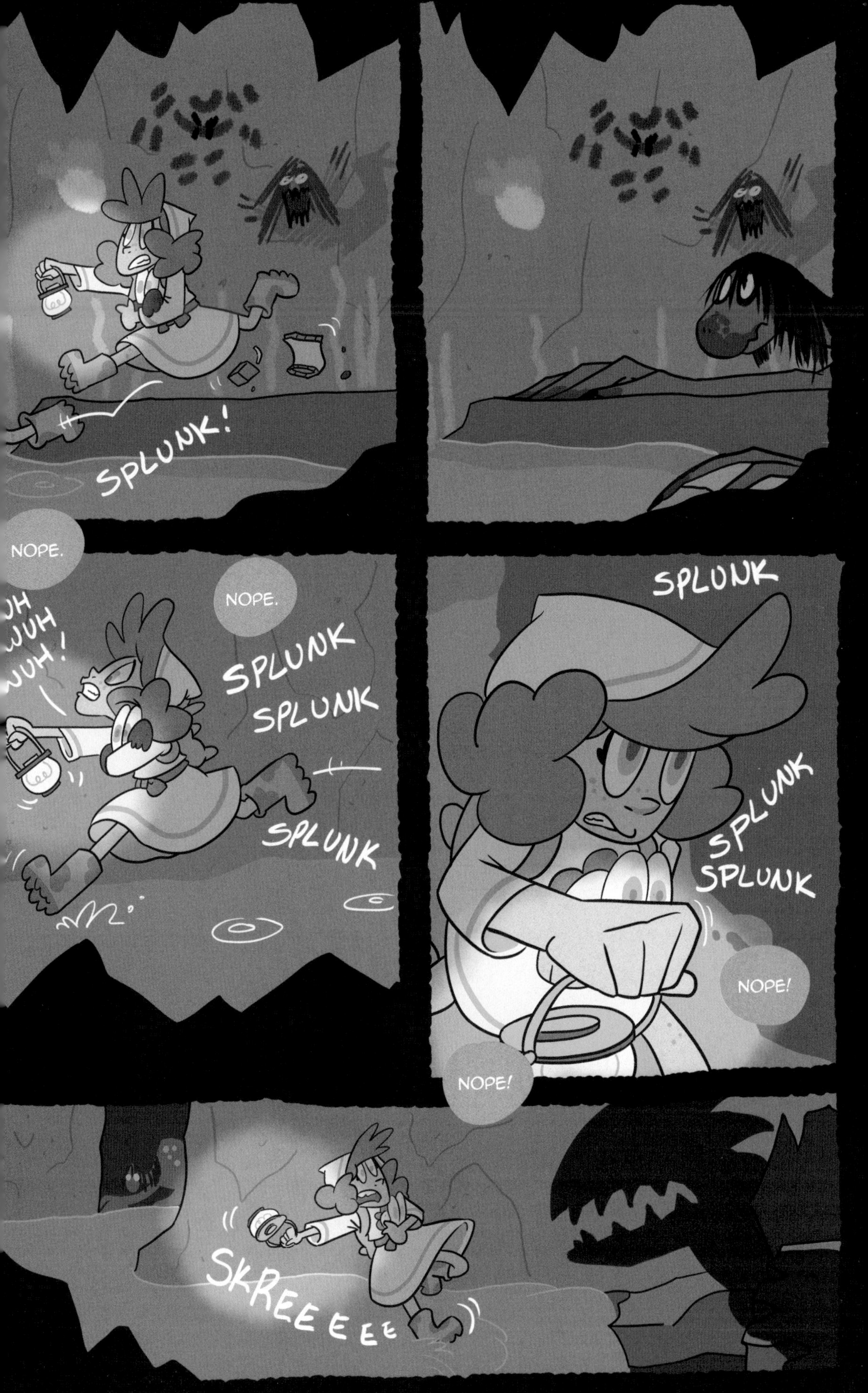

SPLUNK!
NOPE.
UH
WUH
WUH!
NOPE.
SPLUNK
SPLUNK
SPLUNK
SPLUNK
SPLUNK
SPLUNK
NOPE!
NOPE!
SKREEEEEE

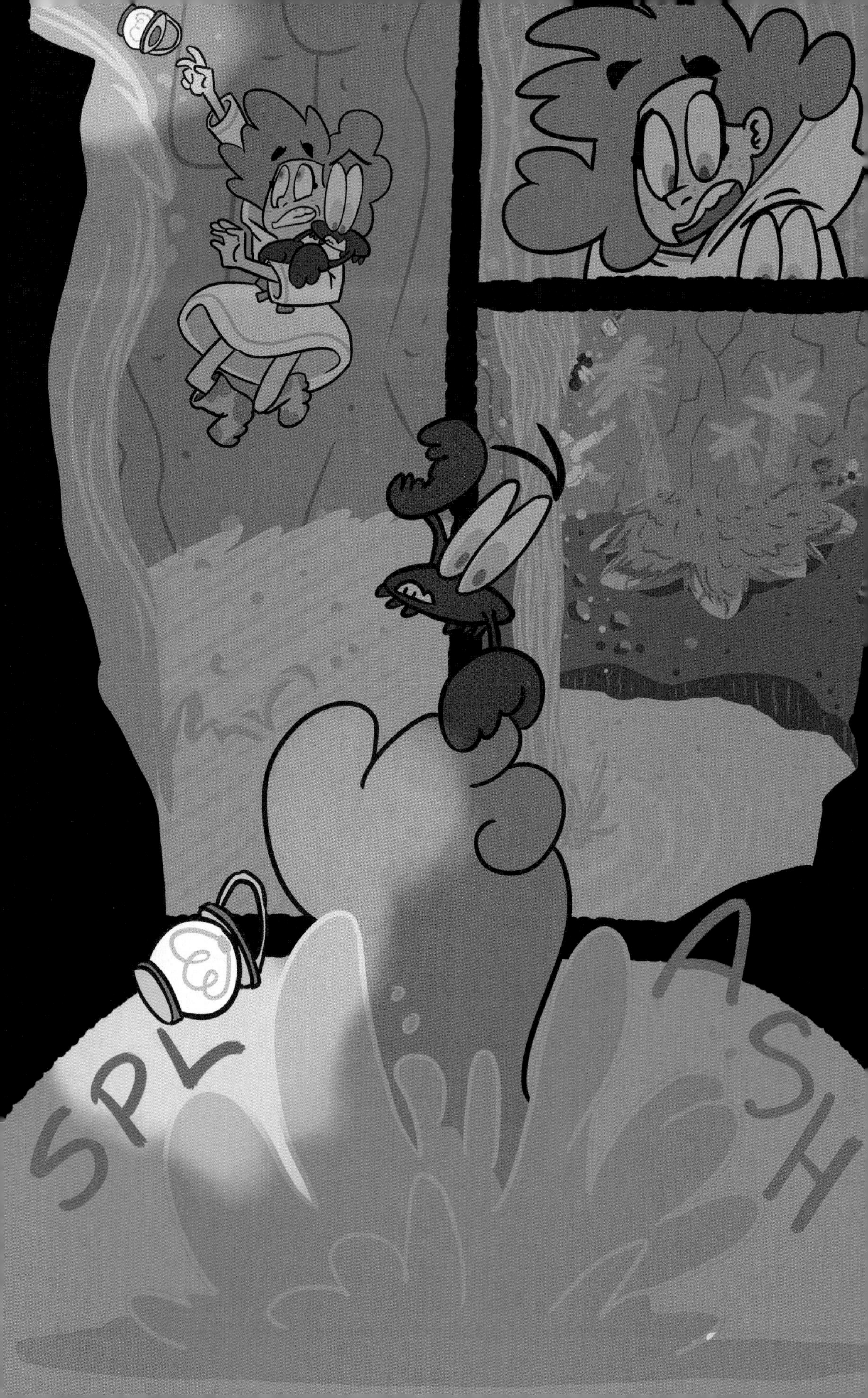
SPLASH

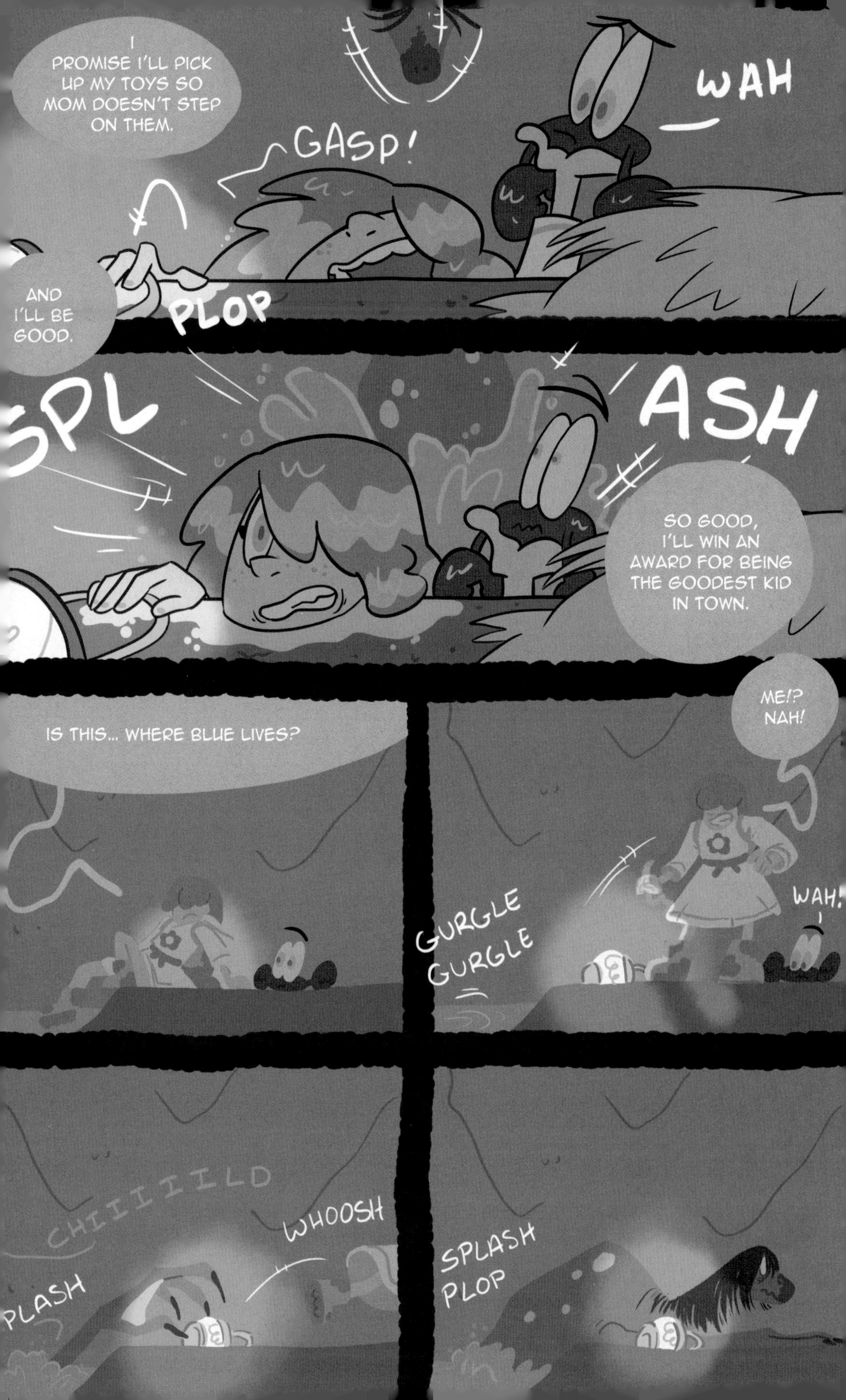
I PROMISE I'LL PICK UP MY TOYS SO MOM DOESN'T STEP ON THEM.
GASP!
WAH
AND I'LL BE GOOD.
PLOP
SPL
ASH
SO GOOD, I'LL WIN AN AWARD FOR BEING THE GOODEST KID IN TOWN.
IS THIS... WHERE BLUE LIVES?
ME!? NAH!
GURGLE GURGLE
WAH!
CHIIIIILD
WHOOSH
PLASH
SPLASH
PLOP

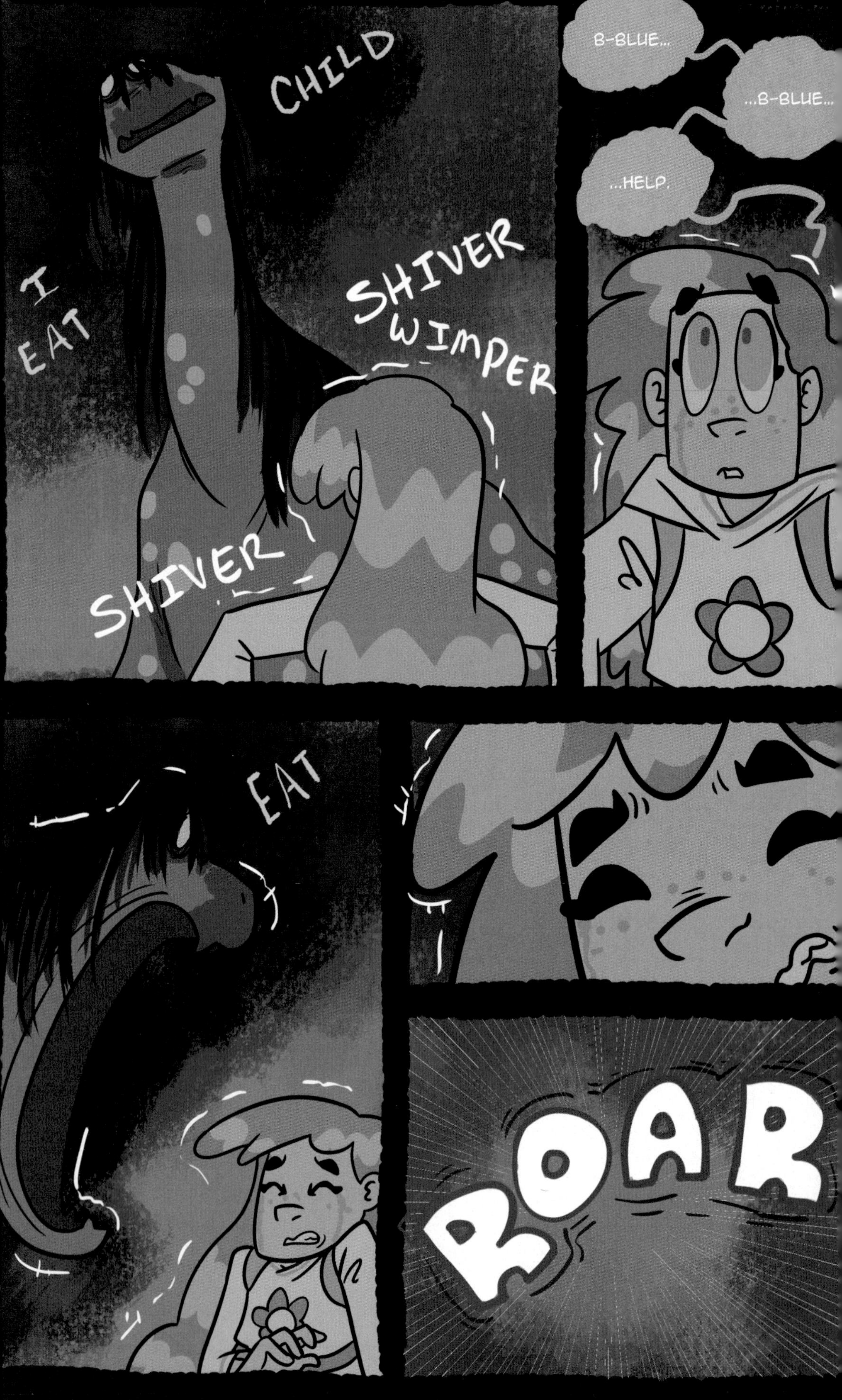
CHILD
I EAT
SHIVER
WIMPER
SHIVER
B-BLUE...
...B-BLUE...
...HELP.
EAT
ROAR

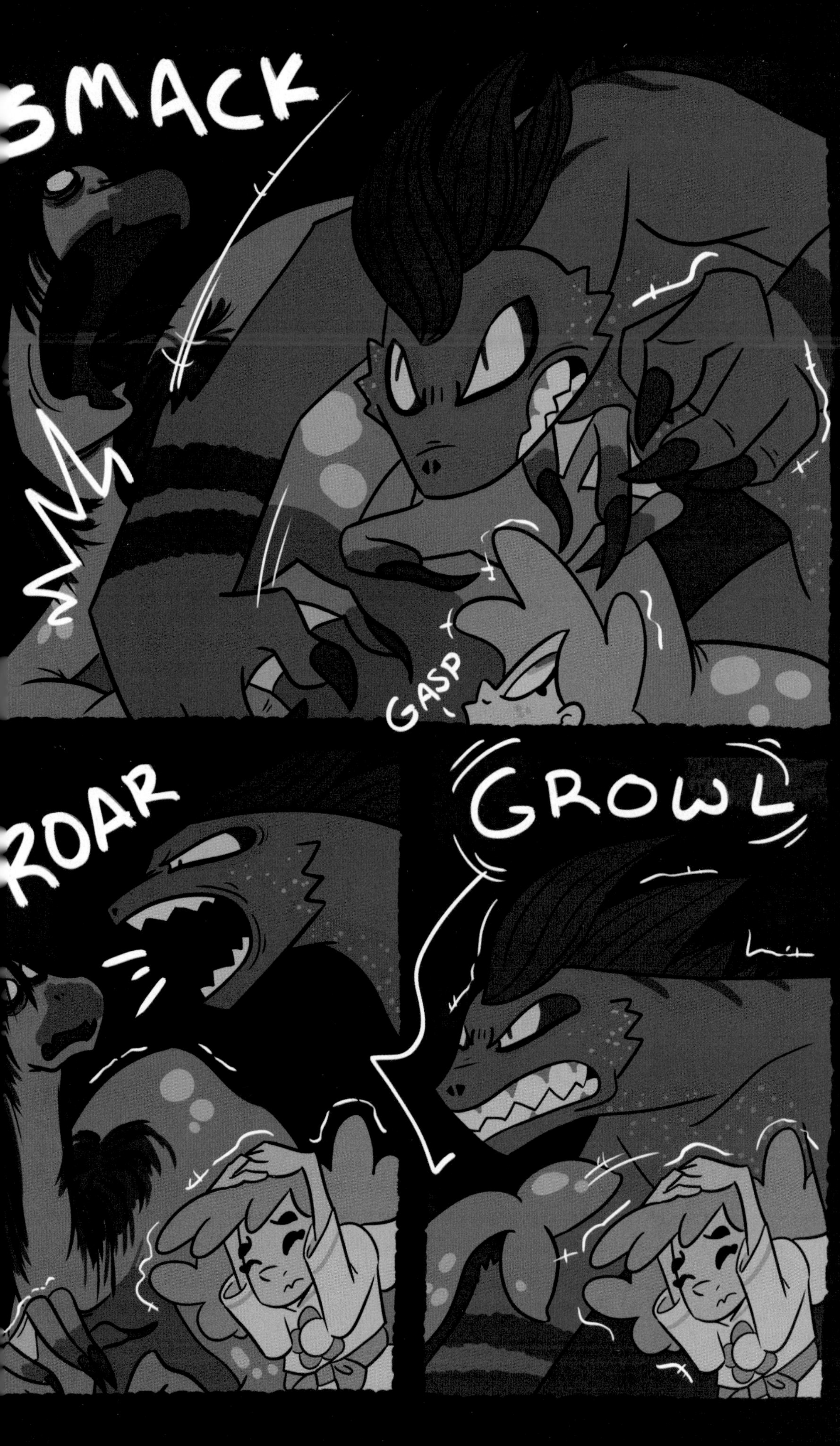
SMACK
GASP
ROAR
GROWL

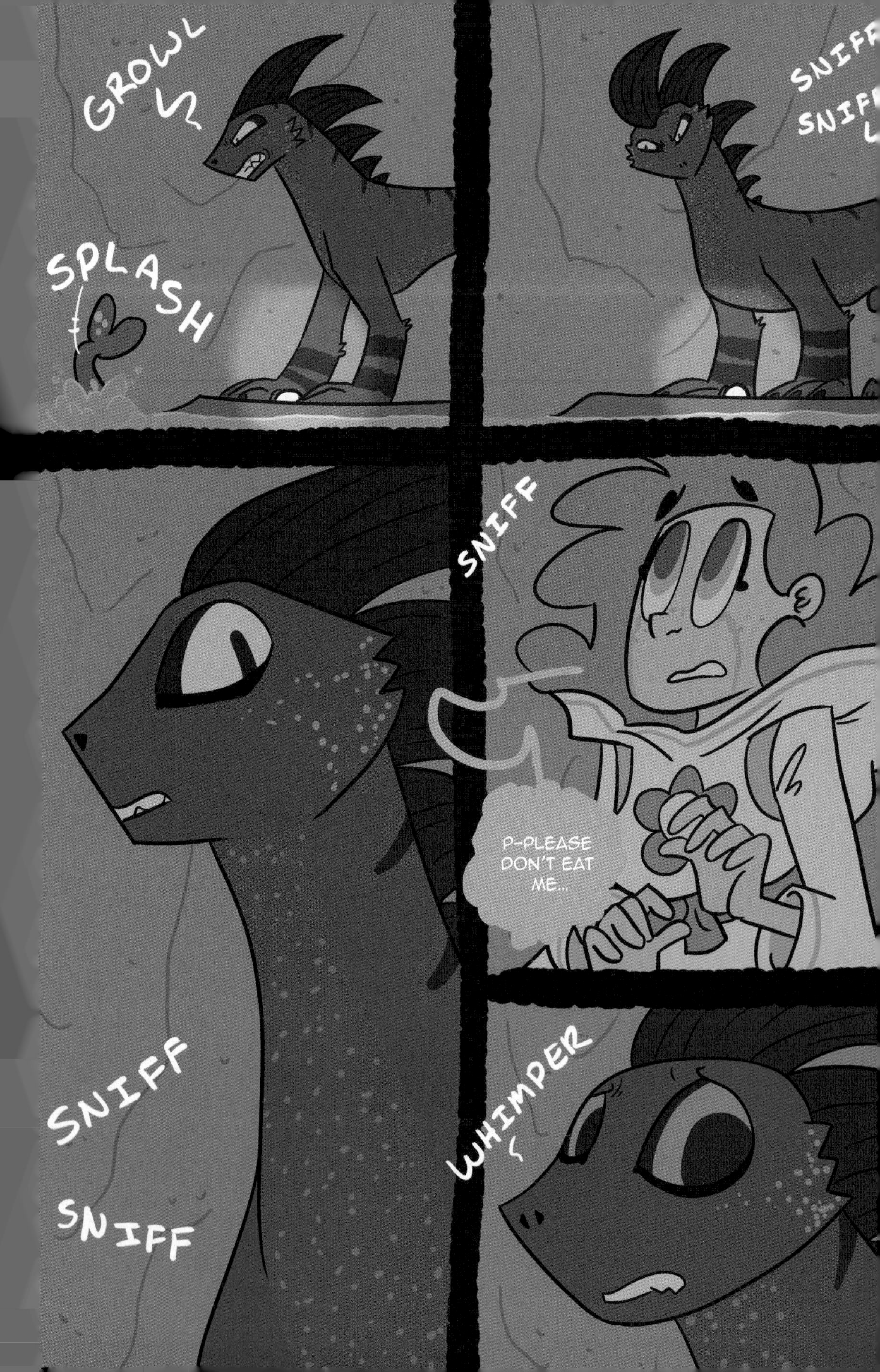
GROWL
SPLASH
SNIFF
SNIFF
SNIFF
P-PLEASE DON'T EAT ME...
SNIFF
SNIFF
WHIMPER

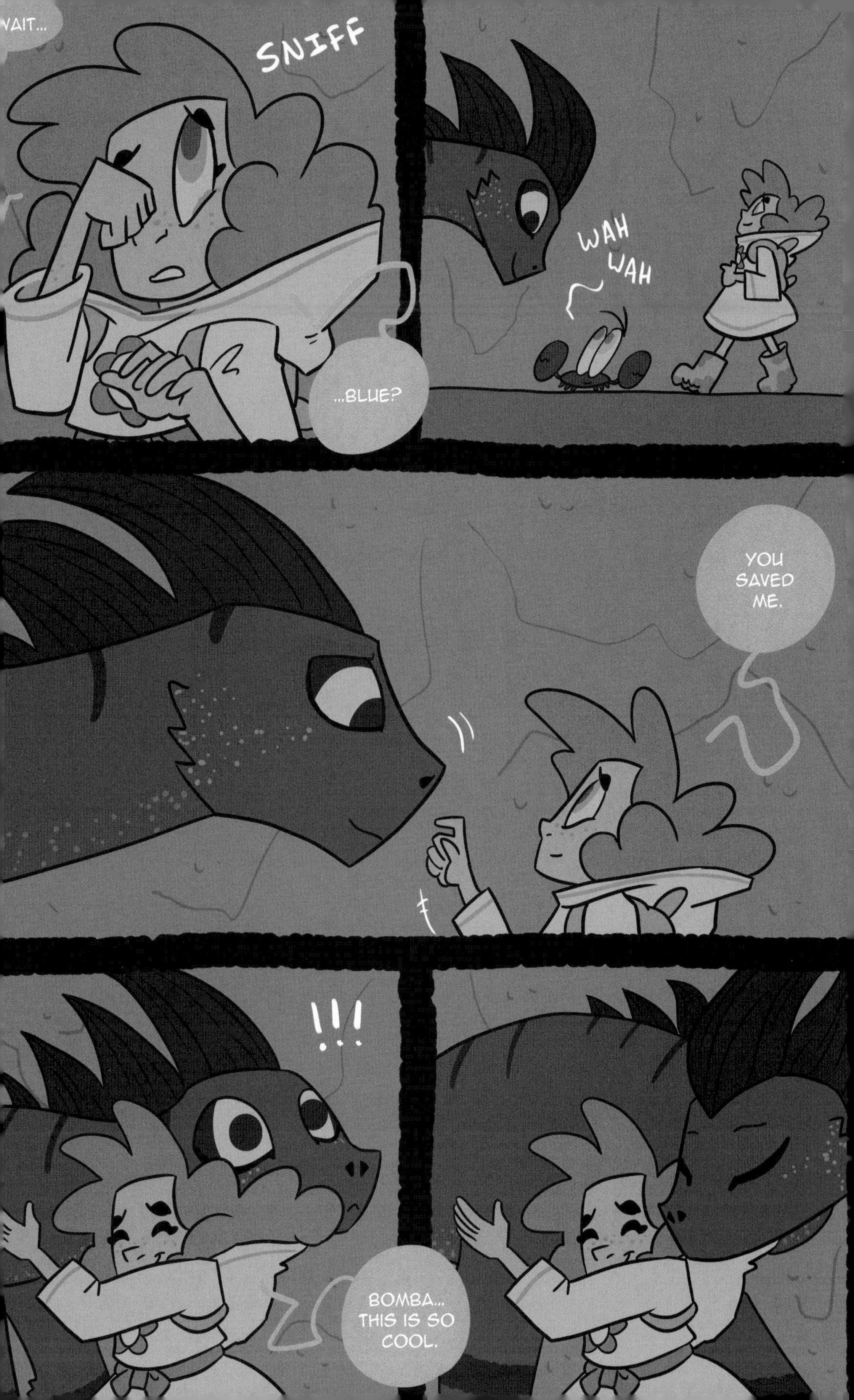

WAIT...
SNIFF
...BLUE?
WAH
WAH
YOU
SAVED
ME.
!!!
BOMBA...
THIS IS SO
COOL.

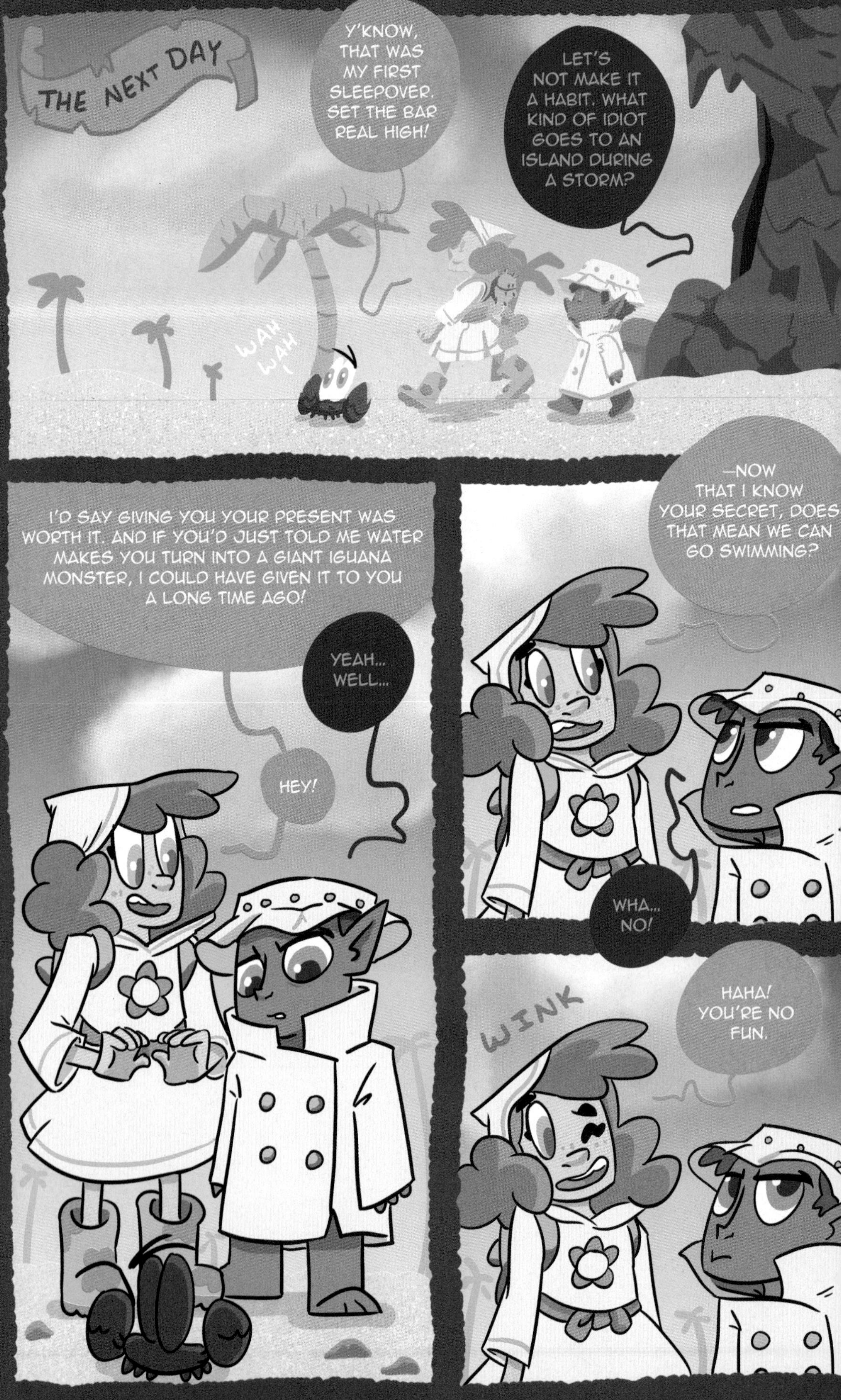
THE NEXT DAY
Y'KNOW, THAT WAS MY FIRST SLEEPOVER. SET THE BAR REAL HIGH!
LET'S NOT MAKE IT A HABIT. WHAT KIND OF IDIOT GOES TO AN ISLAND DURING A STORM?
WAH WAH
I'D SAY GIVING YOU YOUR PRESENT WAS WORTH IT. AND IF YOU'D JUST TOLD ME WATER MAKES YOU TURN INTO A GIANT IGUANA MONSTER, I COULD HAVE GIVEN IT TO YOU A LONG TIME AGO!
YEAH... WELL...
HEY!
—NOW THAT I KNOW YOUR SECRET, DOES THAT MEAN WE CAN GO SWIMMING?
WHA... NO!
WINK
HAHA! YOU'RE NO FUN.

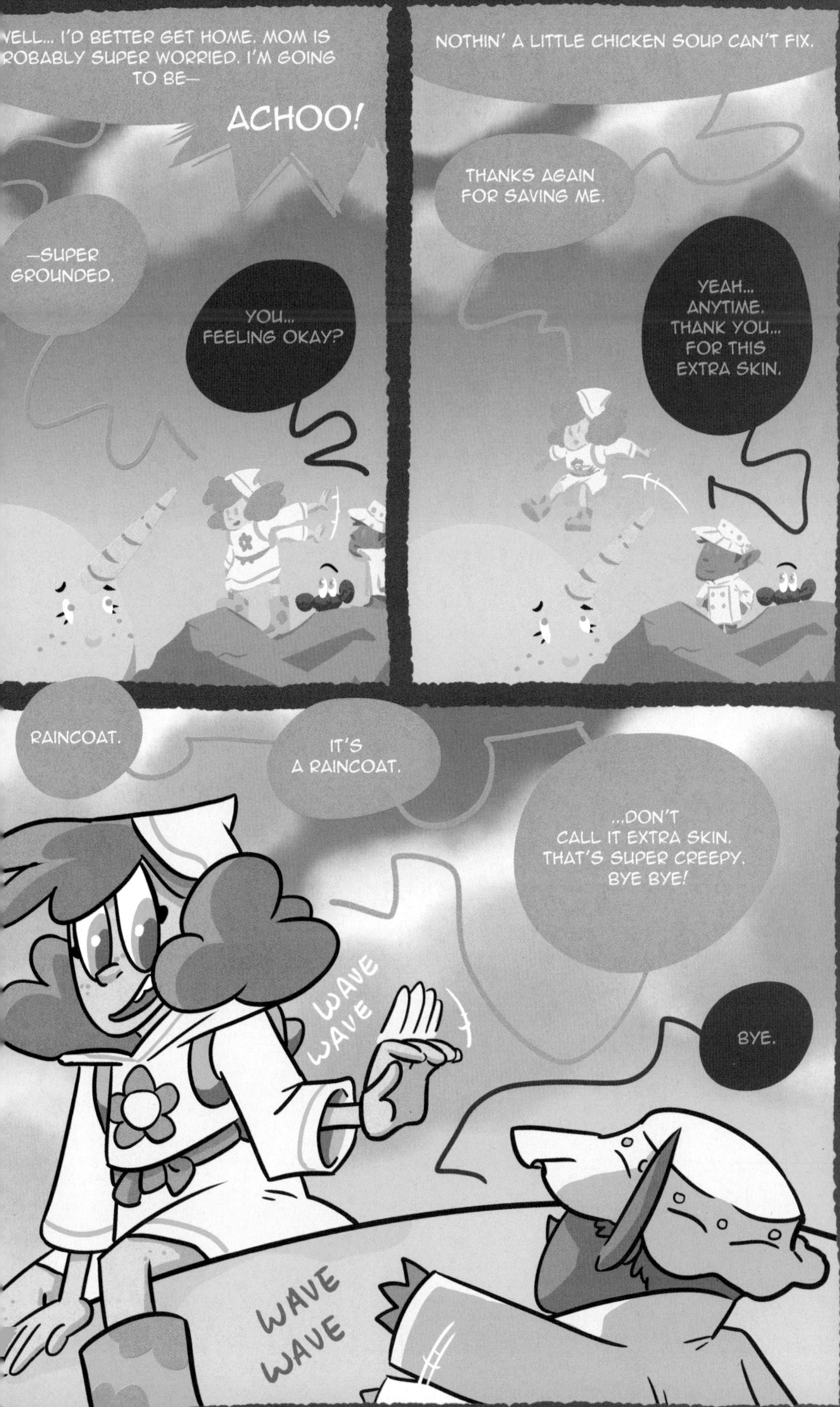
WELL... I'D BETTER GET HOME. MOM IS PROBABLY SUPER WORRIED. I'M GOING TO BE—
ACHOO!
—SUPER GROUNDED.
YOU... FEELING OKAY?
NOTHIN' A LITTLE CHICKEN SOUP CAN'T FIX.
THANKS AGAIN FOR SAVING ME.
YEAH... ANYTIME. THANK YOU... FOR THIS EXTRA SKIN.
RAINCOAT.
IT'S A RAINCOAT.
...DON'T CALL IT EXTRA SKIN. THAT'S SUPER CREEPY. BYE BYE!
WAVE WAVE
BYE.
WAVE WAVE

CONCEPT ART

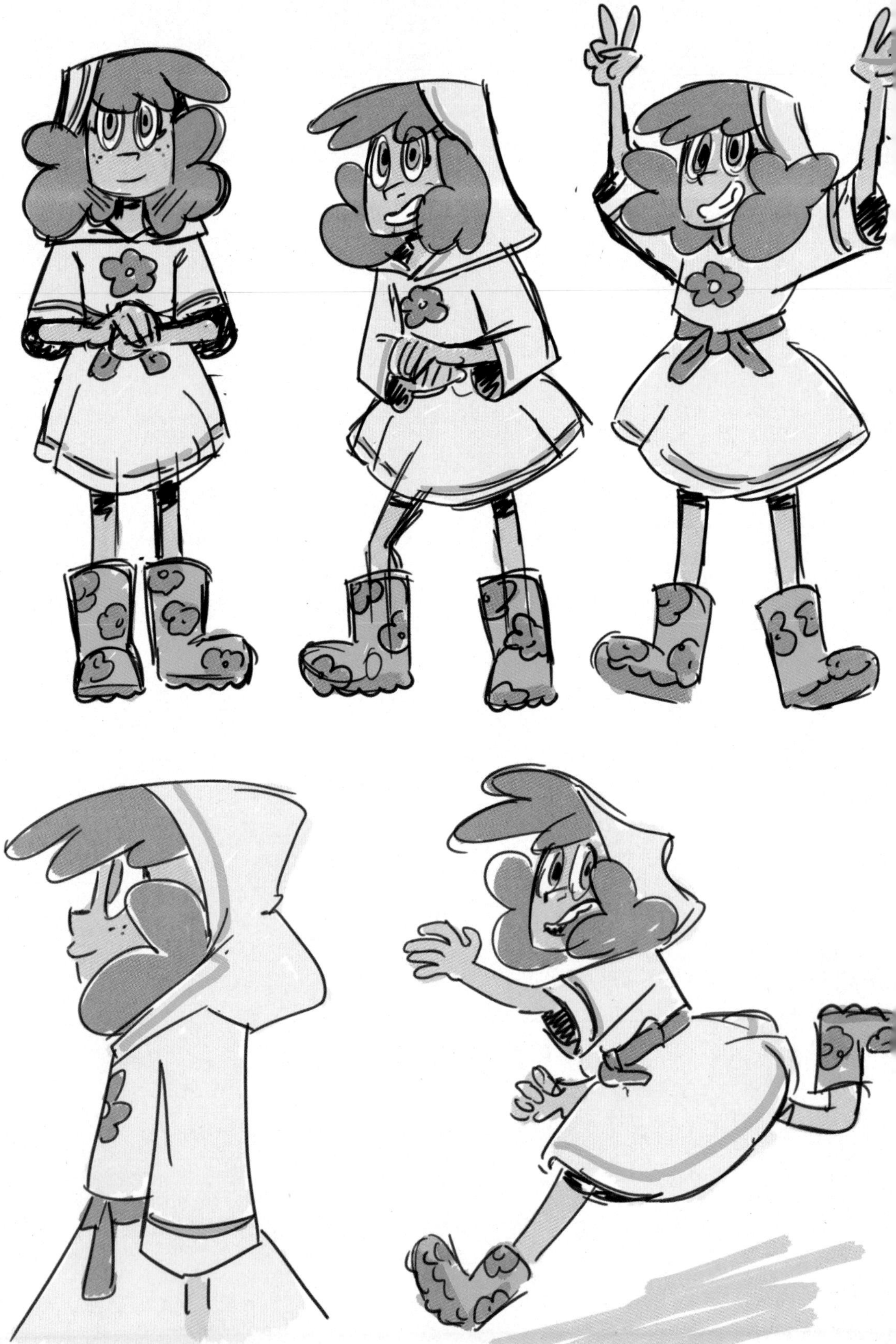